THE FALL
OF
LUCIFER

THE FALL OF LUCIFER

A GREG QUAINTANCE NOVEL

JOHN PEYTON COOKE

**Éditions
Cuir Noir**
Toronto

cuirnoir.com

THE FALL OF LUCIFER is a work of fiction. Any resemblance to persons living or dead is entirely coincidental.

ISBN 978-0-9810047-0-9

Éditions Cuir Noir
J. P. Cooke, Publisher
206-99 Avenue Road
Toronto, Ontario M5R 2G5
Canada

cuirnoir.com

johnpeytoncooke.com

jpcooke@sympatico.ca

This book is for

Keng

FAUSTUS: Was not that Lucifer an angel once?

MEPHOSTOPHILIS: Yes, Faustus, and most dearly loved of God.

FAUSTUS: How comes it then that he is prince of devils?

MEPHOSTOPHILIS: Oh, by aspiring pride and insolence,
For which God threw him from the face of
heaven.

FAUSTUS: And what are you that live with Lucifer?

MEPHOSTOPHILIS: Unhappy spirits that fell with Lucifer,
Conspired against our God with Lucifer,
And are for ever damned with Lucifer.

FAUSTUS: Where are you damned?

MEPHOSTOPHILIS: In hell.

FAUSTUS: How comes it then that thou art out of hell?

MEPHOSTOPHILIS: Why, this is hell, nor am I out of it.

— CHRISTOPHER MARLOWE
The Tragical History of Doctor Faustus
act i, sc. iii

ONE

MY THIRTIETH BIRTHDAY hit me like a sucker punch to the kidneys. Intimations of mortality weren't supposed to come until forty, when your coworkers broke out the black crepe and bunting. I had no coworkers to dress up my office, but that cold October night a few game friends dragged me out to the bars and poured enough liquor down my throat to make me forget I would someday die. I went home alone and awoke late the next morning with my worst hangover in years, wishing somebody would come put me out of my misery. Instead, my friends came and dragged me out again, for brunch. It was only after some eggs Benedict and hair of the dog that I revived and went in to work. It was a Saturday afternoon, and I didn't have to, but I owed a client a final report and wanted to finish it so I could send a final reckoning.

At four o'clock, someone trudged up the staircase to the second floor landing and entered my waiting room, jangling my bell. I couldn't see who it was; the Venetian blinds on the glass partition were shut, and my office door was closed. I shouted that I'd be out in a minute. My report was hanging there on my computer screen with the cursor flashing, waiting for a suitable finale that I was unsuited today to compose. I put out my cigarette, closed up my file, and peeked through the blinds.

The man in my waiting room was of middle years and had the solemn look of a plateaued professional—neither young enough to be upwardly mobile nor old enough to be in a downward spiral. His neat wavy hair was various shades of gray. He was dressed like a suburbanite, in khaki slacks and a navy Ralph Lauren canvas jacket over a cherry-red polo shirt. His briefcase lay flat on the seat beside him. He was sitting casually with legs crossed, showing me one clean rubber sole of his weekend loafers while he rummaged without pleasure through the magazines I kept on the glass coffee table: *Out, The Advocate, Genre, Men's Style, Vanity Fair, Movieline,* and *Architectural Digest.* He frowned, searching for a *Time* or a *Money* but settling for the *Archy D.*

I opened my office door and stepped into the waiting room, still feeling lightheaded from my birthday bacchanalia.

"Greg Quaintance," I said, offering my hand to shake.

"Henry Foster." His knees popped as he stood. He winced at a stab of pain. He clasped my hand and shook it firmly.

"What can I do for you?" I asked.

"I'd like to hire you for a job—if you're available."

"That depends on what you had in mind," I said, stating the obvious. "Come into my office. We'll talk it over."

Foster grabbed his briefcase, and I motioned him through the door. I closed it for privacy, though chances were, not another soul would come in for days. Business had fallen off.

Some months ago, after collecting a particularly large fee, I'd had my office redecorated by someone with more taste than I. The decorator, a fellow Chelsea boy with an office just up Eighth

Avenue from mine, was taken with the fact that I was a private investigator and sold me on a forties retro look. He scoured Manhattan for all the right pieces of old office furniture and found a good set of heavy steel chairs for my clients and a huge steel desk for me. He tore out the indoor-outdoor carpeting and redid the floors in gray linoleum tiles with black speckling. He installed one ceiling fan each in the waiting room and office and was also responsible for the glass partition and Venetian blinds. He located a 1942 street map of Manhattan in an old print shop, had it framed, and put it up on one of my office walls. By the door stood a walnut coat and hat stand. Textured steel filing cabinets lined the opposite wall, most of them empty. On my desk were wooden inboxes, an incandescent desk lamp, and a stainless steel ashtray with a wavy bridge across the bowl that could park six cigarettes at a time. My computer, phone, fax machine, ten-inch TV, and mini-fridge all looked out of place in these surroundings, but I felt at home.

Foster sat in one of the guest chairs, sniffing theatrically at the air. "You're a smoker, Mr. Quaintance?"

"I'll open this if it bothers you." I went to raise the middle window, on which my name and occupation were lettered in gold paint—another retro touch my decorator had talked me into—but looking outside, I balked. The awnings and rainbow flags in front of the Eighth Avenue businesses were fluttering madly in a strong northeasterly wind. Chelsea shoppers were clutching at caps and struggling with tote bags. Fallen leaves from unseen trees were blowing along in tiny maëlstroms at their feet.

"Never mind that," Foster said. "But you *should* quit."

"You're either a doctor or an ex-smoker." I left the window alone and sat at my desk, grabbing a pen for something to hold.

"Both," Foster said, chuckling. "But I don't mind breathing in your remnants. Brings back the good old days, before they were class A carcinogens. Now everything is. You can't win."

"We're all going to die someday," I said sagely. All this talk of cigarettes was making me want to walk a mile for a Camel.

"The older you get, the less you want to hurry it along," Foster countered. "I've seen enough death in my time."

I hoped he would get to the point. Sometimes a gentle prod is all they need: "What kind of a doctor are you, if I may ask?"

"You may," he said cheerily, "and I'm a rheumatologist."

"Do you live here in the city?"

"No, just outside of Hartford," he said. "I'm chief of rheumatology at Hartford Hospital."

"What brings you in to New York?" And to me.

Foster's face darkened. Small talk was over. He was a doctor, though, and he knew how to give it to me straight: "I came into the city today to identify a dead body that I thought would turn out to be my son. Thankfully, it wasn't—but that doesn't solve my problem."

"Your son is missing, then?"

"In a manner of speaking, yes. The police would disagree."

"Have you discussed it with the police?"

"No, Mr. Quaintance, I haven't."

"I see. How old is your son?"

"He turned twenty in July."

"Had he been staying with you?"

"No, he was living here in New York, the last I know of."

"And your son is not mentally impaired or otherwise handicapped or physically dependent on you in any way?"

"No, he's a perfectly normal boy—in that sense."

"If that's the case, you may be right about the police," I said sympathetically. "They'll write up a report, but they won't waste any legwork on it. Not unless you give them a reason to suspect that a crime is involved. Otherwise, since your son is over eighteen and can take care of himself, they'll figure he has the right to disappear if he wants to."

"That's why I came to you."

"Why me and not some other private dick?"

"You're the one who found that child of a neighbor of mine — not really a neighbor, but a fellow Connecticutter. You know, that young girl who went missing from the Lollipop Festival."

"Lollapalooza," I said. Lorelei Matheson was sixteen, and I was lucky to have found her, living in a drugged-out daze among a biker gang in Schenectady. She was lucky to have been found.

"At any rate," Foster said, growing impatient, "what I want is for you to find my son and bring him home to me."

"I'll need more details," I said, "starting with his name."

"Jared," Foster said, spelling it for me unnecessarily.

"When was the last time you heard from Jared?"

"My wife talked to him on the phone about seven weeks ago, just before Labor Day. I haven't seen him since mid-August."

"Your wife — is she also Jared's mother?"

"No, his mother and I divorced when he was twelve. That's old news. I'm not sure what difference it makes now."

"Maybe not much to you, but it probably does to Jared," I said. Foster glared at me. I went on: "When did you remarry?"

"Eight years ago now." Foster was annoyed. "But I don't see why we have to go into my marriages. I saw a boy on a slab this morning that no one can identify, and until they lifted the sheet from his face, I was convinced it would be Jared. I don't want to go through that again. It put the fear of God into me."

"What about Jared's mother? Has she heard from him?"

"Not since he was last out there, back in July."

"Where is that?"

"Turlock, California."

"And you're sure Jared's not out there now?"

"I'm sure. Jared hates California. He says it's too bright, the sun hurts his eyes."

"But he likes it in New York?"

"Yes. I suspect he's still here in Manhattan. That's another reason I came to you instead of someone in Connecticut. You're right here in the middle of the action."

"Have you got a recent photo of Jared?"

"I brought some with me." Foster opened up his gold-monogrammed briefcase and handed me two color photographs. "The first one is Jared the way I like to think of him, when he was starting college—so it's a couple years old. The other is how he looked the last time I saw him, back in August."

The first photo presented a handsome, healthy boy of about eighteen with a summer tan and sun-bleached hair falling straight to his shoulders, wearing a white T-shirt and khaki shorts, sitting on a sofa, reading a book. Jared seemed taken by surprise but was relaxed and smiling agreeably at the camera operator. His solid facial bone structure and broad, cleft chin made him naturally photogenic.

"Good-looking kid," I said.

"Try the next one," Foster said.

The second photo showed Jared with much longer hair dyed a dull, flat black. It was another indoor shot, though of lesser quality, taken with a flash that made him stand out sharply against the redbrick fireplace in the background. Skinnier than in the first photo, face chalky white. His pale forearms were crawling with dark blue tattoos resembling twisted hawthorn branches. He wore a black T-shirt and black jeans, silver necklaces, rings on his fingers, bracelets on his wrists, multiple earrings, two eyebrow rings, a nose ring, and a silvery ball at his lower lip. Jared appeared to be taken off guard again. This time, he was scowling a threat into the lens.

"These were both taken at your house near Hartford?"

"Yes."

"What were the circumstances of Jared's disappearance?"

"I—I'm not really sure of the exact circumstances."

I looked up from my notes and gave Foster a hard stare.

"Let me tell you how it is," he ventured to explain. "We've been out of contact. He didn't return to school this semester, and I was upset with him over it. He was stubborn and wouldn't speak to me after that. The last time he called, he would only talk to my wife. I suppose I was as stubborn—I didn't want to speak to him until he came to his senses and reenrolled. I wanted to be able to tell him I told him so. Before I knew it, here it was, October, and then last night I see this report on the news about the unidentified boy."

"I'm sorry," I said. "I'm not familiar with the story."

"It was all over the news. Didn't you watch?"

"I didn't see any TV last night," I said. Some of the bars we'd been in had TVs, but all they showed were dance videos and naked male flesh. "This boy—he was about Jared's age?"

"I'd say a little younger—eighteen or nineteen."

"They showed his picture on the news?"

"No, it would have been too gruesome for TV. They only gave out a verbal description and flashed a rough sketch and said that anybody who thought they knew him should go down to the medical examiner's office and try to help with an identification. I'm telling you what I saw firsthand at the city mortuary. The kid was skinny, emaciated, with tell-tale tracks on his arms."

"Are you telling me Jared is also a heroin addict?"

Foster hesitated. "I suspect he is. God only knows. It would certainly fit in with his lifestyle. The kids these days, they think they'll live forever . . ." He trailed off, shifting uncomfortably, his hands rubbing at his temples.

I went to my mini-fridge and offered Foster something to drink—bottled water, soda, beer? I also had hard stuff in my desk. He asked for lime sparkling water. I grabbed one as well.

"Thank you," he said. "I'm sorry. My nerves are rattled."

"Take your time." I sipped at my water and waited for him.

Foster downed his water quickly but didn't seem to relax. He also stopped talking. He started staring out my windows.

Finally, I said, "Can we go back to this kid at the morgue?"

"Go ahead," he said, his voice raspy from the carbonation.

"He's still unidentified?"

"He was when I left, several hours ago."

"What are we talking about here, a drug overdose?"

"Not exactly."

"Well, what is it?"

"The police and the medical examiner aren't giving out much in the way of specifics, but I did get a good look at the body, and I've got a fair idea what happened to him."

"Suspicious death? Possible homicide?"

"Definite homicide," Foster said. "The boy's skin was marble white. There were rope burns on his wrists and ankles and a large puncture wound on his left arm—in the median cubital vein, where a nurse usually goes to take a laboratory sample. All the blood had been methodically drained from his body. Frankly, the detective I spoke with looked a little frightened. The method of killing does suggest some kind of psychopath."

"Yes, it does. What made you think it was going to be Jared? You said all they showed on TV was a sketch. Was there such a strong resemblance?"

"No, not really. Certainly when I saw the body I knew it wasn't my son. But I hadn't seen Jared for a couple of months, and who knows how his appearance may have changed in that time? The weight and height they gave out were about right, and

Jared also has blue eyes. What alarmed me were the descriptions of the tattoos. I was lying there in bed with my wife, and I bolted upright and said, 'My God, that's Jared!'"

"Jared and the dead boy had the same tattoos?"

"Not identical, it turns out. Similar in character, though. I don't know how to describe them—ritualistic, satanic, evil-looking—not your regular sailor and biker tattoos. They're the kind of marks people like Jared tend to have."

"What people?"

"In these vampire cults."

"Are you talking about goths?"

"Pardon me?"

"The gothic underground. I'm not sure it qualifies as a cult. They call themselves goths. You're saying Jared is one?"

"Yes," Foster said in a small, embarrassed voice.

"He dresses all in black and wears silver jewelry," I said, looking again at the second photo. "And he probably wears white pancake makeup and dark lipstick and mascara when he goes out clubbing, and I'll bet he reads Bram Stoker and Anne Rice and Clive Barker and listens to macabre industrial rock music."

"Yes, that's Jared," Foster said spitefully. "He's immersed in this—this—what do you call it?—gothic underground."

"When did he start getting into it?"

"When? Oh, Jared's always been into vampires and horror movies in one way or another. But I didn't ever think of it as a problem until he went off to college and started hanging around with these creeps. Jared's a smart kid. He was pre-med here at N.Y.U.—my alma mater. Second semester his sophomore year, his grades plummeted, and he dropped out just before finals. God only knows how he spent his time here last summer. He promised me he was going to reenroll, but he never did."

"That's when you stopped talking to each other," I said. "Is he really missing, or have you simply lost contact?"

"No, he's missing, all right. I talked to the last girl he was living with, and she hasn't seen Jared for weeks. All his things are still over at her apartment. He left without a word."

"What's her name?"

"That would be Anastasia Cartwright," Foster grumbled. He gave me her phone number and an address on Avenue D.

"Were they boyfriend girlfriend?"

"I assume so, but Jared never said anything to me about her. I've only seen her twice—once last summer, once this morning. Not that she's much to look at. You should have seen Jared's last girlfriend. A real looker, if you know what I mean. Jared lived with her until about six months ago."

"What was her name?"

"Excuse me?" Foster seemed reluctant.

"Her name, number, address. I'd like to talk to her."

"Oh, of course. Juliet Logan." He checked his address book and gave me her phone number and an address on MacDougal Street.

"Any odd personal habits Jared developed in the last year?"

"Only odd study habits, far as I know. Overnight, he went from being a straight A student to getting F's and incompletes."

"Can you pinpoint the timing of that?"

"Sometime before spring midterms this year," Foster said. "His midterm grades showed the slide. He dropped out in May."

"How many times did you see him this summer?"

"He came out to Hartford twice, and I came into the city once. I didn't stay with him, of course. Each time I saw him, he was uncommunicative and withdrawn. I asked him if he was doing drugs. He said he wasn't. We were growing apart. I couldn't get through to him. I'm not sure I tried that hard."

"You're saying that he disappeared several weeks ago, but I

get the impression you weren't very worried about him until you had this scare today."

"I've always been worried about him, Mr. Quaintance. Those tattoos, that awful music, this unhealthy obsession with death. I started worrying about drugs when his grades went into free fall. I used to think Jared was too smart to succumb to them—but all it takes is mixing with the wrong people."

"Relax," I said. "Jared may be perfectly fine. He may not be doing any drugs or anything else harmful. I think for most of these goths, it's just a way of dressing up and going out on the town. You say Jared's smart. Maybe we shouldn't jump to any conclusions until we've had a chance to talk to him."

"It's not just the drugs I'm worried about," Foster said. "This body I saw today . . ." He trailed off again.

"You're worried that the same thing might happen to Jared."

"Yes, exactly. This dead kid, he's one of them, one of those goths. He had the same kinds of tattoos. Even fangs."

"Fangs?"

"His canines had been filed down to sharp points, like a vampire's. I'm sure he hung around the same crowd as Jared."

"There are thousands of goths in this city."

"I don't care. I want you to find my son before this or something like it happens to him. As far as I'm concerned, it's no different than if he were in that damned Heaven's Gate cult. I want you to find my Jared before it's too late."

"I'll give it a shot."

"Does that mean you'll take the case?"

"As long as you agree to my rates."

I handed Foster my fee schedule, run off neatly on white three-by-five cards in heavy black ink. I don't like to haggle, and it's nice to have it all spelled out for the client in cold print ahead of time to avoid confusion when I send out my bill.

"These are reasonable enough," Foster judged, sliding the card inside his jacket. "I've got no problem with your rates."

"I don't want you to have any false hopes, Dr. Foster," I said. "I'll try to locate Jared for you, but I've got to warn you about one thing. Even if I do find him, I can't force him to come back to you if he doesn't want to."

"Why wouldn't he want to?"

"It's not the same deal as with that sixteen-year-old girl. Missing adults aren't always eager to be found, and I can't bring them back short of kidnapping. Let's say I do find Jared—I might only be able to tell you where he is. That might be all."

"But what if he's in danger?"

"If he is and I find him and it's not too late, I'll try to get him out of it." I was going out on a bit of a limb.

"Thank you," Foster said, exhaling a sigh of relief.

"I'll need you to give me any other information you can. Anyone else you can think of who's known him these last two years in New York. Any college friends, professors, other ex-roommates, any of his goth friends you might be aware of."

"I don't know much beyond what I've told you. I'm not sure who all his professors were, but you could talk to his adviser, Dr. Willem Kirst." Foster spelled it out for me. "Willem is a fellow alum. We were classmates together."

"An old friend?"

"Old acquaintance, is more like. Willem and I were never close, not even professionally. He was a brilliant student, at the top of our class. We veered off into different specialties, and of course he also teaches. All of my close professional colleagues are either in rheumatology or else work with me in Hartford. When Jared was about to start at N.Y.U., I noticed Willem listed among the faculty advisers. I asked him to be Jared's adviser and help him prepare a solid pre-med curriculum as well as long-range scenarios. Willem was eager to help. He really took Jared under his wing."

"Have you been in contact with him recently?"

"I talked with him this morning. He's as upset over all this as I am. I'm not sure he can tell you any more than I have—but as you said, he can tell you who Jared's professors were."

"Good," I said. "I'll also need the number of Jared's mother out in California."

"Evelyn Grosse. I'll write it all down for you."

"And I want to talk to your current wife."

"Why?" Foster was protective.

"She spoke with Jared the last time he called your house."

"Oh, right. Her name is Gloria," he said, scribbling furiously with a fountain pen on a yellow legal pad from his briefcase. "Gloria Glendenning-Foster, hyphenated."

I asked him to write down anything else he could think of, and he nodded. He spent a couple of minutes on it. He tore it out neatly and reached across the desk to hand it to me.

"I'd also like a two-thousand-dollar advance, in cash."

"I was anticipating something like that," Foster said, obligingly counting out twenty stiff hundreds.

I took the cash from him and put it in my wallet.

"Here's my card, Mr. Quaintance." It included his home phone and fax, work phone and fax, answering service, and pager numbers. Foster grasped my hand and shook it warmly once more. "Thanks again, really."

"Don't thank me now." I handed him my business card from a small black-enameled tray on my desk. "Let me find Jared first."

"Yes," Foster said. "You're very sensible. I like that."

I accepted the compliment and stood up and showed him through the waiting room and out the front door with a goodbye. His weak knees made him take the stairs slowly down to the street. I was suddenly thankful to be thirty and not fifty.

I shut the door to my office and went and stared out my window. I watched Foster cross the street to a fire-engine red Ford Expedition, climb in, and drive off. He made an illegal right on red at West Eighteenth Street and was gone.

I wondered why my acceptance of the case meant so much to him. If I'd refused, he could have gone out and hired another starving gumshoe. It had to be that he was stuck on the fact I'd retrieved that girl who'd been snatched from Lollapalooza. If I didn't find his son, he was going to be in for a big letdown.

He might be in for one anyway. Jared, once found, might very well tell his dad to go to hell.

TWO

I BOUGHT A COPY of the *Post* at a Korean grocer's and ducked into the Paradise Cafe to escape the wind and quaff a double espresso. The hangover was gone, but the fuzzy thinking remained. If I'd known a case was going to come in and bite me today, I would have put off my friends last night with some lame excuse. They would have pitied me, and I'd have been out some free drinks.

I found the story along the gutter on page nine: VAMPIRE 'CLUB KID' SLAIN. The *Post* hadn't run any photos; the narrow column was crowded out by a big ad for a cookware sale at Macy's. The gist of the story was that the body of an unidentified white male, approximately eighteen years of age, was discovered early Friday morning by two police officers from the Sixth Precinct, lying on the sidewalk behind a meat warehouse on West Thirteenth Street between Eighth Avenue and Hudson Street. A police spokesperson refused to comment about the circumstances of the young man's death, other than that it was considered suspicious.

However, the *Post* reporter had it on good authority from an anonymous source within the department that nearly all the blood had been drained from the victim's body through a puncture wound.

Det. Octavio Orjuedos of the N.Y.P.D. was quoted as saying that the victim was "most likely one of these kids who hang out in these vampire nightclubs." The victim was five feet eleven inches tall, a hundred-thirty pounds, with long black hair that appeared to have been dyed. He had blue eyes and was wearing soft contact lenses. His canines had been filed down to resemble fangs. Tattoos included the branches on both arms, an Egyptian scarab on his left pectoral, large bat wings across his scapulae, an ankh on his stomach, a spider's web spreading from his navel across his lower abdomen, and a black widow spider on the right buttock. On the right biceps was a black rose above the name KAREL in scarlet calligraphic script. "Whether or not that is the victim's own name is unknown at the present time," Detective Orjuedos said. "It could be a nickname or someone else's name." Anyone who thought they might be able to identify the victim was urged to contact the medical examiner's office.

I carefully tore out the story, folded it up in thirds, and put it in my wallet, leaving the rest of the *Post* lying around for someone else to read. I went outside and hailed a cab.

"I'm not going to tell you much," said Det. Octavio Orjuedos, whom I met over at the Sixth Precinct house on West Tenth Street, in Greenwich Village. He was a lean man in his mid thirties with the kind of cheek bones models had their back molars pulled to achieve. He could have given every other police detective in New York a seminar on personal grooming. Under the tan shoulder holster holding a shiny .38 Special, he wore a tailored white shirt that was clean and pressed and fit snugly across his shoulders and chest, narrowing down to a firm thirty-inch waist. His nails were clean and manicured. His dusky skin was smooth and well cared for. His hair was styled in a Roman cut, and he kept a neat goatee. Nature had given him long, thick eyelashes. His new investigation had given him bleary, bloodshot eyes.

"Come on, Orjuedos, I'm an agent of the State of New York," I said, trying not to sound whiny. He had my private detective's license before him on his desk. "Whatever you've briefed other officers or agencies with you ought to be able to tell me."

"Bullshit. The investigation's ongoing. It's sensitive."

"You can trust me. I might be able to help you."

Point blank, Orjuedos asked, "Who are you working for?" and leaned back in his desk chair, hands folded behind his neck.

"You know I can't tell you that."

"Come on, you can trust me," Orjuedos said. "I'm a cop."

"My client's paying me for my discretion."

"And the people of the City of New York are paying me to catch killers—especially nuts like this one." Orjuedos rocked gently back and forth on squeaky springs. "I'd love to help you earn your fee, Quaintance, but how do I know the killer himself didn't hire you to come over here and dig information out of me?"

"I doubt that my client has killed anybody, Orjuedos."

"Hey, how do you know? Even around here, facts are told only to those who need to know. That's how we manage to solve so many more violent crimes than we used to. I can't tell you a damned thing. I want to solve this one. Sue me if you like."

"I'm not going to sue you. I'm not even sure your case is relevant to mine. I just want to explore every avenue."

"What kind of case are you working on?"

"A missing adult who may or may not be missing," I said. "The kind you guys don't waste your time on."

"Funny—the doctor I ran into this morning at the city mortuary thought our John Doe was going to be his missing son." The corners of Orjuedos's mouth rose into tight dimples, pulling up his goatee and uncovering white teeth. "What a coincidence."

"He told me that the whole case seemed to 'frighten' the investigating detective," I said. "Who I gather is you."

"Me, frightened?" His smile collapsed. "Why should I be?"

"That's a good question. You're a homicide detective. You see messed-up corpses all the time. Why should this one shake you up? Is it because all the blood was drained out of him?"

"Don't believe everything you read in the *Post*, man."

"I don't," I said. "My client saw the body for himself. He saw the puncture wound in the arm, and he could tell the blood was lost. The *Post* was right, even if they didn't mention the rope burns on the extremities. The body's still unidentified?"

"Yes," Orjuedos said. "I can tell you that, at least."

"You can also show me the photos. I could go down to the M.E.'s office and have a look for myself. You could be a pal and spare me the trip."

"You think you'll be able to identify him?"

"You never know. It can't hurt."

Orjuedos sat up and pulled a manila envelope off his desk. He unclasped the envelope and dumped a set of eight-by-ten color glossies into my lap. The close-ups of the tattoos were striking, especially the black rose, with the name KAREL looking like it had been etched with a quill pen and inked in blood.

"This is fine tattoo work," I said. "Much nicer than my Army tattoo. You ought to be able to track down the artist."

"Yeah, sure." Orjuedos was morose. "Do you know how many tattoo artists there are in the tri-state area? We'll have better luck with the body piercings. I mean, look at this shit. Rings up and down his ears, in his eyebrows, in his nose, a ball on his tongue, rings through his nipples and his navel. Jesus. And check out that next pic, if you can stomach it."

It mostly showed the spiderweb tattoo across the victim's lower abdomen, visible because his pubic hair was shaved down to stubble. There was only one piercing in the picture, but it was a biggie—a Prince Albert, a large silver ring coming up through the underside of the glans and out the eye of the penis.

"Ouch," I said.

"Not too many guys have one of those," Orjuedos said.

"You've been counting?" I asked. "And did the M.E. shave his pubic hair?"

"It was like that when we found him."

I spent some time examining the victim's face, and I had no trouble distinguishing between him and Jared Foster. The victim had a small, pointy chin, whereas Jared's was broader and had a cleft. The victim had a slightly upturned, puggish nose; Jared's was narrower and descended to a slim tip. The victim had a higher forehead than Jared, and the shape and pattern of their ears were completely different. This was not Jared Foster.

"You have any idea who it is?" Orjuedos asked.

"Never seen him before. The body was found just a couple of blocks south of Chelsea, where I live and work. Maybe the guy's been seen there or in the Village. Not by me, unfortunately."

Orjuedos collected the photos from me, squared off the edges, and slid them all back into his envelope.

"Chelsea boy, are you?" he asked slyly.

"I'm not in the closet, if that's what you're wondering."

"I don't know what else I can do for you, Quaintance."

"Call me Greg," I suggested, hoping I didn't sound fresh.

"My friends call me Tavo." He smiled thinly, encouragingly. "Maybe you can be of some help to me, though. You're looking for a missing goth—which means you and I are going to be covering some of the same territory. I'll be searching for a killer, and you'll be looking for this doctor's kid."

"Not much of a kid anymore."

"Whatever. If you run across any information that I ought to know, you give me a call and let me in on it, all right?"

Orjuedos handed me his business card, with the N.Y.P.D. logo alongside his name, title, and phone numbers.

"You might run across my missing goth yourself, Tavo."

"Then why don't you tell me about him, Greg? If I run across him, I'll give you a call. You know—you scratch my back, I scratch yours?"

"Sounds fun," I said, handing over my business card. I'd give him some information, if only to buy more cooperation. "As long as you don't say anything about it to anyone. This has to remain between us, or I'm screwed. My client can't know."

"You have my word of honor, Greg."

"Okay. His name's Jared Foster, and yes, he's the son of the doctor you met this morning. He's twenty, and the details of his disappearance aren't mysterious enough for your Missing Persons to take it seriously. Basically, he's dropped out of school and tried to alienate his parents. If he's in New York, I'll probably find him in a day or two and let his father know where he is, and that'll be that. I've got a photo here."

I showed him only the devilish Jared all in black before the fireplace. There was no point in showing him the angelic Jared; he had already fallen from grace and was unlikely to be restored.

"Jesus," Orjuedos muttered, scanning the photo assiduously before returning it. "I'll know this joker if I see him."

"Good," I said. "If you do find Jared, *don't* tell him his father's looking for him. Just let me know where he is, okay?"

"Sure thing, Greg."

"Now maybe you can tell me more about your dead vampire

kid. You want me to be able to help you, don't you?"

"Ask me some yes-or-no questions."

"Well, first of all, I'm assuming he was *not* killed where you guys found the body, on West Thirteenth Street."

"Yes, that's right."

"You didn't find any of the victim's blood at the scene?"

"No, we did not."

"And the method of killing was the draining of the blood? I mean, the procedure wasn't performed after he was killed, right?"

"Yes," Orjuedos said warily. "He died of heart failure brought on by massive blood loss. You're a good guesser."

"Seems pretty obvious. Was the body naked or clothed?"

"Not exactly a yes or no question." Orjuedos looked like he was going to hedge on me, but he went on: "He was naked, but hidden under an old trenchcoat. Our patrol officers thought all they were doing was rousting a sleeping homeless guy."

"The body looked clean in the pics. Was it found that way?"

"Yes. It was all scrubbed down before we got it."

"Not even any bloodstains?"

"None."

"So any blood evidence is essentially missing."

"Eight pints of it," Orjuedos said merrily. "Hardly a drop left for us. That's pretty unusual, in my experience."

"Sounds like a killer who takes pride in his work."

"Or one who was very thirsty." Orjuedos crossed himself by rote and then laughed to show me he wasn't serious.

"Is that that frightened look I was warned about?"

"Shit, no," he said. "I was crossing myself for luck."

"That's okay, I won't tell anybody." I stood up and grabbed my jacket. Orjuedos watched me get into it. His eyes roved a bit. I added, "Thanks for the back scratching, Tavo."

"Yeah, sure. Tell me something to help me clear this friggin' case, and I'll give you a Swedish massage."

"Find Jared Foster for me, and I'll do you one better."

"Get out of here, Greg." He handed me back my P.I. license and shook his head in frustration. "I've got work to do, and you're turning into something of a distraction."

"I like you, too," I said.

It took me five minutes and one cigarette to walk the rest of the way up Hudson Street, past the triangle that was Abingdon Square, to the spot where the unknown goth was found.

The crime scene had been cleared, and the only evidence I saw that the police had been there was a two-inch scrap of yellow tape still affixed to the wall of the warehouse, flapping in the wind. In the absence of bloodstains, I had no way of knowing exactly where the body had been dumped. It was a lonely site, on a block with no nearby residences. I'd often witnessed plenty of foot traffic in this area late into the evening, but very early in the morning it was probably dead.

The killer could have driven by around four or five Friday morning, let his car idle, checked to make sure no one was watching, and taken out his bundle wrapped in the trenchcoat. Any man in good physical shape could heft a hundred-thirty-pound body for the two or three steps it would take to get it from the curb to the wall. All he had to do was dump it, arrange the coat over any exposed flesh, take another look around, hop back in his car, and drive off. The West Side Highway was only a few blocks distant, and from there he could return to any part of the city — or go through a tunnel or over a bridge to Long Island, New Jersey, Connecticut, upstate, anywhere.

I hoped Orjuedos would luck out and get a positive I.D. on the victim.

I also hoped my case would have nothing to do with his.

THREE

I TRIED Anastasia Cartwright's number a few times from my office but reached only a busy signal. I double-checked my Glock 17L, replaced it in my shoulder holster, put on my jacket, and set out to speak with her face to face if she was home. I hailed a taxi on Eighth Avenue and gave the driver her address on Avenue D.

The cabbie took me east of the East Village, into Alphabet City, which begins smartly at gentrified Avenue A and restored Tompkins Square Park and ends ignominiously at Avenue D and the moldering Jacob Riis housing projects. The blocks between Avenues B and D were among the bleakest in Manhattan. Some old apartment buildings stood empty, with charring above busted-out windows. Other tenements survived in rows that were broken up by vacant lots scattered with the bricks of razed neighbors. Some empty lots had been turned into gray, cheerless public spaces, with benches made out of used slabs of reinforced concrete and hand-lettered signs wired to the chain-link fencing to announce THIS IS A COMMUNITY PARK – NO DRINKING, NO DRUGS.

I'd been to Alphabet City before. The neighborhood was tolerable by day, when young mothers went out walking their baby strollers and the younger kids played roller hockey in the streets after school. By night, though, it could be minatory, with transvestite hookers competing with female hookers for territory, armed drug dealers whispering their wares to passersby, homeless alcoholics and drug addicts doing their stuff murkily in the shadows, spiky-haired punks clomping around in plaid pants, and chalky-faced goths stalking off to their clubs and issuing homicidal glares from behind blackened eyes.

It was late afternoon and still daylight out when the taxi driver let me off at the southwest corner of East Ninth Street and Avenue D, where Jared Foster was last known to have lived with Anastasia Cartwright in a five-story nineteenth-century brick apartment building facing the Jacob Riis Houses. The ground floor was a generic Chinese take-out joint whose sign bragged of Hunan, Szechuan, and Cantonese cuisine. I put a quarter in the pay phone out front and tried Ms. Cartwright's number but was met once more with the annoying busy buzz.

My stomach grumbled an unsubtle hint that Jared Foster must have popped downstairs for cheap Chinese food once in a while. I went in and nodded at the Chinese counterman, who was busy taking an order over a cordless phone. I stood at the counter and scanned the all-encompassing menu. Most items were printed in black, but my eyes were drawn to the hot and spicy dishes in red, marked in the margins with red iconic chili peppers. A note at the bottom of the menu claimed ominously: WE CAN ALTER YOUR TASTE.

"Yes, sir?" asked the counterman, hanging up the phone. He was about twenty-five, wearing a thin pocket tee that stretched tightly around his pecs and delts and bared his sinewy arms. A hard pack of Marlboro reds showed through the chest pocket. He had a sideways jag to his nose and the washboard abs of a boxer. Stubbly growth of a few days defined his scalp like a Buddhist monk's. He smiled at my equally bald head. We were comrades.

I smiled at his smile and said, "Small order of Szechuan beef with hot peppers, extra hot and spicy, with white rice."

"You want extra hot and spicy?" he said, looking up at me seriously from under his furrowed brow. His accent was thick but perfectly understandable. "You sure?"

"Positive," I insisted. "Extra, extra hot and spicy."

"Okay," he said, like it was my funeral. He shouted my order over his shoulder in some kind of Chinese dialect to the glowering cook, an older, skinnier man with stringy arms who snapped back a number of abusive-sounding things that made the counterman blush and probably had nothing to do with my order.

"You new 'round here?" the counterman asked.

"Actually, I'm looking for someone," I said.

I pulled out the photo of Jared and showed it to him. He smeared the pads of his fingers across his stomach and grabbed the picture, considering it for a few seconds before he spoke:

"Sure. Guy live upstairs, dress like a Dracula?"

"That's him," I said. "Have you seen him around recently?"

"No, sir. Not for long time."

"Do you remember the last time you saw him?"

"Maybe last month. Who are you, a cop?"

"Private detective," I said, digging out a business card.

The counterman regarded my card with one eye closed, like a jeweler trying to spot a fake. His eyes must have had different focal lengths—perhaps the result of a solid punch to the head.

"You fight around here?" I asked.

"Me?" He colored again. "No, back home, Guangzhou."

"Boxing?"

"Kickboxing." He pulled his fists in tight against his chest and demonstrated a high snapping side kick to the air.

"Impressive," I said. "You make any money doing that?"

"Enough to get me here."

Since it took about a million dollars' worth of investments to convince the U.S. government to simply hand over a green card to someone without close blood relations in the States, he had probably managed to save some thirty to forty thousand dollars, which he forked over to Chinese gangsters, who smuggled him over here illegally in a stinking rathole of a ship like the *Golden Venture* that had run aground off Rockaway Point a few years ago. Once here, he was indentured to the tongs, given fake papers, and forced to work whatever lousy job they chose for him for as long as they wanted so they could skim the lion's share of his salary and waste the most productive years of his life. The fact that he preferred slavery in America to being a professional kickboxer in China either said a lot about China or a lot about what he didn't know when he got himself mixed up with gangsters.

"About this Dracula guy," I said, taking up the photo. If I kept thinking about the counterman's travails, it was going to put me into a funk. I could never help him. "Um, do you remember anything else about him? Did he ever act funny, strange? Like, did he ever come here with any weird friends?"

"Weird friends? Sure. That girl-Dracula live upstairs."

"Anastasia Cartwright?"

"I don't know her name," he said. "All I know she always order chicken with broccoli."

"Never with garlic sauce?" It was my own little joke. I had no idea it was going to get me anywhere.

"How you know about the garlic sauce? You a mind-reader? The boy-Dracula, he never like garlic sauce. He always asking me, 'Does this have garlic? Does that have garlic?' Give me a break.

Sometimes his order have garlic and I don't tell him. He don't even know the difference, crazy fucking idiot."

"How did he treat you when he came in?"

"Oh, like he all superior. He stare at me with those eyes like he trying to hypnotize me, like he want me to give him free food. That boy-Dracula fucking crazy."

"What about the girl-Dracula? What's she like?"

"Oh, she nice and friendly. I like her okay. Good thing the boy-Dracula don't come no more. She better off without him."

"Thanks," I said. "Your cook—does he speak English?"

"No, only Cantonese."

"Would you mind showing him this photo?"

"Okay, no problem."

"Ask him if he remembers the last time he saw him."

The counterman went back to the flaming stoves and tried to thrust the photo into the cook's face. The cook waved him away, finishing with my dish and pouring it from the wok into a small white paper box. The counterman traded the box for the photo and spoke to the cook harshly. The cook looked at the photo and was further antagonized by it, shouting animatedly at the counterman.

The counterman returned with the photo and spoke to me while he put my order together on a red plastic tray:

"My brother say he see him two weeks ago, Friday night."

"October Fifth," I said, looking at the calendar on the wall beneath a poorly registered color photo of a buxom Chinese girl in a thong bikini. "Your brother's sure about that?"

"I ask him, and he say he sure. He got good memory."

"Were you working that night?"

The counterman laughed gruffly. "Me? Work every night. Maybe out making delivery or down in storeroom. Don't know."

"Ask your brother if the boy-Dracula was alone. If he was

with somebody, ask him to give me a complete description."

The counterman went back and had a brief, reasonably civil conversation with the cook, who nodded several times and answered each of the counterman's questions succinctly, accompanied by wide gesticulations with a long-handled aluminum ladle.

"He say the boy-Dracula with a man, all black head to toe."

"The man was black skinned?"

"Leather," the counterman said. "White man, black leather."

"Head to toe," I repeated. "He means boots, pants, jacket?"

"Yeah, yeah, yeah."

"How old was this man?"

"My brother not sure. Man's face cover up." The counterman waved his fingers in front of his face. "He wearing a mask."

"What kind of mask? Can your brother describe it?"

The counterman asked the cook, who shook his head and said a few words, drawing a line in front of his neck with the ladle.

"No," the counterman said. "He say it a black leather mask over whole head. Lace up in back like a shoe."

"Well, that's something," I said. "So he couldn't see the man's face? Were there holes for eyes? Open mouth? Zipper?"

The counterman relayed this to the cook, who said a few more words and shook his head apologetically.

"He say holes at eyes, nose, and mouth. He never see the face. I ask, but he don't know what color eyes."

I thanked the counterman for his help and asked him to thank his brother. He asked if he could keep my business card, and I said of course. I asked him to write down both of their names for me and any phone numbers where they could be reached, in case I needed to contact them again. He wrote down Cheung Lee Ho (himself) and Cheung Lee Fong (his brother), both with identical work and home numbers.

"You two came over together?"

"Yes," said Lee Ho, surprised that I was asking.

I wanted to ask him if he had paid his brother's way, but I decided that was too personal a question. Lee Ho would probably clam up on me, thinking I was going to run off and report them to the I.N.S. I might need to speak with them again in the future and didn't want to cross an inexcusable line.

I paid for my food and sat down with my tray. Lee Fong's cooking was excellent—truly extra hot and spicy and pretty close to Szechuan cuisine for a humble cook from Guangzhou. I was glad his brother had helped him come over.

Then I started trying to imagine them doing this day after day here on Avenue D for the next twenty years until the gangsters they were paying off were suitably satisfied.

It kind of ruined my appetite.

FOUR

I DIDN'T SEE any point in trying to call Anastasia Cartwright again. I stepped inside the foyer of her building and smelled the reek of cigarette smoke left behind by tenants who had to get their butts up and lit before they ventured out into the cold, cruel world. I pressed the buzzer of 4B, labelled CARTWRIGHT.

"Ye-e-ss?" came a female voice over the speaker.

"I'm looking for Anastasia Cartwright," I said.

"Who are you?"

"I'd like to talk with you about Jared Foster."

"Who are you?" she repeated dully.

"Greg Quaintance," I said. "I'm a private investigator. Do you mind letting me come up so I could ask a few questions?"

The door buzzer sounded for several seconds. I opened the inner door. I climbed up the narrow stairs to the fourth floor, where I found the door to her apartment, painted in black enamel and decorated haphazardly with stickers of goth-industrial rock bands: Skinny Puppy, Ministry, Front 242, KMFDM, Bauhaus,

Front Line Assembly, Christian Death, Leæther Strip, The Sisters of Mercy, My Life With The Thrill Kill Kult, and Type-O Negative.

I rapped a few times on the Bauhaus sticker. A shadow passed before the peephole, the stem of which perforated the left eye socket of an x-ray of a fractured human skull. This was the artwork from the old Ministry recording *The Mind is a Terrible Thing to Taste*, which I happened to have in my collection. I'd been listening to Ministry and Bauhaus since high school. I'd heard of these other bands but was unfamiliar with their music.

Someone unlocked the door and opened it partway, chain lock in place. I caught a glimpse of black hair before a pale face.

"I want to see your identification," she said.

I dug out my private eye's license and driver's license and held them up close enough for her to read. I passed a business card through the gap and told her she could keep it. Satisfied, she shut the door, undid its chain, and opened it wide again.

"Anastasia Cartwright?" I asked.

"That's me." She tossed her hair back to reveal the slightly plump face of a fallen cherub. A silver ring pierced one of her nostrils. Several more decorated her earlobes with burnished images of knives and bones. A filigreed crucifix dangled from a black-beaded necklace between the curves of her breasts. She was looking casual in a black oversized Tones on Tail T-shirt, black jeans, and bare feet. Her toenails and fingernails were polished black. She wore no makeup on her face.

"Could I come in?" I asked. The entryway was dark, only a little light filtering in from the hallway behind me.

"I guess cops are like vampires," she said with an amused chuckle. "They both have to be invited across a threshold."

"I'm not a cop," I said and stepped inside. I followed a slanting ray of dusty light that peeked through a draped doorway and glinted off delicate glass objects and picture frames on a lace doily on a table against the wall. I was careful to avoid bumping into it and breaking things. I wasn't insured for it.

"Through there," she said, locking the door behind her.

I parted the drapes of black velvet and stepped into a small living room lighted by two north-facing windows draped with more of the same, sashed open to reveal cream-colored shifts. The creak of the floorboards was muffled by a faded rug. A red velvet Victorian couch sagged like a piece out of an Old West bordello, flanked by a couple of similar chairs. The coffee table was tidy, with a large black candle in a blue porcelain bowl, a clean glass ashtray, and some issues of the goth zines *Blue Blood* and *Propaganda*. Second-hand bookshelves housed a variety of horror novels, books on the occult, biographies, true crime, dark erotica, graphic novels, several collections of Romantic poets, and various books with names on the spines like Kant, Hegel, Nietzsche, Jung, and Foucault. A compact disc player sat atop an amplifier, and I spotted four Bose speakers tucked discreetly around the room. The TV and VCR sat in the corner on a rolling stand. A disorganized desk held a Macintosh with a seventeen-inch monitor, turned on and running Netscape.

"I won't take long," I said. "Just a few nosy questions."

"Doesn't matter," Anastasia Cartwright said, still examining my business card as she came into the room. "I've been needing a break. I've got a fresh pot of coffee. Want some?"

"Yes, please. Light."

"Skim okay?"

"It'll do." Barely.

Anastasia vanished behind the drapes. A black cat emerged from another room, meowing at me and sauntering over with tail held high. I tried to pet its head, but it flinched away and ran off through the gap in the drapes to find its mistress.

The walls of the room were hung with blown-up gothic-themed photographs in gaudily carved dark wood frames, professionally shot but amateurishly staged. On either side of each picture were iron sconces holding unlit white candles. I made a circuit and took in the images. A ghostly figure in a gray robe, face hidden by a shadowed cowl, leaning over the stretched neck of a prone, bare-breasted woman. An overwrought still-life featuring a dripping red candle in a silver candlestick, a quill pen lying across pages of parchment, a stack of moldy books, and a yellowed human skull. A woman draped in gauzy fabric, with black hollows around her eyes and black hair flowing over her breasts, walking spookily through a mossy graveyard. A Byronic youth lying in a casket with long black hair, frilly white shirt, arms folded across his chest, a ruby ring on one finger, face powdered, dark eyelids closed, with a knowing smile on his blood-smeared lips.

"Did you take these pictures, Ms. Cartwright?"

"Anastasia, please," she said, coming into the room with two steaming mugs. "I'm never Ms. Cartwright. And no—actually, they're the work of my friend Sebastian de Leon. Have a seat."

The cat followed at Anastasia's heels, padding softly.

"Is that your real name?" I took a corner of the red sofa.

The windows rattled behind me, and a draft stroked the back of my neck. Maybe it was a cold spot. Yeah, right.

"I know what you're thinking." Anastasia tossed her hair out of her face again as she handed me my coffee. She sat in one of the chairs. "A lot of goths take on more exotic names—like Sebastian. He'd kill me if I told you his real name. But Anastasia *is* mine. My mother always liked the Ingrid Bergman movie. I grew up as Stacy, sometimes Stace. Ugh!"

"Where did you grow up? Or am I being too nosy already?"

The cat came over and started sniffing my trouser leg.

"Cleveland—but that's history. I had to come here to become Anastasia. Stacy Cartwright from Cleveland is dead."

"Fair enough," I said. Something similar was true of a lot of other people who came to New York from the provinces, goth or not. In my own case, the city had been a last refuge after I was blackballed from the Army and found I couldn't go home again.

"You wanted to see me about Jared?" Anastasia said, speaking evenly, without any apparent anxiety or surprise.

"I tried calling you all afternoon," I said, "but you were on your computer."

"Yes, sorry," she said. "I've only got the one phone line. It gets tied up when I'm online."

"Looks like you're still on." I nodded at her monitor.

"I maintain a homepage that lists goth events in the area," she said. "I usually spend Saturday afternoons updating it."

"Aren't you racking up charges while we speak?"

"No, I've got unlimited access. I don't pay for a thing. I work for a local internet provider—my mundane day job, Monday throught Friday, doing HTML and Java coding for the big, bad corporate clients. Jared's father hired you, didn't he?"

"It shouldn't make any difference who hired me—"

"That asshole." Anastasia exhaled heavily through her nose. "He came by around noon today and woke me up. I only went to bed at sunrise. See, Friday nights I co-deejay with Sebastian over at Bedlam, down here on Houston at Avenue A? . . . Jared's father was real insistent, so I threw on a robe and let him come up, though he knew Jared wasn't here. He came stomping in, acting all aggressive. He wanted to clean out Jared's room, take all his things. I didn't let him. I told him to get out."

"Did he?"

"Only after I threatened to call the police."

"What did he want with Jared's things?"

"I don't know," Anastasia said. "But they're Jared's, and his father has no right to them. I'm sure Jared's coming back."

"How do you know?" I said. "Do you know where he is?"

"No, but I'm sure he's coming back. He always does."

The cat leapt up unexpectedly into my lap. I managed somehow to keep my coffee from spilling. The cat curled up to sleep and began to purr.

"Peter!" Anastasia said. "Get down!"

"It's okay," I said, smoothing down his fur. "You named your cat Peter? Not Beelzebub or Mephistopheles?"

"No, just Peter," she said, laughing. "After Peter Murphy."

"The lead singer of Bauhaus."

"You listen to Bauhaus?"

"I did in high school," I said. "Out in Wyoming."

"Wyoming?" she said, as if this were a worse place to come from than Cleveland. "I don't even know where that is. How did you ever hear of Bauhaus out there? From *The Hunger*?"

"Yes," I said, only bothering to get sidetracked onto this subject so I could gain Anastasia's trust. This was one area where her interests and mine seemed to cross. "Laramie had this little art cinema called The Trout. They showed *The Hunger* a year after it came out, and at the beginning Bauhaus performed 'Bela Lugosi's Dead.' I liked the music, and I thought Peter Murphy was cute. I couldn't get Bauhaus albums in Laramie. I had to buy them as imports down at Wax Trax in Denver."

"You listened to Bauhaus, but you never became a goth?"

"I joined the Army," I said. "I wanted to follow in my dad's footsteps. He went missing in action in Vietnam."

"You had a death wish?" The idea seemed to excite her.

"No," I corrected. "I wanted to be a professional soldier. My checkered career consisted of a few years of servitude, then several months of fighting Saddam in the Gulf War, then getting kicked out because I had the wrong sexual preference."

"It's just as well, isn't it?"

"I guess so," I said, though I still wished crazily that it had never happened and that I was still down at Ft. Bragg working my way up the military career ladder. In the Army, I'd felt a part of a sacred brotherhood of other guys like me—and they *were* like me, even if nine out of ten preferred Venus to Apollo.

Most of these goths were looking for the same thing I thought I'd found in the Army—comradeship and a sense of belonging. They would have been misfits all through high school, and misfits were loners. They read books, watched horror movies, dabbled with computers, and basically had a lot of time alone to brood. Once they left home, whether off to college or to the big city, they found like-minded souls, and it evolved into a way of life, with its own uniforms, hairstyles, tattoos, and codes of conduct—like the military. We were all looking for someplace to belong. Maybe we all had a death wish. Guns, drugs, booze, cigarettes, and smart bombs were all just a means to an end.

Anastasia looked at me interestedly: "How old are you?"

"I turned thirty yesterday," I said. "Black Friday."

"Happy birthday." She was ironic. "I can't call you 'Mr. Quaintance' anymore. I'm the same age as you."

"You thought I was older?"

"Must be the shaved head. Looks nice, by the way."

"I'm sorry I got on the subject of me," I said. "It's not what I came for. How long did Jared Foster live here with you?"

"He moved in back in April. I haven't seen him for a month. Somebody paid his October rent—I assume it was Jared."

"When was this?"

"Two weeks ago Friday," she said. "A little late, just after the first of the month. I was doing my usual Friday-night stint with Sebastian at Bedlam. When I came home at dawn, I found the envelope on my computer keyboard. Cash, no note."

"Is that unusual, for him to pay in cash?"

"No, not at all."

"Was the envelope addressed or marked on in any way?"

"No, it was blank. I have no way of knowing if it was left by Jared, but I'm assuming it means he intends to come back."

"Was anything taken from your apartment?"

"No," she said. "And I checked."

"I've already spoken with a certain witness who saw Jared in this building on that exact evening," I said. "Jared wasn't alone. He was with some man dressed all in black leather, wearing a full-head mask. Sound like anyone you know?"

Anastasia shook her head in the negative. "I have no idea who that could be. I wish Jared would contact me, though. If he's found someone else to move in with, I wish he'd take his stuff and go. Sebastian's been looking for a place, and I'd like to let him move in with me. I probably will, anyway, but there's only the two bedrooms. If Jared comes back, it'll be tight."

"So you don't think Jared's missing at all?"

"Missing? No. Jared has disappeared before, if you want to call it that. He's always come back, eventually."

"Did he ever tell you where he went? Or with whom?"

"No, and I didn't ask. I'm not his mother."

"What's the longest he ever disappeared?"

"Ten days."

"It's already been longer than that. Jared never attempted to contact you during any of those other times?"

"No. He's not the most thoughtful person. He'd go out to some club and just wouldn't come home. I worried about him the first time. I called the hospitals. I even went to the police. They made a note of it but didn't take it very seriously. The next day, Jared returned, smiling like the cat who ate the canary. The same thing's happened four other times. I no longer worry, but I do sometimes wonder about the boy who cried wolf."

"There are a lot of wolves out there," I said.

Something in the way I said it made Anastasia hesitate, like she'd missed something. She sat forward and set her coffee down.

"What do you mean by that?"

"Don't you read the papers?"

"No. The world's running down, and I find it depressing. I've forced myself to become uninterested. I'd rather not know."

"You haven't seen today's paper, then?"

"No, why?"

"Did you hear anything last night about a body that was found yesterday morning? The police think it's a murdered goth."

"A goth?" Anastasia shrank back in her seat. Peter raised his head up to look at her. "Murdered?"

I withdrew the folded-up *Post* story from my wallet and reached across Peter to hand it to Anastasia.

She scanned through it like Evelyn Wood's pet pupil.

"Karel?" she said. "I don't believe it. My God!"

"You knew him?"

"A little," she qualified. "I've seen him at the clubs, anyway. I never really knew him. Jesus! Murdered?"

"That's why Jared's father was so agitated when you saw him this morning," I said. "He went down to the city mortuary to try and identify the body. He thought it was going to be Jared. He was probably still shaken up when he came here."

"I was in the booth with Sebastian all night," Anastasia said. "We never heard a word about it."

"Maybe no one who goes to Bedlam watches the TV news."

"That's likely." She rescanned the story.

"Do you know if Karel's his real name or an assumed one?"

"I wouldn't know. I remember that tattoo, and someone

introduced him to me as Karel. He looked young—too young to drink, anyway. Bedlam and the other clubs let eighteen-year-olds in but don't allow them to drink. I remember he had a kind of accent. He was from Prague or Budapest. Someplace like that."

"Maybe you should go down to the mortuary to confirm that he's the one. Though even if it is him, you won't be able to properly identify him. You don't really know who Karel is."

"I may know people who do—people I used to see him with. Now that I think of it, I haven't seen Karel around the clubs for a while. Though people do come and go."

"That they do," I agreed. I took out my pen, tore a page from my notepad, and pulled Detective Orjuedos's card from my wallet. "I'm writing down the name and numbers of the police detective working this case. You should get in touch with him right away and give him any information you have about Karel."

"But I've told you everything I know."

"It's not my case. I'm not with the police, and I don't want to do any of their dirty work for them."

"I'll call him as soon as you go," Anastasia promised.

"Jared Foster is my case," I said, "and my client is hoping that I find him before he winds up like Karel. Whoever killed Karel did it in a vampirish fashion, and Karel does resemble Jared. It's natural for my client to be worried. What if there's someone stalking these clubs who's gone over the edge?"

"I don't know any goths who like to actually murder people." Anastasia was defensive. "Most of us are in the scene because we like the music. No one takes it as far as you seem to think."

I didn't blame her for feeling the way she did. I would have felt the same if anyone had come up to me at Ft. Bragg and suggested that some guy in my unit had murdered one of our own.

"No matter what's happened to Jared, it's in everyone's interests that we find him," I said. "You're absolutely certain that you have no idea where he is?"

"Yes."

"You wouldn't be protecting him or anything, would you?"

"Why should I do that?"

"In case he didn't want to speak with his father anymore."

"He wasn't on great terms with his father, that's for sure, but that has nothing to do with me. I'm not helping Jared."

"Did you and Jared have an intimate relationship?"

"That's a personal question." Anastasia smirked.

"I'm not asking out of prurience," I said. "All I know is, a breakup might be reason enough for Jared to spend long periods away from your apartment, until he got settled in elsewhere."

"Intimate relations among goths can be fairly tangled."

"That doesn't tell me much about you and Jared."

"Doesn't it?"

"No. Call me dim."

"This is a two-bedroom apartment," she said. "I live in one room. Jared lives in another. He moved in as my friend. If we were intimate on a few occasions, it was purely for fun."

"You were never boyfriend girlfriend, then?"

"No, not in any conventional sense. We were always just good, close friends. That's the best I can describe it to you."

"Friends fall out," I said. "You never had a falling out?"

"Not at all. I like Jared. I think he likes me. He just wasn't the type who would interest me for any long-term deal."

"In what way?"

"In every way—romantically, spiritually, sexually."

"Why not?"

"Why not?" Anastasia repeated, amused. "You sound more like a psychiatrist than a detective. Anyone can tell you, I prefer guys who are more effeminate. More passive. Less intense."

"What makes Jared so intense?"

"I don't suppose you've ever met him, have you?"

"No," I said. "I've only seen his photo."

"It's not going to come through in a photo. It's all in his physical presence—and in his eyes, the way he looks at you, like he wants to impose his will on yours."

"For real? Does it work?"

"On some of them it does. It's always amusing to watch Jared place others under his spell. It doesn't work on me. I'm too strong-willed to become one of his victims."

"Victims?"

"That's what he calls them. Greg, it's a joke. He likes to meet new people all the time. Sometimes he brings them back to his room, but more often he likes to go home with them. It's like what I said about vampires not being able to cross a threshold until they're invited. Jared sees it as a challenge to make people he's just met invite him into their apartments."

"Not easy to do in New York," I said. "Just who exactly are we talking about? Women? Men?"

"Men, women, both—singles, couples, groups, whatever."

"What does he do with them—or to them?"

"How should I know?" Anastasia said. "I never went off with them, and I never participated."

"I've heard that some goths like to drink their partner's blood," I said, becoming more serious. "Does Jared?"

"I see you've been watching the TV talk shows," Anastasia said, shaking her head dismissively. "I'm sure there are a few goths who are into it. I'm also sure there are many more who tell people they do it just for the shock value, to see the look on their faces. As for Jared, I wouldn't know. You'd have to ask him. I think he'd tell you that's a very personal question. Even if he told you that he drank blood, I wouldn't believe him."

"Does Jared ever really think he's a vampire? I mean, does he avoid sunlight, garlic, mirrors, running water, and all that?"

"Please," Anastasia said. "Maybe he likes to play-act a little more than most. But I'm sure he has a grip on reality."

"How about you? Have you ever drank blood? Or tried it?"

"No, Greg, never." She sighed. "Nor is it anything I want to get into. I consider it dangerous. The only way it can be at all safe is if you're in a monogamous relationship with someone you can trust. There are a lot of goths out there having casual sex and injecting drugs. How many of them are being safe about it is anyone's guess. Most of my friends are pretty much single, and there's been a lot of musical beds going on."

"No long-term relationships?"

"I know some long-term couples. I also know a few long-term triads and one quad—and even they aren't what you'd consider monogamous. It's a different world."

"You're telling me Jared could be going off with just about anybody and doing just about anything with them. Drugs, alcohol, blood-drinking, unsafe sex, anything. You have no idea what he does with them, and sometimes he doesn't come back for days."

"Something like that."

"You're never jealous?"

"Why should I be? I don't care what Jared does."

"You haven't seen him out in the clubs in the last month?"

"That's not unusual. There are a lot of goth clubs in Manhattan and other clubs with goth nights. I'm active on the scene, but I don't always go to the same place. I don't even go out every night. Jared could be out at one club while I'm at another. Maybe he's sick of it. Maybe he's found somebody he likes spending private time with. Anything's possible."

"You can't think of any reason why I ought to be concerned about his welfare? He hasn't been hanging out with any psychos?"

"Depends on what you consider a psycho."

"I'm sure there are a few on the scene."

"All kinds of people on the scene, from trendy kids from the suburbs who like to come into the city and do it for fashion's sake, to the Wiccans and Satan worshippers and the hardcore SM fetishists. Most of us fall somewhere in between, thankfully."

"Where exactly did Jared fall?"

"Now that's an interesting question," she said, as if none of my others had been up to snuff. "When I met Jared, he struck me as the wannabe type—just some college kid from the 'burbs. But there was this rabid goth inside him waiting to come out."

"How rabid?"

"More rabid than I."

"When did you first meet him?"

"Last January. Not sure of the exact date. Must have been a Monday night, though, 'cause it was over at CB's Gallery on the Bowery. Kind of a goth crowd there on Mondays. Jared looked like he was testing the waters. He hadn't done a very good job with his makeup. He overdid it, looked kind of clownish."

"He was still in school at the time?"

"Yes. I didn't see him out much back then. After a while, I gave him my number, and we started spending time together outside of the clubs. That's when we became friends."

"How soon after that did you ask him to move in?"

"He's the one who asked me. It was the first week of April. My old roommate was moving out. Jared had been wanting out of the place where he was living with his ex-girlfriend—"

"This would be Juliet Logan?"

"Yes, that's the one."

"Did you ever meet her? Is she a goth?"

"Yes, I've met Juliet. No, she's not a goth."

"How do you like her?"

"I don't."

"Jealousy?"

"You're stuck on that word, aren't you? I told you, Jared was never my boyfriend. He moved in after my old roommate moved out, and Juliet would come by and pester us. She couldn't get it through her head that he didn't want to have anything more to do with her. She kept trying to force her way back into his life."

"Could I see Jared's room?"

"I don't know about that."

"You consider that too much of a violation of his privacy?"

"Yes."

"What if he's in some kind of danger?"

"I doubt it," she said. "But even if he is, how would looking at his room help you do anything about it?"

"I'm only trying to learn as much as I can about him."

"What are you planning to do once you find him?"

"I'm not going to hurt him. The rest is my business."

"I can't let you search through Jared's things, not without a warrant, but I guess I can let you see what's out in the open."

"A quick once-over is all I'm asking."

"Come with me, then." Anastasia stood up, and so did I.

I had to eject Peter from my lap. He wasn't happy about it.

FIVE

IT WAS A SMALL ROOM with no windows, like the cell of a depraved monk. The first thing I saw was Charles Manson's face, with eyebrows turned in and eyes staring out demoniacally, in a tight close-up on a black-and-white poster opposite the bed. On another wall was a similarly giant-sized photograph of Grigory Rasputin, with a wild look that was eerily identical to Manson's — cunning, possessive, hypnotic.

"Not what I'd want to wake up to every morning," I said.

"You're not Jared," Anastasia said.

The rest of the wall space was covered by other, less offensive posters: a collage of photos of a morbid Bauhaus concert circa the early 1980s; the cheerful-looking members of a band called Kevorkian Death Cycle; cover artwork from albums by Mentallo & the Fixer, KMFDM, and Skinny Puppy; a blown-up still of Conrad Veidt as the homicidal somnambulist in *The Cabinet of Dr. Caligari*, carrying the limp form of a woman in a nightgown;

and a grotesque H. R. Giger print depicting fleshy organic structures slithering into gray, necrotic orifices. On the back of Jared's door was one more human face—but it was only Lon Chaney as the top-hatted vampire in *London After Midnight*, baring his razor-sharp teeth. His black-ringed eyes stared wide, in mockery of Manson and Rasputin. Army surplus camouflage netting hung loosely from the four corners of the ceiling, bathing the walls with spiderweb shadows.

"Would you consider this a typical goth's room?"

"Depends on whether you like posters all over your walls," Anastasia said. "Jared's young yet. He still has that teen sensibility that every wall has to be covered with something. You don't still have posters all over your apartment, do you?"

"No, I don't."

"But I bet you did in high school."

"Sure. No Bauhaus posters, though. I used to write away for free Army recruiting posters. I put them up on every wall. Cute young soldiers being all that they could be, preparing to die for their country. These books are all Jared's, I take it?"

The tall shelves next to the bed were filled mostly with paperbacks. The spines were thoroughly creased. The selection here was not as diverse as Anastasia's out in the living room. There were some horror novels, many books about vampires, and a disproportionate number of true-crime titles that added up to a *Who's Who* of serial killers: Jeffrey Dahmer, Joel Rifkin, Richard Ramirez, Ted Bundy, John Wayne Gacy, Richard Speck, David Berkowitz, Albert de Salvo, Ian Brady & Myra Hindley, Henry Lee Lucas, Ed Gein, Peter Kurten (the Vampire of Düsseldorf), and Herman Mudgett, as well as the still unknown Green River Killer, Zodiac Killer, Cleveland Torso Killer, and Jack the Ripper.

"Jared's really into this stuff," I said.

"He and a million other people," Anastasia said. "Otherwise

the big publishers wouldn't print these books, would they?"

"Does Jared act perfectly sane most of the time?"

"I don't know any guys who are perfectly sane."

"Did he ever do anything you thought totally irrational?"

"My idea of rationality and yours are bound to differ."

"You know what I'm trying to get at, don't you?" I asked, wondering how I could dig through her goth defenses and reach the real person beneath. She simply stood there and waited for me to put it into my own words. "You're all obsessed with death. I can appreciate that. Believe me, it doesn't make me jump to any conclusion that you're all a bunch of psychos. I enjoy a good horror novel as much as the next guy, and I even like some of your bands. But there's a danger in taking it too far—"

"Taking anything too far can be dangerous," Anastasia said.

"Has Jared ever taken it too far?"

"By whose standard? What do you consider too far?"

"Let's say harming someone without their consent."

"You mean like rape?"

"Rape, torture, giving someone bad drugs, drinking their blood without their consent. You know, anything violent."

"I doubt it," Anastasia said. "I wouldn't put too much stock in that fact that Jared calls people his victims. There's a lot of theater going on in the scene—that's one thing a lot of people outside it don't realize. Most of us keep our sense of humor. It might be black, and it might not translate, but it's there. Jared can be funny at times, in a sick sort of way."

"You're saying you don't think I should take any of this too seriously—Charlie Manson and Rasputin on his walls? A whole library detailing every sick act of every last mass murderer?"

"Haven't you ever read a book about a serial killer?"

"Yeah, sure, but—"

"It didn't turn you into one, did it?" she said. "Greg, lighten up. If Jared likes to pick people up for sex and call them victims, it doesn't mean he's intentionally hurting them."

"It doesn't?"

"Don't you think that anyone who's been harmed the way you're describing would report it to the police?"

"Most people would," I admitted. "Has Jared ever hurt you?"

"No, and he never expressed any desire to, either."

My attention drew itself to a mirror in an old picture frame over Jared's dresser. Snapshots were tucked along the edges of the frame, curving slightly outward: various people in goth makeup and clothing—everyday shots that looked like other people's Halloween, with people mugging and posing for the camera. Jared was in only a few of his own pictures.

"I thought vampires didn't like mirrors," I said.

"Vampires don't cast a reflection," Anastasia corrected. "Anyway, Jared isn't a vampire. Neither am I. How could any of us put on our makeup if we couldn't see ourselves in a mirror?"

"I didn't mean to imply that I actually believed in the supernatural," I said. "Only that Jared wants to be a vampire."

"Some kids want to grow up to be firemen," she said. "Some want to be nurses. Some want to be stockbrokers. Some want to be vampires. Every occupation has a costume and a look."

"These people in the photos—all friends of Jared?"

"And other people he's met."

"Victims?"

"Who knows? I know most of them myself. Regulars on the New York scene. Some of these were taken in Boston at a goth convention—New York goths mingling with Boston goths. I was there. See? Standing next to Jared, with a little more makeup."

I recognized Anastasia once she pointed it out. She was in full makeup—a pale, lightly powdered face with a line of rouge under her cheek bones, dark eyeliner and mascara, and what looked like black lipstick. She was decked out in a lot of silver jewelry and wearing a black silk shirt with deep cleavage. She was laughing, holding a green bottle of Rolling Rock in one hand, the other arm draped around Jared's waist. Jared had a beer, too, and was looking at the camera operator with one eyebrow raised and with a kindly sidewise grin. His long black hair was pulled off to one side, exposing one ear and falling across the other shoulder. He wore a billowy white shirt, loose in the sleeves and with a ruffled collar, entirely unbuttoned to reveal his flat, bony chest. I made out a dragon tattoo serpentining up his right side and a shrunken head tattoo on his left pectoral. He had silver rings through his nipples and one in his navel, in addition to the many trimming his ears, the two in his eyebrows, the one in his nose, and the ball and post on the lower lip.

"Looks like you were having fun," I said.

"It was a good convention," she said.

"What's this one?" I asked, catching a glimpse of something.

I had nearly missed it, there at the bottom of the frame, curling down and away from my sight. I smoothed it flat against the mirror to get a better look. It was of Jared and another young man who I recognized from the medical examiner's photos.

"Oh my God!" Anastasia drew in a breath. "That's Karel!"

Jared and Karel were standing up against each other with their shirts off, mugging for the camera. They had similar hawthorn-branch tattoos going up both arms, but Karel's other tattoos differed from Jared's considerably: the black rose and the red-lettered name, the scarab, the ankh, and the spider web emerging from his navel and disappearing into the waist of his black velvet trousers. Jared had his arm around Karel and was biting his ear. Karel was smiling giddily, showing his filed-down fangs, with his eyes half-closed and his arm around Jared.

"Did you know that they knew each other?" I asked.

"No," Anastasia said, unconvincingly.

"You'd better tell Detective Orjuedos about this."

"Why?" she asked with a hint of indignation.

"I don't mean to suggest anything about Jared. Right now, the N.Y.P.D. doesn't have a positive identification on your Karel. The only person either of us know of who may have known him is Jared. If I find Jared, he might be able to identify Karel for the medical examiner. He might also be able to give some names of people Karel knew, one of whom might be his killer. Jared Foster could be of great help to the police investigation."

"Oh my God," Anastasia repeated, staring closely at the photo. "They do look a lot alike, don't they?"

"Except for the tattoos," I said, almost to myself.

I wondered just which of Karel's tattoos had been mentioned in the description given out on last night's news broadcasts. I would think they would want to list all of them. The only ones that were similar to Jared's were the hawthorn branches. It was certainly possible that the only ones Henry Foster had heard given out were those, or that he had only been half paying attention. Mention of any of the other tattoos should have been enough to make him lie back down in bed and get a good night's sleep and not have to take a drive down to New York first thing the next morning—unless Foster had paid so little attention to his son that he had no idea what Jared's tattoos looked like.

"I'm going to tell Orjuedos about this photo the next time I speak with him. You will have called him already. If you neglected to mention it, he'll think you're being obstructive."

"Why don't you take it, then, if it's so damned important?"

"I'm not a cop, and it's not my case. If Orjuedos wants to consider this evidence, he'll need to see it in its natural setting. I can't take it. Leave it for him to see for himself."

"Okay," she said soberly. "You're right. I'll leave it."

"Do you know where the picture was shot?"

"Looks like The Lot."

"The Loft?"

"No, The Lot. It's a club."

"Oh," I said. "Where?"

"Corner of Houston and Norfolk."

"Any idea when?"

"Hard to say—no more than three months ago, though."

"Why's that?"

"Jared didn't have that shrunken head tattoo until July."

"I see," I said. "Can you help me with names of Jared's friends? Maybe some of these people on his mirror?"

"Sure, I can," she said hesitantly. "But Jared's met tons of other people that I've never met and don't know about."

"All I need is a shove in the right direction," I said. "I'm not immune to footwork. I was planning on going out to your clubs and asking around. You could still give me some names."

"If I were you, I'd start with Lucrezia," she said.

"Last name?"

"I've never asked. She's a friend of Jared's, not mine."

"Do you have her phone number?"

"No, but you might find her tonight at Bedlam or The Lot."

"Okay," I said. "Who else?"

"Theophrastus."

"Is that one name or two?" I asked, licking my pencil tip.

"One." She spelled it out for me. "I know his last name. It's Jones. But don't use it. He'll get angry. Theophrastus owns The Lot. Come by tonight, and I'll introduce you."

"Do I need a goth look to get in?"

"Not really. Don't bother with any makeup. The shaved head is good. You've got white-enough skin. You'll be a minimalist. Wear black. No Day-Glo colors. No white athletic shoes."

"Right," I said. "What time should I meet you?"

"Eleven-thirty," she said. "Meet me inside, at the long bar. No telling when or if Theophrastus will be there, but you can get started asking around. I'm not sure how far you'll get, though. We're kind of a counter-culture bunch and don't much like cops. Some will be doing drugs, and—"

"I'm not going to bust anybody," I said.

"I can also take you over to Bedlam and introduce you to Sebastian de Leon. He's also a good friend of Jared's."

"Then I'll see you at The Lot, at eleven-thirty," I said. "Oh, and one more thing before I go."

"Yes?"

"Jared's been gone for weeks, and he's got a set of keys to your place. Someone used them to get in here. You seem pretty complacent about it, though you admitted that you don't even know if it was Jared. I told you Jared was seen around here that night—but he was with somebody who may be a stranger to you. No one seems to know where Jared is. His pal Karel's dead, and no one knows who killed him. If I were you, I'd call a locksmith and get your locks changed. *Today*. Even before you call Detective Orjuedos."

"But what if Jared comes back? He'll be locked out."

"Don't worry about Jared. If you're here, you can buzz him in. Better for you to be safe. Change the locks, Anastasia."

Peter meowed up at her, seconding the motion.

"I will," she said and absently stroked her neck.

SIX

I SOUGHT AN ADDRESS on MacDougal Street between Bleecker and
West Fourth, once part of a large working-class Italian ghetto just
south of the hanging grounds at Washington Square. It was
narrow and, at any time of day, lent itself to shadows. When I
arrived, at twilight, the old tenements leaned forward to get a
better look at me. Outside, they looked much like any other
1880's apartment buildings, but the quarters within were
notoriously scant on square footage. Tenants these days were
largely N.Y.U. students, and the apartments were situated above
claustrophobic ground-floor and basement-level shops that offered
vintage clothing, used records, used CDs, used paperbacks, bad
jewelry, take-out falafel, comic books, pizza, booze, and coffee.

I found my address easily enough. The ground floor housed a
small T-shirt shop. Peeling black plastic label tape said
LOGAN/FOSTER next to the buzzer for 3A. I pressed it for two
seconds.

"Who is it?" came a female voice over squawky distortion.

"Greg Quaintance. I'm a private detective."

There was an extended silence, and I began to wonder whether she had pressed her listen button while I was talking.

"What do you want?" she came back with, finally.

"I'm looking for Juliet Logan."

"Um, she's not here."

"Who are you?"

"Her friend."

"Could I speak with you, then? Should only take a minute."

"What's this about? Is Juliet in some kind of trouble?"

"I'd rather not get into it over the intercom." I gave myself the voice of authority. "Would you mind letting me up?"

"I don't know about that."

"Or come down yourself and have a look at me."

"Um, okay," she said. "Just let me put some clothes on."

I backed off a few steps onto the sidewalk and stared through the window of the T-shirt shop. The shirts all promoted one rock band or another—mostly newer groups that I'd never heard of or listened to. I did, however, notice an attractive black Bauhaus shirt featuring the eerie cover art for their old album *The Sky's Gone Out*—a perennial favorite of the goths and one that I still had in my crates full of old vinyl.

I saw above that the sky *had* gone out. Twilight had given in to night, and the city lights rendered the stars invisible.

"Hi!"

Under the glow of a single yellow bulb, the building's door was opened by a twenty-year-old girl with long, straight, blond, wet hair. She wore hip-hugging bell-bottom blue jeans and a tight tie-dyed T-shirt over no bra. She had breasts the size of bagels and nipples like plump raisins—which I would never have noticed if she hadn't been showing them off.

"You're the detective?" she said smilingly.

I fixed up a grim, businesslike countenance and showed her my private eye's license. She took a minute to fully peruse it.

"Would you give me your name?" I withdrew notepad and pen.

"Dawn, D-A-W-N. Lewis, L-E-W-I-S." She giggled as I wrote.

"Are you a student?"

"Uh-huh."

"You live with Juliet Logan?"

"Yeah, so?"

"It says Logan and Foster. I don't see any Lewis."

"Oh, Foster was her last roommate."

"What happened to him?"

"How do you know it was a him?" Dawn tried to be coy.

"I'm not here to play games," I said. "He was a he, and his name was Jared Foster. Where is he?"

"He moved out," she said glumly. "Why do you want to know?"

"I'm looking for him."

"You said you were looking for Juliet."

"To ask her about Jared. He might be in trouble."

"Oh?" Her lower lip trembled. "What kind of trouble?"

I wasn't there to answer Dawn Lewis's questions.

"Did you ever meet Jared?"

"A couple of times." Dawn was getting bored with me fast because I refused to smile. Her shoulders started swaying from side to side as if to music. "He came back to get some stuff."

"What did you think of him?"

Dawn shrugged meaninglessly. Some words caught in her throat, and then she said, "I don't know."

"Is any of Jared's stuff still up in the apartment?"

"You'd have to ask Juliet."

"You're sure she's not here?"

"Sure I'm sure." Dawn laughed like something struck her as funny. "In fact, I haven't seen her all day. And I don't know when to expect her home. Sorry."

"Where can I find her?"

"She should be at work. She waits tables at Café Giotto."

"Over on Seventh Avenue, near Charles Street?"

"That's the one." She sighed like she was unbearably bored.

"You don't want to invite me up?"

"What for?" Dawn Lewis took a step back, into shadow. Any man who wanted to come up but wasn't going to smile was trouble.

"Just to have a look around. I won't touch anything. I'd like to see where Jared used to live. How about it?"

"I—I don't know if I can without Juliet's permission." Dawn hastily dredged up an excuse: "My name's not on the lease."

"You don't get to invite people up to your room? What is she, a concierge?"

"I can't."

"I suppose I'll have to talk to her, then?"

"Yeah, that'd be best."

Dawn began to close the door.

I slapped my hand around it and braced it open.

Dawn jumped at the noise. She wanted to be quit of me.

"I'm not finished," I said. I took out the recent photo of Jared Foster and held it up to her. "Come closer, Dawn. Take a good look. Is this the Jared Foster you know?"

"I guess so," she said meekly. She stared at it for a while, nibbling at the already stumpy nail of her index finger.

"Is it or isn't it?"

"Yeah," she said. "That's him."

"And you're a hundred percent certain that you haven't seen him anytime in the last month or so?"

"Positive." Dawn withdrew her finger from her mouth and started working the nail around with her tongue.

"Dawn, if you do see Jared —"

"Why should I see him?"

"Is his name still on the lease with Juliet's?"

"I — How would I know?"

"Are you sure Jared didn't retain a set of keys?"

"Geez, I hope not."

"Why not?"

"He's creepy." She added a giggle that didn't seem to go along with the sentiment. "I don't get what Juliet saw in him."

"Maybe he wasn't creepy when she met him." I doled out a business card. "If you do see Jared, will you give me a call?"

"Yeah, sure." She slid the card into a tight front pocket.

"Day or night, doesn't matter. It's urgent I find him."

"All right," she said. "But I don't think I'll see him."

"You'll call if you do," I said forcefully.

She nodded up and down. "Sorry I couldn't be any more help."

"Sure you are," I said. "You can go dry your hair now."

I removed my hand from the door and allowed her to shut it.

Dawn double-checked to make sure it locked, then ran back up the stairs like it was someplace very important she had to go.

The clerk inside the T-shirt shop was turning his COME ON IN, WE'RE OPEN sign around to SORRY, WE'RE CLOSED. I stopped him by stepping inside. He looked tired but desirous of a sale. I showed him Jared's photo. He asked me if I wanted it transferred to a T-shirt. I said it hadn't come to that yet. I asked him if he'd ever laid eyes on the guy. He said no and shook his head convincingly. I told him the guy used to live upstairs about six months back. He said he'd worked here less than a month and had never

seen him. I thanked him for his time, put Jared's photo away, and
shelled out eighteen bucks cash for the Bauhaus shirt.

Café Giotto was an easy ten-minute walk from MacDougal Street.
The night air had grown colder, and the wind had died. Leaves
blown over from Washington Square had gathered in piles over
the storm drains so they could clog them up and flood the streets
the next time it rained. I smoked some cigarettes along the way
but was drowned out on crowded corners by the reek of others'
cigars.

The walls of Café Giotto were hung with paintings and prints
of Florence and environs. The marble-topped tables were taken up
by single persons reading books and by couples reacting to each
other's faces over espressos and Italian pastries under the warm
light of ancient floor lamps with tasseled shades. The chairs were
an odd collection of stray antiques with uniquely mismatched
upholstery, each more outré than any of their occupants. The
shelves along the back wall behind the bar held colorful bottles of
flavored syrups flanking the central cappuccino machine—a huge
chromium tank sprouting decorative pipes, gauges, and nozzles
and looking like it could have powered the Fulton Ferry.

I didn't spot any women on the wait staff. The men were all
dressed in semiformal waiter's garb, with black trousers, full
aprons, starched shirts, and bow ties, like the penguins in *Mary
Poppins* only without the tailcoats. A young Italian came at me
with a curly mop of hair, melancholy eyes, and winsome lips that
parted to ask me in lightly accented English if I would care for a
table. He motioned toward a choice empty one by the windows,
where I could see and be seen by all of Seventh Avenue.

"No, thanks," I said, though it was a great table. "I'm
looking to talk with one of your waitresses, a Juliet Logan?"

"Excuse me?" he said. "Did you say a waitress?"

I didn't like the uncomprehending look in his eye. We both spoke English, so it wasn't that.

"Is there a waitress on your staff named Juliet Logan?"

"No, sir," he said. "We don't employ waitresses."

"You're quite sure of that?"

"Absolutely, sir." His mouth rose slightly at the corners as if he found my questions diverting. "I train all of our waiters myself, and I can assure you that they are all men."

"And none have a name anywhere close to Juliet Logan?"

"No, sir. Perhaps you wanted a different café?"

"No," I said. "The person who told me Café Giotto was quite specific about it. I even confirmed the address with her. She must have been pulling my leg. Sorry to take up your time."

"Oh," he said, blushing with modesty. "I'm happy to be of service. Perhaps you would like that table after all?"

"That's tempting, but I'm afraid I don't have the time."

"Ah, too bad." He stared warmly at me with an open question on his lips that came out as, "You'll come back again sometime?"

"I will. I'll take a rain check on that table."

"No promises, of course," he said with a chuckle.

"But I have to ask, why an all-male wait staff? Isn't that old-fashioned?"

"The owner prefers it that way." He shrugged to show me that the matter was out of his hands, but then he gave me a wink, just between us: "It's, you know, for aesthetic reasons."

"I see," I said, though I didn't. I certainly found men more enjoyable to look at, but others considered women equally delightful, and it struck me as insufficient disqualification for employment. These kinds of criteria were still rampant in New York—at once the most civilized and most barbaric of cities.

"Men make better waiters," he whispered conspiratorially,

with blind devotion to our sex. "They know that in Europe."

"I wouldn't go around repeating that here if I were you," I whispered back. "Though I do find you aesthetically pleasing."

I gave him my card, and he gave me one of Cafe Giotto's, with his name—Nick—and phone number written on the back.

At least my coming over here wasn't a total bust.

I had trouble hailing a cab, so I walked as fast as I could down Bleecker to MacDougal. It should have taken me less than ten minutes but ended up fifteen. Foot traffic was heavy and difficult to negotiate. I got stuck behind dawdling out-of-towners walking four abreast. I had nothing against them except that they always appeared miraculously whenever I was in a rush.

The lights in the T-shirt shop were dark. It was shut up and gated for the night. I tried Juliet Logan's buzzer but got no answer. I repeated this for ten minutes before giving up. I looked up at the windows but saw no lights on anywhere above. I wasn't sure whether her apartment faced the street, but in any case, there were no signs of life. The entrance door was firmly locked, and there was no point in picking it.

Dawn Lewis, a.k.a. Juliet Logan, wasn't home.

It was only as I was walking back up MacDougal Street that my suspicions were confirmed. Up near Minetta Lane was a cozy-looking Spanish restaurant with a sooty white stucco façade and iron-barred windows. It looked like it had been there for thirty years. A middling review from an old *Zagat's* was enlarged and posted prominently in the window. The wooden sign hanging out front featured a portrait of a smiling, mustachioed Spanish knight and said DON LUIS – SPANISH CUISINE – TAPAS BAR.

Dawn Lewis. Very funny.

I went back down MacDougal and hung out at a table inside the window of a little falafel joint across from Juliet Logan's building, hoping to catch her coming out or returning.

I wasted a lot of time watching and ate a lot of falafel.

SEVEN

I CAME BACK to my studio apartment in Chelsea, rummaged through my record crates, dug out the Bauhaus album *Mask*, and laid it on my turntable for some mood music—what I'd listened to in my lost teen years when I thought our President was going to snuff us out in grand nuclear style: "Kick in the Eye," "Of Lillies and Remains," "Muscle in Plastic," and so on. It was a British import, still with the Wax Trax price tag in the upper corner: $7.98. The cardboard casing folded out to reveal lyrics and some spooky-sexy photos of Peter Murphy, Daniel Ash, and the boys.

I took a shower and reshaved my stubbly head to make it baby smooth. I used to date a hairstylist from the salon below my office who would do it to me for free with a straight razor. Our breaking up forced me to learn how to manage with a twin-blade without shredding my scalp.

I adorned myself with silver jewelry that I'd picked up cheaply on Eighth Street, just north of Washington Square: a necklace with a silver ankh, finger rings decorated with skulls and bones and gargoyles, and a variety of silver bracelets, including one that wrapped around in multiple coils and was textured like a diamondback, with a rattle at one end and open jaws and fangs at the other. I had a pair of silver hoop earrings lying around, and I put them in. I'd had my ears pierced back in high school but stopped wearing earrings when I entered the Army. Lucky for me, the holes had never closed up.

I put on the Bauhaus T-shirt, a pair of tight black stretch jeans, and black motorcycle boots. I made sure my Glock 17L was loaded and ready, with seventeen nine-millimeter hollow-points in the clip and one in the chamber. I secured it in my shoulder holster, making sure my black leather motorcycle jacket hid it fully. It did. I was ready to go.

I arrived at The Lot around eleven fifteen. It was nondescript. The heavy, black, windowless steel door was propped open by an old red brick. The address was clear above the door, but no sign of any kind marked the club. Dim lights and loud goth-industrial music pouring from within told me I was at the right place.

I paid the door girl the Saturday night cover of five bucks and had no trouble getting past her. Her hair was shorn a half-inch long and was dyed fluorescent purple. Her whiteface makeup was caky and clowny—deliberately so—and she wore charcoal eye shadow in oval rings, like Uncle Fester. At her neck was a dull gray steel collar with three-inch spikes sticking out all around. Her lipstick was a glossy black, like six coats of buffed enamel on an old Cadillac. She glanced up at me with a look of bored despair and let me inside.

The early crowd was surprisingly thick. Gloomy boys and girls lined the front hall, standing stock-still and looking like they were waiting for friends, or for their doom. Strobe lights flashed from the big room beyond and showed the glisten of moisture in their eyes that hinted they were alive. Most had big heads of hair—either black as death or stripped a bright yellow blond—teased high, with strands dangling before their woeful eyes. They were powdered and pale and wasted away, with rose-colored eye shadow and deep slashes of rouge across the cheeks. Some looked as young as sixteen, but perhaps that was the intent of their maquillage. They made a gauntlet of deathly beauty for new arrivals to run, standing against the walls with bony knees jutting out, asking for me or anyone else to take them—take them anywhere, deeper into the club or back out into the night and off to oblivion.

I wondered if Karel and Jared had stood along here wishing that. Jared's bookshelf attested to the fact that there were plenty of people out there who were willing to oblige.

I kept moving, following the music. As I drove deeper, the club grew hotter, and I smelled the strong odors of beer, sweat, cigarette smoke, and marijuana. The walls were painted pitch black, and when I touched them they were cold and damp as a cave. The music over the speakers was driving and elemental and echoed off the hard walls. I descended a few steps into a long room crowded with people dressed in black, many of them dancing, showing pallid arms and chests and midriffs covered in tattoos. I had a tattoo on my right biceps—the Army tattoo I'd gotten down in Fayetteville when I came back from Saudi. I was going to keep my jacket on, tattoo hidden. The goths would only laugh.

Eyes followed me, but the attention was as intense and as limited as in any gay bar. They looked but made no contact, too caught up in themselves, too protective of their cliques, too proud to make a move to get to know another. It looked like they were talking, but I could hardly hear any voices over the music.

I negotiated my way through to the bar. I looked up and

down but saw no sign of Anastasia. I was early, though. The early crowd was thick but bound to get much thicker.

I squeezed in between two young grotesqueries—females, I think—and held a fiver across the bartop. I lit a cigarette and puffed. My peripheral vision caught the females eyeing me.

One of the bartenders saw my little glint of Lincoln green and scooted down to me. His big black hair added five inches to an already great height. He was shirtless and wan, with sunken cheekbones and ribs you could count. Here, this qualified as cute. He had a pleasant rictus smile that probably earned him generous tips.

"What's your poison?" he asked. Ha-ha.

The sign behind him advertised a special on snakebites.

"Snakebite," I said. Whatever that was. I didn't have to drink it if it was too horrendous.

The bartender opened a bottle of English cider and a bottle of Rolling Rock and poured them together into a tall, wide glass. He handed it over and gave me my change. I left a couple of quarters on the bartop and motioned for him with my finger. He leaned over, placing his ear within half an inch of my teeth.

I thought of Jared, biting Karel's ear in the photo.

"You heard about Karel?" I tried to split his eardrums.

"The guy who was murdered?" he shouted back. He glanced up and down the bar, but none of the ghouls wanted him at present.

I cupped my hand around my lips: "Did you know him?"

"No, not really," he said. "I remember seeing him. Never talked with him, though. Friend of yours?"

"Friend of a friend. Do you know Jared Foster?"

"If that's the Jared I'm thinking of, sure, I know Jared."

"I've been looking for him. You seen him around?"

"No," he said. "Haven't seen him. Can't help you."

"Did he come to The Lot often?"

"Excuse me, I've got a customer." He stood back up and moved down the bar with the grace of a marionette skeleton.

I gulped at my snakebite and waited for him to return.

"Hey!" said the zombie woman—or girl—on my right. She was obese enough that I couldn't pinpoint her age. She had a baby face and peroxide-blond hair in an asymmetrical cut. She'd drawn cobwebs at the corners of her eyes that looked like they belonged on a goth Barbie. Her breasts were pushed up in a bustier worn over her shirt—Madonna circa 1990.

"Hey, what?"

"What's your name?" She was chewing a big wad of gum that smelled like artificial green apple. She sounded like a Staten Island goth. I wondered whether she came over like that on the ferry. Not that anyone would give a damn in this weird city.

"Grigory," I said, thinking of Jared's thing for Rasputin.

"Grigory?" she said. "I'm Salomé. You come here often?"

I gathered she was one of these suburban goths who came out of the coffin only on the weekends—the kind Anastasia found so odious. Salomé had probably gotten into the scene because the drugs and the sex were easy. It was more convenient to be a hedonist while donning a mask. But a bar was a bar, and she might just as well have been using her lines at some yuppie singles joint on the Upper West Side—if she was old enough.

"No," I told her. "I'm usually at Bedlam. I'm looking for a guy who used to hang out here. Goes by the name of Jared."

"Jared? I don't think I know him."

I dug out the photo and showed it to her.

"Nope," she said. "Don't know him. Can I buy you a drink?"

"No, thanks," I said. "Excuse me."

I backed away and moved down to where the gaunt bartender was polishing glasses. I caught his eye and begged him closer. His head rose up, and he asked what else he could do me for.

I shouted: "Jared Foster—did he come here often?"

"I saw him a lot," he confessed. "Never seen you, though."

The suspicion in his voice made me worry I was sounding too much like a cop. I still believed that it would be a mistake to announce myself. I would have to be more careful in my approach.

"Name's Grigory," I said, taking an empty stool.

"Xerxes," the bartender said, clearing and wiping off the bar before me. He said casually: "How do you know Jared?"

"From Bedlam. I haven't seen him there for a while, so I thought I'd try here. You remember the last time you saw him?"

"No." Xerxes shook his head and looked up. "Do you?"

"Uh, no," I said cautiously.

"Are you like actively looking for him?" Xerxes asked.

"Yeah. I've got something of his I want to return. Why?"

"If you do find him, come back and let me know, will you?"

It was the kind of question I normally reserved for myself.

Xerxes handed me a business card with The Lot spelled out in ghostly lettering framed by two bats in the upper corners, with address and phone numbers below in modern sans serif.

"You can reach me or leave a message at these numbers."

"Why should I?" I asked, placing the card in my wallet.

"Courtesy?" Xerxes suggested. "I know someone else who's looking for Jared, and I'd like to help him out if I can."

"Who," I said derisively, "some cop?"

"A cop?" Xerxes laughed. "Hardly."

"Maybe I could tell him myself and save you the trouble."

"No. It's my business. I'd rather take care of it."

"When I find Jared, maybe I won't bother to tell you."

"Suit yourself." Xerxes shrugged his bony shoulders, deepening the hollows at his clavicles. "No skin off my back."

"You couldn't afford to lose any," I wanted to say.

Xerxes excused himself to go take someone's drink order.

My snakebite was done. I left the glass on the bar.

I went down the line of stools looking for Anastasia. I didn't see her. I quit the long bar and headed out onto the floor, scanning the ashen faces. No Anastasia. It was only eleven-forty-five, though. Manhattanites always showed up late for rendez-vous. I didn't give it much more thought than that.

I bumped into a guy who couldn't help bumping into me, in a white canvas institutional straitjacket with arms strapped across him and crotch straps drawn down into place over his black jeans. A brown leather harness encased his whole head in a multitude of straps and a thick, firm gag. He was fully made-up and with a shaved head like mine, eyelashes carefully done in thick mascara like the ultraviolent punks in *A Clockwork Orange*, eyes wide open and showing frenzied whites.

He didn't look anything like Jared. For one thing, he was too short. He also had no earrings or facial piercings. Whoever he was, though, he appeared to be comfy-cozy in his get-up. His bound arms were lashed to a bulky chain that dangled between him and a woman who stood a whole head taller, with a spiky black mohawk, black lipstick, and a slim cigarette dangling in her mouth. She wore glossy black latex that smelled agreeably of Armor-All, ending in knee-high boots with stiletto heels. She wore ten earrings in each ear, one through her bottom lip, and a choker that was strung all around with what looked like yellowed human teeth. Her waist was corseted like an hourglass. She had the best body I'd seen on any woman in The Lot—but then, it was the body of a woman, not a little girl. She had the kind of old-fashioned curves you needed if you dared to dress in latex—the kind over which any number of straight men would allow themselves to be straitjacketed.

"You there, Bauhaus!" she barked, like a British army commander about to order me over the top at Gallipoli.

I pointed at my chest and raised my eyebrows innocently.

"Yes, you!" She handed me her end of the chain and gently stroked my cheek with one of her long black fingernails. "Be a chum and look after my minion for me while I go to the loo?"

She sucked up some cigarette smoke and looked like she was about to blow it in my face.

I gave her some of mine instead.

"Did you say chum or chump?" I asked.

The point was moot; I was already holding the chain.

She whirled niftily on her stilettos, rolling her black rubber hips and blowing smoke up into the ceiling, carrying her cigarette in one hand and a green beer bottle in the other. She vanished into the crowd, leaving me standing there with this fugitive from a padded cell, arms tucked formally around him and a gag plugging his conversational skills. His head harness was latched in back with a small padlock. I didn't even have the keys to him if anything happened—if his girlfriend never came back, say, or if he started choking on the gag. I shouldn't have allowed myself to get stuck with him.

"You look like you should be at Bedlam," I said chattily.

The man on the other end of the chain snorted like a boar.

"Do you know a guy named Jared Foster?" I asked.

He shook his head.

I tried to think of something else to say.

"Do you like that woman you're with?"

He nodded.

I glanced at my watch and said, "If she doesn't come back in five minutes, I'm turning you in to the lost and found."

I let him mull this over.

In the meantime, I watched out for Anastasia. I could see over most of the crowd. It was impossible to tell how old most of them were under all that pancake. From the glazed look on the door girl's face, I imagined she let just about anyone in. I felt like I was in never-never land.

The tall rubberwoman returned and reclaimed her property, telling me thanks in a deep, dull voice.

"Don't mention it," I said. "Maybe you can do me a return favor, though."

"I wouldn't wager on it," she said.

"I'm looking for someone named Lucrezia. Do you know her?"

"Lucrezia? I know her, all right."

"Is she here tonight?"

"She's here."

"Can you take me to her?"

"I'm busy, love. See over there? That gaggle of girls by the wall, under the likeness of Bela Lugosi? She's the blonde."

"Thanks," I said. "I was also wondering—"

I had hoped to ask her if she knew Jared, but she had already turned back to coo to her pet psycho:

"Oh, the poor ogre looks thirsty, doesn't it? Here you go, my little ugly." She unfastened the gag, but his jaws were still held open by an O ring fixed behind his teeth and strapped in place by the harness. She pushed his head back and tipped the contents of her beer bottle into his mouth. Some spilled down his chin. Her smile widened appreciatively as he chugged it down his throat. She reinserted the gag and locked it back in place, telling him, "There's a good lad."

I was mildly disgusted by this and decided not to stick around and ask her whether she knew Jared. I had a line now on Lucrezia, who ought to be of more use to me. I wormed my way toward the fine black-and-white Bela painted directly on the bricks, through a roiling vampire circus.

It was midnight, and I had yet to see Anastasia materialize. Although I'd seen the photo of her in full makeup, I wondered whether I'd be able to recognize her in her nocturnal guise.

The girls under the sign of Bela were all dressed in black and standing in a cluster of three, like the witches in *Macbeth* or the weird sisters in *Dracula*. The center one had platinum blond hair, parted in the middle and streaming down onto her shoulders in loosely crimped curls. The other two had long, straight black hair halfway down their backs like the early Cher. All three saw me coming; their dark eyes fixed menacingly onto my approaching figure as if to ward me off by force of will.

It was a feeble attempt. I kept coming at them, like the terminator. They grouped closer together, stood their ground.

"I'm looking for Lucrezia," I said, looking at the blonde.

"And you've found her," she said with a smirk, continuing to stare me down—or stare me up. She was six inches shorter and about five years younger than I, in black leather pants and a black mesh shirt with long sleeves that hooked over her thumbs. The holes in the mesh were wide, exposing her pale tattooed flesh, small breasts, and rosy nipples pierced by heavy silver rings. A broad surgical scar descended from her sternum to her navel. She wore it proudly. I couldn't blame her. If I'd undergone open-heart surgery at a young age and lived to tell about it, I'd show everyone, too. Lucrezia's two companions declined to introduce themselves. They set their jaws grimly and continued their vigil against me.

"Pardon the intrusion," I said, which seemed appropriate.

"Somebody sent you to me," Lucrezia said, as if divining it.

"Yes and no. I was seeking you out."

"On whose suggestion?" She smiled a smile with teeth.

"Anastasia."

"I know her, but who are you?"

"Just some guy. Name's Grigory."

"Oh, yeah?" she said, giving knowing looks to either of her companions, like she'd spotted a cubic zirconium at Tiffany's.

I wasn't impressed. The Lot was full of fakes, not the least of whom was any girl named Lucrezia with Jean Harlow hair.

"Anastasia was supposed to meet me here, but she hasn't shown," I said. "Somebody else pointed you out to me. I've been looking for a friend of mine. Anastasia told me you know Jared."

"Jared, yes, I know Jared," Lucrezia said warily. "But I'd be surprised if he's a friend of yours. I know all of Jared's friends. All of his goth friends, anyway. You may be dressed right, Grigory, but—oh, how can I put it in some way your mind can understand?—you haven't got the mark of Cain."

"Cain," I said. "Hero of yours?"

"Nitocris, Eurydice, it's all right," Lucrezia said to her friends. "Leave me alone so I can focus my energies. Don't worry, I'll be perfectly safe. He's harmless enough."

I almost expected to hear them say, "Yes, mistress," and give her a bow. Instead, one jerked her head at the other, and they vanished into the crowd, in the direction of the bar.

"How can you tell I'm harmless?" I asked.

"I know everything about you," Lucrezia said.

"What's my mother's maiden name?"

"Don't ask me to play parlor games, Grigory. What I mean is, I can tell from your aura what kind of guy you are. Women frighten you, for one thing."

"Oh?"

"But you don't let that stop you when you're determined to learn something. And you know that we have a lot to teach you. You may not want to have anything to do with us, but you're practical enough to know that you can't live without us. You're irresistibly drawn to us, despite your fears. But what you're truly afraid of, Grigory, is the feminine side of yourself."

"You're better than a Chinese horoscope," I said, making a show of taking out my wallet. "How much do I owe you?"

"That's not what you came for."

"No, it's not." While I had my wallet out, I went ahead and removed a business card. She was suspicious enough already, and no amount of play-acting was going to overcome it. I had to take a chance. I handed her the card.

"Someone hired you to look for Jared," Lucrezia said. She tucked the card into the front pocket of her leather pants.

"Do you know where I can find him?"

"I can't help you," she said and looked away, at the crowd.

"Then why'd you take my card?"

"Whatever became of Jared is beyond my ability to see."

"You speak of him in the past tense," I said.

"The only sense I have about Jared is that he's in a transition. If he's in hiding, it's because he's preparing for something. If he's gone away, it's only to return. I can't see anything for certain. The images are vague. Perhaps Jared has constructed a wall to keep me out. He's learned a lot from me."

"I didn't come for your psychic mumbo jumbo," I said. "I want facts. You're Jared's friend. You know his other friends. If you don't have any knowledge of his whereabouts, maybe one of them does. I'm asking you to help me in any way you can. Jared is nowhere to be found, and a friend of his is dead."

"You're talking about Karel," she said coolly. "I only heard about that today, this afternoon. I can't help you."

"Are you going to talk to police about it?"

"Why should I? I don't know who killed him."

"Maybe you know Karel's real name," I suggested.

"Just Karel, as far as I know. He's a Czech. I never asked him his last name. No one I know likes to use theirs, anyway."

"Sounds like a convenient excuse. Maybe you could tell me your last name, while we're at it." Pad and pen found their way into my hands. "And your address and phone number."

"It's Rosenblatt," she said harshly. She gave me an address on the Bowery, within blocks of here, and a home phone number.

"No work number?"

"I'm currently unemployed."

"Why don't you use your powers and set up shop as a psychic investigator or open a one-nine-hundred line?"

"I don't know why you're giving me all this negativity," she said, pitying me with a shake of her head. "I'm willing to deal with you on your spiritually bound level, Mr. Quaintance."

"Sorry. I'll nix the rude comments. It's my natural defense mechanism. It springs up whenever I feel like I'm getting the runaround. I'd really like to talk with you in more detail about Jared, since you and he were such good friends. But first I have to know if you're being straight with me. If you have any idea where Jared is, I want to know, now. The fact that Karel turned up dead makes me worry about Jared's safety."

"I don't know where Jared is. In all honesty."

"You remember the last time you saw him?"

"Yes, I do. Vividly. It was right here at The Lot."

"When was this?"

"About three weeks ago," she said, squinting her eyes in an attempt to recall. "Yes, it was just after the High Holies."

"You observe the High Holies?" I asked dubiously.

"I do the family thing. I don't observe, no."

"So you came back after Yom Kippur and saw Jared here."

"Yes," she said. "I was going down to the office to see Theophrastus—he's the owner—but I didn't make it, because Jared was in there arguing with him. I didn't want to get in the middle of it, so I turned around and went back out. That's it."

"You saw them arguing, or did you just hear their voices?"

"No, I was allowed downstairs where the office is. I peeked around the corner and saw them only for a moment. They didn't see me. I didn't want them to. I went back upstairs."

"What were they arguing about?"

"Money," Lucrezia said. "Theophrastus was asking Jared where the money was. Jared said he'd get it for him."

"Nothing more specific than that?"

"Listen, Theophrastus is a friend of mine. I don't want to get him in trouble. You should ask him yourself."

"I'm not the police. I'm only private. All I want to do is find Jared. You're sure you don't know what kind of deal they were talking about? Why Jared might have owed him money?"

"I only heard that little bit," she said. "I don't know."

"Okay. I'll ask Theophrastus myself."

"Don't tell him I said anything." She looked frightened.

"Okay, I'll leave your name out of it. What did they look like when you saw them?"

"It's not going to sound good. They're friends, and I'm sure Theophrastus wasn't really trying to hurt him."

"Come on, Lucrezia. Jared might be hurt now, somewhere nobody seems to know about. What was Theophrastus doing?"

"Well, he's a big guy, and he had Jared up against his office wall. He was holding him at the neck with one hand."

"Did he look like he was choking him?"

"No, just pinning him."

"And demanding money."

"I don't know what he wanted."

"How often had you seen Jared in the weeks before this?"

"Not often," she said. "Let's see, I was in New Jersey for a week with my family, and I hadn't seen much of Jared during the previous week. I saw him regularly through mid September."

"You saw him that once after you came back, and no more?"

"Yes."

"You never thought anything might have happened to him?"

"No. Why should I?"

"How well do you know Anastasia?"

"Anastasia? Well enough. We don't hang."

"Is it like her to make an appointment and not keep it?"

"When did she say she was meeting you?"

"Eleven-thirty." I pressed the illuminator button on my watch. "It's twelve-thirty now. I don't see her, do you?"

"No," Lucrezia said apprehensively. "Let's look around."

We made a quick circuit of the club, poking into the nooks and crannies. Lucrezia searched the women's room, and I checked the men's. The light in the men's room was dim, but I could make out a few guys in the corners with lengths of rubber hose on their upper arms and syringes poking their flesh—no Anastasia.

"One more place to look," Lucrezia said. "The office."

She grabbed my hand and dragged me over toward a muscular bouncer-type with long, scraggly hair and a gray beard who looked more like a biker than a goth and probably was. He was standing before a black door with a sign that said NO ADMITTANCE – NOT AN EXIT. Going in ahead of us were two lithe blond girls who looked about fifteen. The bouncer nodded and opened the door, letting them in. Beyond the doorway was a dark stairwell; all I saw were two blond heads going down. Their giggles echoed darkly. The door closed. The bouncer stepped before it and folded his arms.

Lucrezia and I were stopped cold.

"Let me down, Ted," Lucrezia said in her forceful tone.

"You know I love you, but not tonight," Ted said. He looked at me and sized me up. "Who's your friend?"

"Grigory," she said, maintaining my alias. "We're looking for Anastasia. You haven't let her down tonight, have you?"

"Haven't seen her." Ted kept looking at me.

"I'd like to talk with Theophrastus anyway," I said.

"He's busy. Come back some other time, pal. Say, don't I know you from somewhere?"

"I doubt it."

"You play in one of the bands we get in here?"

"No. All us bald guys look alike."

"Let's go," Lucrezia said, squeezing my hand.

"Some other time," I said to the implacable Ted.

"See you around, Ted," Lucrezia said and led me away.

"What now?" I asked.

"We go to Bedlam. Anastasia's best friend works there. She might have stopped by to see him and gotten sidetracked."

"Take me over there?" I played the poor, timorous male.

"Your aura's growing clearer. Must be my purifying influence. Let me go uncheck my jacket first."

"I'll come with you."

I had a feeling Lucrezia knew more than she was letting on, and I didn't want her out of my sight.

EIGHT

RED NEON GUTS spelled out BEDLAM against black sheet metal above broad double doors that were propped open by two professional wrestlers in zombie face who gruntingly let in two goths at a time from a long queue that stretched from Houston to Stanton.

Considering Lucrezia's mesh shirt and nipple rings, I was glad she had donned her leather jacket for our one-block trek. I had wondered at the wisdom of bringing her along, but she was able to take me straight into Bedlam with only a nod at the guards, who stood there like a pair of androsterone-pumped gargoyles. Without her, I would have been stuck at the back of the Bataan death march and wouldn't have made it in for an hour or so—not unless I wanted to show the tag team my credentials and bluster a little and maybe grease them with palm oil.

"I'll take you right to Sebastian," Lucrezia said. "If Anastasia's here, she will have said hello to him already."

Yellowed human skulls and bones lined the walls of the low-

vaulted hallway, like Parisian catacombs. I touched the pate of
one of the skulls and felt the varnished softness of plaster; they
were chipped in spots, showing chalky whiteness. Industrial music
echoed off the bones cacophonously, but as we emerged from the
ossuary into the huge main room, the music gained in clarity and
attained untold decibel levels. The walls were of padded
institutional-strength canvas. The main floor was encircled by two
levels of mezzanine. All floors were chock full of goths.

"Sebastian's up there," Lucrezia said, pointing to a dim light
in a small glass booth way up on the second mezzanine. She
dragged me through the crowd, around some chain-link fencing,
and up two flights of iron stairs.

"If she's not with him, we'll never find her," I said.

"Yes we will," Lucrezia said with the confidence of a seer.

The faces surrounding me were generally five to ten years
older than those I'd seen at The Lot. Most were closer to my age,
some even older. The overriding look was still vampirish, but
there was greater diversity in dress and more obvious originality in
makeup and attitude. A small minority didn't look gothic at all. If
Anastasia preferred Bedlam to The Lot, I could see why.

On the second mezzanine, we had to squeeze ourselves all the
way through to the back, where the deejay booth stood like a box
seat high above the dance floor. The smoke of a thousand
cigarettes wafted up below the rafters to create an ethereal fog.
Lights and strobes were shot down from up here by a computer,
like Zeus casting thunderbolts. Video monitors large and small
hung above the crowd and on the padded walls, showing the
bloody nightmare dreamscapes of goth-industrial Grand Guignol.

Lucrezia rose up on her toes to look through a glass and wire-
mesh window and pounded against the door of Sebastian's booth
with the palm of her hand.

"Sebastian! Open up! It's me, Lucrezia!"

I leaned over the mezzanine railing and peeked around the corner of the booth to look in. Sebastian de Leon was a flat-chested, skinny Hispanic man of twenty-five or so in black ribbed T-shirt, leather jeans, and boots. He sat before a rack of CD players, headphones on, knees bouncing up and down as he rummaged through a disordered pile of CD jewel cases. His long, fine hair was bleached to almost as light a shade as Lucrezia's. His smooth, light-brown skin was stretched taut over the bony prominences of his face. He wore two silver earrings in the form of Byzantine crucifixes; the rest of his flesh was refreshingly devoid of piercings. His naturally dark hair color was revealed in his arched eyebrows and a sharply defined, diabolic goatee.

Sebastian removed his headphones and opened the door.

Lucrezia went in.

I followed her.

"Hi, Lu," Sebastian said, nonplussed.

"Sebastian, this is Grigory, a friend of Anastasia's."

Lucrezia shut the door, closing off half the club noise.

"How come I've never met you?" Sebastian asked, reaching out to shake my hand. He had a nice smile: straight teeth, no fangs.

I cut out the small talk: "Have you seen Anastasia tonight?"

"No," Sebastian said, shaking his head. "Haven't talked with her since the end of our shift yesterday. Why?"

"Let's go look for her on the floor," Lucrezia said to me.

"Forget looking for her," I said. "You said yourself she wouldn't be here if she hasn't stopped by to see Sebastian."

"Well—"

"That's right," Sebastian said, looking back and forth at the worry in our faces. "Anastasia would have come up. She's my best girlfriend. What's the matter? Is something wrong?"

"Have you seen Jared Foster recently?"

"No, not for a while. Does this have something to do with Karel?"

"It might. What do you know about Karel?"

"Only that he and Jared were close friends."

"Sebastian, can I use your phone?"

"Sure, Grigory, go ahead. I've got to set up another program." Sebastian put his headphones back on and started pressing buttons on one of the CD players, but he kept glancing up at me, hoping to learn what was going on.

Lucrezia stepped back quietly like she wanted to leave.

"Don't go anywhere," I told her. "I still need you."

She stayed, eyeing me with uncertainty.

I picked up the phone and dialed Anastasia's number. No busy signal. This time it just rang forever. Lucrezia blinked a few times while we waited. Her mascara-teased eyelashes made me think of a Venus flytrap. After the tenth ring, I hung up.

"Come on, Lucrezia," I said. "We're going over there."

"What do you need me for?"

"There's still a lot I need to learn about Jared Foster, as soon as possible. You know him best, but there's no time now. We'll talk later. I don't want you out of my sight, understand?"

"Okay," Lucrezia said in the meekest voice she was likely ever to produce.

"Wait!" Sebastian said, removing his headphones. "Where are you guys going?"

"To Anastasia's apartment," I said.

"What for?"

"To check on her. She was supposed to meet me tonight at The Lot, and she never showed. We thought she might be here."

"I'm coming with you," Sebastian said.

"You're busy."

"I can get someone else up here to take over for me,"

Sebastian said. "It'll only take a couple of minutes."

"Can't wait that long. But I'll talk with you later."

"Hey, wait, come on, guys!"

But I'd already turned and was going out the door, dragging Lucrezia behind me, one hand clamped around her small wrist.

A cab picked us up on Houston at the corner with Avenue A. The driver wasn't too thrilled that we were only going to Ninth Street and Avenue D. There wasn't much he could do about it. I gave him his fare and more tip than he earned, and I held on to Lucrezia's wrist again as I got out, to make sure she came with. I shut the door with a *chunk* and slapped the back fender lightly like a trusted steed I was sending off on its way.

A drunk clothed in rags shambled toward us dragging his left foot and a bag of aluminum cans. Loud rap music thumped at us from competing Saturday night parties in lighted windows high up in the Jacob Riis Houses. A young woman in threadbare fishnet stockings, short red leather skirt, and high heels walked halfway up the block Lucrezia and I were crossing to, then ambled back to her corner. The lights in the Chinese restaurant were off, all except one small fluorescent over a countertop far back in the kitchen work space. The OPEN sign still faced the street.

The outer entry door to Anastasia's building was open, like before. The inner door of the foyer should have been locked, but instead the deadbolt had been thrown outside of its hole so the door could never close until someone threw it back with a key.

I removed my Glock from my shoulder holster and held it up toward the ceiling. The stairwell lights were out.

"I don't want to go in." Lucrezia wrenched free of me but remained there in the foyer. "I'm staying right here."

"You might be safer with me," I said, though I wasn't sure what we might run into upstairs. If she came along, I could be leading her into danger. "I've got a gun."

"I can see that."

"I'll protect you."

"I doubt that."

"You don't know what'll happen if you stay down here."

"Nor if I go up."

"I'd rather you kept right behind me. I can't make you."

"I'm staying."

"Okay," I said. "But *stay*, you got me? I'm going up to Anastasia's apartment. It's 4B. I might run into some trouble up there. If you hear anything, call the police, okay?"

"Sure."

"There's a pay phone right on the corner."

"Okay," she said. "And don't worry. I've got quarters."

"Right," I said.

I wanted to bound up the stairs by twos, but they were old, and the racket would have been thunderous. I made my ascent slowly, minimizing the noise and allowing my eyes to adjust to the dark.

Down the dim fourth-floor hallway, a glow-in-the-dark skull sticker shone out from Anastasia Cartwright's door. I reached out to touch it, and the door opened on its squeaky hinges.

I jumped back against the hallway wall and listened closely but heard no sounds from within. Gingerly, I placed my arm against the door and opened it the rest of the way with the back of my hand, stepping inside with my gun at the ready. I felt my way up the wall for the light switch with my knuckles and used the side of my finger to turn on the entry hall light. The door had a circular hole and worn threads where the cylinder had been punched out. The cylinder itself lay on the rug.

I went deeper inside, unable to see past the velvet curtain. I went into the kitchen and turned on the lights—nothing but pots and pans, neatly ordered, and Peter's dish on the floor, half full of dry cat food. My boots crunched a few stray pieces.

I parted the curtain with the muzzle of my Glock. I felt for the lights with my knuckle, found them, and flipped them on.

The living room was a mess. The black drapes and creamy shifts had been torn from the windows and julienned into strips lying in heaps on the floor. The red velvet couch had had its foam stuffing knocked out of it and lay on its back with three broken legs. The chairs were similarly smashed. The coffee table was caved in at the middle as if by karate chop, its contents assembled together in the wood-splintered valley. All the shelves had been cleaned of books, *objets*, and dust, all of which ended up on the floor, along with the smashed stereo, TV, and VCR. The Macintosh's CPU tower seemed intact, still in its perch on the desk, but the monitor showed spiderweb cracks.

The gothic photos by Sebastian hung askew on the walls, the glass in the frames busted and slivery. I determined that one shot was missing: the sated vampire at rest in his coffin. I glanced around the tornado-stricken room but saw no sign of it.

Everything was missing from Jared's room: the posters from his walls, the snapshots from around his mirror, the books from his shelves, the camouflage netting from the ceiling. The dresser drawers were empty. I opened the closet, which was dark.

Reaching for the string to turn on the light, I jangled a collection of wire hangers with no clothes on. The bright yellow overhead bulb starkly revealed nothing else.

I kept my Glock ahead of me as I went back out into the hall. I hadn't heard any noises other than my own since entering the apartment, but I didn't want to grow complacent. I carefully pushed open the door across from Jared's room and turned on the lights. It was the bathroom, fairly intact compared with the rest of the place. The medicine chest mirror was unbroken, and the contents within were reasonably ordered. I checked the labels of the amber plastic medicine vials but found only minor, uninteresting prescriptions, all for Anastasia, none for Jared. Peter's litter box had been dumped in the bathtub, and the air remained clouded from the fine dust particles. The clear shower curtain had been yanked down from its wire hooks to spill half onto the floor, as if Janet Leigh had been there.

Anastasia's bedroom was as disordered as the living room, but I had no way of knowing what it had looked like before. The odor of urine was strong in the air. The bedding was shredded like the living room curtains and piled up at the head of the naked bed. In the center of the mattress was a damp yellow stain. I doubted it had been made by the cat. Polyester filling from the slashed pillows lay in clumps on the bed and the floor, where glass objects from the dresser lay broken. Her dresser mirror was shattered and clinging for life to its cheap wood frame; one jarring movement and it would all come down in fragments. More framed photos on the walls were now crooked and smashed. I wouldn't know if any more were missing. I stepped with care around the debris and opened the door to the closet. I yanked on the string, and the light revealed boxes dumped from the upper shelves onto a sizable pile of clothing emptied off hangers.

I stuck my hand down into the piled garments, brushing past leather, velvet, and polyester, wondering if anything was buried beneath—but there was nothing that I could find.

"Oh, fuck! My place! What am I going to—look at this!"

Anastasia's voice was coming from the front of the apartment. Extending my Glock out in front of me, I went down the hall and peeked around the corner of the living room.

She stood there in front of the black drapes, made up and dressed for the clubs, her black-lipsticked mouth hanging agape. She was cradling Peter at her chest. Sebastian emerged from behind her. Neither of them was armed or appeared threatening.

"Where have you been?" I asked, stepping into the room and lowering my gun toward the floor.

"Oh, Jesus!" Anastasia said. "Greg! You scared me!"

"I told you he was coming up here," Sebastian said to her.

"What happened?" Anastasia asked, stroking the cat. Peter squirmed and writhed like he wanted to be let down, but Anastasia kept him up and away from the broken glass.

"You tell me," I said. "Jared's things have been taken, and most of the rest of the place has been trashed. It doesn't look like a typical burglary. It's the kind of thing ex-boyfriends or ex-girlfriends do. I didn't witness it. I wasn't here. I came up because you missed our rendezvous, and I was worried something might have happened. Now where have you been?"

I approached them and reholstered my Glock.

"I was late getting over to The Lot tonight," Anastasia said. "I just missed you. Ted, one of the bouncers—"

"Biker type?"

"That's him. He said he saw you leave with Lucrezia. I went over to Bedlam and found Sebastian. He told me he saw you guys, and he was heading over to my place to catch up with you and look for me. I can't believe this! What am I going to do?"

"Did you see Lucrezia downstairs?"

"Lucrezia?" Sebastian said. "No, we didn't see anyone."

"Except Peter," Anastasia added. "Thank God."

"Lucrezia was supposed to wait for me," I said.

"She must have split," Sebastian said. "Lu's a flake."

"Where was Peter?"

"I heard him in the darkness on the second floor," Anastasia said. "He came running to me. I guess they left my door open?"

"Hard to close it the way they left it," I said. "Do you have any idea who did it? Could it have been Jared?"

"It's not like Jared. And I told you he was never my boyfriend. He doesn't have any animosity toward me."

"That you know of," I said. "He did still had a key. Looks like someone used a key to enter the building, but they got brutal with your front door. Did you change your locks today?"

"Yes," Anastasia said. "Didn't do me much good. Maybe the locksmith saw something he wanted and came back."

"It wasn't the locksmith," I said. "Did you get in touch with that police detective, Orjuedos?"

"Yes, and I told him a little. He wants to see me, but he was too busy today. He was going to come by tomorrow."

"He never got to see the photo of Jared and Karel, then," I said. "It was taken along with all the rest of Jared's stuff."

"Maybe it was your client," she said. "Jared's father. He wanted Jared's things, and I made him leave. He waited until I was gone. Then he came back and did this."

"When did you leave your apartment tonight?"

"About ten-thirty. I went over to a café on St. Mark's Place and had some dinner and some coffee and read in a magazine for a while before going over to The Lot. I guess I lost track of time, and I missed you. Now what do I do?"

"Call the police. Report this."

"Should I call that detective?"

"No, just let some patrol officers come and do a report. Have them give you the case number. Keep your appointment with Orjuedos tomorrow and tell him what happened. Refer him to the case number. There's no way of telling if Jared's connected in any way to Karel's murder. And this, whatever happened here, we don't know what it means. It could have been Jared, maybe his father, maybe someone else. Anyone with a grudge against you?"

"Not that I'm aware of, no," Anastasia said.

"Someone wanted to remove Jared's things. They must have

brought a truck. The rest was either directed at you personally, or they wanted to make it look like more of a routine burglary. But it doesn't look to me like they took any of *your* things, only destroyed them. Take a look around and correct me if I'm wrong, but the only thing of yours I know that's missing is that photo Sebastian did of the young vampire in the coffin."

"That's Jared," Sebastian said.

"Who's Jared?"

"The vampire in the photo."

"It is?" I hadn't recognized him—but then I'd only seen Jared in two standard-quality photos taken by some amateur in the Foster household. The costume, makeup, and lighting must have been enough to throw me off.

"Didn't I tell you that was Jared?" Anastasia said, looking at the bare spot on the wall where the frame should have been.

"No," I said. "Anastasia, will you do a favor for me? When you go through this mess, will you let me know if any trace of Jared has been left behind? I suspect you'll find nothing."

"Sure," she said. "But I'm not doing anything tonight. I don't feel safe here."

"Do you have a place to stay?"

"She can stay with me," Sebastian said.

"I'd like that," Anastasia said. "So would Peter."

I had Sebastian give me his address and phone numbers. He wrote it all down on the back of a business card that advertised SEBASTIAN DE LEON – GOTH INDUSTRIAL DJ – MACABRE PHOTOGRAPHY.

Anastasia disappeared with Peter into the kitchen.

I handed Sebastian one of my own cards. "I guess Anastasia told you who I was. It's not Grigory, it's Greg. I'm trying to find Jared Foster. I don't suppose you know where he is?"

"Not on your life," he said. "Haven't seen him for weeks."

"I'd like to talk with you about him. Maybe tonight, maybe tomorrow. Depends on how ambitious I get. Is that okay?"

"Fine," he said. "But I don't know how I can help you."

"You and Anastasia planning to be up late tonight?"

"Maybe we'll go back to Bedlam so I can finish my shift. You might find us there. We probably won't be going back to my place till dawn."

"Either Bedlam or your apartment," I confirmed.

I went into the kitchen to find Anastasia. She was opening a can of wet cat food and spooning half of it into Peter's dish.

"You're going to call and make that report?"

"Right away," she said. "Are you leaving?"

"If I stay, I'll be stuck here until the cops are finished. I have other things to do, like finding Lucrezia. All I did here was check to see if anyone was still in your apartment. I haven't touched anything, and I haven't taken anything."

"Don't worry, I believe you." Anastasia put a square of aluminum foil over the half-empty can and put it in the fridge. Peter gobbled away at the fishy stuff, ignoring the dry forms in the other section of his dish. Cat comfort food.

"You think Lucrezia could read Peter's mind for us and tell us who was here?" I asked.

"You can't be serious." She gave me a disbelieving look.

"I'm not. I only wanted to know if you bought into her."

"I don't. Neither does Sebastian or anyone else I know."

"How about Jared?"

"He thought she could teach him hypnosis. She can do that, at least. She regresses people back to their childhood and supposedly to past lives. But I don't believe she's psychic."

"I'm going back out to look for her," I said. "The apartment's clear. I'm glad you weren't here when they came."

"Yeah, me too," she said. "I would have had time to call 911, at least. They chose a time when they knew I'd be out."

I told her I was sure she was right.

The lights were back on in the stairwell. Anastasia must have known where to find the switch. I stayed on guard as I went down, though, keeping my gun holstered but my hand on the grip.

I went back down to the street and looked up and down it for Lucrezia, but she had booked on me. The same whore we'd seen earlier was still walking her beat, and the parties in the windows across the street were still raging, but Lucrezia was long gone.

I went to the corner hoping for a cab—but it was unlikely I'd luck out and get one at this location this late at night. I paced back and forth a little, like the hooker a block down from me. I kept walking past the Chinese restaurant. The OPEN sign bugged me. Along the top of the establishment was a rusted metal hexagonal tube housing the steel gate that was supposed to be rolled down like a garage door to protect the business at night. It hadn't been rolled down tonight. I considered the possibility that it was rusted in place and couldn't be brought down.

I tried the door. It opened. I stepped inside.

"Hello?" I called, drawing my gun and holding it at my side. "Is anybody here?"

I didn't hear any noise. The only light came from the street and from the single fluorescent tube over one of the kitchen counters. The cash register was turned off and showed no signs of forced entry. The drawer was shut. I lifted the hinged countertop and went deeper, back into the kitchen. The gas jets on the burners were turned off, but nothing looked as if it had been cleaned at the end of the day. Woks still sat atop burners, one with uncooked vegetables swimming in grease. The butcher-block counter along the other wall was slick with blood and fluids, from chicken and fish carcasses, I figured.

I saw no one hiding, nor any bodies on the floor.

Lee Ho had mentioned a basement storage room. There were two doors at the back of the kitchen. One opened on the bathroom and the other, on a stairwell. I flipped the light switch and listened for any noise from down below, but there was nothing.

I went down, covering myself. The storeroom contained crates of vegetables waiting to be sliced up and stir-fried. The door to the office was open. There was no one inside. I went back up the stairs and turned off the light behind me.

The freezer was upstairs, at the back of the kitchen. As I went past, I slipped slightly on a viscous liquid that might have been more chicken blood. Or might not.

I pressed the flat knob of the freezer handle. The door sprang open, and a light came on. Shelves along all three walls contained frozen meats and fishes. Lying side by side on the floor were the frost-covered bodies of Cheung Lee Ho and Cheung Lee Fong, both stained with dark blood from several large bullet wounds that pierced Lee Fong's apron and Lee Ho's T-shirt, in the neighborhood of their hearts.

A third body lay face-down alongside them, with long blond hair framing the massive, bloody hole made in the back of her head by a high-caliber slug fired from close range. She had round hips and was wearing bell-bottom jeans and a tie-dyed T-shirt to which a voluminous spatter of red had just been added.

I didn't want to disturb the crime scene any more than I already had, so I didn't bother to step inside and lift up her head. I had a pretty good idea I was looking at Juliet Logan.

I went back outside to the pay phone on the corner, dropped a quarter in the slot, and placed a call to Detective Orjuedos.

NINE

THE GUYS FROM THE N.Y.P.D. Crime Scene Unit examined my Glock thoroughly and were perfectly satisfied that it hadn't been fired anytime recently. They tested my hands for powder traces, which came up negative. Detective Orjuedos said it was all just a formality, to rule me out of any involvement. I took no offense.

The special investigators proceeded to snap their photos and take their measurements of the scene, attempting to determine where and how the victims had stood when they were shot and what trajectories the bullets might have followed to end up in the bodies. One corpse would have been time-consuming enough; a triple event was going to keep them busy for a while.

Orjuedos took this opportunity to get my statement. We sat in the red vinyl chairs at the wobbly table where I'd eaten Cheung Lee Fong's cooking half a day ago. He made a few smarmy re- marks about my get-up, though he knew before I explained anything that I'd gone to the goth clubs looking for Jared Foster. I recounted my actions from entering the restaurant to phoning him. Orjuedos listened with professional bemusement.

"Tell me what this has to do with Karel." Orjuedos's eyes were red and glassy, bags a deeper purple than before. This case was pushing him hard.

I lit a cigarette and offered him one. He accepted. I lit his against the tip of mine and handed it over. Our fingers touched, and his tired eyes looked up at mine steadily. A smile began to creep up in the corner of his mouth. He blushed.

I exhaled a lungful of smoke and got down to business:

"I met earlier today with Anastasia Cartwright, who shared an apartment upstairs in this building with Jared Foster until Jared vanished about a month ago. I took a look around Jared's room and found a photograph of him with Karel. I asked Anastasia to call you and tell you about it. Did she?"

"Yes, she did. We made an appointment for tomorrow."

"Good. That's what she told me. She's met Karel herself, but she doesn't know him by any other names, and she wouldn't be able to give you any better identification on him than you already have. She says Jared knew him better. It's possible that if Jared turns up, he could identify Karel for you. Though it's also possible some other goth can help you out on that."

"So far, no one's come forward," Orjuedos said.

"Too bad. I met two tonight, a Lucrezia Rosenblatt,"—I spelled this for him—"who's good friends with Jared and might know Karel, and a Sebastian de Leon, who you'll find upstairs. I didn't have time to get much out of them."

"Why's that?"

I told him all about missing Anastasia at The Lot, growing worried about her, and coming back to find her apartment sacked. Another set of policemen were upstairs now, taking her report. Orjuedos knew that but didn't know why it was connected. I gave him an account of the general devastation and how all of Jared's things had been removed from his room—including the photo of him and Karel that Orjuedos had lost his chance to see.

"The destruction to Anastasia's living room and bedroom is the kind you see in domestic disputes," I said. "It looks like the work of an ex-lover or a jealous rival."

"How so?"

"I'm sure you've seen plenty of burglaries. How many burglars bother to take the time to shred the drapes and bed sheets, smash pictures, and pee on the mattress?"

"You're right. I'd better go up and have a look myself. You're saying you think it was Jared?"

"Anastasia insists that she and Jared were never steady lovers, even though they sometimes got intimate."

"Jared's the most likely one to have taken his own things," Orjuedos said. "Who else could it be?"

"I have no idea," I said. I hesitated to tell him about Henry Foster, but he would hear of it soon enough from Anastasia, so I went on: "Actually, no, I've got a couple of ideas. Anastasia told me that Jared's father, Henry Foster—"

"Your client," Orjuedos put in.

"Yes. This morning—excuse me, *yesterday* morning, before he ever came to my office, Anastasia let him up to her apartment. He wanted to take Jared's things. She wouldn't let him. She made him leave."

"That's very interesting. What's your other idea?"

"Anastasia and Jared had been harassed on and off by Jared's ex-girlfriend and ex-roommate, Juliet Logan. If I'm not mistaken, you're going to find that the dead girl back there is her. I spoke with her just after sundown. She was wearing those same jeans and that same shirt, and the hair looks like hers."

I told Orjuedos about the Dawn Lewis alias Juliet had given me and the misdirection to Café Giotto that had bought her enough time to give me the slip. Where she had gone, I had no idea.

"What do you know about the other two?" Orjuedos asked.

"They work here," I said. "The older one in the apron is Cheung Lee Fong, the cook. The one in the T-shirt is his kid brother, Cheung Lee Ho, the counterman. They came here from Canton, probably illegally. I spoke with them in the afternoon, and they described to me the last time they'd seen Jared Foster in the building, about two weeks ago."

I gave Orjuedos as complete a description as I could of the leather-clad and hooded man who accompanied him on that occasion.

"Any idea who that might be?"

"None, sorry," I said. "I figure tonight, the two Chinese happened to witness Jared's things being moved out. There had to have been a truck right outside. You might find witnesses across the street in the housing projects. Juliet Logan was probably an accomplice to both the burglary and the murders of the brothers. It looks to me like they were shot somewhere in the kitchen. Juliet helped her associate drag the bodies into the freezer, after which her services were no longer needed."

"She was a dupe?"

"That's my guess. Unless she happened to be eating in the restaurant when the killers came in. Which I doubt."

"Are you still going to be looking for Jared after tonight?"

"As long as my client approves of what I've been doing."

"All I want to say is," Orjuedos said, "if you do find Jared, I want you to consider him armed and dangerous. Don't do anything foolish. Call us immediately, and we'll take it from there. I want to bring Jared in, at least for questioning."

"At least." I was in general agreement with Orjuedos.

"Do you want to come up with me to Anastasia's

apartment?"

"No, Tavo," I said. "I've seen it, and I've already told you everything I know. I've had enough for one night. I'm going to go home and crawl into bed."

"Ah, bed," Orjuedos said. "I remember what mine looks like. Just when I think it's safe to get in, I get a call like yours."

"The wife must love that," I said to provoke something.

"Wife?" he said like the idea was ridiculous. "I haven't got a wife. Or a partner. All I got is Max."

"Who's Max?"

"My Airedale."

"Lonely dog."

"Lonely me." Orjuedos sighed miserably.

"A man like you?"

"What sort of man is that?"

"Dedicated, intelligent, charming, beautiful."

Orjuedos blushed again. He looked behind him at the special investigators, still active in their work. He turned back to me and lowered his voice: "Greg, are you always this aggressive?"

"No, Tavo. Forget it. I'm sorry. I've got no right."

"Go on home, Greg, and get some rest. You're delirious."

"That's one word for it." My sigh was not so miserable.

Orjuedos smiled despite himself and turned away from me. He went behind the counter and joined the others at the freezer.

I went out the door and off into the cold night. The hooker was gone from her little corner of the world. I appropriated it and waited ten minutes for a cab and had the driver take me home.

TEN

I TOSSED AND TURNED on my futon for a few hours. In my waking moments, I'd spin erotic fantasies of Tavo Orjuedos. Whenever I drifted back to sleep, I had nightmares of Jared Foster facing me down like a coiled snake, widening his jaws and baring his fangs, and I'd stand there frozen. If I flinched, he'd track me. I'd panic and take a step back. Jared would lunge and sink his teeth into my neck, and I'd feel the blood coursing out of my veins.

Then I'd wake up in a cold sweat and try to settle myself by removing Orjuedos's clothes and surveying the lay of his flesh. It was a chimerical map—like one of Tolkein's worlds—and it only made me want to see the real thing for myself, someday soon.

I was finally hitting a restful stride when the phone began to chirp. The sparrows were chirping, too, away in some tree. The sunlight streaming in was harsh. A trio of nosy pigeons outside on the fire escape were staring in at me and warbling in unison— loud, overfed, and pompous, like the Three Tenors.

I fumbled for the receiver, nailing it on the third chirp.

"Quaintance here," I slurred like a drunk.

"Greg Quaintance?" asked a woman's voice I didn't recognize. She sounded distressed and anxious. I didn't like the sound.

"That's me." I sat myself up on my phone elbow and rapped a knuckle against the windowpane, asking the pigeons to mind their own business. They flew away looking put out. "Who's this?"

"We haven't spoken," she said. "I'm Gloria Glendenning-Foster. My husband talked with you yesterday about Jared."

"What can I do for you?" I asked, neither confirming nor denying that I'd spoken with Henry Foster. Discretion was one of the few things that kept my name passing from the lips of one client into the ears of another, and I tried to be mindful of it even at six-thirty on a Sunday morning when I'd gone to bed at three and slept miserably. Though Foster had given me the okay to speak with his wife, I knew nothing of what she really knew of why her husband had come to see me.

"I'm worried about Hank," she said with a nice vibrato that went a little toward authenticating the emotion described. "He hasn't come home, and no one at the hospital has heard from him."

"You were expecting him back home yesterday?"

"Yes, or early this morning at the very latest. When Hank left for New York yesterday morning, he wasn't sure when he'd be back. He thought he might have to stay the night. But in the afternoon, he called me from his car phone to tell me that he'd spoken with you and that you were going to find Jared for us—"

"I said I'd try," I told her, for the record. "I'm sorry. Go on. What else did he say?"

"That he wanted to run a few errands while he was in the city. He was explicit about not getting a hotel room. He was going to drive back and be home before midnight, and we were planning on attending church today. I didn't even wait up for him. I woke up in the middle of the night, and Hank wasn't beside me or anywhere in the house. I told myself not to get excited, and I sat up for a while, expecting him to come walking through the front door. I phoned the New York Hilton, which is where he usually stays when he's in the city, but he hadn't checked in. I've tried a few others, but none of them have him listed. I've called the police and the hospitals. Nothing."

"Calm down, Ms. Glendenning-Foster," I said, prefatory to saying that I was sure there was a reasonable explanation, etc.

Gloria didn't let me get that far:

"Don't tell me to calm down, Mr. Quaintance. All morning long, I've had people humoring me and telling me to calm down. I've been trying my best to keep a level head. But I think I have reason to be worried. This is not at all like Hank."

"Okay, I apologize. I only wanted to proceed rationally."

"I am being rational."

I never wholly trusted anything said over the phone, and our exchange was beginning to illustrate why. Disembodied voices without the accompanying facial expressions and physical tics had an uncanny knack for saying something while telling nothing (as in her case) and for giving unintended offense (as in mine). No amount of digital clarity over fiber-optic cables was ever going to make up for that fact. Nor would a picture phone, thank you.

"Ms. Glendenning-Foster—"

I was about to ask if I could drive in to Connecticut and meet up with her later. The sun was bearing down on me like an interrogation lamp, and I was lacking the mental wherewithal to scare up any niceties. Morning was the cruelest part of the day, and it could make me crude. If we kept on the phone much longer, I was liable to start ruffling more than pigeon feathers.

"Please don't interrupt me," Gloria said. "I'm saddled with

this terrible feeling that something has happened to my husband."

"Can you be more specific?" I suppressed the audio portion of an unbidden yawn. "Terrible feelings can be pretty vague. Technically, he's only been missing for what, six hours or so?"

"Considering that my husband is your client, Mr. Quaintance, I'd think that you'd take a natural interest in the case."

"Not like a duck to water, ma'am, if that's what you mean."

"Ma'am?" Gloria repeated, like a courtroom objection. She was starting to walk, talk, and strut like a pigeon.

I'd given offense again, but I trundled on:

"I'm only interested in cases that pay. So far, I've spent the better part of a day looking for your stepson. Your husband gave me a two-day retainer. If anything *has* happened to him, I'd take an interest in whether I'd ever see payment if the job goes to three days."

"I'll settle our account today," Gloria said, like she was taking out her checkbook, "if that's all you care about."

"That would be fine—except for the fact that your husband contracted me to do a job, and I intend to finish it or keep plugging away at it until he says stop. For now, I'd like to go on assuming that he'll be signing the check himself."

"You seem to be implying that I know something more about what happened to my husband than I'm willing to tell you."

"I wasn't aware that I was implying that."

"If I knew anything more about Hank, why would I try to hire you to find him?"

"Is that what you're trying to do?" I asked innocently. I didn't even know why I was needling her, but I seemed to have struck a nerve. It wasn't exactly a gusher, but what there was could be pumped.

"Yes," Gloria said. "I'll pay you with my own money."

"I appreciate the offer, but I've already got my hands full

looking for Jared. Maybe you should look into hiring another private dick. I could even refer you."

"No, no, no," Gloria said, getting worked up to the point of exasperation. "I want you. I know your track record. I saw your picture in the paper when you rescued the Matheson girl from those bikers."

"The what girl?" I said, priming the pump. You never knew what a person was going to reveal when they started explaining themselves. I wished she would never stop.

"Don't tell me you forgot her name, Mr. Quaintance." Gloria was understandably appalled. "The sixteen-year-old girl who was kidnapped from the Lollapalooza festival?"

"At least you can pronounce it," I said, realizing that she hadn't prepared Henry Foster well enough before our interview.

"The Mathesons hired you, and you managed to track the girl down to some awful Hell's Angels' clubhouse in Poughkeepsie."

"They were Z.Z. Ryders," I said, "and it was Schenectady."

"I knew that, Mr. Quaintance." Gloria gave me a laugh of triumph—the first of any kind I'd heard from her. "I wanted to beat you at your own game. It was your most celebrated case, and you're not likely to forget any of the details. Your male ego wouldn't let me get away with getting all the facts wrong."

"You give my male ego way too much credit, ma'am."

"Try Gloria," she said. "It works wonders. Are you always this difficult with potential clients?"

"I've already got a client. Anyway, you've got me at a disadvantage. I was up most of last night wading through the murk that's gathered around your stepson. I spent the last three hours trying to sleep, and failing. Your call woke me up, and I'm lying here naked in bed with a heavy head and eyes that won't stay open."

"I appreciate the effort you're making on Jared's behalf,"

Gloria said. "And I'm sorry if I disturbed your beauty rest. But I think my husband disappeared there in New York while looking for his son. The two cases are bound be connected. You suggested that I hire another detective. I can't help but feel that that would be like starting from scratch."

"That's what I just don't get. If your husband went to all the trouble of hiring me, why would he stick around and go on looking for Jared himself? You told me all he wanted to do was run some errands."

"'Running some errands' is rather ambiguous, isn't it?"

"Did your husband have any reason to be ambiguous?"

"I'm not sure what you mean."

"I'm only wondering if there might be some aspect of the case that he was unwilling to share with me."

"Such as?"

"You tell me. The only reason I can see him staying and looking for Jared is if there was something he didn't want to reveal up front. I wouldn't even want to guess at what it could be. Perhaps it's something he kept from you, as well. But he is your husband, Gloria. I thought you might know."

"Nothing I can think of," she said, throwing in a pause that acted something like a shrug. "Nothing important, anyway."

"I'd rather decide that for myself. You may already know why your husband didn't come home last night—without knowing it, so to speak."

This was met with a glacial silence—cold and slow.

"Gloria?" I said. "Do you follow me?"

"Of course I follow you."

"I'd like to talk with you in person, if that's possible. I'm told you were the last one in your household to speak with Jared, and maybe you can shed some more light on your husband's behavior. I can't promise that I'll take the case. If they turn out to be unrelated, I'd be selling both my clients short. I could drive out there this morning if you like—"

"No!" Gloria said hastily. "I mean—yes, I'll see you—no, don't bother to come out here. I'm coming into the city."

"There's no need for you to go to the trouble," I said, suddenly eager to have a look at the house outside of Hartford.

"If you won't look for my husband, I'll have no choice but to hire another detective or maybe go find him myself."

"You'll want to know my rates first."

"I don't care about your rates. I want you."

"You warmed up to me awfully fast."

"Why shouldn't I? You're quick, even after a rude awakening. I would never hire a dullard."

"The jury's still out on that. Now about my rates—"

"We can discuss that when I meet you."

"You still insist on coming in? I thought you said something about going to church this morning."

"I never go if Hank's out of town, much less missing."

"Very well," I said. "Leave a note for Hank, telling him where you're going. If he shows up at home unexpectedly, you don't want him having the same morbid thoughts about you that you're having about him."

"I'm not having morbid thoughts. When should I meet you?"

I told her to choose.

"Let's make it ten sharp," she said. "Where's your office?"

I agreed to the time and gave her the address, making sure she knew how to find it. She said she'd have no trouble; she'd spent a lot of time in Manhattan.

"One more thing," I said, trying to stay quick: "Does your husband own a handgun?"

"Yes, he does," Gloria said. "Why do you ask?"

"Do you know where he keeps it?"

"Yes, he puts it right in the—"

"I don't need to know where. Do me a favor. Go take a look and see if it's there. If it is, don't remove it. Leave it. I only want to know whether it's there. Will you do that for me?"

"Uh, sure. Give me a minute."

Gloria's phone made a dull *bonk* as it fell onto a surface.

I waited. I turned my head to find that the three pigeons had returned. They were looking in again with their black, beady eyes, about to erupt into a birdie aria. I slapped the filthy pane of glass with my palm and made them scatter.

"Mr. Quaintance?" Gloria said. "It isn't there."

"It isn't. Do you know what kind of gun it is?"

"I'm sorry, I don't know anything about guns."

"Can you tell me whether it's a revolver or an automatic?"

"I wouldn't know the difference," she claimed.

"Sure you would," I said and gave her the scoop: "A revolver has a hammer and a cylindrical chamber just above the trigger, where the bullets are loaded. The chamber revolves, which is why they call it a revolver. An automatic has no such cylinder, and the bullets are loaded up into the grip. When you squeeze the trigger, the bullets fly out of the muzzle one after another, like popcorn. Got it?"

"I guess it's an automatic, then." Gloria was trying to sound dippy and not succeeding. "I remember it doesn't have one of those revolving cylinder thingies. I know what you mean now. They use those revolvers for what-do-you-call, Russian roulette."

"That's right," I said, and offered a piece of advice: "You wouldn't want to play Russian roulette with an automatic. Though you could take your chances on it jamming. They do do that."

I was on the receiving end of that glacial silence again. Perhaps it wasn't wise to joke about Russian roulette with a woman who was worried about losing her lost, armed husband.

"Well," Gloria said after enough time to clear the dreadful thoughts from her mind. "I'll see you at ten, then."

I said goodbye and hung up. Ten was very agreeable. I could crawl back under the covers and sleep for another three hours. I needed it, and I had nothing better to do. The people I most needed to interview about Jared had probably gone to bed this morning about the time Gloria woke me up. I wouldn't try for them again until sundown.

The three pigeons were back to warble me to sleep.

I let them. They gave me little choice.

ELEVEN

AT NINE-THIRTY, I went to a Chelsea bake shop that offered the best baked goods in New York, sold by the surliest cashiers. The painted wood façade and mini-boardwalk out front made it appear inviting, like some mom-and-pop country store. This was a ruse.

I was faced with the task of trying to gain the attention of the vacant, hapless twentysomethings behind the counter. One of them, in sailor stripes, stood with his back to me, engaged in a personal phone conversation. The other two were standing around chatting amiably with each other. One was a tall freckle-faced guy with long, kinky red hair and a love brush. The other was a short Puerto Rican woman with shaved eyebrows, a buzzcut, and more facial piercings than any goth I'd seen at The Lot. They looked like leftovers from the cast of *Rent*.

I had to resort to a shouted "Hey!" The girl continued to ignore me. The redhead gave me a look that was hostile to the point of psychopathy. I told him I'd like a cranberry scone. He reached for a pumpkin oat-bran cranberry scone. I said that wasn't what I wanted, and he told me yes, it was. I said no, it wasn't. I pointed out the real cranberry scone, right there in front of me with its own little laminated sign. He told me he thought it was a blueberry scone. I said blueberries aren't red and told him to give it to me. He grabbed it, plucked out the CRANBERRY SCONE sign, and rang me up, overcharging me by fifty cents. I mentioned this to him, and he grudgingly gave me my correct change as he handed over the brown paper sack.

And they had the nerve to set up a tip jar on the counter.

At ten-ten, I swept the scone crumbs off my desk, got up, lit a cigarette, heaved the window open, and stuck my head out to look for Gloria. My eyes were still tired, and the white sun in the stark sky made them squint. The air had a nip, but the wind was yesterday's news. I entertained myself by checking out the guys passing below me on their way to Sunday brunch in the company of oldish friends and newish lovers. Some were cute, but it was funny how when you were fixating on one ideal, no one else measured up. Det. Octavio Orjuedos had become my latest yardstick, leaving the rest in the dust.

I couldn't help but notice a racing green Mercedes 560SL convertible with the top up that hovered strategically on Eighth Avenue for a minute at the tail of a battered white Chevy van that was pulling out of a space. Once the van was gone, the Mercedes slipped in easily like an eel into a coral cave. A woman with big black sunglasses and a shaggy mane of yellow hair got out in a knee-length, pearly-gray chinchilla coat. She looked up and down the street apprehensively, as if guarding against a spray-paint ambush by crazed New York animal-rightists.

I drew back inside, shut and latched the window, and crushed my butt in the stainless steel ashtray. A woman's high heels clicked briskly up the stairs. I sat back down in my swivel chair, grabbed some papers from my inbox, and busied myself.

A burst of staccato knocks like M16 fire shook the outer door and rattled the pebbled glass. It was either Gloria Glendenning-Foster or Woody Woodpecker.

"Mr. Quaintance?" came the muffled voice.

"Come on in," I said absently. "It's open."

She came tripping in with that layered, sunbleached mop on her head and those I-want-to-be-alone shades and that giant mouse pelt shroud and said, "Hi, I'm Gloria. Sorry I'm late."

I stood and shook her hand and told her that was okay and offered to take her coat. I showed her the fine wooden hanger on my coat and hat stand. Gloria didn't like the looks of it.

"No, thanks," she said, pressing her lips together and then her knees as she planted herself in one of my cold steel guest chairs. She folded up her sunglasses, slid them into a black kidskin sleeve, and placed them in her handbag, which bore a gold-plated oval stamped with GUCCI. "I'll be fine. You don't look exactly the way you did in that photograph in the paper."

"I'm older," I said, plopping down into my chair.

"It's not that. In the photo, you had hair."

"Usually, I like to keep it shaved smooth. When I started searching for Lorelei Matheson, I decided not to cut my hair again till I found her. Every day when I looked in the mirror, I'd see how far it had grown, and it would remind me of how long it had been since Lorelei's parents had seen their little girl. I was worried I'd end up like Rip van Winkle. But I had a lucky break. What you saw was nearly a month's growth."

"I'm glad you found her," Gloria said simply, studying the shiny curves of my head.

I'd been studying her myself while I was talking, trying to guess her age. Gloria had green eyes that were bright and reflective and may have been colored contact lenses. The hair looked very California—thick as a collie's ruff but the brash color of a cocker. Her flesh was hard and brown like leather upholstery and prematurely wrinkled. It was the kind of skin that had too much leisure time for sunbathing in the summer and skiing in the winter, and I'd seen it even on girls my own age. Gloria wore a skirt as short as her coat, and her fine legs were sheathed in a filmy hose that successfully masked their years—but legs were a poor indicator. The hands were usually the key, and hers were smooth. I put her at thirty-five, forty tops.

She had trophy wife written all over her, though she looked a little tarnished. Either she'd come that way or it had been a long while since Henry Foster had given her a good polish.

"I shouldn't think it would be too difficult for you to find Hank," Gloria said, leaning thoughtfully into the armrests.

I handed her my rate card.

"I don't even care about this," she said, scanning it and then dropping it into her handbag. "Just find him and bill me."

"I told you over the phone, it would be unfair for me to look for your husband while I look for Jared. Double-timing."

"Unfair to whom? I have no objections. The only other person with a right to object is Hank—if you could ask him."

"What about Jared?" I swiveled to and fro.

"I'm not asking you to stop looking for Jared. If you keep working the case, you'll probably find his father as well."

"I don't have any reason to believe that I would. Do you?"

"I don't suppose you mind if I smoke," she said, sliding the ashtray closer to her. She pulled out a pack of Virginia Slims 100s and slid one between her cherry-red nails. "Got a light?"

I unhooded my Zippo and did the honors automatically. Not wanting her to feel lonely, I lit up one of my own Lucky Strikes.

Gloria blew out turbulent gray smoke through pursed lips,

sounding like a jetliner's overhead air-conditioning duct.

It was too early for a break, so I plunged ahead:

"Your husband knew before he ever came to New York that the body at the morgue wasn't going to be Jared. Isn't that right?"

"Yes," Gloria said. "He could tell from the description."

"Jared didn't have any tattoo on his arm that said Karel, did he?" My tone was accusatory, the question rhetorical.

"No, he did not." Her response was square enough for court.

"I didn't see the TV news, but I'd be surprised if they didn't give out solid descriptions of the boy's tattoos like they did in the *Post*. Your husband would have me believe they sounded like Jared's, which is supposedly what prompted him to hire me."

"You're right on a couple of counts," Gloria said. "The news did mention the Karel tattoo, and Hank did know it wasn't Jared. But that doesn't mean he wasn't concerned about his son."

"Why should the Karel tattoo mean anything to him?"

"I didn't say that it did."

"You didn't have to. The TV news is full of murders. I'd buy your husband's story the way he originally gave it, but now it doesn't hold any water. If he heard about a murdered goth and perked his ears up and learned to his satisfaction that it wasn't Jared, he'd lose interest in the story altogether."

"No," she said, shaking her head to match. "It doesn't mean that at all." She was determined to stick as closely as possible to the originally agreed-on facts. "Hank had been out of touch with Jared, and the news report made him realize he had to do something to find Jared before it was too late."

"I'd buy that, too, if it weren't for the fact that he went down to the medical examiner's to have a look at Karel's body."

"How would you know he did that?" she said. "If he did."

"He told me so. A nice police detective corroborated it."

Gloria needed a drag on her cigarette to think about this.

"What's your husband worried about?" It was too general a question, and I didn't have much right to an answer.

"Jared brought Karel home," she said, seeming to deflate.

"When was that?"

"August." The word came out weighted like a stone.

"What's wrong with that? It's not a crime."

"You don't seem surprised."

"I was aware that Jared and Karel knew each other."

"The unholy duo." Gloria was droll. "How did you know?"

"Divine inspiration."

"Is that how you solve your cases, too?"

"You wouldn't happen to know if Karel is his real name?"

"No, I wouldn't."

"Do you know his last name or anything about his identity?"

"No, I don't. If I did, I would have told the police. I'd be interested to know how much else you've learned about Jared."

"It's quite a lot—but not enough. Not that I'd tell you any of it. You're not the one who hired me to find it out."

"Husbands and wives share everything," she said slyly.

"Except the past before they met," I said, checking her.

Gloria pulled her fur closer around her, looking chilled.

"How did a girl like you meet Dr. Henry Foster, anyway?"

"What do you mean, a girl like me?"

"Nothing, actually. Just trying to break the ice. You're his second wife. I was curious how the two of you got together."

"It's a funny story, really." Gloria laughed nervously to show me how funny it was. "Maybe awful is more like it. It was an unfortunate accident, not the best of starts. I was driving through the neighborhood, and I—well, I ran over Jared's dog."

"You're kidding."

"No, I'm not. This black lab came running out of nowhere, right into my grille, and I stopped to see if it was all right. The thing died in my arms and got blood all over my outfit. Then here's this boy running out, calling me a murderer. His father's following fast on his heels. I'm sitting there in the street covered in blood, and the dog is a mess, and Jared's pushing at me and crying. Hank was *so* nice. He parked my car for me, and we brought the dog inside. Jared asked Hank to help his dog, but it was too late. I was a little hysterical. I told them I'd pay for the dog. Hank just kept trying to calm me down. He told me to go clean up in their shower, and he let me borrow some of his wife's clothes—which I later returned."

"Was he still married at the time?"

"Yes, but he and Evelyn were already on the outs."

"Uh-huh," I said.

"She was away for the weekend visiting relatives, and Hank was feeling so bad for me, he said he'd treat me to dinner."

"He was feeling bad for you? What about Jared?"

"There wasn't anything we could do about his dog. It was an accident. Hank was trying to keep me from feeling too guilty."

"What were you doing when you met him?"

"I was a pharmaceutical rep for Merck," she said. "I'd met Hank before, actually, when I was pushing some new drugs at Hartford Hospital, but he wouldn't give me the time of day. Some doctors hate being bothered by drug salespeople. It paid well, but it was a high-stress job. I'm glad I'm out."

"What did you think of him the first time you met him?"

"Oh, he was impressive. Who wouldn't be impressed by Hank?"

I wanted to ask her how she happened to be driving past his house that day when his wife happened to be out of town—but I decided to let it go. I was drifting off into tangents.

"Do you do anything now?"

"No," Gloria said smugly. "And that's how Hank likes it."

"Does Jared have anything against you for killing his dog?"

"You mean still? No, I don't think so. He had a rough time of it when his father divorced Evelyn and married me. We didn't get along very well for a few years, but that changed over time."

"What happened?"

"Jared grew up."

"I see. Are there any other children in the family?"

"No, Jared's an only child. I never wanted any myself."

"Your husband told me that you were the last one in the house to speak with Jared, sometime back in September?"

"That's right." Gloria crossed her legs and yanked the hem of her skirt forward half an inch over her knee. "It was the Friday before Labor Day weekend, if I remember correctly."

"That's roughly what I heard. I take it Jared phoned you? Can you give me an idea of what you said to each other?"

"Yes, well—" Gloria searched my ceiling tiles for an escape hatch. "He wasn't going back to school, for one thing."

"Did he say why not?"

"He didn't like school."

"Okay, go on. What did he say and what did you say?"

"I'm not sure I can remember everything. He wanted money."

"How much and what for?"

"He always wanted money. Rent, I suppose."

"I asked you how much."

"Five thousand."

"That's a lot of rent for someone living on Avenue D and splitting with a roomie. Did you pay it?"

Gloria shrugged and scratched at her knee. "I would have, if Hank hadn't gotten wise to it. He wouldn't let me."

"Does he control your bank account? You told me you had your own money. It's what you were going to pay me with."

"Sure, I've got my own, and it's not an allowance. I've got my own bank account. Hank doesn't control it. He only made it clear that I'd be going against him if I gave Jared the money."

"Why wouldn't he go along?"

"I assume because he was hoping to teach Jared a lesson. It happens all the time in monied families. The kid gets it in his idea to drop out of school and expects to keep pulling a steady income from the parents. Once Jared dropped out, back in May, Hank cut him off."

"But Jared kept going to you for money during the summer?"

"Yes," Gloria said. "How did you figure that?"

"As far as I know, he wasn't working," I said. "He had to get money from somewhere. Your husband wasn't aware of it until that last phone call?"

"That's right."

"I don't see how he could have found out, unless he was listening in."

"He wasn't listening," she said. "He suspected something somehow and went rifling through my bank statements. He found my cancelled checks made out to Jared, going back to May. He was furious. He told me to stop. It was a day or two after I last spoke with Jared. It was a long weekend, and I hadn't gotten around to writing out the check yet. Hank stopped me."

"Jared never got that five thousand you agreed to send him?"

"No, he never did," Gloria said. "And I never called to let him know it wasn't coming. I couldn't afford to take the risk."

"And that was the last either of you heard from Jared."

"Yes," she said with a slight sniffle. She rubbed her nose.

"How much money had you given Jared since May?"

"I don't see that it's that important."

"You don't have to tell me. I'm not your husband."

That did the trick.

"All told, I guess it was fifteen thousand. He may have gotten some more from his mother. He was out there in July for his twentieth birthday. I'm sure she gave him at least *some*."

"This would be Ms. Evelyn Grosse of Turlock, California?"

"That's her."

"What do you think of her?"

"Not much, but she deserved better than what she got."

"That's a nice way of passing the buck," I said.

"I resent that remark."

"You should," I said. "Do you and Evelyn get along?"

"Better than she does with Hank."

"I'm getting the idea Hank can be a hard guy."

"Sometimes, but I know how to soften him up."

"And you have absolutely no idea where he might have gone."

"If I did, I wouldn't have come to you. It's that simple."

"Nothing's ever that simple."

"Did anyone ever tell you that you're a little paranoid?"

"Oh, sure, my old C.O. down at Fort Bragg used to tell me that all the time. He tried to reassure me that the Army wasn't out to get me or any of my buddies. Guess what? They were. As a result, I don't trust in much anymore. Serves me well in this line of work. Now, you're sure you don't know where Hank is?"

"You're nuts."

"Yet you still insist on trying to hire me."

"I thought I'd hired you already."

"We haven't shaken on anything," I said. "I like settling things like a gentleman, even with the ladies."

"Let's settle it now. Are you taking the case or not?"

"I'll take it, but it's not exactly ethical of me. I'll have to set some conditions, just to make me feel better."

"What sort of conditions?"

"Listen carefully. I'm only going to explain myself once, and I don't want any misunderstandings down the road. I'm going to continue looking for your stepson, and it will remain my primary focus for as long as it takes. Since you haven't offered me any leads on your husband, I'll have to take what I can from the Jared investigation. If I judge that I have the time and resources to follow any leads on your husband, I'll certainly do so, but Jared will have priority. If the two cases seem totally unrelated, I'll keep track of the time spent on each and bill you and your husband accordingly. If they're related, I'll draw up one bill and hope that one of you is willing to pay it."

"I'll make sure that whatever bill you send is taken care of, whether for one case or two. If my husband is with Jared, Mr. Quaintance, it probably won't be of his own free will."

"You're suggesting Jared would have kidnapped his father?"

"I don't know what I'm saying. Forget I said anything."

"I'll try, but it won't be easy. Can you think of any reason why your husband might have wanted to remove Jared's personal possessions from the apartment on Avenue D?"

"I couldn't guess at Hank's motives, no. Why?"

"Hank wanted to take out Jared's stuff yesterday morning, but Anastasia Cartwright wouldn't let him," I said, watching Gloria's face to gauge her reaction, if any. "Late last night, somebody went up there and did just that—burglarized the apartment, destroyed many of Anastasia's things, and took all of Jared's. It could have been Jared. Maybe it was your husband."

Gloria kept a poker face throughout.

Finally, she said, "What do you mean, destroyed?"

"Torn curtains, smashed furniture, broken glass, you know."

"And all of Jared's things stolen?"

"Baffling, isn't it?"

"It doesn't sound like Jared to me."

"What about your husband? Does his blood ever boil?"

"No, he wasn't—he isn't violent. Neither is Jared."

"Hank's handgun," I said. "The automatic pistol—just for household protection? Do you know what caliber it is?"

"I have no idea. Why?"

"There were three witnesses to last night's burglary. One of them may have been an accomplice. At any rate, all three of them were shot dead. I'm not sure of the exact caliber, but it was on the high end, like a nine-millimeter or a forty-five."

"I can't imagine Jared or Hank ever killing anybody."

"With any luck, we'll find out whether your imagination jibes with reality," I said. "That's what you're paying me for."

"It's a deal, then, Mr. Quaintance?"

"You agree to my conditions?"

"Yes. I'll trust you to use your best judgment."

"Then it's a deal, Gloria."

With that, I leaned across my desk and held out my hand.

Gloria sat up a bit and shook it. Her hand was clammy.

"You're sure you'll want to know the truth?"

"I want you to find my husband," she said. "And Jared."

"I'll do my best, but I can't guarantee a happy reunion."

"I understand," Gloria said, though it still looked to me like she was expecting everything to come up roses in the end.

"Are you driving back to Connecticut or staying here?"

"I'm spending the night at the Plaza."

"Not the Hilton?"

"Hank likes the Hilton. I like the Plaza."

"Fair enough," I said, and let her go.

Gloria left some of herself behind: gray chinchilla fibers clinging to her chair and wafting dreamily in the air.

TWELVE

I DUG OUT Dr. Henry Foster's business card and tilted it leisurely between thumb and forefinger to make the raised black ink glisten under my desk lamp. I wondered at the panoply of phone, fax, and pager numbers that some poor designer had gone through hell to set. I was taunted by the same notion that drove the state lottery: more numbers meant more chances to win. Gloria might have already tried them all, sure, but there was always the odd chance that Foster had returned from wherever he'd been and was now available at one of them. There was also the chance, perhaps not so odd, that Foster had screened his wife's calls and declined to return her pages. Or he might be lying in a gutter somewhere, dead of exsanguination. Or he might have been struck with amnesia or run off to join the French Foreign Legion.

Hell, I thought, and called the first number.

"Department of Rheumatology," said a woman.

"Dr. Foster, please."

"Dr. Foster is out of the office."

"Was he supposed to be?"

It wasn't the question she was expecting. A pause of a few beats elapsed before her thoughts could regroup:

"I'm sorry, sir. I'm not at liberty to divulge the doctor's schedule. Would you care to leave a message? I'll be sure that he gets it as soon as he comes in."

"I suppose he's usually at church Sunday mornings."

"I'm sure I wouldn't know," she said primly.

"Do you know where I could reach him? It's important."

"You sound too young to be one of his patients."

"I'm not. One of his patients, I mean. Not yet, anyway. The name's Greg Quaintance. I'm a private investigator. I'm calling from New York City on business."

"I thought you sounded like a cop."

"Is that good or bad?"

"Maybe that depends on whether Dr. Foster is in trouble."

"Would you say that's likely? You know him better than I."

"I only work for him," she said sprightly. "I'm not his therapist. I'm Nina. Nina Keynes. Keynes like the economist."

"But no relation."

"None. What do you want Dr. Foster for?"

"Just to talk to him. I'm having trouble reaching him."

"So is his wife," Nina said, then gasped. I could see her putting her hand to her lips. "Oh, I shouldn't have said that."

"That's all right. It's nothing I didn't know already."

"Of course, you could try his answering service."

"I plan to, Nina."

"That's area code eight six oh—"

"I've got the number, thanks," I said. "Nina, I'm sure you could help me with one thing, at least. Has Dr. Foster been acting strange recently? I mean, out of the ordinary."

"Not that I can think of, no. He maintains an even keel."

"Are you aware of anything happening recently that might have upset him?"

"I don't know anything about the doctor's personal life."

"It doesn't have to be personal. Could be professional."

"I can't think of anything recent," Nina said. "He's been upset for a few years about the changeover to managed care. It's been a constant source of frustration for him—but we're talking about a long-term thing that's been lingering, not anything that's happened overnight. And Hartford's been through a rough decade, what with the collapse of the insurance industry. It's made a lot of longtime residents kind of depressed."

"Is Henry Foster depressed?" I latched onto this easily enough, after Gloria's offhand mention of Russian roulette.

"I think he's just tired," Nina said. "Aren't we all?"

"Yes," I said thoughtfully. "Thanks for your time, Nina."

"No trouble at all, Greg. I'm sure I haven't been much help. You're not really worried that something might have happened to him, are you?"

"No, nothing to be alarmed about. If you do hear from him, tell him I called and have him call me back A.S.A.P."

"Will do," Nina said, and we hung up.

Depression wasn't necessarily that much to worry about. Plenty of medications were available to treat it, and Henry Foster ought to be enlightened enough to seek help if he was having trouble. On the other hand, a lot of people never recognized clinical depression until it tried to devour them whole. Foster might be the kind of guy who would live in denial for too long or was too proud or too stubborn to allow himself to be medicated. This could lead to a variety of rash acts.

I called Foster's home number.

"Foster residence," said a woman with some kind of south-of-the-border accent.

"Who am I speaking to?"

"I am Carmelita. I am the housekeeper. Who are jew?"

"Is Dr. Foster at home?"

"No, señor. Dr. and Mrs. Foster no are at home. Who can I say them is calling, please?"

"Greg Quaintance." I spelled it. "I'm a detective."

"*Mierda*, another detective!" Carmelita said deeply as if the subject bored her. "Jour friends come here this morning."

"What friends?"

"The three detectives from New Jork."

"How do you know I'm from New York?"

"Caller I.D. say *dos uno dos*. Maybe jew was one of them, how do I know, eh? I forget their names, but one—Orjuedos."

"Hard to forget Detective Orjuedos," I said. "He's a friend of mine, all right. Did they, um, get what they came for?"

"What they came for?" Carmelita repeated. "Jew mean Herod?"

This threw me for a moment, and I had a wild vision of the frightened Hebrew king slaughtering the male babies of Bethlehem.

"Yes," I said. "I take it Jared Foster is not at home?"

Carmelita sighed with exasperation. "As I told jour friends, so am I telling jew that joung Herod no is at home. He no live here. *Me entiendes?*"

"So you sent my friends away, or did they come inside?"

"No, they no enter the house to talk. Then they go."

"I see. Is there anyone else staying there at the house?"

"No, señor. Lonely house. Very lonely house."

"One more question, Carmelita."

"*Sí*, señor?"

"Do you remember a young man who came to visit along

with Jared sometime in August? I believe his name was Karel?"

"Karel. *Sí*, señor." Carmelita sounded like she wanted to register a complaint. She was speaking to the right department.

"Is it a good memory or a bad memory?"

"Bad memory. That boy give Carmelita much to clean up."

"Karel, you mean?"

"*Sí.* Bad guest. I no want to see him ever again."

"What kind of a mess did he make?"

"Oh, señor! Blood everywhere. On the sheets, soaked through to the mattress. I had to throw the sheets away."

"What about the mattress?"

"I call Dial-a-Mattress, they come pick it up and give us a new one."

"What happened? Was somebody hurt?"

"No, señor, nobody hurt. I no have no idea what happen in there. Carmelita yust get stuck with the mess."

"Whose bed are we talking about?"

"I no should be talking at all, Señor Quaintance."

"Yes, you should, Carmelita. You're being very helpful."

"Well, since jew are the police—" Carmelita paused, waiting for me to reconfirm that I was what she had assumed.

"Actually, I'm a private detective," I said, "but I'm working closely with the New York police on this."

"Private detective, eh?" she said. "Like *Magnum, P.I.*?"

"Sort of," I said. "Though not half as good-looking."

Carmelita giggled like not even schoolgirls giggle. "Jew no fool me. I can tell a man by his voice. Jew very sexy man."

"Thank you. Whose bed had the bloody sheets?"

"The master bedroom, señor. I ask Mrs. Foster, how can this happen? She say, Carmelita, yust clean it up and mind jour own business. She ask me no to tell Dr. Foster nothing about it."

"Did Karel cause any other trouble?"

"I no can tell nothing more, señor. Jew ask Mrs. Foster."

"Did you tell any of this to Detective Orjuedos?"

"No, señor. Orjuedos no ask nothing about Karel. He only looking for Herod. He want Mrs. Foster to call him pronto."

"*Gracias*, Carmelita," I said. "*Muchas gracias. Adiós.*"

"Yeah, yeah," she sang. She hung up abruptly.

My burgeoning search for Henry Foster was assuming some urgency. There were a lot of new answers I wanted out of him. He hadn't been dealing straight with me—more like from the bottom of the deck. He wasn't the first client to do so, and he wouldn't be the last. I didn't have to like it. In fact, I didn't.

I called the next number on his business card.

The woman on the other end told me I'd reached Dr. Foster's answering service and asked if I cared to leave a message.

"Could you forward my call to the doctor?"

"I'm sorry, sir. Not at the present time."

"Why not?"

"We can only do that when the doctor tells us where he is and what number he wants us to forward to."

"And you don't know where he is or where I could reach him?"

"No, I don't. But I'd be happy to take a message. Dr. Foster will get it the next time he calls in for his messages."

"When do you think that will be?"

"I couldn't say."

"How often does he usually call for his messages?"

"Sir, I can't tell you that."

"Maybe you ought to," I said. "My name's Greg Quaintance. I'm a private detective working for Dr. Foster. It's important that I get in touch with him. He was supposed to call me this morning and hasn't. Tell him I called and ask him to call me."

"I will do that, Mr. Quaintance. How is that spelled?"

"Just like acquaintance but without the A.C.," I said, and gave her my work phone and pager numbers. "Don't hang up just yet, ma'am. Any more information you can give me could be very useful. Specifically, I'd like to know how often he calls to pick up his messages and when he did so last."

"I'm not sure if I—"

"This is official business, ma'am." I gave her my best cop-like manner. "I'm licensed by the State of New York and deputized by New York County. The work I'm doing for Dr. Foster is related to an ongoing official police investigation."

"I'm still not sure—"

"What do you require? A copy of my private eye's license? I'll be happy to fax one to you. What's your fax number?"

"Okay, I'll see what I can do. Please hold a moment."

I didn't like her putting me on hold. She could be turning to her shift supervisor and asking about the propriety of this. If she got her supervisor involved, even a fax of my license wasn't likely to help me get the information.

"Sir?"

"Yes?"

"Dr. Foster's got quite a backup of messages. The records show that he usually calls in four or five times a day. The last time he called in was yesterday afternoon, at two-thirty P.M."

"Under normal circumstances, then, he would have already called in another two or three times yesterday, right?"

"I guess so," she said. "Maybe he went on vacation."

"Right," I said. "Thanks for your help. I appreciate it."

"You're welcome."

"And don't forget to leave him my message."

"I won't," she said. "That's my job."

I wanted to say good girl but figured it would get me in

trouble. You couldn't say good girl to anyone anymore without catching hell. You couldn't hold the door open for most women without getting a ball-busting glare. Political correctness made you have to handle people with kid gloves. Handling people with kid gloves took a lot of the fun out of handling people.

"Thank you very much," I said pleasantly. "Goodbye."

Foster had two pagers, for some reason. Perhaps he wore one around the hospital and the other when he was off-duty. I called both numbers a few times and left various phone numbers where I could be reached, including work, home, and pager. Wherever Foster was, one of his pagers ought to be on him. I hoped he had his wits about him as well as the good sense to return my page. If I didn't hear from him, I was going to start to really worry.

I didn't want to have to worry about him. I had enough to worry about. Jared Foster was up to his eyeballs in this mess that his father had gotten me into, and I probably couldn't get him out. If Henry Foster had vanished on purpose, he was leaving me high and dry. I liked handling a case my way, and normally I liked it when a client left me alone—but I also liked having them available to confer with.

Call me, Foster.

If you're still alive.

THIRTEEN

IT WAS NOON when I tried to reach Evelyn Grosse. It was nine in the morning clear across the country in Turlock, and I wasn't at all surprised to reach an answering machine. The message was in the cheerful voice of a middle-aged woman who had been standing too far away from the microphone. It sounded muffled, as if she had recorded it from across the room—or in a wind tunnel:

"Hello, you've reached the home of Gustav and Evelyn Grosse. We're sorry we're not here to take your call. If you'd be so kind as to leave us your name and phone number after the beep, we'll be sure to return your call as soon as we can. Thank you!"

"Yes, this is Greg Quaintance calling from New York. I'm a private investigator. I'd like to speak with you about your son Jared Foster. Please give me a call back." I gave out my numbers. "You can reverse the charges, if you like. Otherwise, I'll call again later. Looking forward to hearing from you."

I waited for a few minutes. If they were screening, they would call back soon enough. But I had a nagging feeling that they were out of the house. It was still morning in California, and some people did go to church on Sundays. The voice on the machine sounded like one that might.

Not that I had anything against churchgoers. I was eager to talk with Evelyn Grosse. If she was getting herself all gussied up and heading out with Gustav to hear the preacher's sermon, they'd probably hang around afterward in the reception hall for social hour and soft beverages, then head on out to a nice Sunday lunch at their favorite greasy cafeteria. If so, they would be out of the house for the next three or four hours.

I was assuming a lot, of course.

Whatever the reason, they weren't home. I watched the phone for fifteen more minutes, but it refused to ring.

I closed up my office. I couldn't afford to sit around all day twiddling my thumbs. I had somewhere to go and someone to see who might be able to help me with both Henry and Jared.

FOURTEEN

IT TOOK ME fifteen minutes to walk to East Sixteenth between Irving Place and Third, the north side of which was taken up by Washington Irving High School, a beige behemoth with bars on the windows designed by the same guy who did the Bastille. That was Irving's bust in bronze out front, facing onto his place. Try telling that to the kids who went to his school. They'll care.

I wanted a townhouse on the south side of East Sixteenth. The one to its left had work permits taped up on the doors and heavy plastic tarpaulins draped over scaffolding, but no one was doing any work today. A giant garbage receptacle was taking up two parking spaces out front, piled to overflowing with the detritus of a gutting—rotted planks, white plaster chunks, cement-caked bricks, and radiators coiled up like iron sausages.

The townhouse I wanted had already been through the works, or at least a facelift. It was a five-story redbrick thing from about 1850, and I didn't like the job that had been done on it—or to it. The first thing owners liked to do when they got their hands on an old townhouse was remove all the old layers of paint and find some new skin beneath. They would hire an outfit to come over, spread thick acidic gook on the paint, and go at it with sandblasters. The tarpaulins were there to keep pedestrians from getting drenched. When the process was done, the owners were out several thousand bucks and had themselves a brand-spanking-new façade that looked like shit.

Like the one I was staring at now—half an inch of the brickface had been professionally eroded away, leaving behind a wavy, uneven, pockmarked surface that revealed the raw interior of bricks that had been baked in Washington Irving's day, now flush with the cement instead of jutting out smartly like a good brick should. If I were to come into possession of this house, I'd want to throw up three coats of Sears Weatherbeater to cover its nakedness. Those neighbors who thought sandblasting such a good idea would probably sue me for lowering property values.

Dream on, Quaintance. As if you'd ever make enough money in this line of work to buy a townhouse in Manhattan—or anywhere.

I put away my envy, went up the steps, and rang the buzzer.

"Yes?" came a man's voice.

"Greg Quaintance. I'm a private investigator."

"I'm sorry, did you say private investigator?"

"Yes, I did."

"Well, what do you want?"

"I'd like to speak with Dr. Willem Kirst if he's at home."

"I'm Kirst. Give me a minute. I'll be right down."

He wasn't, though. I gave him an extra five minutes.

"Sorry to keep you waiting, but I'm in the middle of writing a grant proposal," Willem Kirst said as he opened the door. His bright hazel eyes were made buggy by thick lenses that didn't look right for their polished Donna Karan frames. The bags under

Kirst's eyes were magnified as well. His hair was peppery gray, cropped to three-quarters of an inch and groomed into a narrow chinstrap down around the jaw and up over the lip. He stood in bare feet, faded blue jeans, and a navy pullover sweatshirt that said NYU MEDICAL CENTER in yellow block caps.

"Don't you have grant writers for that?"

"I do," Kirst said. "I leave some of it to them, but they don't know everything. It's not an easy thing to milk people."

I handed over a business card. "Can I come in?"

"Um," he said, frowning. "Is this going to take long?"

"Not if I can help it."

"By all means, then." Kirst held the door open and stepped aside, shutting and deadbolting it after me. "Have a seat in the front room, to your left. What you might call the parlor."

You might, I thought. What I said was:

"Nice house. You live here all by yourself?"

"Yes," Kirst said.

The polished mahogany staircase reminded me of the one in the *Psycho* house—the one my fellow private dick, Arbogast, took a tumble down with a bit of chocolate syrup on his forehead after meeting Norman's mother. I skirted the stairs and ducked under the mahogany-framed archway to my left. It was a roomy parlor, with a fourteen-foot ceiling, elaborate plaster cornices, an original-looking red granite fireplace, and two tall windows overlooking the giant garbage receptacle. The furnishings were sleek Scandinavian on top of an antique Persian.

"Looks like you do pretty well for yourself," I said.

"I'm good at writing grant proposals," Kirst said cagily. "You have to be good, when there's less money going around. The cardiologists are competing with the AIDS researchers and the breast cancer crowd. It can get bitchy. Go on, have a seat."

"What kind of research do you do, Dr. Kirst?" I planted

myself in a squat, square-backed armchair with square legs, a square seat, and tall, square arms that rose up under my square shoulders like the marble throne at the Lincoln Memorial.

"Neurological," Kirst said, grunting as he leaned over a long, low-rising cabinet that opened to reveal several long rows of tall-rising bottles. "Dealing with sleep, mostly. Can I get you something to drink, Mr. Quaintance? My bar is well stocked."

"Ginger ale."

"I have milk, too," Kirst said smarmily.

"I don't like milk in my ginger ale."

"One ginger ale," Kirst reaffirmed, rising with an audible exhalation. "I'll have to go to the kitchen. Be right back."

Willem Kirst disappeared under the archway and padded past the dark staircase and down the hall toward his kitchen.

I got up. Lying atop the liquor cabinet was a neat pile of outgoing mail, stamped, sealed, and ready to go. Bills, mostly: Con Edison, NYNEX, American Express, Time Warner Cable. One was a piece of professional correspondence addressed to some M.D. at Stanford with an unpronounceable Indian name. The address was typed on an ivory laid stationery envelope that bore Kirst's overachieving titles in embossed ink in the upper right corner:

WILLEM P. KIRST, M.D., PH.D., F.A.A.N., F.A.C.N.

DEPARTMENT OF NEUROLOGY, NYU MEDICAL CENTER

PROFESSOR OF NEUROLOGY, NYU MEDICAL SCHOOL

DIRECTOR, J. WALKER HAMILTON SLEEP DISORDERS CLINIC

Somewhere far away a refrigerator closed. I arranged the mail as it had been and sat down again in the nice square chair.

Kirst came in and handed me a tall glass of ginger ale with bubbles crawling up the sides of the three clinking ice cubes.

"Your drink, Mr. Quaintance." He smiled like a pedant.

"Thanks." I took it and sipped it with feigned interest.

I didn't like that smile he gave me. Around well-educated types, I was in danger of sprouting a chip on my shoulder. I was always worried that my smattering of junior college and years at the Ft. Bragg Finishing School showed on my face. I wasn't ashamed—it was only that I resented it when people with college degrees made a big deal out of feeling sorry for me.

"I suppose you're looking for Jared Foster," Kirst said, bending over his wet bar and pouring cognac into a snifter.

"Who said that I was?"

"A little bird named Henry." He brought it back with him to the slinky couch across the coffee table from me and sat.

"Is that all he is to you? A little bird?"

"Figure of speech," he said and wolfed down a gulp. "Did I say something wrong? I didn't mean to insult your client."

"Who said anybody was my client?"

"Aren't we defensive!" Kirst clucked his tongue. "You don't have to keep it a secret from me. Hank Foster came to see me yesterday morning and said that he believed Jared was missing. He was considering hiring a private eye to find him. I don't get private eyes ringing my doorbell every day, Mr. Quaintance."

"I don't suppose you do," I admitted. "You're right, I am looking for Jared Foster. That's the main reason I'm here. Maybe you could begin by telling me what you told his father."

"There's nothing to tell."

"I'd still like to hear it."

"I'd be the last person to know anything about Jared."

"Maybe you'd like to offer me your learned opinion."

"How can I have an opinion on nothing?" he said calmly.

"You were Jared's academic adviser, weren't you?"

"Yes, that's right." He took a small sip of his cognac.

"And you and Henry Foster went to medical school together here at N.Y.U.—same graduating class."

"Right again." Kirst pursed his lips and narrowed his eyes.

"When Henry came yesterday, were you surprised to see him?"

"Naturally," he said and sucked air through his teeth. "I had no idea Jared was missing."

"Right. Why would you? Jared dropped out in May. I'd assume you wouldn't have seen him at all since then."

Kirst didn't say anything but swirled more cognac onto his tongue. It was the sort of thing you'd drink to soothe your nerves, and Kirst was an expert on nerves if not cognac.

I went on: "Did Henry Foster have any reason to think you might have had any recent contact with Jared?"

"I don't know how he could. Why he would, I mean."

"*Have* you had recent contact with Jared?"

"Sure I have," he said, like it was the most natural thing.

"Did you tell Henry about it?"

"No."

"Why not?"

"I didn't think it relevant."

"Maybe you could tell me."

"I still don't think it relevant."

"I'd be willing to sit through a mountain of irrelevancy."

"Oh, I like that. That's very good. 'A mountain of irrelevancy.' I'll have to remember to use that on my students."

"Look, Dr. Kirst, Jared may be in trouble." I didn't mind spinning and parrying with him in conversation a little, but I had to try to communicate the gravity of the situation. "Over the last few days, two of Jared's friends have been murdered."

Kirst raised his eyebrows at this.

"What you think is irrelevant could very well be key," I

continued. "I'm trying to find Jared. You may know something. It may be important, and maybe you can't see it. You can take as long as you like, but I want it now, and I want it straight."

Kirst lowered his eyebrows but didn't say a word.

"Come on, let's have it." My teeth were beginning to grind.

"I could claim doctor-patient confidentiality," Kirst said.

I stood up. I had the urge to throw my glass of ginger ale into the fireplace to get his attention. I suppressed it. I took a sip instead. Then I said: "Stop wasting my time."

"Sit down, Mr. Quaintance. Relax. I was about to say that I certainly *could* claim doctor-patient privilege—but that I don't believe in this case that will be necessary. I'll tell you whatever you want to know about Jared's condition. You can decide for yourself whether it's relevant. Or not."

"What condition?" I said, lowering myself into the chair. I wished now that I had a real drink, but I wasn't going to ask.

"Jared came to me a few times over the summer and allowed himself to be observed at the sleep disorders clinic."

"What clinic is that?" If I hadn't already dug through his mail, it would have been the next obvious question.

"The J. Walker Hamilton Sleep Disorders Clinic," Kirst said with all the weight and pomposity that came with it.

"Was Jared having trouble sleeping?"

"'Having trouble sleeping' implies insomnia. Jared wasn't suffering from insomnia. The International Classification of Sleep Disorders encompasses a great deal more than that. Nearly everybody has a sleep disorder of one kind or another that the clinic would be willing to observe and treat. Snoring is common, of course, as are the insomnias. Many suffer from hypersomnia, or excessive daytime somnolence. You've heard of narcolepsy?"

"Yes." I had to show I was paying attention to the lecture.

"There's restless legs syndrome and obstructive sleep apnea, which are physiological problems, of course. Many other sleep disorders can be psychological or psychiatric in nature—caused by anxiety, depression—or, say, personality disorders."

"Was Jared suffering from a personality disorder?"

"It won't do much good for you to guess," Kirst said. "Bear with me. I want you to understand why Jared came to see me."

"All right," I said. "It's your ball, doctor."

"There are sleep disorders caused by drug and alcohol use, and by irregular work hours, and by jet lag, and any number of other causes. Some disorders are sexual. Every boy going through puberty has nocturnal emissions, and there are many adults who fall asleep the very instant they reach orgasm."

Kirst paused, as if expecting one of my witty remarks.

"What about Jared?" I asked.

"Be patient, Mr. Quaintance. I'm getting to it. There are also what are termed the parasomnias, which can be described as disorders of partial arousal."

"What do you mean exactly by partial arousal?"

"Let me explain it this way. Normal sleep proceeds from the arousal stage, when we are fully conscious, to non-REM sleep, and then on to REM sleep."

"By REM, you mean rapid eye movement?"

"You're trying for brownie points. Yes, that's correct. During the course of normal sleep, we cycle from non-REM to REM and back again, generally two or three times, until we awaken, when we're back at the arousal stage again and in full control of our faculties. REM is the deepest sleep and provides the most vivid dreams. It's sometimes hard to awaken someone who's in the middle of an REM period. Non-REM sleep is lighter and generally less restful. A parasomnia could be just about anything that qualifies as a disturbance of a certain sleep stage or a disorder of partial arousal. Many parasomnias are idiopathic, which means we can find no underlying cause—but such disorders are almost always neurological at some level."

"Jared was suffering from some kind of parasomnia, then?"

"Indeed he was. Probably still is. We certainly didn't manage to cure him of anything. Jared is a somnambulist, a—"

"A sleepwalker," I finished for him.

"Good for you," Kirst said smugly.

"I know some ten-dollar words. When did Jared come to you?"

"I don't recall the exact dates. Since May, I must have checked him in for observation on four, maybe five occasions. I'd have to go over his whole file to tell you exactly."

"You wouldn't happen to have his file here, would you?"

"Of course not. It's at the clinic."

"Would it be possible for me to see it?"

"No." Kirst swallowed the last of his drink. "I don't mind telling you man to man about Jared's case, but his file must remain strictly confidential. You understand."

"When you say you checked him in, you mean that he stayed there twenty-four hours a day, maybe for a few days or more?"

"Correct. We like to monitor both sleeping and waking."

"What was the longest Jared stayed there?"

"I believe about ten days. Give or take."

"He wouldn't be staying there now, would he?"

"If he were, I would have told you at the outset."

"When was the last time he was checked in?"

"Late August. He'd just come back from Connecticut."

"I see," I said, though I wasn't at all sure what it was that I saw. "I'm curious. How do you get patients to come? Jared wasn't employed, but most of your patients must have jobs. They'd have to take time off. Maybe their sick time covers it?"

"In some cases it does. But we pay them, anyway."

"You pay them?" I said, surprised. "You mean, like blood centers pay people to come in and give plasma? You pay people for their sleep?"

"That's one way of looking at it," Kirst said. "The clinic conducts several ongoing studies, and when we meet candidates who meet our criteria, we enroll them and pay them for their time. Not handsomely, but adequately."

"So you paid Jared, then."

"Yes, of course."

"Is there any possibility he was faking his sleepwalking?"

"Nonsense," Kirst said gruffly. "Somnambulism can't be faked. Anyway, we have twenty-four-hour videotape monitoring, handwritten records of our direct visual observation, and electrophysiological polysomnographic recordings to prove it."

"Who do you intend to prove it to?"

"I'm not entirely sure what you're getting at."

"Sounds like the kind of evidence Jared's defense attorney would love to get his hands on."

"Defense attorney?" Kirst's eyes widened appreciably.

"Assuming we can find the kid." I sighed heavily. "The police are interested in questioning him about the four murders."

"Four? I thought you said there were two."

"I said two of Jared's friends had been killed. There were also two bystanders, guys who worked in a Chinese restaurant. Jared is the police's only connection to any of them. If they find Jared, they're going to book him."

"But that's preposterous! Jared's no murderer!"

"Maybe he is, maybe he isn't," I said. "I don't know enough to be able to judge. But I'm telling you, even a public defender would know what to do with the kind of data you've got on Jared —and Jared Foster won't be getting a public defender, I bet."

"Somnambulists are not homicidal maniacs, Mr. Quaintance!"

"Perhaps not." I thought of Jared's *Cabinet of Dr. Caligari* poster. But in the movie, everything was only a dream, anyway.

"They're far more likely to be a danger to themselves!"

"You've got to admit, it wouldn't be too hard to convince a few out of twelve jurors that a sleepwalker wasn't responsible for his actions. It opens up a big can of reasonable doubts."

"Aren't you getting ahead of yourself? Jared hasn't been charged with any crime."

"Not yet," I said. "But he will be. And it's never too early to start thinking ahead. Jared Foster is in big trouble."

"Just whose side are you on?" Kirst blustered.

"I don't take sides. I just poke around for answers."

"It doesn't sound to me as if you have Jared's best interests at heart."

"That's not my job. I was hired to find him, that's all. I'm concerned about his welfare. Considering all the death that seems to be surrounding him, I'd like to know that he's still alive. Once we find him, the police either arrest him, or they don't. That's their business. My client pays me regardless."

"Have you ever met Jared?" Kirst's eyes went all twinkly.

"No," I said.

"Quite an amazing young man."

"In what way?"

"Not at all like his father. Hank doesn't understand his son, I'm afraid. Jared was lucky I was there to advise him. He and his father talked at cross purposes. Jared needed a kind of replacement father who could listen to him and help guide him."

"You didn't advise him to drop out of college, did you?"

"No, of course not. But he wasn't cut out for medicine."

"And you told him that?"

"I would have been derelict not to. The field is not for

everyone. Jared has more of an artistic bent, only he didn't know how to let it out. Hank had always been overbearing with him, especially since his divorce and remarriage."

"Jared spoke to you of things like that?"

"He had no one else to confide in—no one older, anyway."

"What other sorts of things did Jared tell you?"

"That's an awfully general question."

"So call me a generalist," I said. He didn't find it funny.

"Jared talked about everything. School, home, his college friends, his dreams, and his nightmares. There's too much to tell. I don't have the time, and surely you don't."

"You and he spent quite a lot of time talking, then. How did you ever make the time for him? You practice, you teach, you volunteer as a student adviser, you conduct your research at the clinic, you write grant proposals, you probably write papers for the medical journals, and I bet you write for the textbooks. There must be a couple of neurological conventions every year, too. I can't figure you academic doctors out, always juggling a thousand things. How did you ever have time enough for Jared?"

"I admit I spent a little extra time with him than with my other students. He seemed to need it. His wasn't a happy home."

"I'll bet." I thought of Miss Gloria Glendenning running over Jared's poor dog on her way into Foster's pants.

"I never agreed with his dropping out of school," Kirst went on in defense of himself. "He didn't consult me, anyway. He had talked of it, but I always told him, as long as his father's paying for his schooling, he might as well take it and make something of it. All I suggested was a change of direction, away from medicine, toward something else."

"Like?"

"The dramatic arts, perhaps."

"So what went wrong? Why didn't he listen to you?"

"It wasn't my fault," Kirst groused. "It was his father's."

"How?"

"Hank Foster wouldn't hear of his only son turning away from medical school. That's the kind of man Hank is. He wants to have utter control over every part of his world. Hell, if he couldn't recognize Jared wasn't suited for a career as a doctor, he must have been half mad. Hank had a strong hold over Jared. Jared suffered through nearly two years of school before he got the courage to admit he didn't want to be a doctor."

"Admitted it to his father, you mean? How'd it go over?"

"Badly. Hank threatened to cut him off and pull the plug on his education. Makes him sound quite the monster, doesn't it? I'm afraid Hank was in denial, thinking Jared was simply going through a phase and was bound to get over it. He thought his son would thank him someday for setting him straight."

"Only it didn't work, did it?"

"Oh, no, it backfired right in Hank's face!"

"Sounds like you got some kind of sick glee out of it."

"That's not a very nice thing to say!"

"I said it because it was true," I said. "You don't like Henry Foster much, do you, Dr. Kirst?"

"I hardly know the man. I knew him better in college."

"Maybe I'm tuning in to the remnants of some old rivalry."

"Hank and I were never rivals. I was at the top of our class, while Hank floundered around somewhere in the middle. He's been off at Hartford trying to treat old people's joints for twenty some-odd years. What does he have to show for it?"

"He's chief of his department, isn't he?" I said, since Foster wasn't around to defend himself. "And he made a family—or an attempt at one. You don't have a wife or kids, do you?"

"Never had the time for it," Kirst said dismissively.

"Then you can't know what it's like for Foster to see his own son throwing away his education, drifting off into some alien subculture, maybe doing drugs, maybe hurting himself. You were his adviser all this time. You must have seen him go through all these changes. Didn't you ever get concerned about it?"

"What should I have been concerned about? The piercings? The tattoos? The hair?" Kirst laughed. "Do you know how many of my students look like that?—even the serious ones? I never noticed that Jared was hurting himself. If he was. We examined him at the clinic, and I never saw any evidence of drug use."

"No tracks?"

"No."

"Did he ever talk about the girl he was living with?"

"Which one?"

"The first one. The student. Juliet Logan."

"All I know is she was madly in love with him." Kirst got up and went back to the liquor cabinet for more cognac. "Madly. Obsession is not too strong a word for it. The way Jared told it, Juliet would have done anything for him—I mean *anything*."

"Such as?"

"Are you sure you wouldn't like a glass of something real?"

"I'll take a tequila straight up, if you've got it."

"If I've got it," Kirst scoffed. He had it, but he had to dig for it. It was the last bottle on the end of the back row.

"What things do you think Juliet would do for Jared?"

"Oh, I don't know." Kirst poured me a shot, neat, up to the rim. "Lie, cheat, steal—the usual. Jared couldn't take her."

"So he got out," I said. "Moved in with the other girl."

Kirst handed me my shot and told me to enjoy it. He sat back down with his refilled snifter and said: "Juliet was a minor casualty of Jared's major crisis. Once he told off his father, he couldn't focus on his studies. His grades suffered. He couldn't stand the sight of Juliet, and he'd found some new friends, so yes, he got out. He had no stamina left to finish the semester. That's also when he first started experiencing his somnambulistic episodes. In May. After he dropped out."

"And came to see you at the clinic," I said.

My shot was done. I set it on the coffee table.

"That was the first time, in May," Kirst confirmed.

"Did you ever determine what was causing his sleepwalking?"

Kirst gave me a professional doctor's shrug. "Psychological factors, mostly—the dispute with his father, the breakup with the girl, the anxieties over school—coupled with an underlying neurological disruption, perhaps caused by malnourishment and lack of sleep."

"Malnourishment. That could be caused by drug use, couldn't it? Such as a heroin addiction?"

"Or by not eating properly. Jared wasn't on drugs."

"So you keep insisting. Whenever he checked himself into the clinic, he never told anyone where he was going, did he?"

"No, I don't believe he did."

"So no one ever knew that he was with you."

"The rest of the staff at the clinic knew."

"I mean on the outside. None of his friends or family would have known where to reach him, would they?"

"Probably not."

Encouraged by the warm tequila in my stomach, I asked again:

"Jared wouldn't be at your clinic now, would he, Dr. Kirst?"

"Certainly not. You'd be wasting your time going there."

I wasn't sure I believed him. I wanted to press him on the subject, but that would be an exceedingly bad idea. Kirst knew now, if he didn't before, that the police had an acute interest in Jared. If he was keeping him at the clinic or here in his house or anywhere else, I'd given him ample opportunity to share that with me, and I wasn't about to get it now simply by asking.

Instead, I stared hard at him and said nothing.

Kirst went on by himself, like a wind-up doll: "I told you, Mr. Quaintance, I haven't seen Jared since late August. Two full months ago. I have no knowledge of his present whereabouts, nor has he been in contact with me in any way."

My curiosity was tempting me to ask him to show me around his house, but that would amount to revealing my hand. It was a pretty sad hand to begin with. It wasn't always safe to go around relying on hunches. Kirst may have been a creep, but I had no real reason to believe he was hiding Jared from the cops.

Kirst poured all the rest of his cognac down his throat and stood up. He looked at his watch and faked shock at the hour.

"I'm sorry," he said. "I'm afraid I've spent all the time with you that I can afford. I'm hard at work on a proposal—"

"You've said that three times," I said. "Do you usually drink this heavily when you're writing grant proposals?"

"In case you missed my meaning, I think it's time you left."

"Well, if that's how you feel . . ." I stood up to go.

Kirst was all smiles as he showed me out. He threw back the deadbolt and opened the door for me. He gave me a gentle nudge on my shoulder—out—and added, "This has been a most interesting chat. Let's do it—"

"I had one more thing to ask you," I said. "You said you spoke with Henry Foster yesterday morning. He told me the same thing when I met with him in the afternoon. After he left my office, he didn't happen to stop by to see you again, did he?"

"No," Kirst said, shaking his head no.

I wondered if that counted as a double negative.

"Why do you ask?" he asked.

"Foster didn't come home last night," I said. "After he said that he would. Gloria considers him missing. I thought maybe since you're his only friend in New York—"

"I doubt that I am! Did Gloria say I was? You must have spoken to her today."

"She came into the city to see me."

"I should ring her up. Is she staying at the Plaza? I'm sure she is. Gloria wouldn't stay anyplace else. That girl!"

"You know her well?"

"Yes, of course. I knew her way back when she was hanging around the medical center selling pharmaceuticals. And I went to their wedding, naturally. Gloria and I sometimes do lunch when she's in town. Is she the one who suggested Hank might have dropped in to see me before getting it in his head to disappear?"

"She never even mentioned you. It was my idea. I thought Foster might have stopped by, to catch up on old times."

"Hank has disappeared and *I'm* your only lead? Good luck!"

"He didn't tell anyone where he was going. I was hoping he might have told you. If not, my leads amount to zilch."

"I only saw him that once, yesterday morning," Kirst said, starting to close the door on me. "I wish I could help you."

I smiled in resignation and said: "That's okay."

"Goodbye, Mr. Quaintance," Kirst said.

He closed the massive door after me and locked it up tight.

FIFTEEN

I FOUND THE J. Walker Hamilton Sleep Disorders Clinic in the phone book and had a taxi take me up to its location, on East Thirtieth Street between Second and First. The clinic was a relatively modern structure that must have displaced an old townhouse like the one that stood next to it. It had a face of industrial-grade white porcelain tiles, with columns and rows of glass bricks where windows ought to be, and a pair of misaligned glass doors in aluminum frames. I threw away the stub of my cigarette and opened one of them. It grated across the lip of aluminum at my feet, where a grimy half-moon had been etched from all the openings and closings since the door went out of whack.

The interior went a long way toward perpetuating the general aura of shabbiness. The gray indoor-outdoor carpeting looked like it might have spent more time outdoors. The potted banana tree was dying a slow, agonizing death brought on by the northward-facing glass bricks and likely by a lack of attention. I was just as inept at taking care of plants, but at least I'd given up torturing them by bringing them into my home. There were a few other potted plants about the reception area, but they fared no better than the banana tree, and I couldn't bear to look at them. The oil paintings on the walls were tired seascapes and quiet mountain vistas—the sort of so-called starving-artist specials you might find at a so-called liquidation sale at some Ramada Inn in Pennsylvania. The chairs were upholstered in a thick gray weave, with sagging cushions I couldn't quite figure out: did people really sit out here and wait while their loved ones were inside sleeping? The reception desk was of yellowed formica, chipped at the corners to reveal a deep, corrupt brown like one of those unpopular shades Crayola decided to nix. Above the desk hung an oversized portrait in oils of a withered old man in a bow tie who bore a strong resemblance to our national bird.

I approached the receptionist, who wasn't shabby at all.

"May I help you?" he said, looking up from his *People.* He was a wiry youth not much more than twenty, with shoulder-length sun-bleached hair parted in the middle and drawn back over his ears. His skin was a light gold from a fading summer tan, and his dark lips were the kind of full, round things you don't see often enough on guys. He also had a nice Adam's apple; sometimes it's those forgotten little parts you fall in love with the most.

"Yes," I said, trying to get over the momentary distraction. I handed him one of my business cards. "I'm a private detective. I'm looking for a guy named Jared Foster, about your age. He's been a patient here before. I was wondering if he's here now."

"Oh, man," he said, sounding bummed. "I'd tell you if I could, but stuff about patients is like confidential."

"I know Jared Foster's been here before," I said. "Maybe you could at least confirm that for me."

I smelled the sickly sweet odor of marijuana in the air.

"Sorry, guy," he said. "I'm just the weekend receptionist, anyway. I'm really like not the guy to ask about stuff. We've got this lady, see, she's public relations? If she knew I was giving out stuff like that, she'd like chew me a new asshole."

"We wouldn't want that," I said. "Maybe you could tell me who that is behind you?"

"What?" The young man turned with a start, like he was expecting Hannibal Lecter or maybe the public relations lady. Then he looked up at the portrait and laughed, sort of a half-baked chortle. "Oh, that! That's like the old fart we're named after. J. Walker Hamilton. Stern-looking old geezer, isn't he?"

"Before your time, I guess."

"You got that right, bud."

"What's your name?"

"Ray." He chortled again. "As in, 'You can call me Ray.'"

"What did you do, Ray, go smoke a joint on your break?"

"No." Ray looked around as if somebody had betrayed him.

"I can smell it all over you. It's nice being the weekend receptionist, isn't it, Ray? Nobody looking over your shoulder?"

"Well, yeah," he said.

"What is this, some little gig you do on the side while going to school?"

"Yeah."

"You wouldn't want to lose it, would you? Which you probably would if someone ratted on your pot smoking, right?"

"Who's going to rat on me?"

"I could, if you don't give me the information I want. All it would take would be a few words with that nice P.R. lady."

"Hey, bud, it would be like your word against mine. You don't have any proof. I ate the roach."

"I could take it straight to Dr. Kirst. How do you think he'd handle it?"

Ray chortled again. It was beginning to erode his beauty.

"What's so funny?" I said.

"Dr. Kirst?" he said. "Go ahead! Go right on ahead, guy!"

"Why? What's the deal with Kirst? Are you some little pet of his, or does he simply tolerate drug use at his clinic?"

"It's not his clinic anymore, Mr. Private Eye."

"Since when?"

"Since we got a new director," Ray said cheerfully. "Kirst is out, man! He got his ass canned!"

"Why? What for?"

"Some kind of sexual harassment deal."

"A lawsuit?"

"Yeah, I guess."

"Brought on by whom? A staff member? A patient?"

"Some patient, I think. But it's still pending or something. We're not supposed to talk about it."

"Was Kirst canned temporarily, or permanently?"

"Oh, he's out, man, out for good. It's a pretty big deal."

"Do you know the name of the patient who brought suit?"

Ray shook his head and said, "Naw, no clue."

"What happened? The patient was asleep and woke up with Kirst fondling her—or him?"

"I don't know any of the details, bud. You can try asking public relations, but I bet they don't tell you shit, either."

"It wasn't Jared Foster, was it?"

"I know nothing," Ray said, chortling.

"I don't suppose I'd be allowed into the clinic, would I?"

"Not without an escort, and she's like not working today."

"The P.R. lady," I said.

"Her name's Jennifer Millhauser," Ray said. "I got like one of her cards here, somewhere." The top drawer of the desk was off its runners, but Ray managed to yank it out. He rummaged around inside among the colored paper clips until he came up with a business card, slightly dog-eared like everything else. "Come back tomorrow for the Magical Millhauser Mystery Tour."

"I will," I said, putting the card in my wallet. I could hardly restrain myself from giving out the unsolicited wisdom of a guy who'd just turned thirty: "In the meantime, Ray, go easy on the pot, will you? And you could find yourself something more nourishing to read than *People*."

"In other words, get a life, right?" Ray looked up at me and smiled, like I was the fool.

"No, Ray," I said, giving him a good look in the eye. "I'm sure you've got one already. Maybe it's a good one. How do I know? All I'm saying is, drugs are a big time-waster. Life is too short, and you should waste as little of it as possible."

"I hear you, man." Ray cast his eyes down at the *People*, but it didn't look like he was reading it anymore.

"I hope you do," I said. "Thanks for all the information."

"What information?" Ray wanted to know.

Thank you, pot.

I didn't answer Ray. I was already pushing the door open, scraping another scar into the flat aluminum lip. The pneumatic door-closer shut it slowly behind me with a fun noise like a bear's claw on a blackboard. I hoped Ray got a kick out of it.

SIXTEEN

I'D HAD MY pager with me all day, but so far not a single beep from anyone, much less Henry Foster. Back at my office, there was a single message on my answering machine. It was Detective Orjuedos, asking me to call him back.

I called, but I didn't get him. The detective on the line told me he'd convey my message via Dispatch, but he couldn't promise that Orjuedos would call me right back. I said fine.

Hanging around my office was not what I wanted to be doing, but there was no telling what Orjuedos wanted, so I waited, with the help of a few smokes. Ten minutes later, the phone rang.

"Greg, it's Tavo. You got a minute?"

"What's on your mind?"

"We found the gun," Orjuedos said. "The one the shooter used at the Chinese place. We found it in the garbage."

"What's the make?"

"Llama M87 nine-millimeter. Nice little piece of weaponry."

"I'll say," I said. "Why are you telling me?"

"The gun's registered in Connecticut under your client, Dr. Henry Foster."

"Is that so?"

"I hope you haven't been sharing any sensitive information with him, Greg. If you have, I'll ask you to cease and desist."

"Relax," I said. "I haven't even spoken with Foster since he hired me yesterday afternoon."

"Can you tell me where I might find him?"

"Honestly, no."

"I'd like to ask him a few questions."

"Me, too, Tavo. I don't know where he is, and now I'm looking for both him and Jared. I'll tell you if I find them."

"You better. If you don't, I'll hit you with obstruction and see what I can do about yanking that cute license of yours."

"That would be sweet of you."

"Don't make me do it," Orjuedos cautioned.

"I wasn't even thinking about it. I'm playing square."

"As long as you are, where can I find the wife?"

"Why do you want her?"

"She's the next best thing. Her husband and stepson are both wanted for questioning. She might be worth a squeeze."

"I've already tried it," I said. "To the extent that I squeeze. She came to see me this morning. Called me up at six-thirty, in fact, woke me up. She drove in later, and we talked in my office. Henry Foster was supposed to come home last night and didn't, and she wanted me to find him. I told her I would, if the two cases turned out to be connected."

"They sure the fuck are," Orjuedos said. "A couple of us went out to Hartford to surprise her this morning, but she was on her way in to see you, I suppose. You must know where she is."

"She's staying the night at the Plaza. At least that's what she told me. I haven't tried to recontact her just yet."

"Thanks, Greg."

"Don't mention it. I told you I was playing square. Are your boys sure the Llama is the same gun used in the killings?"

"Absolutely. The slugs retrieved from the corpses show the markings of the Llama's barrel. The Llama's clip holds fifteen, and it's down three, and there were only the three shots fired."

"Any latents?"

"*Nada.*"

"Okay, Tavo," I said. "So if I do find Foster or his son, you want me to bring them in?"

"Call us," Orjuedos said. "We'll handle it. Both of them may be armed and dangerous. You're only one man, Greg."

"I'll try to remember that."

"Don't do anything foolish."

"I won't, Mom," I said.

Orjuedos sighed worriedly, like he didn't believe me.

I retried Evelyn Grosse and got the answering machine again. I left another message. I'd try back again, or she could call me back if she liked. I slipped into my shoulder holster, rechecked my Glock, put on my leather jacket, and closed up shop.

I walked the two long blocks over to Kotby's Garage on West Sixteenth Street between Tenth Avenue and the West Side Highway and asked for my car. The attendant in the booth was Alejandro, a friendly kid of about twenty with a strong, handsome Mexican face. He'd shaved his head last summer in emulation of me but was now growing his hair back, sporting a spiky inch all around.

"*Hola*, Alejandro," I said, about to exhaust half my knowledge of Spanish. "*Como estás?*"

"Hey, Greg!" Alejandro said, smiling, happy to see me. He

reached for the keys to my car without even looking at the rack.

"Growing out the hair," I said, motioning with my chin.

"My mother, she don't like it so good with no hair."

"No one asked her to shave her head," I said.

Alejandro laughed, charitably. He always laughed at my jokes, but then he was used to my tips. He also liked my car.

"Getting cold, anyway," he said. "I can't get used to this New York weather, man. It don't get like this in Matamoros."

"It's not even cold yet," I said. "And you don't want to go back to Matamoros, do you?"

"Shit, no, man!" Alejandro frowned. "You *loco?*"

"Maybe a little."

"Take me out in your Barracuda sometime," he proposed.

"If you're ever not working, and if I ever have the time. You can drive me somewhere."

"I'd love that, man. I want to see how she handles."

I wanted to tell Alejandro that the 'Cuda wasn't a *she* but an *it*—but I didn't want him to think I was trying to correct his English, which was fine. The 'Cuda was still an it.

"I'll go get your car." He kept laughing as he walked up the garage ramp, maybe imagining what his mother would look like without her hair, and shaking his head at poor Greg, *el loco.*

While I waited, I stared at the yellow, windowless Manhattan Mini-Storage building across the street, and it made me wonder about the vehicle that must have taken Jared's things away after the burglary. There might have been someone hanging out the window of one of those parties in the Jacob Riis Houses who saw people loading it up. It would be a big help to know the make of the vehicle and try to track it down.

I hoped Orjuedos was following up on it. If not, I would see what I could find out myself—but later.

Now was the time, while Gloria Glendenning-Foster was in

the city and Henry Foster was nowhere, for me to get the 'Cuda
out of mothballs and take it on an excursion into suburban
Connecticut.

SEVENTEEN

I LOVED THE 'CUDA, and the 'Cuda loved me. It was the longest romance of my life, dating back to my basic training days at Ft. Bliss, when I hopped a ride into El Paso with some buddies and saw this '70 model's chromium grille grinning at me from the corner spot of a pennanted lot. Since then, I'd given it a glossy black finish, upped the torque by having the cylinders rebored, and generally souped it up with a couple of extras that were kosher in some states but not in New York. The rent at Kotby's Garage was killing me, but I didn't have the heart to leave the 'Cuda on the street, and whenever I got it in my head to sell it, I was prevented by a guilt that tied my stomach in knots. The 'Cuda was one of the few things I could depend on, and the twists my cases took me through proved I still had a use for it. It needed to be treated right, though, and I didn't get it out on the road often enough.

Hartford was a convenient excuse. Carmelita seemed to know things, and I was wondering if she had a use for some tax-free supplementary income. That was another thing the phone was no good for. It would be much easier to hand Carmelita some bills than to send them Western Union. It so happened I'd brought a pocketful of crispies with me, like miracles.

The traffic was thicker than I'd expected. People were out for fall Sunday drives to look at the changing leaves, and they weren't in rush about it. It took me two-and-a-half hours to reach Hartford, and I wondered whether this little side-trip was worth the time. I still had to get back. By the time I did, it would be dark. The goths would be out of their crypts.

The house outside of Hartford was cut off from the world by a private swatch of weathered old trees bearing fall foliage in bitter red and rotten yellow. The drive was paved in coal-black asphalt that took me up a rise and leveled off at the front door of a wide house that looked like a pile of flagstone into which somebody had popped a few windows. They had set an A-shaped roof on top and squashed it nearly flat.

The 'Cuda shut off well. I was pleased with the way it sounded. I got out and stretched. Birds twittered on all sides of me like they were in Surround Sound. Woodpeckers pecked. Hummingbirds hummed. A gang of squirrels was seen pinching nuts and making a clean getaway back to their hideout.

I rang the doorbell, which had a good chimy *ding-dong* to it.

Carmelita opened it, and her hand stayed clutched on the knob, the cords in her forearm tightening. She was lean, with sharp features, skin she took care of, and dark raven eyes with the black hair to match, drawn taut off her forehead like a ballerina. She wasn't a day over thirty-five. The Fosters had her in an old woman's gray uniform and white apron, and it didn't suit her. Carmelita belonged in bright Miami colors, in the bright Miami sunshine, lounging at poolside with some Miami stud—who didn't have to be bright. Too bad my money couldn't work that kind of miracle for her. If it could, I'd be there myself, looking for the same dim stud.

"I'm Greg Quaintance," I said, showing my license and giving out another business card. "We spoke on the phone. That is, if you're Carmelita, the housekeeper."

She nodded dolefully and tried to hand me back the card. I told her she could keep it. She dropped it in her apron pocket, where it could keep her gray dust rag company.

"I am sorry, señor," Carmelita said, her hand gripping and anxious to close up the house against me. "Nobody at home."

"Good," I said. "It's you I wanted to talk to. Alone."

"I?" Her reddish flesh went a slight shade deeper.

"Is there anyone else here today? Maybe other help?"

"No, señor. Like I tell you, is a lonely house."

"Can I come in?"

Carmelita eyed me up and down the way I was sometimes eyed at Eighteenth and Eighth. She said: "If jew insist."

"Thanks."

I went in, and she closed the steel door after me. It made a sucking sound like the closing of an airlock. The sound of her black pumps followed me along the parquet floor of the foyer and ended when we hit the carpet that led to the sunken living room. The ceiling was textured, spray-on style, with random holes for lights, vaulted by dark squarish beams bolted together in huge cast-iron braces at the peak of the squashed A. The fireplace was cobbled together out of more flagstone, tapering as an exposed chimney up to the ceiling. The farthest wall was glass, with doors onto a redwood deck and an outdoor jacuzzi. Beyond that were the woods, crowded, sunny, and shallow.

"Nice house." I was growing tired of saying this about other people's houses, but there was nothing in the cards to change that.

"If jew say so, señor." Carmelita was probably growing tired of working in it. "What jew want to talk about?"

"Let's sit down," I said, to get her off her feet.

"Eh, hokay." She sounded reluctant, or suspicious.

I let her sit first. She chose the overly pillowed corner of the wraparound leather couch. I sat a few cushions down from her, hoping to quell any thoughts that I had ulterior motives.

"Is cold in here, no?" Carmelita said, clutching her elbows.

"I'm fine."

"The hot air, it goes up there and out and away from me."

"They could install ceiling fans to push the air down," I said. "And put in triple-pane windows."

"They no will do that." She laughed. "Fosters are cheap."

"They're paying me well enough."

She laughed again. "They no pay me well enough, señor!"

"How long have you been working for them, Carmelita?"

"Two jeers, six months."

"Do you live here with them?"

"Jase," she said. "That make the pay not so bad, maybe."

"Would you like a cigarette?"

"Jase, but I cannot. Dr. Foster no like it in the house."

"Dr. Foster isn't here," I said, bringing out my pack. "The smoke will drift up to the ceiling. I'd like one. Would you?"

"Hokay." A rebellious smile crept up at the corners.

We leaned closer together, and she put the Lucky Strike to her lips. I lit it with my Zippo and did the same for myself.

"We have no ashtray," she said thoughtfully, blowing the smoke above her to encourage it on its upward trek.

"Will this do?" I removed a coffee table candle from its cut crystal base and set the base on the cushion between us.

"I like jew, Señor Quaintance." Carmelita's eyes narrowed.

"I'm beginning to like you, too, Carmelita. I'll like you even more if you answer some questions for me."

"I am the housekeeper," she pronounced again, as evenly as she had over the phone. "I am no supposed to give out secrets."

"Even when lives may be in danger?"

"Whose lives, señor?"

"Jared Foster. Henry Foster. Others, maybe."

"It make no difference to me, maybe."

"You don't care for the Fosters, Carmelita?"

"I no have to. All I paid to care for is their dust."

"You and me both, sister," I said. "The Fosters seem to need a lot of cleaning up after."

Carmelita smiled at that. This was the way private eyes were supposed to talk. She'd seen *Magnum, P.I.*, if nothing else. She was beginning to see right through me. All to the good.

"What sort of questions jew want to ask, Señor Quaintance?"

"Personal questions about the family you work for."

"Some family."

"So I'm beginning to discover."

"What make jew think I tell jew anything?"

"Because I'm in the market for information, and from where I'm sitting, you've got a corner on it."

"A corner?" Carmelita missed the idiom.

"You've got some information I want," I said. "I think."

"How much jew willing to bet?"

"Now you're catching on, sister."

"I am not jour sister, mister." Carmelita blew smoke. "Jew think because Carmelita make little money cleaning up dust, jew can hand her twenty dollars and learn all the Fosters' secrets?"

"Something like that," I said, blowing smoke of my own. "Only I was thinking of a slightly larger sum than twenty."

"Jew were thinking of exploiting me for jour own profit, like any other gringo."

"Nothing exploitative about it, Carmelita. It's commerce. And I'm no gringo, not the way you mean it. You have something I want. I'm willing to pay for it, and I'll give you good money."

"How good?"

I took the bills from my pocket and laid them out on the cushion: five fresh hundred-dollar bills—the new kind with the life-size portrait of Benjamin Franklin taking over the front.

Carmelita was quietly impressed. She lifted them up and sifted through them, arranging them like a poker hand. Then she folded them neatly in half and put them in her apron pocket to join my card and her rag for an inanimate-object party.

"I no sure what jew want to know first," she said. "Jew must promise jew no tell Fosters what I tell jew, hokay?"

"You can trust me," I said. "I live by discretion."

"Jew live by it, eh? I live by what I do here. Maybe I no like it so much, but I want to keep doing it."

"You took the money."

"Jew no say nothing to get me fired."

"That's the last thing I would ever do. If you're not going to answer my questions, I'll take the money back."

"Jew no have asked me no questions. Jew want to start?"

"I was too busy giving you promises. I'm ready if you are."

"I am ready," Carmelita said, snuffing out her butt in the Waterford crystal she would have to clean later. "Jew have another one of these for me?"

I lit another couple of cigarettes and handed her one.

"Go ahead," she said, settling against the pillows.

"First, I'd like to let you in on something that may give you some idea what this is about. I asked you before about Karel, the kid Jared brought home with him back in August? A couple of nights ago, this same Karel was murdered and his body dumped on a New York backstreet. The killer hasn't been caught."

"Did jew say murdered?"

"I did say murdered. The police are thinking Jared did it."

"Herod?" Carmelita's dark eyebrows fell in concern. "No, no, no. The police make a mistake. Herod, he no kill nobody."

"How would you know?"

"I know nothing. I feel it is no true, is a lie."

"Feelings don't count for much in court," I said. "That's where Jared will end up unless some evidence turns up that points to someone else. The prospects for that don't look good."

"I no have no evidence," Carmelita said. "I know nothing about Karel's murder. Here, take back jour money."

"No. I don't expect you to know anything about Karel. I want to know about the bloody sheets you found in the master bedroom that time Karel was staying here. You told me nobody was hurt. I find that hard to believe, unless it was chicken blood."

"It no chicken blood, señor, but nobody go to hospital."

"Now you're telling me something different."

"Jew want to hear something different, no?"

"Only if it's the truth. So somebody was hurt?"

"Jase," Carmelita said, casting her eyes down. "Only a little bit. Mrs. Foster. It was Mrs. Foster's blood."

"Do you know what happened?"

"I no see nothing happen, Señor Quaintance, but I have an idea. I no as stupid as Mrs. Foster think, eh?"

"Was Dr. Foster around when it happened?"

"No, señor," she said with a sly grin. "Mrs. Foster never would have done it with her husband home. She never do."

"Are you saying she sleeps with men behind Foster's back?"

"I might be saying that, maybe."

"For five hundred, I want more than mights and maybes."

"Jase," Carmelita said with a note of impatience. "Mrs. Foster, she is one of these lonely wives, living in a lonely house. Her husband, he no spend so much time at home. Dr. Foster, he keep busy at hospital, he travel all the time, he often go away. Me, I am always around, but Mrs. Foster no treat me like a human being, no? She treat me more like a vacuum cleaner. She no even notice me in the same room with her."

"You haven't been in the same room when she was sleeping with other men, have you?"

"No, señor!" Color brightened Carmelita's face again.

"Then how do you know what she does with them?"

"I am no stupid! What jew think she do with them! She pick them up from the country club or the food market. She bring them back home. They go up to her room. They shut the door. Some are good-looking, like jew. Some are fat, old, ugly men."

"I'm glad you didn't place me in the second category," I said. "And she brought this Karel with her up to her room?"

"Jew must be thinking I am stealing jour money, señor. I no am giving jew five hundred dollars of information. I no am only one in Hartford who know about Mrs. Foster and her men."

"Does Dr. Foster know?"

"No, señor!" Carmelita laughed and shook her head. "He is—what you say in English?"

"A cuckold?"

"How you say again?"

"Cuckold," I said.

"Cuckold," she repeated. "Funny word. Sounds like a bird. It mean husband being fooled by his wife?"

"Yes, it does. It's a good word to know."

"I remember it if I ever meet a husband."

"You will, if a husband's what you want."

"I have wanted many things I never got."

"Keep going," I said, leaning forward to look more closely at her. "You were going to tell me what you know about Karel."

"I tell jew what I know about all of them." She raised her eyebrows as if to impress me, then lowered them again and frowned at the burned-down butt in her fingers. "But my Lucky Strike is done. Light me another, señor. I tell jew everything."

I tapped another Lucky out quick. I lit it and let Carmelita get comfortable with it before asking: "Do you remember what day it was that you saw the bloody sheets?"

"No, I no remember. Each day like the other in this house."

"You called Dial-a-Mattress that same day?"

"Jase. Mrs. Foster want it done pronto."

"Do you still have the invoice?"

"I do." Carmelita set her cigarette in the candle base and stood up. "I go get it for jew."

"Mind if I come with you?"

"If jew insist."

I laid my cigarette next to hers and followed her out of the living room and down a long hall, past closed doors. We went down the carpeted stairs, into the basement, and down another long hall, past the laundry room where the washer was churning through the spin cycle. Beyond the laundry room was Carmelita's room. She opened it with a key from a chain on her waist. It was a small room, barely big enough for the two of us. It had a statuette of the Virgin on the dresser and a portrait of Jesus on the wall and a tightly made single bed covered by a brightly colored blanket. Carmelita had a writing desk in the corner with two drawers, one of filing-cabinet depth with a lock on it. She unlocked it, paged through some file folders, and came up with a sheet of pink carbonless paper with the Dial-a-Mattress logo printed on top. She handed it to me.

"Here it is," Carmelita said. "August twenty."

I looked it over. Delivered was one queen-size Sealy

Posturepedic mattress, paid for in cash and signed for by Carmelita Solano. I gave it back to her.

"These are your housekeeping files?" I asked, and she nodded. "Does anyone else have access to them?"

"No," she said. "It is my desk. I have the only key."

"Are you sure Dr. Foster never knew anything about Karel?"

"That depends on what jew mean, Señor Quaintance." She looked at me hot and smolderingly in a way that had nothing to do with the words she was speaking. There was something in it that almost made me want to change my sexual preference.

"I'm not sure what I mean," I said, unnerved by the sexual tension and the incongruity of our conversation. I wondered when the last time was Carmelita had had a man in her bedroom.

I opted for an out:

"Why don't you show me the master bedroom?"

Carmelita took her eyes off me and turned around to replace the slip of paper and lock up her drawer.

"Come," she said. "I show jew where it all happen."

She took me back up the stairs to a large bedroom at the back of the house with floor-to-ceiling drapes on the back wall. The queen-size bed stood in the middle—a four-poster with mirrored canopy. Recent bestsellers lay in two stacks on either night table. On one side we had Tom Clancy and John le Carré. On the other, Patricia Cornwell and Anne Rice. Opposite the bed was an entertainment center with a thirty-inch TV and a VCR and shelves of hardcover books, prerecorded videotapes, and assorted knickknacks. In the corner by the drapes stood a tripod with a VHS video camera on top, aimed at the bed, with the lens cap on.

Carmelita watched as I went over to the drapes and peeked out. More glass here, with a section of the redwood deck jutting out and stepping down to the backyard woods. I let the drapes fall back and went over to the video camera. I stood behind it and removed the lens cap and got a good look at the bed. I pressed the eject button, but there was no tape inside.

"The Fosters like to make movies?"

"Would jew like to see one?" Carmelita folded her arms under her breasts and gave me a smirk.

"I don't have the time, and it wouldn't be germane."

Carmelita asked what I meant by germane.

"Nothing to do with my case," I said. "Not if they're movies of Dr. Foster and his wife in bed. I have a good-enough imagination to know what they'd be like. Not to my taste."

"I know what jew mean. They movies are pretty boring."

"You've seen them?"

"They keep them here," Carmelita said, leading me into a walk-in closet on the other side of the room lighted by fluorescent tubing. She pointed to a locked drawer. "I no have the key, but still I can open it for jew. I have before."

"If they're so boring, why do you watch?"

"It amuses me, señor. They fuck like two old dogs. Jew want I can show jew."

"Open it up," I said. "I only want to see the tapes."

Carmelita took out a small pocketknife and jimmied the lock in two seconds flat. She slid the drawer open. Inside were three rows of VHS videotapes labeled with dates and filed chronologically. The Fosters appeared to have made a movie about once every three months, going back eight years. I wondered if that was how often they had sex.

"These are just the doctor and his wife, right?"

"Jase," Carmelita said. "Nobody else. Some toys, maybe." She held up a tape marked 2-14-95. "*This* one is *very* amusing."

"Close it up," I said.

"Jew the boss," she said, jimmying the lock shut again.

Perhaps Carmelita got some vengeful satisfaction out of

watching her employers going at it, but I didn't give a damn what
the Fosters did in the privacy of their bedroom. All I was hoping
was that it would lead me to something else.

"Has Mrs. Foster ever made tapes of herself with other men?"

"Jase, a few times. But she no stupid enough to keep them."

"What did she do with them?"

"She give them to her lovers."

"That's even more foolish."

"Sometimes she no think straight." Carmelita tapped her
forefinger three times against her temple. "She no can help it."

"Why's that?"

"Mrs. Foster, she have problems."

"What kind of problems?"

"Like I tell jew before, she very lonely woman living in this
lonely house with nothing to do. She have some bad habits."

"Stop drawing it out," I said. "What sort of habits?"

"She take many pills."

"And?"

Carmelita illustrated Gloria Glendenning-Foster's next habit
by rolling up her sleeve and giving herself a mock injection with
an invisible syringe. "Jew know what I talking about, señor."

"Heroin?" I said with a certain surprise. "How do you know
about it? Do you spend all your time spying on her?"

Carmelita raised her chin sharply in offense. "I no spy on
nobody, Señor Quaintance. I no want to get fired."

"How long have you known about the heroin?"

"Only since September. She come to me one day in the laundry room and ask me if I know how to get some for her. I no
know nothing about getting drugs, señor. I no want get mixed up
in that. Mrs. Foster, she desperate, she pleading with me to 'ask
around.' Like she think Carmelita such great friends with the drug
dealers. She tell me she know *Mexicanos* all involved in heroin

trade across the Texas border. I tell her go get help. She think I
mean drug dealers, but I tell her I mean hospital. Mrs. Foster not
in good health that day, very tired, act all crazy in the head. She
accuse me of lying. I no can do nothing. I want to tell Dr. Foster,
but I so afraid of being fired, I do nothing. After that, Mrs. Foster,
she take her pills and she drink her liquor to cover up. Dr. Foster,
he think she becoming alcoholic. They have a big argument one
night, two, maybe three weeks ago. Things settle down some after
that."

"Dr. Foster has no idea about her heroin addiction?"

"No, señor." Carmelita's lip was trembling. Recounting the
story had given her another taste of the fear she must have felt.

"Why not? He's a doctor. He ought to see the injections
marks, the tracks on her arms. He can't be blind to it."

"Jase he can. Mrs. Foster always have those things, from the
beginning. She is diabetic. She inject insulin. She even train me to
do it for her."

"Did she ever ask you to inject her with heroin?"

"No, señor." Carmelita acted suitably horrified.

"You might not know the difference if she'd already prepared
the syringe. How long do you think Gloria's been an addict?"

"I no can say. Is no something jew can see on the face. I knew
some addicts in Mexico—friends of my brothers—and jew no can
always tell, no?"

Carmelita was absolutely right. Plenty of young New York
professionals had gotten themselves hooked on heroin because it
was trendy. They'd been written up in the papers and shown in
silhouette in investigative news reports. You didn't get a lot of
stories in the press about the indigent addicts. Give them a stock-
broker or a lawyer or a book editor, though, and they'd give you a
heartbreaking tale about all the lies and deceit and financial problems these unfortunate yuppies succumbed to.

"So Henry Foster is twice a cuckold," I said. "You think he doesn't even suspect?"

"I no have seen no sign that he knows. Dr. Foster only think his wife take too many pills and drink too much."

"How sure are you of that?"

"I no can be sure, señor." Carmelita shrugged.

I took her with me out of the closet to stand by the bed.

"What happened here on August the twentieth?" I asked.

"It start the night before and go into the next morning."

"Dr. Foster was away?"

"Jase," she said. "He down in Key West for some meeting."

"I see. And Jared and Karel had been here how long?"

"Three days. Dr. Foster was here for two before he fly down to Florida. Herod and Karel, they stay in Herod's old room. I no like that Karel from when I see his face. Karel, he look cute like other teenage boys, but when he smile, he have these fangs like a vampire bat. I cross myself and pray he no come near me."

"What about Jared? Did he frighten you, too?"

"Maybe he would have, but I know him too well, I know Herod is hokay boy. His father treat him badly, and I always feel a little something for him. Herod, I no like his clothes or his tattoos, but I no afraid of him."

"What happened the night Dr. Foster left for Florida?"

"Karel sneak in here."

"Uninvited?"

"I no standing around spying, señor. I no can say if Mrs. Foster invite him. I did come by late that night, maybe midnight, on my rounds. I do this every night, check every corner of the house so I can lock the doors before bed. I walk by the door of the master bedroom, and I hear them inside."

"Do you know what they were doing?"

"What jew think they were doing?"

"A lot of things," I said. "Having sex, shooting up heroin, making movies. Maybe drinking blood."

Carmelita snapped her eyes up to mine, and the color drained out of her face.

"Why jew say drinking blood? How jew know about *that?*"

"How do *you* know?" I said. "Did they make a movie of it?"

"Jase," she said and shivered. She clutched her hands to her elbows as she'd done on the couch when she felt the draft. "I no can tell jew how *horrible*— "

"You only passed by the door once that night, correct?"

"Correct."

"And the next day, Mrs. Foster asked you to destroy the bedding and replace the mattress."

"Correct, señor. I do all these things. I no like it, but I do it. She my boss, and I do what she say. Everything look hokay when the mattress come and I put on fresh bedding."

"Where was Mrs. Foster while you were doing this?"

"She go out with Herod and Karel."

"Do you know where they went?"

Carmelita shook her head. "No, señor."

"Is that when you looked at the tape?"

"The way you say that, it sound so bad, like I get some pleasure out of it." She acted horribly insulted. "The truth is, I go all over the master bedroom, setting everything back the way it supposed to be, so Dr. Foster know nothing when he come home, hokay? I get down on my hands and knees and scrub out some tiny drops of blood on the carpet. I polish the bedposts. I check everything four, five times, afraid of missing something. I go over and check that camera. I am dusting it off, and I hit that button, and the tape comes out."

"Uh-huh," I said dubiously.

"Of course I was curious, señor. I no deny that. But maybe I am expecting the funny kind of movie Dr. and Mrs. Foster make together." She shook her head slowly from side to side. "No. This movie no funny. This more like a horror movie. Very bad."

"Horror movies can be like that, only they're not real."

"This is real, señor. I see it myself, with my two eyes."

"What did you see, Carmelita?"

"Is too horrible, Señor Quaintance."

Carmelita looked all around her, at the bed, at the drapes, at the video camera, at the TV set altar. She shivered and clutched herself again. The master bedroom was smothering her.

"Maybe you'd like to go back out to the living room and tell me about it over a cigarette."

I put my arm around Carmelita's shoulders. She put one around my waist. We went back to the couch and sat, where our burned-down cigarette butts lay side by side in the crystal dish.

Carmelita smoked one cigarette in silence and started a second before she felt bolstered enough to speak. The sun cast skeletal shadows in the woods beyond the glass. I looked nervously at my watch. It was getting late. I had to get back to New York.

"I fast-forward through most of it," she said. "Stopping when I wonder what they are doing. It no make no sense to me."

"Did you see them do any drugs?"

"No, señor. I never see no drugs in the tape. I no looking for drugs when I watch it. I no know Mrs. Foster doing drugs at that time. Maybe they do it before they start to make the movie. I no can say. They must be doing *something* before the tape start, because they both naked already. First thing I see is Karel walking back from the camera to the bed."

"What did he look like to you?"

"Oh, he have his long hair tied back in a ponytail, and I see these big bat wings tattooed on his back and what look like a spider crawling up his rear."

"That's Karel," I said. "I've seen photos of his tattoos."

"He get onto the bed, and she take him in her arms. They fuck for a long time. This part of the tape is hokay. They kind of romantic and passionate, like on a soap opera. No like with her husband. No like two dogs. More like two lovers."

"Mrs. Foster was enjoying herself? Karel wasn't forcing anything on her?"

"No, señor. But I only watch because I am curious, so I fast-forward for a while. Then Karel brings out some rope. He tie Mrs. Foster to the bed."

"Did she fight him?"

"No, she seem to want to be tied down. After she tied down, I no can say if she want it no more. They fuck again. I fast-forward some more. Karel start hurting Mrs. Foster, using things on her, getting rough. I no like what I see. She look like she no like it. After a while, he stop doing that. I no want to watch no more, and I am about to take the tape out and put it back in the camera. Then I see Karel lean over, and I think he going to bite her on the neck, but he no do that. He take out a knife, and he make a cut on Mrs. Foster's arm. I see the blood. He put his mouth on it, and I see him sucking and the blood on his lips, and his chest heaving on top of Mrs. Foster. When he finish, she is passed out. He swab her arm with alcohol, and he fix up a bandage. Then he start touching her again, only she no wake up. He fuck her again while she lie there asleep."

"How did the blood get all over the sheets?"

"That was the last thing I see." Carmelita took a long drag on her cigarette before she would tell me.

"Did her wound open up?"

"No, señor," she said. "Karel, he no can hold it in."

"What do you mean? He vomited it up?"

"Jase."

I didn't want to ask Carmelita any more questions, but I had to know one thing:

"What happened to the tape?"

"I no can say," she said coolly. "I rewind it and put it back in the camera. I no thinking about what going to happen to it. I only glad nobody see me watching it. I no more want to touch it. I put it back in, and I check the room one more time. Everything look hokay for Dr. Foster, and then I leave. I no know what happen to the tape, and I no want to know. That tape no belong in this house, señor. It belong with the devil."

I stood up to go. "I don't know how to thank you."

Carmelita stood along with me, came a little closer, and touched my cheek with her hand. "Jew have to go? So soon?"

"I'm afraid I do." I brought her hand back down, gently.

"Jew no have to be afraid." She saw something in my face that made her flinch. "What is wrong? Jew no like Latinas?"

"I like Latinos. The last guy I dated was named Juan."

"Oh," Carmelita said sadly. "No wonder I like jew so much."

"I'm sorry I had to put you through all this, Carmelita."

"I no am sorry," she said, patting her apron pocket.

Guilt struck me: "Is there anything else I can do for you?"

"Maybe jew can find me a new position, eh? Maybe in New Jork? Jew have any rich friends who need a housekeeper?"

"I'll ask around, Carmelita."

"Jew mean that, Señor Quaintance?" She didn't believe me.

"I mean it," I said, and I did, and I would. "Nobody deserves to have to work for the Fosters. That includes me."

Carmelita smiled at that. She escorted me to the door.

I gave her a kiss on the cheek and went out to the 'Cuda.

Cumulus clouds were taking on color as the sun made its last ditch for the horizon. New York suddenly felt very far away.

EIGHTEEN

MY BEEPER WENT OFF three times as I was driving into the city. I didn't look at it. I kept my eyes on the road, trying to avoid trailer trucks and trying hard not to think about blood.

When I reached Manhattan, it was going on nine. The sky was dark, the stars blocked out by a blanket of luminescent clouds hovering over the skyscrapers. I stopped off at a Mobil station and treated the 'Cuda to a tank of high-octane superpremium. I thought about turning it in to Kotby's Garage but cancelled that. I was going to have more running around to do and didn't want to have to rely on taxis. I found a spot for the 'Cuda on West Sixteenth Street off Eighth Avenue and walked around the corner and up the flight of stairs to my darkened office.

The air in my office was warm and stale. I bolted the door behind me, turned on my desk lamp, and opened a stubborn window.

I checked the numbers on my beeper's display. I wasn't sure who any of them were. I wrote them down and cleared my beeper.

My answering machine had some messages for me as well:

Beep. "Yes, hello? Mr. Quaintance? This is Evelyn Grosse returning your call from California. Is Jared in some kind of trouble? You've got me all worried. We should be home the rest of the day. I'll be here waiting for your call. Bye."

Beep. "Greg, this is Lucrezia. It was rude of me to run off like that last night, and I apologize. I let you down. I panicked. There were black emanations coming at me from that building. Now I know why. The news said three people were killed there. I knew one of them. I'll try to explain—that is, if you still want to talk with me about Jared. Feel free to call me back at my home number. I think I gave it to you."

Beep. "Yeah, Greg, Tavo Orjuedos. We need to talk."

Beep. "This is Gloria Glendenning-Foster, Mr. Quaintance. I just tried your pager, but you failed to return my call, so I'm calling you here. You've got a lot of nerve telling the police where to find me. They're looking for Hank now themselves, in case you didn't know. They're trying to pin some murders on him. It's urgent that you find him before they do. I *have* to talk to Hank. I know you didn't promise me much, but I'd like to know what sort of progress you're making. Please call me here at the Plaza or come up to my room if you have time. It's room 913."

I wasn't ready for another round with Gloria Glendenning-Foster, so I found the number of the Plaza Hotel in the Manhattan telephone directory and matched it up with one of the ones from my beeper. I would save it for last or maybe go up and see her. I certainly couldn't give her much of a progress report. Willem Kirst hadn't helped me find her husband, and I couldn't tell her what I'd learned from Carmelita or even that I'd spoken to her. She was going to have to sit in her room and stew for a while.

*   *   *

I placed a call to one of the other numbers from my beeper.

"Hello?" a man said.

"Greg Quaintance. You paged me?"

"Oh, Greg, yes. This is Sebastian, Anastasia's friend? She and I talked most of the night last night, and together we came up with some information you might be interested in. I knew Karel better than she did, and—"

"Have you taken any of this to the police?"

"Not yet," Sebastian said. "Anastasia thought I ought to talk to you about it first. Did I do the right thing?"

"As far as I'm concerned, yeah. The police are liable to disagree with me. Can I come over to your apartment? I'd rather get this face-to-face. If you don't mind."

"No, not at all. When can you make it over?"

I checked my watch. "Ten o'clock? I have a few more phone calls to make. One of them might take a while."

"Ten's fine," Sebastian said.

"How's Anastasia doing?"

"She's okay. A little depressed. I think it didn't sink in until she woke up. Her whole life was in that apartment, and it was pretty trashed."

"Do you have to work tonight?"

"No. Sunday's my night off. I'll have time to talk."

"Good," I said. "I'd like to talk to Anastasia, too."

"She's not planning on going anywhere," Sebastian said.

I thanked him, said I'd be there at ten, and hung up.

I called back the last number that had tried to reach my beeper. The other end of the line picked up, but no one said anything.

"Hello? This is Greg Quaintance. Did you page me?"

The line sounded live, but barely.

"Hello?" I tried again. "Is there anyone there?"

I thought I heard breathing. Maybe it was me.

"Dr. Foster?"

A moment later, I damned myself for saying anything at all.

The phone on the other end fumbled around noisily in somebody's hand. There were clicks and a sudden disconnect.

I was left listening to the dial tone.

I hung up the receiver like it was a hot rock.

NINETEEN

IT TOOK A FEW CIGARETTES to calm me down. I shut the window and locked it and felt a little safer. It was getting cold, anyway.

The most pressing thing I had to do was call Evelyn Grosse. I hadn't intended to get her upset. She had a mother's instinct for bad news, and she was waiting for me to give confirmation or reassurance. I couldn't give her either, but I had to call.

I went to my mini-fridge and opened up a Rolling Rock and brought it back to my desk. I picked up the phone and called.

"Grosse residence." It was the voice of an older man with some kind of European accent that zeroed in on the consonants.

"I'd like to speak with Evelyn Grosse," I said.

"I am her husband," he said irrelevantly. "Who is this?"

"My name is Greg Quaintance, Mr. Grosse. I'm calling from New York. I left a couple of messages earlier, and your wife was good enough to return my call. Unfortunately, I wasn't here, but she left a message and wanted me to call back. Is she around?"

"Yes," he said with an ess that hissed. "I will put her on." He called to her like a Prussian general: "Evelyn! Evelyn! You are wanted on the telephone!" Then he came back to me: "Wait one minute. She is coming. This is about Jared, yes?"

"That's between me and your wife," I said.

Grosse said nothing to that.

"Yes? Hello?" Evelyn Grosse said. Before I could respond, she went on to her husband: "You can hang up, Gustav. I'm on the phone in the bedroom."

I heard the noise of Gustav Grosse hanging up, and the line became clearer.

"I'm sorry," Evelyn said. "Is this Mr. Quaintance?"

"It is," I said. "Thank you for calling me back."

"How could I not? You got me so worried! Is Jared all right?"

"That's what I'm trying to find out, ma'am."

"Are you asking me?"

"Not necessarily. As I think I told you in my message, I'm a private investigator here in New York. Your ex-husband, Henry Foster, determined that Jared was missing and retained me to find him. It might help if I could ask you a few questions."

"What do you mean, missing?"

"The last Henry Foster spoke with him was August, when Jared was at the house in Connecticut. Gloria Glendenning-Foster spoke with him on the phone around Labor Day. He hasn't stayed at his apartment since mid-September, though I did speak with someone who apparently saw him the night of October fifth, a Friday. I haven't found anyone who's seen him since then."

"Hank didn't say anything to me about it."

"When was the last time you spoke with your ex-husband?"

"I called him in August. We didn't talk for long."

"So after he decided Jared was missing, he never even called you to find out whether Jared might out there in Turlock?"

"No, he didn't," Evelyn said. "I wish he had. Why do you

keep saying Hank 'decided' or 'determined' Jared was missing?"

"It seems to have been a sudden decision on his part," I said. "Or on Gloria's. There are some other circumstances I'll get into in a moment. First, you can tell me whether Jared is out there now."

"Out here? With me? No, Mr. Quaintance. No, he's not."

"He did visit you sometime in July, correct?"

"Yes, that's right. I flew him in for his birthday."

"Have you spoken with him at all since then?"

"Yes, I have, in August, when he was at the old house."

"Henry Foster didn't think you had," I said. "He said you hadn't spoken with Jared since July."

"Hank knows I talked to him. He handed off the phone."

"Why would he want to say that you hadn't?"

"I don't know. Is Hank there? Can I talk to him?"

"No, he's not here. In fact, I don't know where he is."

"What do you mean?"

"I mean I don't know where he is," I repeated. "I'm looking for both of them now. Gloria has hired me to do that."

"Gloria," Evelyn said like a curse.

"Gloria thought you might have given Jared some money when he was out there," I said.

"Is that an accusation? I gave him some birthday money."

"How much?"

"I don't think that's any of your business."

I took a sip of my Rolling Rock and tried to figure out how to proceed. I was getting off on the wrong foot with Evelyn Grosse, and I didn't want that. It was too easy to lose people or make them so mad they hung up. I had no time to fly out to Turlock. I'd have to stay nonconfrontational.

"You misunderstand me," I said. "I'm not trying to blame anything on you. The way it's been laid out for me, Henry Foster pretty much cut Jared off after he dropped out of school. Jared hasn't been working, as near as I can tell. Gloria admitted to giving him some money to help him out, and she thought you might have, too. It may seem like personal business, but you can trust me, Mrs. Grosse. I have your best interests at heart. All I'm trying to do is find your son—and your ex."

"Well," Evelyn said grudgingly. "I did give Jared about two thousand dollars. He said he needed it for rent."

"What was he like when he was out there? Did he seem like the same old Jared to you?"

"No, Mr. Quaintance. If you know anything about Jared, you must know that he's changed. I didn't think it was the best visit we've ever had. We didn't really get a lot of visiting in, to tell you the truth. He spent most of his time out of the house. He stayed out late and sometimes came home drunk. He's not even of legal drinking age!"

"What was Jared like growing up? Was he a good boy?"

"Yes, he was good, always very bright. I certainly did what I could with him. I was a stay-at-home mom, which was good for him, since he was sort of a lonely boy. I was always there for him, at least. Until Gloria Glendenning came into our lives."

"Did Gloria really meet your husband after she ran over Jared's dog?"

"Yes, it's true. She killed Pardner, Jared's black lab."

"Pardner? That's a good dog's name."

"He was a good dog. But how in the world did you ever hear about how he died?"

"Gloria told me so herself," I said.

"That was the beginning of the end."

"The end of what? Your marriage?"

"The end of everything," she said. "Not just me and Henry. Jared, too. He was never quite the same after Gloria did that."

"How did Jared change?"

"He became highly antisocial. He was distant. He didn't like to be touched. Even by me. He'd shrink away."

"Isn't it common enough for twelve-year-olds to go through changes like that? Aren't those normal adolescent problems?"

"No, Mr. Quaintance. Jared's problems were not normal. I think the combination of Gloria killing his dog, his father and I getting divorced, and Gloria marrying Hank caused some kind of deep psychological trauma. And Hank did nothing to help him."

"Why didn't you?"

"I didn't have custody."

"Why not?"

"I didn't seek it. It's not that I didn't love Jared. It wouldn't have been fair to him, that's all. I had work lined up that was going to take me abroad. I didn't know for how long. Jared wanted to be with his father, and I didn't want to hurt him even more by fighting over it. So I let him stay with Hank."

"And with Gloria."

"And with Gloria," Evelyn said.

She left it at that, and I didn't want to push her on it.

"When Jared was out there visiting you, did you ever notice any evidence that he might be doing drugs?"

"You mean like marijuana?"

"Well, that and—"

"I smelled his breath a few times, but all I could ever smell was alcohol. And cigarettes. I don't like him doing those things. I worry about his health. But I try to understand. I mean, he's not a boy anymore, and a lot of people do still drink and smoke."

"You don't drink or smoke, Mrs. Grosse?" I asked, putting down my beer and lighting myself a cigarette.

"No, I don't, and I won't allow them in this house. The body is a temple, Mr. Quaintance, and—"

"Okay, okay," I said. "I get the picture. You never saw any evidence that he was doing drugs, then? I don't mean just marijuana. I mean ecstasy, LSD, cocaine, heroin?"

"Good Lord!" Evelyn said. "I certainly did not! One night I did catch him smoking in the guest bedroom with our foreign exchange student. I made them take it outside."

"You had a foreign exchange student staying with you?"

"Yes," she said cheerfully. "Gustav and I don't have any children of our own. We like to play host family every year to a different student. We set up the program, actually, through our church and the local high school. Last year, we had an opportunity to host a boy from Prague, which we thought would be nice, since that's where Gustav is from. You see, after the divorce from Hank, I got more involved with my church and poured myself into missionary work. That was about the time Eastern Europe was opening up, and they had a real thirst for Christ's teachings after all those years of communism. I ended up in the Czech Republic—somewhere I never thought I'd be in a million years! That's where I met Gustav. I brought him back with me, and we Americanized his last name and got married. This boy we hosted was the son of a friend of his, actually."

"What was the boy's name?" I asked, feeling my heart drop down into my stomach. I didn't want to be the one to tell her.

"Karel Janáček," Evelyn said. "But it didn't work out so well. Karel was the most difficult young person we've ever housed, even though there was even less of a language problem than usual. There was quite a large gap between us."

"What happened to Karel?" I asked. I felt guilty for going on like this without telling her, but I had to get whatever information I could before I gave her the news. It was possible she would be incapable of answering my questions after that.

"What happened to him?" Evelyn said. "Why do you ask?"

"He's no longer with you, is he? He's returned to his home country by now?"

"Yes and no. I mean, he's no longer with us, sure. But he didn't return to Prague. He was supposed to, but he didn't. Gustav and I saw him off at the San Francisco airport, which is where our responsibility for him ended. Karel was supposed to switch planes in New York, at J.F.K. Airport, so he could catch his flight to Frankfurt and Prague. He never got on the plane."

"He stayed in New York? Have you heard from him?"

"Well." Evelyn sighed discomfitingly. "We heard first from his father, Gustav's friend. He was quite upset that Karel hadn't been on the plane. We had no idea what to tell him. The next day, he got a call from Karel telling him that he was okay, that he was in New York, and that he wasn't going to come home."

"And Karel was how old?"

"He turned eighteen in April," Evelyn said. "April fifth."

"So there was nothing you could do about it."

"That's right. It wasn't up to us. Karel's father considered flying to New York to bring his son back, but he had a good idea Karel would refuse to go with him. He was probably right. Karel's father is poor by our standards, and he could have wasted a great deal of money, so he decided against it."

"Have any of you heard from Karel since then?"

"Yes," Evelyn said. "I did get to speak with him, that time I called the old house, Hank's house, in Connecticut."

"Jared and Karel became friends when Jared visited you?"

"Friends? Well, yes, they did. They had a lot in common."

"You mean they both liked gothic music and tattoos and making themselves up as vampires and going out to clubs?"

"You seem to know a lot, Mr. Quaintance." Evelyn sounded suspicious. She had a right to be. "Karel really didn't fit in here in Turlock. Not that there aren't plenty of kids like that at our high school—but I don't want them in my house! Jared tried to reassure me that it doesn't amount to Satan worship, but isn't that just the way the devil works? He tricks people into doing what he wants, and they don't even know they're doing it!"

I looked around my darkened office, with only the desk lamp on and the wind whistling outside my windows. I wished I could be out there in Turlock, where the sun was still shining, so I could look Evelyn Grosse in the eyes and say what I had to say.

"Mrs. Grosse?" I said. "I have some bad news for you. Are you sitting down?"

"Yes," Evelyn said. "I'm sitting on the bed. What do you mean, bad news? I thought you didn't know anything about Jared."

"It's not about Jared," I said. "Not directly, anyway."

"Well, what is it!" she demanded.

I swallowed a gulp of beer to brace myself.

"The police found the body of a young man a few days ago, and they've been unsure of his identity. No one's come forward to claim him, even though it's been all over the news. He has a number of tattoos. The one on the right biceps is a black rose with the name *Karel* underneath it in red, spelled K-A-R-E-L."

"Oh, God! Gustav! Gustav! Get on the other line, hurry!"

Gustav Grosse on the other line was the last thing I needed.

"Yes? Evelyn, I am on. What is this about, sir?" he said.

"I, I—" I said.

"It's about Karel," Evelyn said. "He's dead."

"What?" Gustav Grosse said. "Who are you? What is this?"

"I'm a private investigator working with the police on this investigation," I said, feeling he would respond to the voice of authority.

"I thought you were working for Hank!" Evelyn cried.

"I am, I am," I said. "Henry Foster and his wife are my

clients, and I'm looking for Jared, who's missing. The police think Jared may be involved somehow in Karel's murder, and I'm assisting them in the investigation to that extent."

"Murder?" Gustav said. "Karel Janáček has been murdered?"

"He didn't tell me he was murdered," Evelyn said, sniffling.

"I was getting to it," I said, trying to make a recovery.

"Jared murdered Karel?" Gustav said angrily.

"I didn't say that."

"You said the police think so."

"Yes," I said. "That doesn't mean Jared is guilty."

"Jared would never murder anyone!" Evelyn said.

"I am not so sure about that!" Gustav said.

Evelyn started sobbing noisily into the phone.

"Now, honey," Gustav said. "I did not mean to say that."

"Oh, yes, you did!" she said.

"Please calm down, Evelyn. Maybe Jared did not kill Karel."

"That's the point I've been trying to make," I said. "I've been looking into it, and there may be other possibilities."

"Evelyn, you and I are going to New York," Gustav said.

"That would be a big help," I said. "The police need someone to make a positive identification of the body."

"You said it's been all over the news," Evelyn said, trying to talk through tears and congestion. "Why didn't Hank or Gloria go to the police and tell them who it was? He was a guest in their house! They knew who he was! How could they not do that?"

"That's a very good question, Mrs. Grosse, and one I've been trying to answer for myself for a little while now. It was after the news reports of Karel's murder that Henry Foster came to me and hired me to find Jared. Now we can't locate Henry."

"We are taking the next flight to New York, Evelyn!"

"Yes, Gustav, I think we'd better," she said. "Thank you."

I calmed them down long enough to give them Detective

Orjuedos's name and phone numbers off his business card and
instructions on how to get to his precinct house. I also gave them
my name, phone numbers, and street address and asked them to
get in touch with me as soon as they got to New York.

"Please find Jared for us, Mr. Quaintance," Evelyn said.

"Yes," Gustav concurred. "I want you to find that boy!"

I told them I was working on it.

"Come, Evelyn, we go!" Gustav said, and they both hung up.

TWENTY

I CALLED ORJUEDOS's pager. A beat later, Orjuedos called back.

"Greg?" he said. "Where have you been?"

"Nowhere," I said. "I've got a present for you, though."

"A present? How nice. I've got something for you, too."

"What is it, Tavo?"

"You first."

"Karel Janáček."

"Karel what?"

I spelled it out and told him where he could put the accents.

"Where'd you learn this?" Orjuedos asked.

"From Jared Foster's mother, Evelyn Grosse. Karel was a Czech foreign exchange student living with the Grosses out in California. I just got off the phone with them. I told them to call you. They may be trying to reach you now. They say they're coming in to New York on the next flight to make the I.D."

"That's a break. Jared met Karel out there?"

"Yeah."

"No luck finding Jared, I guess?"

"Nope."

"What about Henry Foster?"

"Nope. You said you had something for me, Tavo."

"It's about Foster."

"Let's have it."

"I'd like you to come over and see for yourself."

"I don't have much time," I said, checking my watch. "I'm meeting someone at ten. If it takes long, I guess I can call them back and reschedule."

"It won't take long. We're in the Village, on MacDougal Street—hold on a sec, I'll tell you the address."

I got to it in my notebook before he got to it in his. I read it off to him and said, "Juliet Logan's apartment?"

"You got it, Greg." Over his line came a beeping. "Oh!"

"What's that?"

"I just got paged from the two-oh-nine area code."

"They're a little shook up. Go easy on them."

"Greg, you're a pussycat. See you in a few."

"That you will," I said.

I tried Lucrezia's number. It rang three times before it was finally picked up with a sleepy hello that sounded like her.

"Greg Quaintance," I said.

"I knew it was you," Lucrezia said.

"Sure you did," I said. "Thanks for calling me. I was worried about you after you ran off. Where did you go?"

"Back to my apartment. I had to escape all that darkness."

"Isn't the whole goth world steeped in darkness?"

"Yes and no," Lucrezia said. "It depends."

"You remind me of a magic eight-ball," I said. "'Should I play the lottery today?' 'That might be a good idea.'"

"Ha, ha. Very funny. Do you want to talk to me or not?"

"I want to talk to you, but not on the phone, and not now. I have some other business to take care of first. Can I—"

"You can come up to my place," Lucrezia said.

"Can we make it—"

"Yes, Greg, we can make it later."

"Let's say about elev—"

"Eleven-fifteen?"

"I was going to say eleven-thirty," I said. I was lying.

"No, you weren't," she said with a laugh. "Eleven-fifteen?"

"Yes, that's fine," I said. "Where's your place again?"

She gave me the address, on the Bowery between Bleecker and Houston. It would be apartment 3-C, with no name on the buzzer. She told me to buzz three shorts, three longs, and three shorts.

I got in the 'Cuda and headed for MacDougal Street. On the way, I noticed in my rearview a pair of headlights following directly behind me. At a stoplight, I managed to get a make on the car. It was a racing green Mercedes 560SL convertible with the top up. I didn't have the time or the inclination to shake her, so I let her tag along. I was glad I could even tell I was being tailed. It wasn't so easy to notice such things when your head was filled with shiny bits of junk tumbling around like a kaleidoscope.

I lost her by accident while I was circling for a space. I ended up parking on busy Houston Street and walking the two blocks up MacDougal, all the while looking over my shoulder for a glimpse of Gloria, who might be tracking me. She wasn't there, but she was somewhere, and she was mad at me.

One marked squad and two unmarkeds were parked in front of the building. The T-shirt shop was closed for the night, but the falafel hut across the street was open, and I was hungry. I went in and bought far more than I could eat and took it out with me and across the street. The door to Juliet Logan's building was being held open by a sturdy eye hook tenants probably used when they wanted to move stuff in and out. I went up to the third floor. An older uniformed patrolman with snow-white hair and ruby-red cheeks stopped me from going into 3A.

"Whoa, buddy! Where do you think you're going, huh?"

"Falafel?" I held one out to him like a peace offering.

"Is that Quaintance?" came Orjuedos's voice from inside. He stepped into the doorway, cute but bedraggled: "It's okay, McCoy, this guy's a private dick. An honest one—at least I think so. He's sort of working with us. Come on in, Greg." He noticed my bag and said, "I hope you brought enough for everybody."

"I think I did."

"Good boy," Orjuedos said. He smiled like the case was beginning to break his way. He didn't know any better.

Officer McCoy smiled congenially at me: "May I?"

"Be my guest." I proffered some falafel to him again.

McCoy plucked it out of my hand and started chomping down.

"What's this about?" I asked, crossing the threshold.

"Like I said, it's about your client," Orjuedos said.

The two other cops in the room dropped what they were doing when they smelled the food. Orjuedos introduced us. The burly white plainclothesman was Tony Doohan, and the uniformed black female officer was Lucille LeComte, both of the Sixth Precinct.

"Take what you like," I said, grabbing some for myself and passing around the bag. "This is on my client's tab."

"I've told them who you are," Orjuedos said. "They're already learning a lot about your client."

I scanned the room while the police took their break. It was, as I suspected, short on square footage. A kitchenette intruded into the living room, which was about the size of a bedroom. There was a stack of handwritten letters on a small desk, where Detective Doohan had been standing before I came in. Officer LeComte had been rummaging through the contents of a gray plastic footlocker that stood open on a ratty old pink couch. I peeked into the footlocker and saw a collection of seven VHS videotapes with homemade labels that bore nothing but dates, in the same handwriting I'd seen in Foster's closet. The dates started in April of this year and continued through September.

The bedroom was about the size of the sagging double bed that was in it. Juliet Logan had put twenty different framed pictures of Jared Foster on her dresser, from his pre-goth days. She had covered her walls with posters from the decade she so loved: Shaun Cassidy, Kiss, Farrah Fawcett, the Bee Gees, Andy Gibb, John Travolta, the Bay City Rollers, Olivia Newton-John. She must have been alive for only a year or two of the seventies, and now she'd never get to see the millennial odometer turn over and do its thing, whatever that was going to be.

The only other thing of interest in the bedroom was a familiar-looking briefcase lying closed on top of the bed. It had the gold initials H.K.F. to one side of the handle. I tried the clasps, but they were shut and locked with a combination.

"That's Henry Foster's briefcase," I said.

"We figured as much," Orjuedos said with his mouth full.

"He had it with him in my office. He's been here, then, sometime after he came to see me."

"And he hasn't been back," Doohan piped in, smacking his lips and wiping his fingers on a paper napkin. "I came here myself and sealed the outer door, about four-thirty this morning. We didn't have time to search it right off. We were too busy looking for Jared Foster."

"Greg's way ahead of us on that, aren't you?" Orjuedos said.

"I've got a few leads," I said grudgingly.

"That's more than we've got."

"Henry Foster could have been here anytime after he left my office, about four-thirty Saturday afternoon, until you sealed up the place. Anytime in those twelve hours. But I can venture a guess when he was here—around seven o'clock last night. I came to see Juliet Logan, but I didn't know what she looked like. She refused to let me up. Henry Foster was probably up there with her. She came down instead. She'd just come out of the shower. She gave me a false name and sent me off on a wild goose chase. I wised up and came back about half an hour later, but she was gone. *They* were gone. And Foster forgot his briefcase."

"Or left it behind to come back and get it later," Orjuedos said. "But he never came back."

"Maybe he came too late, after you sealed it off."

"Don't you want to know why he was here in the first place?" Doohan asked. "All Ms. Logan was to him was his son's roommate, as far as you know, right?"

"Ex-roommate," I said. "My guess is Foster was banging her."

Officer LeComte screwed up her face like she didn't like the word *banging*. I felt slightly apologetic but kept my mouth shut.

"You often jump to such conclusions about people?" Orjuedos asked, with more than a hint in his eyes of the conclusions I'd jumped to about him last night. "What makes you think they were having any kind of liaison?"

"I see love letters on the desk," I said. "And I'd guess these are homemade porno tapes in this footlocker here."

"Greg Quaintance, psychic investigator," Orjuedos said.

"Just intuitive," I said. "Detective Doohan was poring over the love letters when I came in. Officer LeComte, have you had a look at those tapes yet?"

"Enough to know what's on them," LeComte said stiffly.

"What's on them?"

"Male white, approximately fifty years of age, having sexual intercourse with a female white, approximately twenty years of age, on the female's bed—the bed in that bedroom, in there."

"Juliet Logan and Henry Foster," I said.

"I wouldn't know, sir," LeComte said. "I've not seen either one. It would appear they match the descriptors I have of them."

"Doohan, you've read the letters," Orjuedos prompted.

"Steamy, erotic letters from Henry Foster to the decedent," Doohan said.

"She wasn't deceased at the time he wrote them," I said.

Doohan glared at me. He wasn't finished. I'd interrupted him. He went on: "Most of them conclude with mention of an enclosure of money. Amounts unspecified."

"Going back how long?"

"The earliest we have is from April the tenth."

"These letters weren't lying out when you got here," I said.

"No, we had to dig them out of Logan's desk," Doohan said.

"And you dug the trunk out from somewhere, too?"

"Yes," LeComte said. "I found it in the bedroom closet."

"Does Juliet Logan have a video camera?"

"There's one in the closet," LeComte said. "A Sanyo."

"What does all this say to you?" I addressed Orjuedos.

"It says to me your accomplice theory about Juliet Logan is correct," Orjuedos said. "Henry Foster has been keeping her as his mistress ever since Jared moved out on her. She must have needed the money. Foster knew that Karel Janáček was a friend of Jared's, and when he heard about Karel's death, he immediately suspected Jared, for the same reasons we're suspecting him. Foster hired you to find his son—probably to get him in the hands of a good defense lawyer before we could get to him. He hired you because you have a record of being honest. Because of that, though, there was something he couldn't ask you to do. Foster was afraid there might be some damning evidence in his son's apartment. At the very least, there was that photo of Jared and Karel together."

"Hardly damning," I said.

"He tried to get the stuff one way, simply by asking Ms. Cartwright. When that didn't work, he came back, at night, when she was out. With Juliet Logan's assistance, they burglarized the place and loaded Foster's truck with Jared's things."

"Did you manage to find any witnesses to that?"

"We did, as a matter of fact," Orjuedos said. "I've spoken with two different people who were at parties across the street at the Jacob Riis Houses who happened to be looking out the window. They saw what they described as a paunchy older man with short gray hair and a slim younger woman with long blond hair in bell bottoms loading items into a red Ford Expedition."

"They didn't call the police?"

"No," Orjuedos said. "They thought what anybody would think—that this girl's father had brought his truck and was helping her move out. They didn't keep watching. It wasn't of any interest to them. They didn't witness the incident in the Chinese restaurant. They didn't hear any shots, either, over the party music. They didn't see the truck leave. All they know is, after a while, the truck was gone and we were there."

"What's your take on it?"

"We think Jared killed Karel, and Dr. Foster's trying to cover it up or at least damage the case by destroying evidence. All we have to do now is find the two missing Fosters."

"Excuse me," I said, "but that doesn't make any sense."

All three cops stared at me bug-eyed.

"Okay," I admitted, "so you have witnesses who saw what appear to have been Foster and Logan removing Jared's things. They parked Foster's truck right there on the street and took everything out the front door, in full view of the housing projects and the Chinese restaurant. Foster wasn't thinking of it as a burglary. Jared was his son, and he felt he had a right to the stuff. That's how he acted with Anastasia Cartwright. In his own mind, I doubt he considered it a crime."

"He knew he was obstructing justice in a homicide case," Orjuedos said. "Isn't that serious enough?"

"You expect me to believe that Foster would take out his gun and murder his own mistress and two innocent restaurant workers? Commit a triple homicide so he wouldn't get pinned with a charge of obstruction of justice? I don't buy it. Neither should you."

"You're thinking out of the box," Officer LeComte said.

"Out of the box?" I repeated, as if there were some hidden meaning in it that was just out of my reach.

"At the academy, they trained us to think out of the box," LeComte explained sheepishly. "They tried to, anyway."

"I know you're paid to protect your client, Greg." Orjuedos was annoyed by out-of-the-box thinking. "But look at the facts."

"You don't have all the facts, Tavo."

Doohan and LeComte exchanged knowing glances at each other, as if they had just caught me and Orjuedos in a lovers' spat.

"Maybe you can fill me in on what's missing, Greg," Orjuedos went on in a raised tone of voice. He counted off points on his fingers: "We've got Foster linked up with Logan. We've got Logan shot dead with Foster's gun. We've got two witnesses also shot dead with the same gun. We've got witnesses from across the street who place Foster at the scene, with Logan. Maybe they didn't see Foster leave, but he left, didn't he? We know that."

"Foster may have his secrets," I admitted. "And he may be trying to protect his son. But I find it hard to believe that a doctor of his reputation would risk everything by shooting two innocent people in cold blood and executing his mistress. Maybe another party caught them in the act of taking Jared's things, took Foster's gun, and did the killing himself? Or herself?"

Officer LeComte smiled at that, pleased that I'd politically corrected myself.

"Another party?" Orjuedos said. "Like who, Jared Foster?"

"Maybe," I said. "Maybe not."

"Why not?"

"You need a witness who saw the truck leave, Tavo. And it wouldn't hurt to find the truck itself."

"We're working on that," he said, running fingers through his sweat-dampened hair. His Roman cut had seen better days, like yesterday. "We've got his Connecticut license plate numbers, and we know the color and the make. We'll find it."

"Are you going to try to open Foster's briefcase?"

"I think I may need a court order for that. For now, all we can do is place it into evidence. You have any idea what might be in it?"

"Besides a fountain pen and some legal pads? No, I don't."

"We have a warrant out now for Henry Foster's arrest," Orjuedos said. "If you do find him, we want him immediately. If you can't bring him in safely, call us, but watch him. If he's desperate enough to kill three people, he'll kill you, too."

"He can try," I said. "If he's still alive."

"You have reason to believe he's not?"

"Only that he's been missing since last night and won't return my pages. He did hire me to find his son, and you'd think that no matter what he's up to, he'd want a progress report. He and I are completely out of contact. If he's alive, someone may be keeping him that way—but there's been no ransom note as far as I know. Without a ransom note, I'd assume he's dead. I'm going to keep looking for him until I turn up his body, whether it's kicking and breathing or turning up daisies."

Officer McCoy popped his head in and said: "Hey! You guys got any more of that falafel?"

"All gone, McCoy," Orjuedos said. "We're almost through here, anyway. Go across the street and get yourself some."

"Hey! You got a five?"

Orjuedos dug his money clip out of his pocket and peeled off five ones for Officer McCoy. McCoy went down the stairs and out.

"You think Jared would kill his own father?" Orjuedos wanted to know. I'd become their expert on the subject of Fosters.

"I have no idea," I said. "I've never met Jared."

"But you don't think his father would kill anybody."

"Anything's possible, but Foster doesn't strike me as the type."

"We've got a lot of evidence against him," Orjuedos said.

"Not enough to convict."

"In my experience, just about anybody is capable of murder."

"Even they had to have a reason. I can't come up with a good reason why Foster would want to kill his secret nympho lover and two total strangers. We're playing with half a deck."

"You said you had some leads. Any idea where Jared is?"

"No," I said.

"Are you playing straight with me?"

"Yeah."

I had some germs of ideas that I was trying to culture in the fertile mush of my brain. Nothing substantial enough to give to the police. Among other things, I couldn't tell them anything I'd learned from Carmelita. There were too many unanswered questions. If I relayed my suspicions, the police would either dismiss them out of hand or go and harass people I still needed information from. I saw a bigger picture of what had been going on than they did, but it was still too amorphous to describe, even to myself. Let them do their job, and I mine.

"You *do* think Jared killed Karel, don't you?" Orjuedos said, narrowing his eyes and delving into mine as if I knew the answer.

"He may have," I said. "But I have my doubts."

Detective Doohan and Officer LeComte looked confused by all this. Before I came over, their package was neat and tidy.

I looked at my watch. It was seven minutes after ten.

"Excuse me," I said, heading for the door. "I'm late for an appointment."

"Stay in touch," Orjuedos said. His cel phone rang. He picked it up off his belt and said: "Yeah?"

I stayed in the doorway watching him. Officer McCoy came bounding back up the stairs with a sack of smelly food.

"I'll be there as soon as I can," Orjuedos said to his phone. "Greg? How important is that appointment of yours?"

"Fairly," I said. "Why? What's up?"

"We found Henry Foster's truck," Orjuedos said. "It was parked in a bus lane early this morning and towed to a lot in Battery Park City. I'm going there now. Want to come along?"

I debated this for a moment and said:

"Sure."

TWENTY-ONE

I CALLED SEBASTIAN from Juliet Logan's phone and rescheduled for midnight. I figured I ought to be done with Lucrezia by then. Orjuedos left Doohan in charge of Juliet's apartment and the two patrol officers. We went down to Orjuedos's unmarked Crown Vic.

Orjuedos started it up and radioed in to Dispatch to tell him where he was going. They acknowledged. He turned down the volume on the radio unit and wormed us out of the parking space.

"How long you been doing this, Greg?"

"About a year. Before that, I was a security officer at a meat warehouse in Brooklyn."

"And before that?"

We ended up going west on Houston, right past the 'Cuda. Parked directly behind it was Gloria's Mercedes, with Gloria in it. Orjuedos didn't notice her. He wouldn't know her car. I saw Gloria, but she was watching the end of MacDougal Street and didn't see me. I wondered if she'd be there when I got back.

"Before that, I was in the Army," I said with a sigh, leaving out mention of the lost years in between.

"The Army? Did you like it?"

"I liked it, Tavo. It didn't like me. I got booted out. General Sam Nunn said I was a threat to unit cohesion."

"That asshole," Orjuedos said. "You serve in the Gulf?"

"Yeah, I did."

"Military police?"

"Infantry."

"You get any of this Gulf War Syndrome?"

"No. I was one of the lucky ones."

"My pop was an infantryman in Vietnam," Orjuedos said. "Two tours. He wasn't the same when he came back."

"At least he came back." I wondered what my father would have been like if he'd come back. If he was changed, I certainly wouldn't have known the difference. I was a baby then.

"Yeah, there's that," Orjuedos said. "It made me never want to be in the Army, though. They took all the life out of him."

"The Army has a way of doing that to people," I said.

We turned onto the West Side Highway. Orjuedos gunned the Crown Vic the rest of the way down to Battery Park City. We ran out of things to say. I resisted the temptation to turn and look at him in the green glow of the dashboard lights. It was enough to know that he was there, and that he trusted me.

The wind off the Hudson when we got out of the car was strong. Orjuedos brought a long, thin steel hook with him for opening cars through the side windows. The twin towers of the World Trade Center loomed over us, lit up on those floors where the night janitors toiled. The lot was on municipal ground near the entrance to the Brooklyn-Battery Tunnel, surrounded by chain-link fencing. A length of chain was draped around the gate like a pendant, with a heavy-duty padlock as the ornament. A gray-bearded, blue-capped watchman emerged from the dark, looked at Orjuedos's badge, and unlocked the gate for us.

"You fellows lookin' for the Expedition?" he asked with one eye cocked, like a crusty old sea salt trying to sign us up for a whaling voyage. "I got her at the back."

"What time was it towed in?" Orjuedos asked.

"The citation was written at five-twenty-one this morning. She was parked right in a bus lane on Madison Avenue, between Twenty-Seventh and Twenty-Eighth. She was towed into my lot at six-oh-seven. Been here all day. No one's come to claim her."

"No inquiries about it, either?"

"Just yours, detective."

The watchman turned on his flashlight and led us down the narrow path between the rows of towed vehicles. They were an odd assortment, new and old, expensive and worthless, compacts and sedans and sport utilities, staring out at us like unwanted pets at the pound. The long-termers had owners who had to pay unpaid accumulated traffic citations before they could be released.

"There she is!" the watchman said, like *Thar she blows!*

Foster's truck was a whale all right, a big red one on high-testosterone tires. Midlife crises gave rise to such things, not to mention young kept mistresses and homegrown sex videos.

"I'll leave you boys to it," the watchman said. "Gotta get back to my post." He wandered back along the row, touching the noses of the vehicles as he made his way, leaving us in the dark.

Orjuedos took out his huge Maglite.

"Let's have a look," he said.

We went around to the back and started there. The photo of Jared Foster and Karel Janáčekwas taped up in the middle of the back window like a taunt. Jared was still biting Karel's ear.

"That's the famous photo," I pointed out.

Orjuedos leaned in to get a closer look at it.

He said: "A couple of cutie-pies, aren't they?"

The back half of the truck was piled haphazardly with Jared's things, like a homeless person's shopping cart of junk.

"This is Jared's stuff?" Orjuedos said.

"I recognize some of it," I said, looking in. "The serial killer books, the Charlie Manson poster."

"Sounds like a sick kid."

"Lots of black clothing draped over everything," I said. I moved around to the side. There was more stuff dumped in the middle seat. I didn't have the flashlight, though. "I can see the camouflage netting Jared draped from his ceiling."

"Camouflage netting?"

"He liked what it did to the light," I said. "Wait a minute, wait a minute—"

"What, Greg, what?"

"Tavo, come over here. Put your light on this. There's something in the netting."

Orjuedos hustled over and handed me the flashlight.

"See?"

I played the light over it. The bulk of it was buried underneath piles of black clothing, but parts of it were visible. I clearly made out a pair of human feet. Following up the body, I found a few pale fingers poking out of the netting.

"Holy Mother," Orjuedos said.

"Let's have a look at the face."

Orjuedos followed me around to the other side of the truck and jimmied his steel hook into the window groove, wrenching it up and down a few times until he finally managed to unlock the door and open it.

The rotten smell of death rushed out.

I pawed clothing and books onto the floor and uncovered

Henry Foster's naked, corpulent body wrapped up in the netting, like a fly mummified in a spider's cocoon. He was white as a sheet and staring up at the ceiling with his mouth open.

"He doesn't look like he has any blood left in him," I said, shining the flashlight over him. "Rope burns on the wrists, and he's got a puncture wound in the crook of his left elbow, there."

I danced a circle around it with the light.

"I see it." Orjuedos's face was grim, his nostrils flaring at the stench. "Is that your client?"

"That's Foster," I said. "He's been dead all day."

Orjuedos crossed himself and muttered a Spanish curse.

"Close it up," he said, and I did.

The door slammed hard and solid like the seal of a tomb.

TWENTY-TWO

ORJUEDOS HAD TO STAY and wait for the medical examiner to take charge of the body and the N.Y.P.D. Crime Scene Unit to take charge of the truck. We said goodbye for now, and I walked over to the Brooklyn-Battery Tunnel and hailed a cab that was coming out of it. I had the driver take me back to Houston Street.

The 'Cuda was still there, all black and shiny in the reflected street light. It looked unmolested. The green Mercedes was still parked behind it. Gloria Glendenning-Foster was still in the Mercedes. When she saw me ignoring her, unlocking my car instead, she got out and hurried over in her gray chinchilla coat and black alligator-skin heels.

"Where are you going?" Gloria demanded.

"That's my business," I said, turning the key.

"Didn't you see me sitting there?"

"What you do in your own car is *your* business."

"I've been waiting for you for a long time, Quaintance."

"I know that. I'm not sure what you were waiting for."

"Where have you been? I saw you go up with the police into Juliet Logan's apartment. Then you disappeared."

"I'll tell you about it in a minute," I said.

"Was he there? Did Henry go visit that slut of his?"

"He was there. I wouldn't know if she was a slut. You probably don't, either. Whatever she was, she isn't anymore."

"I know that," Gloria said. "The cops told me she was one of the ones killed last night."

"How did you know your husband was seeing Juliet Logan?"

"I followed him into the city a couple of times," she said. "Hank was too stupid to notice me. I've been wanting to see you, Quaintance. Didn't you get my message?"

Taxis and trucks were whizzing past us, too close.

"Let's get out of the street," I said. I took Gloria with me over to the sidewalk and lit myself a cigarette. Plenty of pedestrians were still killed on New York's streets by maniac drivers who didn't understand the vulnerability of human flesh.

"Aren't you going to offer me one?"

"They're not Virginia Slims." I handed her a Lucky Strike and my Zippo to light it with.

"So gallant," she said, lighting the cig herself.

I put my hand out for my lighter. She gave it back.

"I got your message," I said. "Only I couldn't give you a progress report. I hadn't made any progress."

"What have you been doing all day?"

"Trying to find Jared."

"What about my husband?"

"I told you I'd try to look for him, if the cases should intersect." I breathed in a lungful of smoke. "Well, they've intersected, Gloria. I found your husband. He's been murdered."

The leathery skin of her face didn't move.

"Somewhere deep inside me, I guess I was expecting that,"

Gloria said. "As I told you, it's not like Hank to be out of touch with me or the hospital or his answering service. I was fearing the worst. I don't get you, though. You saw me here in my car, and you were going to drive off without telling me Hank was dead?"

"I knew you'd come over to talk to me, Gloria. That's what you've been parked here for. I didn't have to go to you."

"No, we're too proud for that, aren't we?" Gloria said. "What do I owe you for a day's work?"

She said this without a trace of cynicism.

"Nothing," I said. "Your husband gave me a retainer. So far, I'm not owed any more than that. It's all the same case." "What do you mean, all the same case?"

"Your husband was murdered the same way as Karel Janáček."

This time only the skin of her eyelids moved, slightly.

"That's the boy's last name, Janáček, in case you didn't know," I told her. "I think you did. He's the boy Jared brought with him out to Hartford in August. That little detail you and your husband were so eager not to share with me. Karel Janáček's been lying on a slab at the morgue with a John Doe tag on his toe since Friday. Your husband went and had a look at him but pretended not to know his name. You didn't even bother to go down yourself. Because of that, Evelyn Grosse and her husband are having to fly in from California to make the identification."

"It wasn't our responsibility," Gloria said. "It's not like we were Karel's relatives. Neither is Evelyn, for that matter."

"Why didn't you want to help the police?"

"If you won't tell me your business, I won't tell you mine."

"Your husband made it my business when he retained me."

"And look where it got him," Gloria said, as if his death were my fault. "Are they sure it's the same killer?"

"I don't know. The medical examiner hasn't started on him

yet, and I'm no pathologist. I can't say whether it's the same killer or a copycat. Chances are, it's the same. You ought to get on back to your hotel. The police will be calling you soon and inviting you down to the medical examiner's office. I hope you'll at least be willing to identify your own husband."

"I'm not happy you told the police where I was staying."

"I know you're not," I said. "It was necessary."

Gloria opened up her purse and started digging out money.

"I still feel I should pay you for your time," she said, putting together a wad of bills.

"The time's paid for. If I run over, I'll send you a bill."

"You mean you're going to keep looking for Jared?" It didn't sound like something Gloria Glendenning-Foster desired.

"Why shouldn't I?"

"Hank's the one who hired you, and he's dead."

"I assumed you'd be honoring your husband's contract."

"You didn't make Hank sign any contract."

"Call it a gentleman's agreement. There is such a thing."

"Hank wasn't much of a gentleman."

"Why don't you want me to keep looking for Jared?"

"I'm not sure it's safe for you to go on," she said.

"Are you concerned for my safety?" I asked with a laugh. "Or are you threatening it?"

"Neither," Gloria said. "Don't misunderstand me. I think your services are no longer necessary. I'll pay you a kill fee, if that's what you require to terminate the agreement."

"You really don't want me to find your stepson?"

"I'm sure Jared will turn up." She wouldn't look at me. She kept compiling money in her purse, wondering how much I'd be willing to take. She was keeping a lot of money in there.

"He might turn up dead," I said.

Gloria stopped counting, folding the money into her fist.

"Listen, Quaintance," she said with a sudden edge in her voice. She looked up at me and bared her porcelain-capped teeth. "I don't care what happens to you, but I sure as hell care what happens to me. Hank hired you to find Jared, and look where it got him. I don't want to wind up the way he did."

"That's what I've been wanting from you all evening."

"What's that?"

"An honest answer," I said. "While you're being so honest, would you mind telling me where you were last night?"

Gloria rolled her eyes. "You think I killed Hank?"

"I didn't say that. I asked you where you were."

"I was at home, waiting for Hank," she said. "I didn't leave the house until after I called you this morning."

"Can that be corroborated?"

"My housekeeper, Carmelita, was home all evening. She ought to be able to back me up."

"I'll ask her," I said. "Did you have any contact with Carmelita last night?"

"No, not really."

"Then how could she back you up?"

"I don't know," Gloria admitted. "Maybe she can't. You've done a very nice job, Quaintance. I'm sure my husband would have been pleased. I don't want anyone looking for Jared anymore if it means they're going to be killed."

"If we *don't* find Jared, more people might die," I said.

"Here's three thousand dollars." Gloria extended her fist and tried to make me grab the money.

"You're scared, Gloria."

"Just take the money!" she said. "Go on to your next job and forget about Jared! That little shit's not worth finding!"

"I'm not sure Evelyn Grosse would agree with you."

"Evelyn is a naïve simpleton! Here, take the money!"

"Put it back," I said. "It's not for me."

"I said take it!" Gloria looked like a rabid collie.

I grabbed her hand by the wrist and squeezed hard, until her fist opened up and let the bills fall into my other. I snatched her purse off her shoulder, opened it, and stuffed the money inside it. I handed the purse back to her and said:

"Here."

Gloria looked at me as if I'd betrayed her.

"I thought you were smart," she said. "Guess not."

That kind of psychology didn't work on me.

"Did someone tell you to pay me off?" I asked.

"Pay you off?" Gloria's jaw dropped. She shook her head.

"That's what you tried to do," I said. "Pay me off."

"I'm only trying to keep us all out of danger. What use is it going to be to anyone if you find Jared? Hank's the one who wanted him, and Hank's dead. What am I going to do with him?"

"You didn't know Hank was dead," I said. "But you had all that cash put together in your purse for me. Not only that, it's a Sunday. You really came prepared."

"I got it at an ATM machine, for Christ's sake! And I told you already, I feared the worst about Hank."

"That's what you told me, all right." I gave her a look.

"I was right," Gloria said. "You *are* paranoid."

"Who told you to pay me off?"

"Nobody," she said. "No, it was my own stupid idea. I told Hank from the beginning to leave it alone and not get involved."

"You're talking about Karel."

"That's right. We saw it together on the TV news. I told him to forget about it, but no. He had to find Jared. If he'd listened to me, he'd still be alive. These people are nuts."

"What people?"

"These goths," Gloria said disgustedly. "These vampires."

"No such thing as a vampire," I said.

"Yeah, right. Tell that to my husband. And I have just one more thing to say to you, Quaintance, and that's goodbye."

With that, she swept past the grille of her Mercedes and climbed in behind the wheel and pulled out, taking advantage of a break in traffic to do a U-turn in the middle of Houston. She was heading east, toward the Lower East Side—not the direction I would have taken to get to the Plaza Hotel.

I looked up at the night sky, then down at my watch: 11:05.

Time enough to get to Lucrezia's without being scolded.

TWENTY-THREE

I PARKED THE 'CUDA on a stretch of Bowery gutter between Bleecker and Houston where there were no other cars. I double-checked the signage to make sure parking here was legal. It was. The restaurant equipment companies down here—purveyors of items like Vulcan ovens and Hobart mixers—were shut for the night with corrugated steel pocked with dents and embellished with graffiti. The only human activity was a block north, on the other side of the street, outside CBGB and CB's Gallery. Farther north of that, the Amato Opera stood dark. Where I was, it was dead.

I lit a cigarette, alone on the Bowery except for a bearded black man in an olive, oversize winter parka and white sneakers who was excavating recyclables out of a garbage can and dumping everything else out in large handfuls to blow away in whorls along the sidewalk. As I passed, he asked me quietly for one of my cigarettes. I lit a Lucky and passed it into his fingerless gloves. He muttered thanks, coughed, and went back to his dig.

I found the entrance to Lucrezia's building and the buzzer for 3C and tapped out the S.O.S. signal she wanted to hear.

The door buzzer sounded. I went in and up the rickety stairs. The balustrade rocked to and fro when I touched the railing. The stairwell was lighted by dim yellow bulbs sticking straight out from wall fixtures, one on each landing. The walls were marred by small meteor craters that hadn't been replastered but simply painted over, in puce.

As I approached the door to 3C, I put a precautionary hand inside my jacket, on the textured stock of my Glock. I rapped on the door with my left knuckles—the same Morse horseshit. A shadow eclipsed the peephole for a moment, then passed. The locks were undone scrambledly: when the door was tried, it held, and the locks had to be undone and redone and undone again before they were all properly unlocked together. In the process, a few frustrated *fucks* could be heard from the other side.

The door opened to reveal Lucrezia, eyes darting around the hall, saying: "Get in."

She didn't have a gun, and I saw no one behind her.

"Are you alone?" I asked.

"Yes, I'm alone," she said, pulling at my jacket. "Get in!"

As I went past her, I withdrew my gun and held it pointed toward the floor. Lucrezia refixed her locks, then did them again to make sure she'd done them right. Her apartment was a small studio with enough lights on. I made a quick scan of the living-sleep area, poked the bathroom door open and turned on the light, and nosed behind the shower curtain. No one hiding.

"You might check the toilet tank, Greg," Lucrezia advised at my back, calmer than she'd been at the door.

I turned around, noted the smirk on her face, and slammed my gun back into its holster.

"Don't be offended," I said. "I do this to all my friends."

"All two of them?" Lucrezia folded her arms. Her platinum locks fell to her shoulders exactly as they had at The Lot. She was wearing a black lacy see-through shirt over a black bra. The bra covered her nipple rings, but the shirt acted merely as a veil over the pink surgical scar down the middle of her chest. Black stretch jeans hugged her from navel to ankles like the dark casing of a blood sausage. Her feet were bare, toenails red.

"What are you afraid of, Lucrezia?"

"Who says I'm afraid of anything?"

"The secret signal. The locks. The look on your face when I came in. The way you ran from me last night."

"Are we going to keep talking in here?" Her eyes made a circuit of the bathroom. "You like the lighting or something?"

"No."

Lucrezia led me out of there and into the main room, with its posters of Stonehenge, the Great Sphinx, the Great Pyramid, and Machu Picchu. Crystals sat on her coffee table, on her dresser, on her bookshelves, and on the formica counter of her kitchenette, some of them purplish in color and clustered together in a mass. More crystals hung by black threads in her windows. The windows were undraped and gave us our reflections against the night, like Elvises on black velvet. I went over to one, shaded my eyes, and saw fire escapes finely delineated by the moonlight over a black back alley stacked with black plastic bags, the ancient cobbles glistening with black garbage juice.

"You would like a beer," Lucrezia stated matter-of-factly.

She handed me a Rolling Rock. I opened it and sipped.

"Now try to guess my weight," I said.

Lucrezia had a beer of her own. She took it with her to a futon on a pinewood frame that was currently jacked up into the couch position. She patted the other end of it for me. I didn't like being directed where to sit, but my only alternative was a chair far off in the corner, away from her face. I wanted to look at her while we talked. I gave in and sat where she'd pat.

"How long does it take you to crimp that hair?"

"No time at all. It's a wig. I don't like my real hair much. I shave it bald, same as you."

"How about that scar? Is that real or just makeup?"

"It's real," Lucrezia said, lifting her shirt up to just under her bra, half the scar's length. "You want to touch it?"

"Not particularly."

She lowered her shirt. "I had a hole in my heart. They had to open me up and fix it. I was seventeen."

"Must have been rough," I said sincerely.

"Yes and no," she said. "I had a near-death experience on the operating table. I saw the other side."

"You mean the whole dark tunnel and shining light bit?"

"Don't sneer at it, Greg." Lucrezia thought I was tempting fate. "It changed my life. I came back with the sixth sense."

"Six cents?"

"You don't believe in the sixth sense, I can tell."

"No, I don't," I said. "I don't believe in vampires or the Easter Bunny or voodoo economics, and I don't believe in a sixth sense. If I did, I wouldn't believe you've got it."

"I thought you promised to cut the rude remarks."

"That was last night," I said, "before you ran out on me."

"I told you why I ran, in my message."

"Something about black emanations," I said dubiously. "I'd like you to color that in a little for me. At least explain it in some way that my spiritually bound mind can grasp."

"I'm not sure that's possible," Lucrezia said.

"What made you run away?"

"I sensed a presence."

"A presence," I repeated.

"A lingering presence," Lucrezia said, closing her eyes, putting her fingers to her temples, searching for words a mere mortal might hope to understand. "A sort of cosmic residue."

"A residue."

"Something there but not there." She inhaled deeply through her nostrils, tried to focus. "Or a trace of something that had been, or that had left something. Some *thing*, don't you see?"

"A thing," I said flatly. "You mean a ghost? What?"

"No!" Lucrezia opened her eyes and stared at me hard for a moment, then seemed to break her concentration. She took a gulp of beer. "It's useless. You'll never believe me."

"Okay, I'm sorry. I may not believe in the supernatural, but I'm willing to listen if you tell me what you felt. Try again. Just tell me what you remember. If they're your true feelings, that makes them facts. You can't fake what you felt."

"Yes," Lucrezia said, smiling at the common ground we'd managed to find. "You're right, Greg, of course."

"You were even afraid to come up with me," I said. "Start with that. What made you want to stay downstairs in the foyer?"

"The unlocked door, the darkness, the threat that something might have happened to Anastasia—since she hadn't shown."

"Yes," I said. "All tangible facts."

I was worried I might have lost her again for a moment, that she might think I was trying to prove a point. But she went on:

"I felt the lingering presence right there in the doorway. Some *thing* had been through that door and gone up, and had come back down and out, and then vanished. I have a certain sensitivity to psychic residues, and all I can tell you is that these were some of the blackest I've felt."

"Black emanations," I said, throwing her a bone.

"Yes," she said. "Not from the building, really. The residues of what had been in. I planned on waiting for you, really I did. I couldn't go deeper into the building. I tried going out onto the sidewalk, but it was there, too, the darkness. And up along the sidewalk, going into the Chinese restaurant."

"Did you notice anything strange about the restaurant?"

"Only that the open sign was still up. Nothing more."

My mind was feeding me perfectly logical explanations for Lucrezia's bad vibes. The order of the scene had been disrupted by the unlocked doors, the OPEN sign on the closed shop, the night gate not rolled down. She could see these things as well as I, but they were filtered through her "psychic" glasses. Visible evidence of disorder translated into black emanations.

I wondered, though, whether she was giving me her true feelings, or whether they were influenced by what she had learned from the news about the murders in the Chinese restaurant.

"Can you describe this lingering presence?"

"All I can say is that it grew intolerable, like an opposing magnet on all sides of me. It was oppressing me, suffocating me. I had to get away, but I was standing atop a pinnacle surrounded by a void. Finally I found a weak spot and ran through. I ran back here and locked myself in."

"But what was it? This *thing*? Something, what—evil?"

"Evil, yes." Lucrezia gave me a sidewise glance. "I've never felt anything so dark. Evil—if you believe in that."

I smiled and said: "Evil is one thing I do believe in."

"Why?"

"Too much evidence," I said. "Not that I think it's a spiritual force. It's a manmade thing, like the cotton gin. People sell their souls all the time. I've known a few."

"Hmmm," Lucrezia said. "Your aura's clearing up again."

"Thank you. But let's skip the theology. I want to go back to last night a little bit longer. You said in your message that you knew one of the victims."

"Yes, Juliet Logan. She came to The Lot every now and then, after Jared. He didn't want to have anything more to do with her, but she was relentless, like one of those snippy dogs. She knew I was Jared's friend, and sometimes if he was ignoring her she would try to get messages to him through me."

"Were you a friend to her?"

"I put up with her. What worries me is—well, on top of the fact that she was murdered—it's her association with Theophrastus."

"What kind of an association?"

"Purely business," Lucrezia said. "She wouldn't have interested him sexually. She was one of his dealers."

"Drugs?"

"You don't know about Theophrastus?" Lucrezia looked around her, as if he might be lurking outside on the fire escape.

"What does he handle?"

"Ecstasy, pot, cocaine, heroin, whatever. He doesn't do any selling, though. He has operatives for that. Like Juliet."

"Why did her recruit her?"

"Juliet Logan never fit in at The Lot. No matter what she tried, she just wasn't one of us. Theophrastus befriended her and realized he could gain access to a slightly different market through her—N.Y.U. students who didn't make the scene. Juliet dealt out of her apartment. I'm not sure how much. The important thing is, she worked for Theophrastus."

"Important because?" I could take a guess, but I wanted Lucrezia to spell it out. I didn't want to pick up a wrong cue.

"Because of the way she was killed," Lucrezia said. "You know—execution style. That's what they said on TV. Gunshot through the back of the head, point blank, execution style."

"And you think Theophrastus had something to do with it?"

"I have no idea. All I can say is, that lingering presence I felt—

well, I'd felt it before. Not to the same degree, mind you, but it was somewhat reminiscent of Theophrastus."

"Theophrastus gives off these black emanations?"

"He has, sometimes," Lucrezia qualified. Everything she said on this subject seemed slightly hesitant. "I don't know if Theophrastus is evil, but he's not a *good* person. He's no Boy Scout. I don't think he would want to hurt me—though he would if he knew I was talking to you like this. I *have* seen him angry. When he's in one of his rages, the blackness pours out of him. I can feel it, almost see it. It has that same suffocating quality like what I felt last night. Theophrastus has never given off anything quite like that, but if he were pushed far enough, I think he could."

"So that's what you're afraid of," I said. "You think Theophrastus is dangerous."

"He's definitely dangerous. It's just a matter of degrees."

"You'd recommend caution around him."

"You aren't thinking of confronting him, are you?"

"I'd like to ask him some questions."

Lucrezia closed her eyes. "That's not a good idea. You'd be putting yourself in great danger."

"Why would you want to tell me about him if you didn't want me to do something about it?"

"I don't mean for you to get hurt, Greg."

"Theophrastus might have had nothing to do with it. I can't think of a reason why he'd want Jared's things—unless it was meant to cover for that money Jared owed him. He was supposedly downstairs last night, when you and I were talking with Ted the bouncer, when those two girls went down ahead of us—about the same time the burglary and killings must have taken place."

"All we have is Ted's word for it," Lucrezia said.

"I have to find out. If Theophrastus has an alibi, it lets him off."

"Let the police look into it. But when you talk to them, keep me out of it, okay? I don't want my name mentioned in any police report about Theophrastus's drug activities."

"I'll keep you out of it. But I still intend to talk to Theophrastus myself. I have things to ask him about Jared. He might be more cooperative with me than with the police, anyway."

"Theophrastus is uncooperative with just about everybody, and he'll be uncooperative with you. Don't cross him, Greg."

"Could he have had reason to kill Karel Janáček?"

Lucrezia swallowed hard and gave me a frightened look.

"How did you learn Karel's last name?" she asked.

"I learned it, that's enough. You told me you didn't know."

"I lied about that." Her eyes went down to her beer.

"Why didn't you tell the police who Karel was?"

"I don't want to be the one to bring the police down on Theophrastus. Even if he were tried and convicted, he has thugs who might reach people who talked to the police. You've got to promise me you'll keep my name out of it."

"I did. What has Karel got to do with Theophrastus?"

"Karel was another one of his dealers. I'm not the only one keeping silent about Karel. Everyone's afraid. Nobody wants to talk to the police. It would mix things up too much."

"Sure," I said. "If Theophrastus goes to prison, where are you all going to get your drugs? That's more important."

"They're scared, that's all," Lucrezia said defensively.

"If Theophrastus killed Karel, how does Jared Foster's father figure into it?"

"Henry Foster?" Lucrezia uttered the name with disgust.

"He's dead. He was killed the same way as Karel."

"I don't believe it," she said, almost to herself.

"Did you know him?"

"I never met him, but I heard a great deal about him from Jared. In fact, what I've been wanting to tell you about Jared mostly concerns his father—what his father did to him."

I looked at my watch: 11:49. I had to see Sebastian soon.

Lucrezia prodded: "Well, do you want to know or don't you?"

"I want to know," I said and swallowed the last of my beer. "You can start by telling me how you got to know Jared. I'm still looking for him. You were his closest friend. You ought to be able to help me get to know him better. In his absence."

"Yes," Lucrezia said, unnerved by *absence*. "All right."

Nothing in her face made me think she knew where Jared was, either psychically or really. She'd already told me she didn't know, that she sensed Jared was in transition, that perhaps he had gone only to return. But what as? Prophet or devil?

"When did you meet him?"

"March. It was at Bedlam. Theophrastus hadn't opened The Lot just yet. Jared was still living with Juliet, but they had already broken up. He was vulnerable. Ripe for me."

"Ripe?"

"I won't try to explain it all to you," Lucrezia said. "He was overflowing with dark energy. I was drawn to that. I fed off him for the next few months, until after he'd moved in with Anastasia and began to find himself."

"What do you mean, fed off him? You drank his blood?"

"No." She laughed and shook her head. "His lifeforce. I can see you don't believe me, Greg."

"Forget what I believe or don't believe," I said. "I only want to know how you felt about Jared. You and he became boyfriend girlfriend? Or am I being too simplistic again?"

"It evolved beyond that. When I enter into a relationship with another, I never expect it to last. I tap into their energies and take them into myself. I use them up, and I tend to do that rather quickly."

"You're what they call a psychic vampire?" I asked.

"You may call it that, if you wish."

"What was different about Jared?"

"For the first couple of months, it followed the typical pattern. I would drain him one night, and he would replenish, and I would drain him some more, and it went on like that. He had more vitality than most. But then there was a change. I discovered that my own energies were being drained, reciprocally. Jared had his own need. It was always in him, I believe, but I was the one who drew it out."

"How?" I asked, never really buying the psychic angle but still curious. "And when did this shift occur?"

"It happened in May. Jared's energies replenished so easily—he was *so* strong—I decided he must have a rich past life history. I decided to regress him back through hypnosis and catalogue his past lives, look for clues to his current persona."

"Skip the past lives. I'm only interested in Jared Foster."

"That's what I was intending to do. We went first simply back into his childhood. I didn't expect to find anything—but you often stumble on things when you're not looking. Jared regressed with difficulty. He was cooperative, but his mind was trying to keep me away from some guarded secrets."

"Repressed memories?"

"Yes," Lucrezia said. "And if you know about repressed memories, you must know they tend to relate to traumatic events."

"Like sexual abuse," I said. "Was Jared sexually abused?"

"Yes."

"By whom?"

"His father."

"And he was no longer consciously aware of it?"

"That's right," Lucrezia said. "The memories were locked up in his brain until I let them out."

"Isn't that supposed to be done by a licensed therapist?"

"If you're trying to imply that I may have done him harm by opening him up, I disagree. It did Jared a world of good. He was finally able to break the Gordian knot between himself and his father, and that can only be a good thing."

"This was when he dropped out of school," I said. "Do you think that was good for him?"

"I think it was for Jared to decide. It certainly wasn't good for him to let his life be ruled by his father."

"What was the nature of the supposed abuse?"

"Why do you say supposed?"

"I'm not sure repressed memories are always repressed memories. I've read of enough cases when they were suggested to the patient by the therapist."

"You may be right," Lucrezia said. "But as you pointed out, I'm no therapist. I didn't have a political agenda. I wasn't collecting case studies for some book. I tapped into this purely by accident. I think that's reason enough to take it seriously."

"Okay," I said, finding this a reasoned response. "Go on. What was the nature of the abuse? How old was Jared? Was it a one-time deal or a recurrent thing?"

"Recurrent. It seems to have begun when Jared was six years old and continued until around age twelve. Henry Foster abused his son about once a month, and he always went about it the same way. It always happened late at night, around three or four in the morning. Jared would be woken up. His father would turn him on his stomach and bind his wrists and ankles to the bed."

"I don't need to hear all the details," I said. "Please."

"But some are significant," Lucrezia said. "The tying down is important. His father was enjoying this horrible power trip. On several occasions, Henry Foster would tie a noose around Jared's neck. He would cut off Jared's air until he passed out, then revive him. He would do this repeatedly. It put Jared in mortal fear of his father, and of course his father told him that if he ever breathed a word of it to anyone, he would kill him."

"Foster did this for six years? Why did it stop?"

"I don't know. Jared and I discussed it after he was out of the trance, and he seemed to think it had to do with his father's divorce and remarriage. He doesn't know exactly why. Maybe Jared was an outlet for some rage that was percolating in his father during the first marriage. Maybe the second marriage solved whatever problem he was having."

"Or maybe he started taking out his rage on Gloria," I said, wondering now what was on those closeted tapes. "Do you know whether Jared ever confronted his father about the abuse?"

"I don't believe so," she said. "After we uncovered his memories, Jared began to truly hate his father, but he was still intimidated by his father's threats."

"That he'd kill him if Jared ever spoke of it."

"Yes. He was deathly afraid of that."

"And this is the point where your relationship changed?"

"Yes, that's right," Lucrezia said. "Once this was opened up, Jared became more like me, needing to feed off other people's energies. His own lifeforce became shut off to me. I couldn't tap into it anymore. We became even stronger friends, but we were no longer—as you would say—lovers. He started developing an interest in what I do. He wanted to learn hypnosis and how to influence people psychically."

"Is that what you do?"

"Sometimes."

"Are you influencing me psychically now?"

"No," Lucrezia said. "You're not receptive to it."

"That's good to know. Now, in May, when all this came up, that was about the time Jared started sleepwalking, right?"

"How do you know about the sleepwalking? From Anastasia?"

"No, she never mentioned it. I learned about it from Dr. Willem Kirst. Do you know him?"

"Jared's adviser?" Lucrezia asked, sounding unsure. "Never met him. What does he have to do with anything?"

I explained how Dr. Kirst was more than Jared's academic adviser, how he talked regularly with Jared and treated him for his sleepwalking at the sleep disorders clinic.

"Have you witnessed Jared's sleepwalking?" I asked.

"Yes, I have. It was never anything much."

"Did he ever talk while sleepwalking?"

"Just incoherent mutterings. Why?"

"I'm wondering if he ever told Dr. Kirst about his father's abuse, while he was sleepwalking, without knowing about it."

"I doubt it," Lucrezia said. "All it usually amounted to was Jared getting up from bed, shuffling around the apartment, bumping into the coffee table, maybe going to the kitchen. When he spoke, it was just yattering. I never heard him utter a complete sentence when he was sleepwalking."

"Just a thought," I said. "Do you think Jared hated his father so much he would want to kill him?"

"He never expressed anything along those lines to me."

"He wouldn't, most likely, even if he was thinking of it."

"I'd like to think he had nothing to do with it."

"You like Jared a lot."

"I'm fond of him, yes. We're kindred spirits."

"I'd better go," I said. "I'm supposed to see Sebastian and Anastasia, and I'm late. Maybe I should call them."

Lucrezia let me use her phone. My watch said 12:15. I got Sebastian on the line, apologized, and asked them to wait for me.

"Thanks for the beer, Lucrezia," I said at the door. "And for everything else. You've been a big help."

"Though you remain skeptical about my powers," she said.

"At this point, I'll take what I can get. Stay safe."

Lucrezia promised she would and locked the door behind me.

TWENTY-FOUR

I FOUND A SPACE for the 'Cuda on Ludlow Street and walked around the corner to Stanton, where Sebastian lived in an old tenement. I was buzzed in and had to walk up six flights of steep, narrow stairs. By the time I got to the top, I was winded. I waited to catch my breath before knocking on the door. I had no reason not to trust them, but I put my hand on my Glock just the same.

Anastasia opened the door, dressed casually in a T-shirt like the day before, without her club makeup on.

"Are you doing all right?" I asked.

"I'm fine," Anastasia said. "Come on in."

I went past her and took a quick look around without drawing my gun. Sebastian was sitting at his computer, immersed in a video game, and paid little attention to my entrance. Peter was asleep atop the warm computer monitor, his tail dangling.

Sebastian's place was a studio smaller than Lucrezia's, smaller than mine, more the size of a dormitory room. A pinewood loft bed was erected above the windows, leaving room beneath for a computer desk, TV, stereo, record crates, and shelves lined with CDs. More CDs were stacked on the floor and in every available nook. The walls were covered with Sebastian's gothic photographs, large and small, most of them simply tacked into the plaster. The bathroom had a shower, no tub. The kitchenette was adequate, with an ancient refrigerator, meager cabinet space, and a sink barely big enough to wash a plate in. Anastasia had said Sebastian was looking for a new place, and I could see why.

"Sorry I kept having to put you guys off," I said, taking my hand out of my jacket. "Things kept coming up."

I looked over Sebastian's shoulder. He was engaged in a fierce laser battle with an ugly space alien. He took a direct hit and went down, calling the alien a motherfucker. Game over.

"Sorry," Sebastian said, tossing his long blond hair back off his face. "I had to finish that. Have a seat."

There was only one other chair, and the chivalrous side of me couldn't take it if it meant Anastasia would sit on the floor.

"I'll stand," I said. "This won't take long, will it?"

Anastasia brought us all beers from the refrigerator.

"I don't think so," she said. "Sebastian and I just put our heads together and came up with some stuff you ought to know."

"Thanks," I said to the beer in my hands. I took a gulp. "Do you think it'll help me find Jared?"

"We want you to find him," Sebastian said. "He's our friend. We didn't have enough sense to worry about him until you showed up. I guess we just assumed he was okay. But now all this stuff with Karel—"

"How well did you know Karel Janáček?"

"Well enough." Sebastian looked up to Anastasia.

"I knew him better than I let on, Greg," Anastasia said, taking the seat next to Sebastian. "I was too scared to talk."

"Scared of what?" I said. "Theophrastus?"

Sebastian looked at Anastasia again. He put a cigarette to his lips and lit it. Anastasia asked him for one. While they were doing this, I lit up a Lucky Strike. We all sat there blowing smoke for half a minute—three doomed suckers.

"Why do you think I'm scared of him?" Anastasia asked.

"Karel ran drugs for Theophrastus," I said, keeping my word to Lucrezia that I'd keep her name out of it. You never knew when you might be speaking to a rat. "Theophrastus has a dangerous reputation. A lot of people seem to think he might have had a hand in Karel's murder. But they're scared to talk."

Anastasia looked to Sebastian. Sebastian looked at her.

I kept looking at both of them, wondering what was what.

"I could go on," I said, and did: "In mid September, Jared was seen being threatened by Theophrastus. Jared owed him some money. Theophrastus tried choking it out of him. Do either of you know anything about that? Could Jared have had a drug debt?"

"I don't think so," Sebastian said. "Jared wasn't a big drug user. He'd do the occasional ecstasy, but nothing more. He was the kind of guy who'd take drugs offered to him by his friends. He wasn't the type who would buy drugs for himself."

"He never used heroin?" I asked, looking to both of them.

"Not to my knowledge," Anastasia said.

"No," Sebastian said. "Jared was too afraid of an easy overdose. A lot of the junk on the market these days is extra pure, and people sometimes wind up with a lot more of it in their system than they intended. Jared didn't trust the stuff."

"Do either of you?"

"I don't have time for it," Sebastian said.

"I used to, a long time ago," Anastasia said. "I've been away from it for more than five years. Ecstasy is about the most I'd do. Jared was on about the same wavelength."

"Could Jared have been buying heroin from Theophrastus for

a third party?"

"I can't think of who," Sebastian said. "Any of his friends would have known where to get it without going through Jared."

"What about someone who wasn't in the scene?"

Anastasia shrugged. "It's possible, I guess. I wouldn't be surprised if Jared owed Theophrastus money. If he did, it couldn't be for anything else but drugs."

"Why wouldn't you be surprised?"

"Because of the phone call I got last night," she said. "Maybe you were wondering why I happened to be so lucky not to be in my apartment when the burglars came. I was tipped off."

"Why didn't you call the police? Or me?"

"I'll explain. The call came at about ten-thirty, from Juliet Logan. She said Theophrastus had been looking for Jared, that Jared owed him some money. She wanted to warn me that he was sending some guys over to remove Jared's things from my apartment. I asked her how she knew this, and she said I just ought to take her word for it. She told me I should make sure I wasn't around. If I was at my apartment, I'd probably get hurt. She told me not to tell anyone she had called, and she hung up."

"Juliet lied to you. She seems to be good at that."

Anastasia frowned. "How do you know she lied?"

"It was Henry Foster and Juliet Logan who took Jared's things," I said. "Juliet didn't want you around, because she didn't want you to know who'd done it. I'm sure Juliet was the one responsible for the peeing on the mattress and the shredding of the bedsheets and most of the other destruction. She hated you for the fact that you lived with her beloved Jared."

"I know she hated me. I didn't realize how much."

"How do you know Jared's father had anything to do with it?" Sebastian asked. "And with *her?*"

I explained how Henry Foster had been having an affair with

Juliet Logan since April. I mentioned the witnesses who saw Foster and Juliet loading up Foster's truck. I said I could only guess that Foster suspected Jared of Karel's murder and was trying to remove any evidence that might implicate his son.

"Jared couldn't have murdered Karel," Sebastian said with a strong element of protest. "Jared *loved* Karel."

"That doesn't rule anything out," I said. "Murders are often committed by someone close to the victim."

"I don't believe it," he said stubbornly. "I never will."

Anastasia said, "I agree with Sebastian."

"Well, for whatever reason, Foster thought so," I said. "He and Juliet took Jared's things. Someone else came along, though, and took them by surprise. The police found Foster's truck tonight, full of Jared's things. Foster was in it, too. All the blood had been drained out of him, same as Karel. He's dead."

"I don't get it," Anastasia said.

"Neither do I," Sebastian said.

"What else did you guys want to tell me?"

"I almost hesitate to tell you now," Sebastian said.

"Don't hesitate. Just let me have it. You want me to find your friend, don't you?"

"Of course I'm still going to tell you. It just makes me feel uncomfortable, now that I know Henry Foster's been killed. Jared hated his father, and he had reason. I learned a few weeks ago that his father had sexually abused him as a child."

"Jared told you about this?" I asked.

"Me and a lot of other people," Sebastian said. "In front of a whole studio audience—in front of the whole world, in fact, though the whole world hasn't seen it yet. We were on a TV talk show— *The Betsy Morgan Show.*"

"Oh, brother," I said. When the days were slow and the phone wasn't ringing, I sometimes watched it. It came on after my soaps. "You're saying this episode hasn't aired yet?"

"I don't think it has," Sebastian said. "She was taping it for broadcast around Halloween, so it probably won't be shown for another nine or ten days. It was the sort of thing you'd expect—a show about 'real-life vampires.' I was on because of being a DJ at Bedlam, and I brought along some examples of my photos. Theophrastus was there with a couple young girls on his arm, talking about the pleasures of blood-sucking. Lucrezia was there, and also a couple of other goths I don't know. And some nut who claims he's a 'vampire hunter.' And Jared and Karel."

"Who was this nut?"

"I don't remember his name. He called himself a doctor."

"What about you, Anastasia?"

"I wouldn't have any part of that circus," she said. "I was asked, but I didn't go on. I don't want to be made fun of on national television."

"But Sebastian, you didn't mind?"

"Hey," he said. "They pay you."

"And Jared revealed on the show that he had been sexually abused by his father? How did that come up?"

"Betsy Morgan was looking for explanations for why these young people had turned to the so-called vampire lifestyle. Lucrezia talked about putting Jared under hypnosis, and then Jared piped up and said that his father had abused him."

"Do you know whether he told his father about the show?"

"I have no idea," Sebastian said. "I haven't seen Jared since the taping."

"When was that?"

"Sometime in mid September. I really don't remember."

"Where's this show taped?"

"Hell's Kitchen Studios."

"Did Karel or anyone else say anything else provocative?"

"For most of the country, the whole show will be provocative. It was all sort of silly. I wish I'd never had anything to do with it. Anastasia was right."

"The name of this self-styled vampire hunter," I said. "It wouldn't be Dr. Willem Kirst?"

"No. I can't remember what it was, but it wasn't that."

"Have either of you heard Jared talk about Dr. Kirst?"

Anastasia and Sebastian looked at each other and shook their heads no. I didn't have the sense they'd ever heard the name.

"Jared's mysterious disappearances," I said, "were times when he would go check himself into Dr. Kirst's sleep disorders clinic. Anastasia, you never mentioned his sleepwalking to me."

"I didn't think it was important," Anastasia said. "A lot of people sleepwalk. Jared never did anything strange. He would just get up at three or four in the morning and wander around the apartment, sometimes bumping into things. That's it."

"Jared never mentioned the J. Walker Hamilton Sleep Disorders Clinic to either of you?"

"No," Anastasia said. Sebastian had never heard of it.

"Do either of you know where Karel was staying?"

"Sure," Sebastian said. "I was over there once, back in August, just after Karel moved in. It's not far from here."

"Where?"

"On Rivington Street. I should have the address here somewhere." Sebastian grabbed an address book from a cubbyhole on his computer desk and thumbed through it. He read off an address on Rivington, between Norfolk and Suffolk, apartment 1E.

"Was he sharing with anybody?"

"No, I don't think so. It's a small studio like mine. But I can tell you something else. His landlord was Theophrastus."

"More good information."

"Don't the police know this already?"

"Not to my knowledge. They haven't got the identification nailed down on Karel just yet. Jared's mother, Evelyn Grosse, is flying in tomorrow to make it official. She knew Karel was in New York, but I don't think she knew where he was living. The police are going to be very interested in this. In fact, they may want to come and talk with you some more."

"I'm worried about Theophrastus," Anastasia said.

"You can ask the police to keep your identity confidential."

"I'm still worried about him."

"This is just your gut reaction," I said. "We don't have any proof that Theophrastus has anything to do with Karel's murder or Foster's murder or Jared's disappearance."

"I don't feel like giving him the benefit of a doubt."

"Maybe you should," I said. "It seems to me that Theophrastus would have a lot to lose if he started getting mixed up in multiple murders. He's a businessman, he owns property—"

"You're assuming Theophrastus is sane," Anastasia said.

"He's not?" I asked.

Sebastian and Anastasia looked at each other and laughed.

I asked them if there was anything else they left out.

"No," Sebastian said. "You already knew half of what we were going to tell you. Please find Jared. We want him back."

"I'll find him for you," I told them.

I didn't tell them the hourglass was running out of sand.

TWENTY-FIVE

I WALKED DOWN a block and over a couple to Karel's building on narrow Rivington, a seven-story dusky charcoal tenement with a few windows alight. A loud party was going on in one of them. I tried the front door, but it was locked. I had some lock-picking wires in my pocket, but I didn't want to attempt it, exposed to the street as I was. I scanned the array of buzzers, trying to guess which one had the party. They would probably buzz me in without question. But I couldn't guess. I could try pressing all of them down the line. There was always the chance someone would buzz me in without even talking to me. It was one in the morning, though, and I was afraid of disturbing someone and getting the police called on me. I stood back from the building and looked up at the windows to find the party.

I was saved from having to guess. A trio of drunken persons— two girls and a guy—were stumbling down the stairs with beers in their hands, arms draped around each others' shoulders, heading out the front door. I made like a resident on my way in and got my keys out. The giggling, snorting partygoers were kind enough to open the doors for me as they exited. I barely caught the second door with my foot. I heard the partygoers' laughter dissipate into the night´as their boots clopped down the street.

Apartment 1E was tucked behind the stairs, out of sight of the street. I knocked as a precaution. I waited a minute and knocked again. No answer. I tried the knob, but it was locked. It was an old, simple lock, luckily for me. I got out my lock-picking wires, stuck the flat one along the bottom, carefully ticked off the key ridges with the other, and tried the knob. It turned. There was a deadbolt, too, but it hadn't been thrown.

I took out my Glock and held it up alongside my ear.

I opened the door slowly. The hinges squeaked. The lights were off. I flicked on the switch and closed the door behind me. The short jag of lighted hallway took me around a sharp corner into the dark main room. I had to turn on another light, but I couldn't find the switch. It wasn't to my left. Not much light came in from the short hall. I could make out part of a yellow easy chair and the end of a single bed. I reached across with my left to the other wall and fumbled around but failed to find a switch. There had to be a lamp.

I stayed back in the hall and removed a penlight from my jacket. The light didn't stretch far. I stepped into the room and played it around quickly. A lampshade presented itself in the farthest corner of the room, on a small table by the single bed. I didn't see anyone in the room.

I walked over to the lamp and reached for the chain. It clicked, but no light came on. I tried again. No light.

The penlight showed bloodstains on the sheets and strands of rope dangling from the bedposts. Poor Karel. Poor Foster.

I felt a stabbing pain in my left shin and cried out. My leg jerked up reflexively, and I clutched it. Warm blood seeped through my fingers. Something reached out from under the bed and yanked my other foot forward. I went sprawling onto my back, hitting my head on the floor and dropping my gun. I was dazed, slow in getting up, rubbing at the back of my head. I kicked my legs out at my assailant. All I hit was air.

The thing from under the bed got out with a shuffling noise.

All I saw was a dark shadow rising.

I reached for my gun but couldn't find it. A heavy object struck me across the side of the head and shattered. I fell back again, tasting blood and bits of porcelain on my tongue. A pointy-toed shoe nailed me in the soft spot at the base of my skull. I swore and flailed my arms at my attacker. The shoe nailed me again, harder, in the same spot.

The room started spinning in four directions at once. I was in a lifeboat being tossed among the waves. I felt feebly for my gun and cut my hands on porcelain shards. I groaned.

Footsteps hurried across the room. I caught a double-vision glimpse of a fuzzy silhouette disappearing around the sharp-angled corner. The hall light went off. The door slammed shut.

Another wave hit the lifeboat hard, broadside.

I was thrown overboard, into the depths.

TWENTY-SIX

I CAME TO in darkness rubbing the back of my head. I found a
raised lump, a loose layer of scalp, and a gash seeping blood. My
mouth was wet with blood from a cut lip, and my tongue was
playing with sharp bits of something. I turned over slowly and
spat it all out. My left leg was hurting from a deep wound.

I pushed myself up to a sitting position and remembered
where I was. I remembered the hands snatching me from under
the bed, and falling back and dropping my gun. A sharp pair of
shoes had clocked me twice on the head with intent to disable,
then gone running out the door, dousing the hall light.

I remembered the last thing I saw before going down was the
bloodstained sheets and the rope lengths on Karel's bed.

"Shit," I said.

I tried to stand, but my head was reeling and I couldn't put
much weight on my leg. I found the bed and used one of the posts
to help pull myself up. I reached for the lamp that had been on the
night table, but it was no longer there. It was on the floor in

dangerous fragments. I couldn't find my penlight. My palms were cut in several places; I didn't want to get down on my knees to search for anything.

I limped away from the bed, crunching bits of porcelain under my boots, and found the door to the bathroom. I had trouble finding a light switch again, but I discovered a chain at the medicine cabinet that turned on two bright bulbs above it.

My eyes balked at the sudden light. When they got used to it, they weren't happy with what they saw in the mirror.

"Goddamn," I said. Blood was smeared down my chin from a sliced lip that bulged hugely on one side. I had another gash along the side of my head, where the lamp had struck and broke, and a smaller cut along the same cheek.

I turned the faucet and let the water run cold for a bit. I sunk my head into the sink and let the water run over the back of my head and down the sides. Pink runoff swirled down the drain.

The cold flow restored my brain a little. I looked in the mirror again and saw new blood bubbling out of the faultlines in my flesh. I grabbed a handful of toilet paper and daubed at the blood, flushing the red-dotted sheets down the rust-rimmed bowl.

I hitched my left boot up onto the rim of the sink. Blood spread in an oblong shape from a one-inch cut to my jeans. I tore around the fabric a little to have a look. It was a slim puncture wound, probably from a knife. It had felt like a knife jab, all right. It was the kind of cut that needed treatment, but I didn't have time to go to the hospital. My straight-cut jeans were too tight to roll up over the wound. I unbuttoned them and pulled them down to my ankles. I needed a bandage. I ripped my white cotton briefs off at the sides, rolled them up, and tied the resultant strip tight around my shin. I pulled my pants back up. It would have to do for now.

The bathtub was white and clean and smelled strongly of

bleach. I looked around the rim of the drain and found dried flecks of blood someone had been careless enough not to scrub.

The bathroom opened right onto the main room of Karel's apartment, and the light from the medicine chest shone in a wide swath across the floor. The lampshade lay on its side, still attached to its frame and the light socket. The bulb and the porcelain base of the lamp were shattered in a million pieces all over the floor. There were bloodstains on the floor—mine, I supposed—but the dried blood on the bedsheets was not.

I reached down for my gun, dusted it off, and put it back in its holster. I looked for my penlight and found it had rolled under the bed, against the wall. When I got down on my right knee and reached for it, I noticed something else:

The splintery wood flooring had snagged a number of gray chinchilla hairs, presumably off the thing that had attacked me.

I made a search of the place, but it had been cleaned out of any of Karel's personal effects. I was careful not to leave any more fingerprints; I'd disturbed the crime scene enough already.

I picked up the phone with some tissue and called Orjuedos's pager. At the beep, I punched the number for the phone I was at.

It was the same number that had sent me the mystery page, the line I'd called back only to be met with silence.

I didn't like the idea of waiting around for Orjuedos to call back. If he took too long returning the page, I'd have to leave anyway and call him again later. My shin was throbbing, and I tried to keep my weight off it. I spent a few minutes in the bathroom, checking my Glock for damage. It appeared fine.

Finally, the phone rang.

"Hello?" I said.

"Detective Orjuedos," he said.

"Tavo, Greg Quaintance. I found Karel Janáček's apartment."

"Oh, yeah? Where is it?"

I told him where and that I was in it. I described the evidence I'd found and gave him an account of my assault. I left out the part about the chinchilla fibers; they could find them on their own and draw their own conclusions.

"Let me get this straight," Orjuedos said. "Once you found out where Karel lived, instead of calling me and letting me handle it, you went over there yourself, entered illegally, and disturbed the evidence. Am I hearing you correctly?"

"I wouldn't have disturbed anything if I hadn't been attacked," I said. "It wasn't my intention."

"Fuck your intentions."

"I know I screwed up. But look, someone knows I was here. You need to get over here now, before they come back and try to remove evidence. I can wait here and let you in."

"I can't just step in and take over," Orjuedos said. His tone remained calm and level, but I sensed that he was fuming. "The evidence has to stand up in court. If you lived there or owned the place and gave me your consent, that would be fine. As it is, I'm going to have to get a warrant. That may take an hour or two. I'd love it if you could sit there and protect the integrity of the scene, or what's left of it—"

"I can't stay that long," I said. "I've got work to do."

"I'm going to bust your ass, Greg, I swear. If you fuck up this investigation, I'll see you lose your license, maybe even do some prison time. I could book you right now for B and E and obstruction. I might find one or two other charges to tack on."

"That would be fine if you were here to bust me," I said. "Why don't you send a couple of patrol guys over here until you get your warrant? If I'm still around, they can hang onto me for you. If I'm gone, you can post them in front of the building to make sure no one enters apartment 1E until you can get here."

"It's already done," Orjuedos said. "They're on their way."

"I'd think twice before you bust me."

"Why's that, Greg?"

"Without me, you'd be a day behind on all your leads."

"You think I'm an honorable man and that maybe I even like you a little and that you're entitled to a break?"

"Something like that, Tavo."

"You're only half right. If this investigation reaches a satisfactory conclusion, you *might* get a break. If it doesn't, you're going to be my sacrificial lamb. You got it, Greg?"

"Got it," I said. "And one more thing. I'm out of here."

I hung up.

I put my penlight back in my jacket. I looked out the peephole and saw no one in the hall—but peepholes had blind spots, so I drew my Glock before opening the door.

TWENTY-SEVEN

I HAD NO REASON to go back to the 'Cuda on Ludlow just yet. I was heading north up Norfolk, watching out for police. I was in a hurry, and my limp must have looked more like a cocky, bouncy gait. The Lot was only two blocks up, and Theophrastus and I were due for a chat. I didn't think it could wait much longer.

I followed the pull of the thudding music until I came to the gaping doorway and the girl with the fluorescent purple hair and clown-face makeup. I paid the cover, and she let me in.

My watch said 2:03. The front hall was packed with more teenage goths than I'd seen last night—girls and boys scoping me out as I brushed past, hoping I'd want to have something to do with them. I must have seemed all the more succulent with bloody gashes, fat lip, and blood-spattered shirt. I wondered where all these teens had come from, whether they had school tomorrow, whether they were drop-outs.

It took me a few minutes to push my way through the floor throng to get to the door where Ted the bouncer stood guard.

Ted's arms were folded as neatly as last night, with a naked buxom babe tattooed on his left biceps and HARLEY-DAVIDSON on his right. His long hair was tied in back tonight. A string of beer foam clung to his gray bird's-nest beard. Kinky gray hairs poked up out of the stretched collar of his T-shirt. He was wearing a too-small black leather vest I hadn't seen him wearing last night. It bore a machine-embroidered patch on the left breast that I recognized from the Lorelei Matheson case: a grinning human skull in the center, with two Zs spelled out in crossbones up above, and RYDERS decked out in blood-dripping letters below.

I didn't notice the patch until I was right in front of Ted.

"I want to talk to Theophrastus," I blurted. It had been on my lips ever since Rivington Street. I'd been preparing to say it, and I was determined not to take no for an answer. But when it came out of my mouth, it sounded weak—especially over the loud music. Ted had asked me last night if we hadn't met somewhere before. I was sure I'd never met Ted, but he might have recognized me from the newspapers, and he'd had a day to mull it over in his mind until he had me pegged.

"Theophrastus wants to talk to you," Ted said, smiling.

I was about to chicken out and back away into the crowd, but Ted had his meaty arm around me and was opening up the door.

"Why would he want to talk to me?"

"Same reason you want to talk to him, I suppose," Ted said, stepping through the door with me and closing it behind us.

We were at the top of the dimly lighted basement stairs. I was reaching inside my jacket when Ted lurched over me, plunged in his hand, and pulled out my Glock. He yanked my jacket down over my shoulders to my elbows, planted his knee squarely at the top of my ass, and propelled me forward.

"There you go," Ted said.

I was airborne. Then my toes bumped a step. My knees

slammed hard into a lower step. The rest of the stairs sprang up to smack me in the face. I rolled over myself to the bottom and landed on my side on cold concrete, curled up in a fetal position, my arms still half-bound by the screwed-down jacket. My vision faded to black, but I was still aware enough to hear Ted clomping down the stairs, sniggering.

"You son of a bitch," he said. "You're dead."

My sight came back like a flower opening to the sun. Ted's boots were right in front of my eyes, and his apelike hands were reaching down for my armpits. He pulled me up to my feet, but I couldn't stand. My knees had caved in, and my shin was still throbbing. Blood was dripping from my nose into my mouth.

Ted held me up and stood me against the cold stone wall. I saw the grip of my Glock poking out of the waist of his jeans and making an indentation against his beer belly. I hoped it would misfire and send a nine-millimeter hollow-point into Ted's balls.

We were in a dim hall, alone. I saw a couple of dark doors at the far end, both marked PRIVATE. The music and dancing were shaking the foundation. No one upstairs would hear me if I yelled for help, and I doubted Theophrastus or anyone else behind those two doors would come running to save me.

"I know who you are," Ted said.

He slammed his right fist into my stomach, holding me up with his left hand. It was a hard blow, but I'd tightened my abs before he struck, so it didn't quite knock the wind out of me.

"Who?" I eked out.

Ted switched to holding me up with his right hand, and I clenched my abs again to receive the blow from his left. A small package of air rushed out through my teeth.

"You're that private dick who took Lorelei away from us."

Ted head-butted me like a ram.

I had two points of contact—Ted's head and the stone wall

behind me—and I'd already suffered blows to the head tonight.

Stars exploded around me, and I collapsed like a jellyfish.

Ted leaned over, planted his shoulder against my kidney, grabbed my thigh, and hefted me up and over his back. He carried me off toward one of the doors, unlocked it, and stepped inside.

I was looking at the grimy floor. The blood rushed to my head, drowning out all the noise. After that, I was out.

TWENTY-EIGHT

I JOLTED AWAKE, drawing breath. Ice cubes and ice water were spilling down my back. I was on the concrete floor, naked, on my knees, leaning forward, prostrate, my arms out in front of me. My wrists were tied together with tough coils of rope wrapped in tight figure eights. My ankles were bound similarly. I had no strength to try to get up.

"Wakey, wakey!" came Ted's voice from behind me. He tapped my ass with the toe of his boot. "This little piggie looks ready for slaughter, don't he?"

"Hoist him up," came another man's voice, deep and hoarse.

I hadn't realized there was anyone else in the room.

I raised my head and looked around. It was a large storage space half filled with aluminum beer kegs and cardboard cases of beer and liquor piling up toward the ceiling. In the farthest corner was a toilet and an old bathtub on claw feet, with a black curtain that could be drawn around it for privacy. The rest of the space was a kind of lounge area, demarcated by a section of red shag

carpeting and furnished with a black leather couch, black vinyl
bean-bag chairs, and a glass coffee table. Several red candles were
burning on the coffee table, and there were three people sitting on
the couch—one adult, two kids:

The adult was a large, beefy man wearing no shirt. His chest
was overgrown with black hairs, like kudzu, creeping around his
sides and onto his neck and shoulders. His belly, chest, and arms
were covered in blue tattoos. A silver crucifix hung upside-down
on a string of black rosary beads around his neck, and he had
silver rings on most every finger. Curly jet-black hair fell back
from his scalp, long enough for him to be leaning against most of
it. A black beard grew thick and untrimmed along his jaw. He was
in black leather jeans and pointy-toed boots.

The two kids sat on either side of him. They were girls of
fifteen or sixteen, with wildly teased platinum blond hair,
earrings, nose rings, lip rings, black lacy tops, and black velvet
pants. They had powdered the exposed portions of their flesh,
hidden their eyes behind dark eyeliner and mascara, and smeared
bruise-colored lipstick all over their mouths. One of them had her
arm around the man. The other had her hand on his chest,
entwining her black fingernails in his dense overgrowth.

The three of them sat there watching me intensely.

"You must be Theophrastus," I slurred. My lip was fatter
now, my tongue thicker. I must have bit into it when Ted head-
butted me. There was fresh blood in my mouth.

The hairy man smirked at me and gave Ted a go-ahead nod.

Ted reached down in front of me and locked a chain between
my wrists, around the coiled rope. I looked up and saw the other
end of the chain disappear into an engine hoist. Ted grabbed onto
the pulling chains and ran them speedily through his hands, one
over the other, gradually lifting my arms into the air.

"I said you must be Theophrastus," I said to the hairy man.

"Ted, tell your little piggie to shut the fuck up," he said.

"Shut the fuck up, piggie," Ted said, kicking my thigh.

The girls laughed, watching with excitement as my arms came up over my head and started drawing my torso up.

Ted kept up his pace. When my knees came off the ground, my weight pivoted me around. I was completely off balance. Ted hoisted me up until I was hanging straight, barely touching the gritty floor with the tips of my toes. He grabbed me and turned me around so I was facing the audience on the couch.

"If you're Theophrastus," I said, "you'd better let me down. The police are going to be coming by soon to talk with you."

"Ted, I'm tired of hearing all these pig snorts," the hairy man said. "Can't you put a goddamn muzzle on him?"

"I got just the thing," Ted said.

Behind me, Ted laughed. I heard duct tape being pulled off the end of a roll. He slapped the end of it over my mouth and wrapped the roll around the back of my head, going around it four times more before ripping the roll free from the tape. Then he tore off some more and wrapped it from under my jaw over the top of my head and back down. I couldn't open my jaw or speak.

"That's much better," the hairy man said, standing up. "You girls stay put and watch the show. It's going to be a goodie."

The jailbait blondes cozied up into each other's arms.

"Yes, I'm Theophrastus," the hairy man said, coming around the coffee table and off the carpet to stand before me. "And your name is mud, or shit, or piggie, or whatever I say."

All I could do was give him a look.

"Don't you be eyeballing me, piggie," Theophrastus said, landing a punch to my stomach. "I won't have none of that."

"How'd that feel, boss?" Ted asked, standing behind me and grabbing onto my love handles, holding me like a punching bag.

"Damn good," Theophrastus said. "I'll have me another."

Theophrastus punched me on the other side, near a kidney. Then he bent over to the floor, grabbed a handful of ice, and rubbed it over my stomach in the spots where he'd struck.

"Got to keep piggie toned up and ready for more," he said.

"Better than he deserves," Ted said.

"You probably don't even know why we're doing this to you, do you, piggie?" Theophrastus reached around my head and held it while he stared at me with yellowed, bloodshot eyes. "Look at me when I'm talking to you! None of this would be happening to you if you'd left well enough alone. Our Schenectady brothers warned you off once already, but then you came back, stole Lorelei away from them, and got them all busted."

I shook my head, not that it wasn't true. It was only that Theophrastus was misunderstanding why I was nosing around. The Lorelei Matheson case was over, as far as I was concerned. I had no personal vendetta against the Z. Z. Ryders. But I couldn't explain this to him. All I could say was *mmph*.

"Don't you try to tell me it's not true, piggie. We know who you are. Ol' Ted saw you last night with Lucrezia. You going to deny you were here? Ted recognized you. You came here to see me tonight packing a semi-auto. We've been through your wallet, piggie, so we know who you are. You're the same dick, all right. You know, I never got up to the Schenectady clubhouse that often, but I did pay them a visit before you came on the scene, and boy, did I get a good taste of sweet Lorelei!"

I jolted reflexively, wishing I could get at him.

"Easy to press his buttons, isn't it?" Theophrastus said with a toothy grin. "Take him up a little higher, Ted."

"You got it, boss," Ted said.

He hoisted me up so I was hanging entirely by my wrists, my feet a few inches off the floor, fingers numb, circulation nil. My arms were in pain—but it was a certain relief to no longer have any weight bearing down on my wounded shin.

"If you think we want to molest you, piggie, think again," Theophrastus said. "We were going to leave you in your shorts, but you weren't wearing any. Don't worry, I don't go in for gay shit. I'm not sure what all we're going to do with you. If we end up sticking something up your ass, don't think it's 'cause we love you. We just want to cause you some serious pain."

I wondered if what I'd told him was true, that the police would be coming. If Orjuedos was getting a search warrant for Karel's apartment, wouldn't he have to at least make contact with Theophrastus, the building's owner? I clung onto this, even though the thought of Orjuedos and his boys storming the basement and setting me free in the nick of time seemed insanely remote.

Theophrastus and Ted started double-teaming me, throwing punches to any broad section of flesh that turned their way — chest, abdomen, back, thighs. I spun in circles, bouncing off them, trying not to kick one of them for fear of reprisal (though I wondered what I had to lose, and how long I'd last).

As they were going at it, someone new entered the room. It was the tall, gaunt bartender who called himself Xerxes. He was grabbing a case of Rolling Rock down from a tall stack. He threw a casual glance at us, did a double-take, and set the case down.

"Wait, guys," Xerxes said, not very effectively. "Maybe you ought to stop layin' in to this guy."

"Mind your own goddamn business, Xerx," Theophrastus said.

"But this is the guy I was telling you about."

"I know who he is. He's a private dick who's been snooping around our operation. We've got an old grudge against him."

"I don't know anything about that," Xerxes said. "He's the guy I was talking to last night. He's been looking for Jared Foster.

He might be of some use to you, if you don't kill him."

"Wait, hold on a minute," Theophrastus said, putting out his arm to keep Ted from thrashing me some more. " *This* is the guy?"

Xerxes eyed me up and down: "Even beat up, looks like him."

"Lower him a bit, Ted, and get that tape off him."

Xerxes stalked off, hefted his case, and left the room.

I was gently lowered onto the balls of my feet, not that I had any strength left to hold myself up. Ted found the ends of the tape and ripped it all off my skin. My lip opened up afresh.

I was too busy breathing to say anything.

"Is that true?" Theophrastus said. "You're not here looking into my business? You're looking for Jared Foster?"

"Yeah," I said. "Let me down."

"Not so fast. I don't trust you enough."

"Let me down," I huffed. "I can't touch you now."

"Why did you come here looking for Jared?"

"He owed you some money, didn't he?"

"How do you know about that?" Theophrastus's eyes narrowed.

"Let me down, and I'll tell you."

Theophrastus shook his head and grinned: "No way, dick. I've got you where I want you. Who hired you to find Jared?"

"Henry Foster," I said. "His father."

Theophrastus didn't register any reaction to this.

"Maybe you know already where Jared is," he said.

"Maybe I do," I said.

"Maybe you do? Well, maybe you'd better tell me, piggie."

"Stop calling me that. I don't like it."

"Maybe you don't appreciate your situation," Theophrastus said, smacking me open-handed on the stomach. "I can do whatever the hell I want with you, and you can't do jack shit about it."

"The police are coming to talk to you," I said again.

Theophrastus pressed his hand against my trachea and began to squeeze. "How would you know, unless you put them onto me?"

I tried to speak but couldn't until he relaxed his hold.

"Nothing to do with me," I gasped. "They're interested in Karel's apartment."

"Karel?" Theophrastus laughed jovially and looked over at his girls, who just kept sitting there watching. "Karel who?"

"Karel Janáček. The kid who was murdered."

"I had nothing to do with that."

"That remains to be seen."

That earned me a slap across the face.

"Ted," Theophrastus said, not taking his eyes off me.

"Yes, boss?" Ted said.

"Give me the dick's gun."

Ted dug my Glock out of his craw. I hoped again it would go off and maim him. It didn't. Ted slapped it into Theophrastus's sweaty palm. It still didn't go off. Nice, reliable gun.

Theophrastus put it up against my temple.

"I know how to use one of these," he said, breathing hot and heavy into my face. He stank. "And don't kid yourself into thinking I won't do it. I'm trying to get you to realize the situation you've got yourself into, dick. I've got you strung up like a side of beef. Even if I let you down, you'd be too weak to move. I've got a mean, powerful gun aimed at your head."

"Okay," I said. "What do you want?"

"I want you to give me some answers," Theophrastus said, "and you're going to cooperate with me, like they do on *Sesame Street*. You understand? Cooperation, man, that's the name of the game. You cooperate with me, I might let you kiss my ass."

"Got it," I said. "Just like on *Sesame Street*."

"Don't get smart with me, either. I don't like you."

"Put the gun down, Theophrastus. You're making me nervous. You can always pick it up again if you don't like what you hear."

"Piggie has a point, Ted," Theophrastus said. He lowered the Glock and shoved it down the front of his leather pants.

"Start asking," I said. "You guys really fucked me up. I don't know how much longer I can hang here without passing out."

"We'll keep you awake," Ted said. "We got plenty more ice."

"Yeah, that's right," Theophrastus said. "Don't think we're going to try to make you more comfortable."

"What do you want to know?" I asked.

"Why are the cops interested in me?"

"They're searching Karel's apartment right now."

"That doesn't answer my question." Theophrastus spoke through clenched teeth. "What's that got to do with me?"

"Karel was one of your dealers, wasn't he?"

"The cops can't know that." Theophrastus was nervous.

"You were also his landlord, weren't you?"

"Yeah, so what?"

"The police are over there now, gathering evidence." Or they would be in another hour or two, but that didn't help me.

"Evidence?" Theophrastus said. "Evidence of what?"

"The murders were committed there, in Karel's apartment."

"Murders? I thought only Karel was murdered."

"Also Henry Foster," I said.

"I don't know nothing about either one."

"What about Juliet Logan and the two Chinese guys?"

"I heard about that," Theophrastus said. "What about it?"

"Nothing to do with you?" I was pressing my luck.

Theophrastus didn't seem offended by my question.

"I was here at my club all night," he said. "The first I heard of it was this afternoon. Why should I kill Juliet?"

"She was one of your dealers, too. Maybe she was screwing you. Who knows? Could be a lot of reasons."

"You seem to know a lot about me," he said. "For a fucking side of beef." His hand toyed with the butt of my Glock.

"Take it easy. You want to know everything I know, right?"

"It's cool," he said, taking his hand away. "So the cops know about my trade, and Juliet and Karel are dead, and Karel was killed in his apartment, in my building. So they want me?"

"They'll want to talk to you. I don't know what else."

"Oh, man!" Theophrastus paced a few steps in a tight circle like he was practicing his waltz. He slammed his fist against his palm, ran his fingers through his greasy hair. Sweat dripped off his chest, onto the concrete. "This really bites, Ted."

"I hear you," Ted said. "Find out what else he knows."

"You're right, you're right," Theophrastus said. "When you're right, you're right, Ted, and you *are* right. What the fuck has this got to do with Jared Foster?"

"Everything," I said.

"Don't get cryptic on me, man." Theophrastus grabbed my head and shook it and looked me straight in the eye. "Tell me!"

"Okay." I took a few deep breaths and tried to get my bearings. "I'm going to make a guess here. It's only a guess, so if I'm wrong, don't shoot me. You've been looking for Jared. Maybe not actively. You've been keeping your eye out for him. He dropped out of circulation. Mid-September. I'm guessing that was around the last time you saw him. When you demanded your money. Maybe Jared talked you into giving him one more chance. How much was it, a few thousand? Three, four?"

Theophrastus's upper lip twitched. "Three, originally," he said. "But Jared was two weeks late. I gave him a break. He got one more week, but I added another thou. Interest."

Sweet of you, I thought.

I said: "It was money for drugs. Heroin, is my guess. Only Jared never touched the stuff, did he?"

"I never seen him do it," Theophrastus said. "He's been down here in the lounge plenty of times when it was available. Jared never partook. Neither do I, tell you the truth."

"Serious dealers seldom do," I said. "Jared was buying heroin for somebody else. He ever tell you who?"

"You know so goddamn much, why don't you guess?"

"I'd guess it was his stepmother, Gloria."

Theophrastus nodded, grinning. "That's what he told me. Don't that take the cake? He was supplying her!"

"She was supplying him with the cash," I said. "She ran into a snag and couldn't pay. And you put the squeeze on Jared."

"He already had the stuff. I can't do business that way."

"Jared had no money. After Gloria failed to pay him, and after you threatened him, he disappeared." Kind of. I didn't want to bring up the rent money he'd left Anastasia. "Either he went looking for money, or he was trying to get away from you."

Theophrastus pulled absently at his beard, saying, "Huh."

"Maybe he was killed, like Karel and Dr. Foster," I said. "Or maybe Jared killed them himself. I don't know."

"I never met Henry Foster," Theophrastus said, thinking only of himself. He wasn't concerned about what might have happened to Jared, only about his money. "The cops can't tie me to that!"

"Yes, they could," I said. "They might think you killed Foster. To coerce Gloria into paying her drug debts."

"Shit." He'd never thought of that. "You're right."

"You've been tied up in another way," I went on, worrying a little about being the bad-news messenger. "Last night, Juliet Logan called Anastasia. Tipped her off to the burglary. She said you were behind it."

"That's a lie!" Theophrastus said.

"I know it is. Juliet was a compulsive liar. She used your name to frighten Anastasia, to keep her quiet. Anastasia wouldn't tell this to the police. She *is* afraid of you."

"Good," he said. "Let her stay that way."

"But I already told them," I lied. "The police aren't afraid of you. They don't know you from Adam. To them, you're a ready-made sucker. They'll slam the lid on your drug operation, shut down your club, and haul you in. While they're at it, they might as well pin five or so murders on you. Especially if they haven't got a clue who the real killer is. And don't get mad at me for telling you. I'm giving you some valuable information."

"Valuable how?"

"You've got a head start," I said. "You've got time to destroy your drugs, shred documents, whatever you've got to do."

Theophrastus rewarded me by putting the gun to my head.

"How do I know you're telling me the truth, dick?"

"Wait long enough, the police will be coming around."

"How long?"

"I wouldn't know. They're a little slower than I."

"Why'd you want to come see me tonight?"

"I wanted to ask you some questions. We've covered most of it. I wanted to know if you knew where I could find Jared. But you don't. I wasted my time and got the crap beat out of me."

"You've got some mouth," Theophrastus said, shaking my gun at me. "You should thank me and Ted for that beating."

"Yeah, thanks." I risked being shot for sarcasm.

It went over Theophrastus's head. I was safe.

"You said you knew where Jared was," he said.

"I said maybe I do."

"Ted, take this and hold it on him," Theophrastus said,

passing the gun over to his lackey. "Shoot him if he peeps."

Theophrastus spun around, blowing air out of his nose, and stormed out of the storage room, slamming the door. I heard another door slam—the one to his office, I supposed.

Ted stood in front of me with a shit-eating grin, holding my Glock slightly sideways. I wondered whether I could raise my knees quick enough to knock it out of his hands, but it seemed a bad idea. Even if it worked, even if I took him by surprise, the two blondes would probably pounce on the gun and do me in. They kept watching me like couch potatoes curled up with a good movie.

Doors slammed again, and Theophrastus was back. Ted stepped aside to give him room, but he kept the gun aimed at my chest.

"I'm going to give you something real special," Theophrastus said. He held up a large needle, about three millimeters in diameter and four inches long. "See this?"

"Yeah," I said.

"And this?" Theophrastus held up a thick silver ring.

"Yeah."

"Now, do you feel this?"

Theophrastus grabbed my cock in his fist.

"Yeah," I said. "I feel that."

"Don't think I get any kick out of touching it," he said. "No, but I do get a kick out of what I'm going to do to it. You ever seen a Prince Albert?"

"Wait a minute," I said, instinctively pulling away.

"Ted."

Ted stepped closer and jammed my Glock into my ribs.

"I asked if you've ever seen one," Theophrastus repeated.

"Karel had one," I said. "I saw it in the autopsy photos."

"Oh, yeah? Maybe they'll see one in your autopsy photos. I

gave Karel his—sort of an initiation—but I put some stuff on his dickhead to deaden the pain. You're not getting any."

Theophrastus lowered the giant needle toward my cock.

"Stop," I said on the edge of my breath.

"Tell me where Jared is," he said.

"I don't know."

"You said maybe you do."

"I said maybe because I'm not sure."

"I'd advise you to take a guess," he said calmly. "You must be a good dick if you found Lorelei Matheson. You're pretty good at guessing from a rough sketch. Go on, think. I'll give you one minute. Then you'll give me an answer. If you don't give me an answer, I'll pierce your dick, and we'll proceed from there. If you do give me an answer, and if I find Jared, I'll come back and let you go. If I *don't* find him, I *won't* let you go. I'll pierce your dick, and we'll proceed from there. Understand me?"

"Maybe you should give up on finding Jared," I suggested. "There've been five murders already. It might be dangerous."

Theophrastus pricked me lightly with the needle.

I flinched.

"No more shit," he said. "I asked if you understood me."

"I understand," I said, mindful of the needle.

"Good," he said. "Your minute's up. What's your guess?"

"It's a townhouse," I said. "Home of Dr. Willem Kirst. On East Sixteenth, off Irving Place. I can't remember the exact address. It's in my notepad, there, in my jacket."

Theophrastus withdrew the needle from the danger zone, set it down on the coffee table, and said: "For later."

TWENTY-NINE

ON THEOPHRASTUS'S INSTRUCTIONS, Ted lowered me onto the floor but left me bound hand and foot and chained to the engine hoist. I lay there on my sore stomach, with no chance of untying myself. My fingers remained numb and wouldn't respond to my commands.

Theophrastus asked Ted if he could round up some of his boys, and Ted said he was sure he could find a few of them over at a biker bar on West Eleventh. Ted said they could take his van. Theophrastus sent him upstairs, stretched himself into a black T-shirt, and left my Glock with the two young blondes.

"My girls Darcy and Marianna are going to take care of you while I'm gone," Theophrastus said, crouched on one knee and leaning over to look at me. "You heard my instructions to them?"

I nodded a solemn acknowledgment of the fact.

"Don't try anything funny," he warned. "I bet neither one of them has ever touched a semi-auto before. If you make them nervous, they're liable to empty that whole clip into your body."

I nodded again. He was probably right.

I glanced over at Darcy and Marianna, who were studying the gun on the coffee table and looking like a couple of vampirish Clara Bows.

"Me, Ted, and the boys are going to pay a call on this doctor friend of yours. You'd better pray Jared's with him."

"To God or to the Devil?"

Theophrastus pressed my face into the floor.

"A parting gift," he said, and stomped out.

I wanted nothing more than to lie there and recuperate, but I was afraid I'd fall asleep. Theophrastus might conceivably be back within the hour, and I could easily sleep that long. I wanted to get out before then. I wasn't exactly sure how to go about it.

"Don't you girls have school tomorrow?"

"Shut up, piggie!" one of them said from their perch.

"Which one of you is Darcy?"

"I am, and I told you to shut up!"

Darcy had a tattoo of the Grim Reaper on her right arm, and she had more flesh on her bones than her friend. Marianna was gaunt and had some kind of red demon goat on her left shoulder, with baroque curlicues slithering down the length of her arm. Other than that, they were dressed identically, with identical bandages wrapped around their left wrists.

"Did you girls cut yourselves?"

"We gave of our virgin blood to our lord Theophrastus," Marianna said, scratching at the perimeter of the bandage.

"Virgin blood?" I said. "I'll bet."

"He's mocking us," Darcy said to her friend.

Marianna smirked: "Worms can't mock, and that's all he is."

"Pig or worm?" I said. "Make up your minds."

"You were a pig when you were hanging," Darcy said. "Now

you're squirming on the floor, just a stupid worm."

"I'm squirming on the floor because your lord Theophrastus is imprisoning me against my will," I said. "That's a felony."

Darcy and Marianna stared at me dumbly.

"You girls aren't stupid," I said. "Maybe you think it's fun hanging around with Theophrastus, doing drugs and letting him drink your blood. I don't give a damn about that. But do you really want to be caught up in this? You're holding me here for him. You're willing accomplices to a very serious crime."

"I thought I told you to shut up," Darcy said.

"Shutting me up isn't going to change your predicament. Do either of you girls have a criminal record?"

"No," Marianna said, implying that was a stupid question.

"Well, you're going to," I said. "That is, unless you want to kill me now and shut me up forever. But I don't think you want to do that. That would be murder. I don't care how old you are, they'll try you as adults and send you to prison for life."

"Who said anything about killing you?" Darcy asked. "All we're doing is watching you till Theophrastus gets back."

"What if I try to escape? Aren't you supposed to shoot me?"

Neither of them responded.

"Do you really think you could do it? Shoot a man in cold blood?"

"We don't have to kill you," Marianna suggested. "We could just shoot you in the leg, teach you a little lesson."

"And risk letting me bleed to death? You don't know when Theophrastus is coming back. You might hurt me more than you counted on. I'm already in bad shape. If I died on you, what would happen to you? You'd get caught and sent to prison."

"Stop jabbering!" Darcy said. "We'll wait for Theophrastus to come back. You're his problem. We're just your guards."

"What authority does Theophrastus have to lock me up and

put guards on me?"

"He owns The Lot," Darcy said. "He can do what he wants."

"He still has to follow the same laws as everyone else. You heard the spiel I gave him. The police are very interested in Theophrastus. They're going to close this place down. Even if they don't pin those murders on him, they can get him on drug trafficking and dispensing alcohol to minors, if not statutory rape and tax evasion. You still want to worship this guy?"

"Theophrastus cares for us," Marianna said. "He takes us seriously."

"Yeah," Darcy concurred. "He doesn't talk down to us."

"He's just using you," I said. "He looks about thirty-five, and he has a thing for girls half his age. You tell him you're virgins, and he wants to suck your blood. Fine. He'll take it, and after he's had that, he'll take more from you. He'll use you up and throw you out with the garbage. Don't you girls want to have a future?"

Darcy laughed coldly and said: "There is no future."

"I don't know who told you that," I said.

"Nobody had to tell me, okay? I know it myself, for a fact. I could die tomorrow, don't you know that? I want to live and experience things other people are afraid to try. I'd like to do everything before I die. I'm not like other people."

"Marianna," I said. "You feel the same way?"

"Pretty much," Marianna said, shrugging.

"You both think you're special," I said.

"We're into pleasure," Darcy said. "Experiencing pleasure. Most people think they'll get theirs when they get to heaven. I don't want to wait. I want mine now."

"Does this give you pleasure, watching me get pummeled by your lord and master? Waiting for him to come back so he can hurt me some more? If you get pleasure out of that, you're no better than a Nazi. Why don't you get a swastika tattoo?"

"You're wrong," Marianna said. "Goths are anti-fascist."

"What do you know about fascists? You're willing to follow Theophrastus anywhere, just like the Germans did Hitler."

"No." Darcy had a superior smirk. "It's not like that."

"Well, you know what happened to Hitler. He went down. Theophrastus is going down, and there's nothing you or I can do to stop that. Do you girls want to be dragged down with him?"

For the first time, Darcy and Marianna looked at each other with something that might have been mistaken for intelligence.

"Prison is not a place you want to go," I said, hoping to pry myself out of here now that I had some leverage. "If you keep holding me here, you're accessories to a serious felony. There's no telling what Theophrastus might do when he comes back. Sure, he'll pierce my cock, but after that, what? He strikes me as an unstable type. What if he kills me? He'll ask you girls to stay quiet about it. That'll make you accessories to murder. If you want to experience pleasure, all those years in prison are going to be a big disappointment."

"What do you think we should do?" Marianna asked Darcy.

"Nothing," Darcy said. "Let me think."

I stayed quiet for a while to encourage her.

I worried about what I'd done, telling Theophrastus about Willem Kirst's townhouse. I could be way off base, of course. But if Jared really was there, I had put him in danger. There was no telling what Theophrastus might do to him, charged up as he was. For that matter, I had put Kirst in danger, even if he were merely an innocent player in all this. And I'd done all this to stave off a moment of pain that was going to come anyway if I didn't manage to convince the girls to let me go.

"You want some help?" I asked them.

"Shh!" Marianna said. "Darcy's thinking."

"Sorry," I said.

"We can't let him go without getting into trouble," Darcy said. "I don't want to make Theophrastus mad."

"Me, neither," Marianna agreed.

"Hey, girls," I said. "Is my wallet still lying around?"

"Check his pants," Marianna said.

Darcy got up and found the pile of my clothes.

"It might be in my jacket," I said.

"Here it is, I've got it."

"Is there still money in it?"

"There sure is," Darcy said.

"Count it," I said.

Darcy counted audibly until she was done: "Thirteen hundred sixty-two dollars in cash."

"If the two of you agree to cut my ropes and let me go out of here with my clothes, you can have all the cash."

"Really?" Darcy said.

Marianna got up from the couch: "Let me see, Darce!"

"It's a deal," Darcy said without conferring with her pal.

"One of you got a knife?" I asked.

"I do," Marianna said, digging a pocketknife out of a front pocket of her velvet pants. She sprung the largest blade and came over to me.

"Do my hands first," I said.

"Hurry!" Darcy said. "Theophrastus might come back!"

Marianna sawed feebly through the hemp.

"Throw your weight into it," I said. "Use some muscle."

I was saying this to a skeletal girl with little weight and no muscle. She was making progress, though.

Finally, my left wrist snapped free. My hand tingled as the blood surged back into the tissues, but it was still lifeless.

The ropes loosened around my right wrist. Marianna helped

me wriggle out. I slapped my free hands against the floor. My fingers started moving a little. I could barely feel them.

Marianna went to do my feet. One by one, the ropes popped.

My feet were free. I drew them up closer to me.

"Darcy, would you bring me my clothes, please?" I asked.

"Get them yourself," she said.

"My feet are numb," I said. "It'll save me some time if you just bring them over to me, all right?"

"Okay," Darcy said, dumping the pile in front of me.

"You two had better get out of here," I said.

"Thirteen hundred?" Marianna said. "How much do I get?"

Darcy counted out her half and said, "Here."

They ran out of the room. The door slammed behind them.

They never even touched my Glock. It still lay there on the coffee table, fully loaded, apparently undamaged.

Slowly, I worked my aching body into my clothes and my leather jacket. I put on my boots and stood with the assistance of a beer keg. I walked stiff-legged over to the coffee table, picked up my Glock, and put it in my shoulder holster.

I didn't want to risk leaving through the club. There was still a crowd upstairs, and there were probably still bouncers. They might have been given instructions to watch out for me. Worse yet, Darcy and Marianna might have told them I was loose.

There was a loading ramp at the back of the storage room that angled up toward a pair of corrugated iron doors in the ceiling. They were the kind of doors that opened onto the sidewalk so the beer trucks could unload straight down the ramp and into the basement.

I walked up the ramp and checked the doors. They were locked from inside with a heavy padlock. The lazy son of a bitch who last opened the doors had left the key in the lock, or maybe this was their common practice.

I turned the key just as two burly biker types were coming through the door to the storage room, saying: "That's the guy!"

I pushed the iron door open and scrambled up the ramp.

The first biker guy came up after me. I pitched the padlock down on top of his thinning pate, and he went sprawling down the ramp, knocking his buddy off his feet. I slammed the door shut.

I hobbled up to Houston Street and hailed a cab.

I asked the driver to take me to Ludlow Street.

Then I realized I had no money. I had him take me to an ATM machine on Second Avenue in the East Village. I took out some cash, and then we circled back down to Ludlow.

I paid the driver, tipped him well, and watched him go.

I unlocked the 'Cuda and climbed in to safety.

THIRTY

BUT THE 'CUDA was only the first step to the safe haven of my apartment. On my way back, I kept checking my rearview to make sure no one was following. I parked the 'Cuda on the street, half a block down from my building. The walk up to my apartment was murder. I went in, locked the door, and ditched my clothes on the floor. I went to the fridge and guzzled a quart of Gatorade. I went into the bathroom, avoiding all mirrors, and stepped into a steaming hot shower.

I never gave out my residential address to clients or to anyone other than friends, boyfriends, and my mother. My home phone is on my business card, but I'm not in the book. The last thing I needed was someone breaking in and messing with me while I was trying to get some rest—or showering.

My case was still going on without me, out there in the city. I had no choice but to let it play itself out for a while.

I'd be no good to anybody, least of all myself, if I pursued it any further now. I had to get some sleep. If I woke up and someone else was dead, it wouldn't be my fault. I kept playing that in my head like a mantra. I only hoped it was true.

I stayed in the shower until my fingers were pruning. I grabbed a towel and dried myself off. It was a white towel, and it came away with little pink and red stains. The full-length mirror on my bathroom door showed abrasions, bruises, and cuts from my head to my toes. I sat on the edge of the tub and tended to my wounds with rubbing alcohol and cotton balls. I fixed a couple of Band-Aids across the stab wound to my shin. It needed a few stitches, and I needed a tetanus booster, but screw it.

My futon couch was still lying flat in the bed position like I'd left it yesterday morning, sheets and pillows making hills and valleys like some austere alien landscape. My alarm clock said it was four-fifteen. I set the alarm for nine-thirty and double-checked to make sure I had it on A.M.. It wouldn't be enough sleep, but too bad. The pigeons would be showing up in a couple of hours; I was counting on being oblivious. I turned off the ringer on my phone, lay down on the mattress, and crashed.

Another shower on waking, a pot of coffee, and some stretching — some very careful stretching. It had been a long time since I'd had a gut-punching like the one Ted and Theophrastus had given.

I turned the ringer on and checked my answering machine. No one had called, not even Orjuedos. The last we'd spoken, he wanted to bust my ass. Not in the way I wanted him to. I hoped he was getting a good night's sleep. I doubted it, somehow.

I no longer had a client, and I'd donated most of Foster's advance to Carmelita, Darcy, and Marianna. Orjuedos's threats were real enough, though. I couldn't trust him to wrap up the case in a way that left me totally clear. I had to determine what had become of Jared Foster, even if it was now pro bono.

My livelihood, such as it was, was at stake.

I put on blue jeans, white T-shirt, black boots, shoulder holster, Glock, and motorcycle jacket. I was out of cigarettes.

I made one phone call, to some desk guy at the Plaza Hotel:

"I'd like to speak with one of your guests, Gloria Glendenning-Foster," I said, spelling it for the guy and making sure he got the hyphen. "I think she said she's in room 913."

"I'm sorry, sir," the guy said. "Ms. Glendenning-Foster is no longer staying with us. She checked out this morning."

"Thank you very much," I said.

"You've most welcome," he said as I was hanging up on him.

I turned off the coffee pot, locked up my place, and went stiffly down the stairs and out the door. A traffic cop was making her way down the street in a three-wheeled Cushman, two cars down from the illegally parked 'Cuda. I got to it in time and moved along, giving the traffic cop a wave in my rearview.

I kept an eye open for Gloria in her Mercedes.

I planned to keep it open all day.

I drove up Tenth Avenue to West Fifty-Third Street, to the old converted warehouse that housed Hell's Kitchen Studios. A motley crew of vacationing tourists and jobless New Yorkers was queuing up outside, down the block, and around the corner, drinking coffee. A sign at the entrance told me they were the audience-in-waiting for the 11:00 A.M.. taping of *The Betsy Morgan Show*.

A husky black female security guard in a close-fitting blue uniform stopped me with her arms out before I could set foot in the building. At the top of her voice, she chanted at me:

"If you're here for *The Betsy Morgan Show*, the line starts here and goes all the way back. This line is for the eleven o'clock taping *only*. The line for the one o'clock taping will start forming at eleven-thirty. Seats are first-come, first-served. We don't offer advance tickets. No saving seats."

She would brook no interruptions. I let her speech run out. She tried to usher me away from the door.

"I'm not here for the taping," I said.

"Excuse me?"

"I'm not here for the taping. I'm a private investigator. Here's my license. I'd like to go in and talk with one of your producers, if I may."

"In relation to?" She stared dubiously at my P.I. license.

"A murder investigation."

Her eyes darted up to mine, then took in the cuts and bruises all over my stubbly bald head.

"Five murders, actually," I amended.

"I'll have to clear it." She was officious.

She went over to her security desk and picked up a white phone, keeping her eyes on me. She appeared to be on hold.

I stepped in and approached the desk.

"Wait until I say you can come in," she said.

I waited. Finally, she muttered a few words into the phone and read some information off my license. I heard her give a unique, French-Caribbean pronunciation of my last name. She hung up the phone and wrote out my name on a red name-tag sticker so that it read, in toto, "Hello, my name is *Greg Q.*"

"That's your visitor's pass," she said, handing it to me, along with my license.

"Do I have to wear it?" I asked.

"Yes, you do," she said. She waited for me to put it on.

I stuck it on my leather jacket: "How's that?"

"That's just fine. Now go through those double doors and take a left down the hall to reception. But don't you expect to get to talk to Ms. Morgan. She's too busy all day taping."

"I was hoping I wouldn't have to," I said. "Frankly."

*   *   *

I told the receptionist my business and waited for someone to come out and talk to me. I tried to avoid looking at the giant monitors all around the room, which kept showing Betsy Morgan's smiling talk-show face as she fielded audience questions. It was impossible to tune out the audio, though. The guests on this particular show were mother-and-daughter hookers. Betsy Morgan kept promising gleefully that at the end of the show, we were going to meet a grandmother, mother, and daughter who were all still actively turning tricks.

"Is that the show being taped now in the studio?" I asked the receptionist.

She was a big-haired blonde with too much rouge and eye shadow, looking something like the mother-daughter hookers.

"No," she said. "That show's already aired. Ms. Morgan likes us to keep tapes of her show running continuously."

"Oh," I said. "I'm sorry for you."

Eventually, a bookish young woman emerged from a hallway with her arm stretched out toward me. She had stringy brunette hair and crooked wire-framed glasses over a crooked set of tobacco-stained teeth. She wore a beige cardigan over a white turtleneck, with khaki slacks. Her nails were bitten short.

"Roz Ingram," she said. "I'm an assistant producer."

I stood up, shook her hand, and gave her my card. "Greg Quaintance, private investigator."

"You were inquiring about one of our shows?"

"Is there somewhere we could talk?"

"My office," she said. "Come this way."

I followed her to a modular cubicle wrapped in blue burlap with snapshots of her children tacked up all over. Nice office. Roz Ingram had fudged her title a little; she was maybe an assistant to an assistant producer, or maybe an intern. I had to pull up another chair from an unused cubicle. She started to make small talk about her lovely kids.

"I don't have a lot of time," I said. Or interest in your kids. "I'm working with the police on a murder investigation."

"What has that got to do with us?" Roz's smile grew higher.

"Five people have been murdered," I said.

"Oh, my goodness, a serial killer?"

"We don't know," I said. "At least one of the victims, a Karel Janáček, was a guest on one of your shows."

"Oh, dear me," Roz said, frowning for one brief moment before recapturing her professional smile. "Which show?"

"Apparently, you taped a show back in September about real-life vampires. Maybe I should say goths. People who go to goth clubs, dress as vampires, drink blood, stuff like that."

Roz flinched with disgust. "Yes, I remember the show."

"It hasn't aired yet, has it?"

"No, that show is scheduled for Halloween."

"That's what I thought. I was wondering if I could have a look at it?"

"What for?"

I told her the manner in which Karel had been killed. I also told her about Jared Foster's disappearance and mentioned he had also been one of Betsy Morgan's guests.

Roz started taking notes on some pretty pink paper.

"My goodness! This would make a great follow-up show!"

I snatched the pink paper off her pad, crumpled it into a ball, and tossed it into her garbage pail.

"One kid is dead," I said. "Another is missing. The missing kid's father has also been murdered. A few witnesses to an apparently related crime were also killed. Probably all by the same person. I'm pursuing every good lead I've got. All I want is to see the tape of the show, if it's at all possible."

"I'll go ask," Roz said, suitably cowed. She got up and left her cubicle, heading briskly down the carpeted hall.

I sat there pleased with myself. Then I was humbled with the realization that my arrogant macho routine only worked on certain women like Roz and got me nowhere with others, like the security guard outside.

My beeper went off while I was sitting there. I compared it with the ones on my notepad and discovered it was Willem Kirst.

Roz came back and said I had their permission to see the footage, but the show wasn't exactly ready yet. The editors still had to put it together. As it happened, they were scheduled to start work on it this afternoon. I asked if they could maybe drop what they were doing and get to it now. Roz smiled and gave me a polite no. I decided further intimidation tactics would be inappropriate, if not futile; Roz probably wielded less power than the editors. She said I could come back at one o'clock and sit with the editors in their booth while they worked on it, if I promised not to disturb them. I said I could manage that.

I went across the street to a corner deli and bought a pack of unfiltered Lucky Strikes from a middle-aged Korean cashier.

The cashier handed me my change with a chortling laugh and said, "Thanks, Greg Q."

"Hmm?" I said. "Oh, thanks."

I ripped the embarrassing visitor's pass from my jacket and threw it in a garbage can on the street along with the cellophane wrapper. I puffed on a cigarette and limped over to a pay phone.

THIRTY-ONE

"MY HOME WAS burglarized last night, Mr. Quaintance, and I'm holding you responsible." Willem Kirst's voice was shrill.

"Why's that?" The cigarette helped me remain cool.

"You know perfectly well why."

"I'm at a loss. I didn't burglarize your place."

"I didn't say you did," Kirst said. "I said I'm holding you responsible. You said something to somebody that made them want to come over and pay me a visit at three-thirty in the morning."

"You're not making much sense."

"Four men, Mr. Quaintance. Large men wearing women's hose on their heads, waving guns around. One of them sat me down in my own living room and kept me there with a loaded revolver in my mouth while the others ransacked my entire house. They made off with family heirlooms and other valuables. Before they left, they tied me up. It took me hours to untie myself, but by then they were long gone."

"Are you all right?"

"Of course I'm not all right!" Kirst said. "I felt like I was going to have a heart attack! Physically, I'm okay, I suppose. They didn't actually *hurt* me. I still feel violated."

"Anyone would," I said. "I don't understand why you're blaming me. What have four masked burglars got to do with me?"

I was concerned that Theophrastus might actually have given him my name for some perverse reason. If so, Kirst was cryptic.

"They kept asking for Jared Foster," Kirst said. "Several times, as a matter of fact. I was under the impression they came looking for Jared, and when they didn't find him, they decided to make off with my valuables. The only person I've talked to about Jared Foster is you. I put two and two together, and I get you."

"I'm not the only one you talked to, Dr. Kirst."

"Yes, you are."

"You're forgetting Henry Foster."

"Well, yes, but he's—" Kirst's voice faltered.

"Yes?" I prompted.

"Hank's dead," Kirst said with more confidence. "Didn't you read the papers this morning?"

"No," I said.

"It's all over the news. The police think they're on the trail of a serial killer. Hank was killed in the same manner as that Karel person. The one you told me about, the friend of Jared's. The papers are calling him the Downtown Vampire."

"Jared?"

"I didn't mean that," Kirst said. "Whoever the killer is, that's the moniker they've given him."

"Has Gloria Glendenning-Foster been in touch with you?"

"No. Why should she?"

"Just wondering," I said.

"Are you going to continue to deny that you put somebody

up to searching my house?" Kirst was breathing heavily. It came through loud and clear, even over the bad pay phone connection.

"You're giving me a different story now," I said. "All you said at first was that you held me responsible. Now you're suggesting that I put someone up to it. And since when is a burglary a search?"

"Private investigators are not the most reputable of persons," Kirst said.

"Not as reputable as doctors, anyway. Come off it, Kirst. You've been seeing too many movies. Any private eye who tried to pull something like that would lose his license in nothing flat."

"That's what I intend to see happen to you. The truth will out, Mr. Quaintance. You can't get away with an illegal search."

"I had nothing to do with it, Dr. Kirst. If you pursue this, you're going to have egg all over your face."

"I'll pursue it to the fullest," he said with a laugh. "I intend to hire a private investigator of my own to look into what you've been up to. He'll find the evidence. We'll take you to court. I'll sue you for everything you've got."

"You're welcome to it," I said. I made a mental reservation on one point: the 'Cuda. If worse came to worst, I'd transfer the title to my mother's name and hide it in her garage. "Don't waste the effort, Kirst. There's nothing in it. I'm clean."

"I'll find a way, Mr. Quaintance. Whatever it takes, I'll find a way to fix you. You'll be sorry you ever messed with me."

"Is that a threat?"

"You decide," he said.

"Did you stop to consider that maybe Henry Foster mentioned your name to his killer before he died? Seems more likely to me that the killer would be the one hiring armed thugs to go over to your place looking for Jared."

"I thought Jared was the cops' number-one suspect. He

wouldn't send people over to look for himself. Makes no sense."

"It makes no sense if you think Jared's the killer," I said. "I don't happen to think he is. I think it's somebody else."

"If so, it's probably some psycho we've never heard of. Some goth kid he met in one of these vampire nightclubs, someone who developed a weird fixation on Jared. Some very sick person."

"I'm sure he's very sick," I said. "Whoever he is."

"If so," Kirst went on, "he couldn't have know anything about me. Which leads me back to you. I'm mad as hell. No one breaks into my home and gets away with it. I know for a fact that you were behind it. I'm going to ruin you, Mr. Quaintance."

"Talk to my lawyers," I said flippantly. "The next time you want to make wild accusations against somebody, get some evidence first. You're a scientist. You ought to know the value of evidence. Learn the facts before you go off half cocked."

"Oh, I'm fully cocked, Mr. Quaintance," Kirst said with a note of excitement in his voice. "I've got a full complement of bullets in my cylinder and the hammer drawn back. I'm ready."

I was about to tell him good luck when he hung up on me.

The line reverted to the dull drone of the dial tone.

I dropped in another quarter and called Orjuedos's number.

Orjuedos wasn't in.

I tried his beeper and left the number of the pay phone.

I hung around the pay phone like a drug dealer, waiting for it to ring. I waited fifteen minutes, then gave up.

I had things to do and little time to waste.

THIRTY-TWO

IT WAS NOON when I got to the J. Walker Hamilton Sleep Disorders Clinic. The door scraped annoyingly as I entered. The waiting room was just as shabby as it had been yesterday, with nobody waiting in it. The banana tree was still dying, ignominiously. The stoner weekend receptionist was gone, though, replaced by a round-faced woman of fifty with gray-streaked hair, bags under her eyes, and jowls that drooped like a basset hound's. I told her I'd like to experience the Magical Millhauser Mystery Tour.

"Pardon?" she said, blinking extravagantly.

"I'd like to speak with Jennifer Millhauser," I said.

"One moment, please." She pressed a button on her phone bank and spoke into the speaker. "There's a man here to see you. Says he wants the Magical Millhauser Mystery Tour."

"He must have been speaking to Ray," said a woman's voice over the intercom, accompanied by not unpleasant laughter. "Tell the gentleman I'll be right out."

"Ms. Millhauser will be right out," the receptionist said.

I thanked her and took a seat. I leafed through a yellowed trifold pamphlet: *How Do I Know If I Have A Sleep Disorder?*

"I'm Jennifer Millhauser." She was tall and leggy, in dark hose, black pumps, a brown narrow skirt, and a green double-breasted blazer with gold buttons. Her black hair was cut short and choppy in a way that made me think of Vidal Sassoon. She wore wide, narrow glasses in tortoise-shell frames and a golden name tag that said JENNIFER MILLHAUSER – PUBLIC RELATIONS.

I stood to meet her and said, "Greg Quaintance." Her eyes played over my battered face as we shook hands. I handed her a card. She was the first person I'd run across in a long time who seemed impressed. "I'm working with the police on the case of this so-called Downtown Vampire. Maybe you read about it in the papers. I was wondering if I could ask you a few questions."

"By all means," Jennifer Millhauser said with a more genuine smile than I deserved. "Let's talk in my office, shall we?"

Hers was a real office, with real walls and room enough for a real desk and a collection of filing cabinets. The walls were decked with framed posters marking past exhibits at the Whitney. She had no windows, though, and her various potted plants were dying as miserably as those in the waiting room.

"I spoke the other day with Dr. Willem Kirst," I said.

The cords in Jennifer's neck tightened. "And?"

"He told me something about the clinic, but he neglected to mention he'd been let go as director. Either he didn't want me to know, or he's in denial over it. What do you make of that?"

"He is in denial," Jennifer said. "I'm sure of that. He seems to think this will blow over and he'll get his job back."

"No chance?"

"None," she said.

"I bullied Ray into telling me what it was about," I said. "He told me it was some kind of sexual harassment case."

"I can't discuss it. It's a pending legal matter. What has all this got to do with this Downtown Vampire of yours?"

"I'm not sure. I was hoping you could help me with that."

"I don't know how. All I know about the murders is what I read in the papers this morning. Gruesome case, isn't it?"

"Yes, it is," I said. "At the heart of the case is a young man who's been missing these last few weeks. The police consider him a suspect. The victims whose blood was drained were a friend of his and his own father. Three others were killed with guns. I came to you because I'm searching for this young man. He was a frequent patient at your clinic."

"What was his name?"

"It was—and is, I hope—Jared Foster."

Those beautiful tendons grew taut on Jennifer's neck again.

"Jared Foster?" she repeated. "The Downtown Vampire?"

"I didn't say he was. The police think he might be. Jared wouldn't currently be under care here at the clinic, would he?"

"He is not," Jennifer said. "I've been trying to get in touch with him for the last few weeks, as a matter of fact, with no success. I was wondering what had become of him."

"Why would you be trying to reach him? Would it have anything to do with the sexual harassment case against Kirst?"

"I told you I can't discuss it." She looked away briefly.

"It does have something to do with it. Jared Foster was the patient who complained against Kirst, wasn't he?"

Jennifer Millhauser stared impassively, then turned her gaze to avoid me. She swallowed hard and said, "I can't discuss it."

"Jared was here undergoing treatment for sleepwalking. What happened? He woke up to find Kirst fondling him or something?"

"I have no authority to get into the details of the case."

"And Jared filed a complaint, getting Kirst into trouble," I went on. "There must have been some kind of evidence to back Jared up, or Kirst would never have been fired. Videotape of the session, maybe? An unbiased witness? Physical evidence, maybe? It could have been more than fondling. Jared could have been raped. A medical examination would have provided evidence."

"Stop it," Jennifer said, slamming her eyes shut. "It will do you no good to go on like this. I'm forbidden to discuss it."

"Whatever happened," I said, "you basically told me there's no chance in hell that Kirst will get his job back."

"In a nutshell, yes. All for the good of the clinic."

"Did Kirst have a history of complaints?" I asked futilely. "Maybe unfounded ones? Jared's complaint was the last straw?"

"There had been other complaints," Jennifer said. "That's not relevant to the other case, so I'm free to tell you that."

"But they were unproved," I said. "Finally, you had proof."

"We had sufficient cause to terminate Kirst's directorship."

"What was he like to work for?"

"Difficult," Jennifer said. "Demanding, arrogant, possibly corrupt. Since his departure, we've discovered financial irregularities. The structure that was in place was too loose, and it seems Dr. Kirst often took advantage of his privileges."

"As well as his patients," I added drily. "He was a man who took what he wanted, then?"

"Dr. Kirst saw the clinic as his own private domain, where he reigned supreme. He was far too overextended professionally to run the clinic adequately, though. He had too many other responsibilities at the university and at the medical center. Our new director is much better suited to the position, and so far I don't see any signs of megalomania in her."

"So you would describe Kirst as a megalomaniac?"

"I'd say that's accurate," Jennifer said.

"You say it's a pending matter, and you've been trying to get in touch with Jared. Will your case against Kirst be in jeopardy if somehow you were never able to talk to Jared again?"

"I wouldn't put it that way," Jennifer said mildly. "But I certainly hope we get to talk again with Jared."

"Me, too," I said. "Tell me, did you ever have a young man by the name of Karel Janáček here as a patient?"

"I'll check the database." Jennifer turned to her computer and ran through a series of screens. I spelled the name out for her, not bothering with the accents. They wouldn't have entered them, anyway. "Sorry, no record of that name. I tried a few alternate spellings, just in case, but I can find nothing."

"It was worth a shot," I said. "I'm just trying to figure out all the connections here. It's not easy. Could you check two more names for me? Juliet Logan and Henry Foster."

"I recognize those names from the paper," Jennifer said as she keyed in her query. "Is this Karel Janáček the one who's unidentified? I remember reading there was a tattoo."

"Yes," I said. "The official identification is being made today, but that's him." I wondered whether Evelyn and Gustav Grosse had made it into the city yet. I'd asked them to call me when they got in. They had a lot on their minds, though.

"No record of Juliet Logan or Henry Foster," Jennifer said. She turned to face me, and one of her eyebrows went up. "Since you dug so much information out of me without my even telling it to you, maybe you can do the same for me."

"Shoot," I said.

"You wouldn't be thinking that maybe Willem Kirst is your Downtown Vampire, would you?"

"I'm afraid I can't discuss it," I said apologetically.

"If he is," she said, "I hope you nail the son of a bitch."

"Or drive a stake through his heart," I suggested.

Jennifer Millhauser smiled with pleasure at the thought.

THIRTY-THREE

I GOT BACK to Hell's Kitchen Studios by one o'clock and was issued another visitor's pass. Roz Ingram took me back to the editing booth, a dark room full of television monitors and stacks of three-quarter-inch videotapes and computer equipment and tiny lights and switches. Roz introduced me to the two editors. One was a forty-year-old Italian guy named Vince with a thick head of hair and two days' growth of stubble along a nicely shaped jaw. I shook his hand, and he looked right up into my eyes. He had a darkly tanned arm covered with long black hairs. Vince was sexy. The other guy was closer to my age, with thinning blond hair and a dark beard, named Curt. I shook his hand, too, but my eyes didn't stray as long on him. Curt was no Vince.

Roz smiled painfully at us and backed out of the room.

"What's the story with Roz?" I asked after the door closed.

"She doesn't get enough," Curt said.

"So give her some," Vince suggested.

"I don't do charity cases."

"I don't see you datin' no Drew Barrymores."

They turned to face their monitors, but all the screens showed were colored stripes. I was left looking at the backs of their heads. Vince's hair had a feathery texture. I wanted to reach out and stroke it. He was wearing a thin knit shirt that draped over his shoulders. He kept reaching forward, pressing buttons and pushing videotapes into slots. I watched his shoulders move.

"So you're a private dick, huh?" Vince said, still with his back turned. "What's this about?"

I briskly ran through some of it, basically letting him know I was searching for the police's number-one suspect, who was one of the guests on the *Betsy Morgan* they were about to edit.

"You shittin' me?" Vince looked over his shoulder at me.

I shook my head no and tried to give him a charming smile— though I didn't know how much charm I had left, beat up as I was.

"It's the truth," I said. "I promise not to bother you guys. I'll just sit here and watch you do your stuff."

"What are you lookin' for on the show?" Vince asked.

"I don't know," I said. "If there is anything, I'll know it when I see it. This could be a bust, for all I know."

"This show's always a bust," Curt said snidely.

"Ghosts and goblins, witches and warlocks," Betsy Morgan said, speaking deadpan into the camera with a phallic microphone beneath her button chin. "Today is Halloween, that favorite day of children—and of dentists—when our little girls and boys dress up in spooky costumes and play ghoul for a day. Well, on today's show, we're going to introduce you to some girls and boys who grew up and decided that one day out of the year just wasn't enough for them. You can see them all over the streets of New York, and yes, even at the suburban malls. They like to dress up as vampires. Some of them even want to *be* vampires. They call themselves 'goths,' and for them, *every* day is Halloween. Stay tuned, and we'll be right back with today's show: 'The Invasion of the Goths.' I'm Betsy Morgan, and we'll be right back."

"Ugh," Curt said.

They hadn't had to do any editing on the intro, but now they had to add material indicating the time-out till the end of the commercial break. Vince and Curt worked together effortlessly. For them, every day was *The Betsy Morgan Show*. Ugh, indeed.

The first guest to be introduced was Sebastian, identified as a goth club deejay and goth photographer. He was looking good, in skin-tight black leather pants and a ruffly crimson shirt with loosened lacings crisscrossing his smooth chest. Examples of his photography were cut into the mix.

Betsy Morgan asked him some softball questions about how the goth subculture started, and Sebastian did his best to explain how a few new wave bands in Britain in the early 1980s were described as "gothic" by a pop music magazine because of their look, the introspection of their lyrics, and the darkness of their sound. Cut to Betsy Morgan nodding and smiling. Sebastian took the hint and sped up the history, explaining how the fans adopted the look of their favorite bands and started calling themselves goths.

"So this really started with the music," Betsy Morgan said. "What is it that would attract teenagers to morbid songs about death, blood, and gore? How did we get to where we are now, where the kids actually want to *be* vampires? Is there something in the music that's infecting their minds?"

"No," Sebastian said. "Life can be pretty horrific. Pop culture reflects that. Horror has been a part of the mass media since people began telling stories. The most popular stories of today are in the lyrics of popular songs. You could think of goth songs as being the musical equivalent of horror fiction."

"And a lot of you do read Stephen King novels, am I right?"

"Anne Rice," Lucrezia peeped up from the far end of chairs.

Cut to the audience, where some goth types were sitting, all made up and wearing their best club clothes. They cheered the mention of Anne Rice—and Lucrezia's swipe at the host.

"Same difference, isn't it?" Betsy Morgan said.

"Noooo," Lucrezia said, shaking her head from side to side.

"Whatever." Betsy Morgan turned back to Sebastian.

It went on like this for a while. I admired Sebastian for coming on and trying to show that goths were regular, sane folk. But I knew this wouldn't last long. The guests would have been interviewed by assistant assistants like Roz before they went on, and Betsy Morgan's questions were carefully scripted to allow the show to slide ever deeper into sensationalism.

The seating arrangement itself dictated this. It began on the far right with Sebastian and a couple of goth club kids I'd never met. Betsy Morgan was talking to these kids now, asking them what they got out of the music and the fashion, which was evidently all it was to these particular goths. After them, moving to the left, we were going to meet Jared and Karel, who were sitting for now with amused smirks on their faces. Then would come Lucrezia. Betsy Morgan was saving the best for last: the Satanic-looking Theophrastus himself, flanked on either side by Darcy and Marianna, who kept reaching over and touching him.

The show didn't play out in realtime for me. Vince and Curt kept stopping it here and there, choosing the right spots to cut away from the guests to the host or the audience. I'd already been in the booth forty-five minutes by the time we got through the first fifteen minutes of what would be an hour-long show.

After another commercial break, we got to Jared and Karel. Their chairs were positioned close together, and they were shown in a two-shot. Jared had his arm around Karel's shoulders. They both had pale, powdered faces, black eyeliner and mascara, slight swaths of rouge under their gaunt cheek bones, and deep red lipstick. Their makeup was similar enough, I assumed they had done each other. They both wore black stretch jeans. Jared was in the same Byronic frilly white shirt he'd worn in the photo on Anastasia's wall, unbuttoned to his waist and falling open to reveal the dragon and shrunken head tattoos and his small pink nipples with large silver rings through them. Karel was wearing a tight black T-shirt advertising the band Marilyn Manson.

"Now, Jared and Karel are an anomaly among our guests," Betsy Morgan went on, "in that those are their actual names. Everyone else on our panel today has dropped what they consider their boring, square given names and chosen a more exotic name for themselves. Jared, Karel, why did you keep your names?"

"That's a boring question," Jared said, turning to smile at Karel. The goths in the audience whistled their approval.

The show was going to degenerate from here. Betsy Morgan came across as every rebellious teenager's worst nightmare of a never-understanding suburban mother, and it wasn't going to help her much with today's guests and their allies in the audience.

"Okay, we'll skip the names," Betsy Morgan said. "Karel, you're from Eastern Europe, are you not?"

"I'm from Prague," Karel said. "What's your point?"

"Only that many of us associate vampires with Eastern Europe, countries like Romania, for instance. I was wondering if your interest in vampires stems in any way from your heritage."

Karel emitted a curt laugh: "No. I don't know of any vampires in my family. My dad was a Communist bureaucrat."

"I notice you actually have fangs," Betsy Morgan said. Then, to the cameramen: "Can we get in there tight and show everybody on the monitors?"

Karel obediently widened his mouth into a grimace.

Vince cut to the close-up of Karel's filed-down incisors.

"Jesus Christ," Curt said. "Will you look at that."

"That's the first one who was killed," I told them.

"Now, you filed those down yourself," Betsy Morgan said.

The same close-up footage was being shown on a monitor for the studio audience. The non-goths among them groaned in revulsion. Vince spliced in a reaction shot of the audience looking grossed out. They hadn't seen anything yet, I thought.

"Why do you want vampire teeth, Karel?"

"So I can suck people's blood," Karel said with bravado.

Back to the audience for a reaction shot and more groans.

"Now, I've heard of this," Betsy Morgan allowed. "There are actually some goths who are into drinking the blood of their sex partners. I assume it's always consensual?"

"Usually," Karel said with a half-smirk.

"Aren't you worried, I mean, in this day and age—"

"In this day and age," Vince muttered disgustedly. "The all-purpose euphemism for AIDS. Why can't she just say it?"

Karel explained that he only sucked the blood of people he was seriously involved with, people he trusted were being honest with him when they informed him of their HIV status.

"Jared is one of your closest friends, is he not?"

"Yeah," Karel said, grinning with pleasure and giving Jared a sweet, intimate glance. "Jared's my best mate."

"Are you just friends?" Betsy Morgan was nosy. "Or are the two of you lovers? I guess what we all want to know is, Karel, do you suck Jared's blood?"

"Jared doesn't let me suck his blood," Karel said. "But I do suck his cock."

"Whoa," Curt said. "Stop it right there. Are we going to bleep that out, or just cut the whole thing, or what?"

"No, wait," Vince said. "Let it run for a bit. We'll come back and deal with it."

The audience had a curiously mixed response—clapping, groans of disgust, laughing, whistling, cheering, folded arms.

"I have to tell him to watch the teeth," Jared said.

Betsy Morgan's jaw had by this time dropped to the floor.

Karel turned to Jared and gave him a look. Jared drew Karel closer. They locked lips and began sucking each other's tongues. Karel's hand went onto Jared's chest and dove all the way down into his pants. You could see Karel's hand moving around inside.

"Okay," Vince said, stopping it. "I say we just cut Karel and Jared's audio from the cocksucking part on, and for the rest of it, we'll just stay on Betsy's jaw-dropping and the audience squirming. We'll leave the rest to the viewers' imaginations."

"Fine with me," Curt said. "Let's try it."

To keep us from lingering too long on Betsy Morgan, they worked in a variety of audience shots. I was watching their master monitor. Suddenly, a couple of familiar faces leapt out at me from the audience—a couple of non-goth faces.

"Wait," I said. "I'm sorry, guys, can you go back to that shot for a second? The last one you used of the audience?"

"Sure thing," Vince said. "What's so special about it?"

I leaned closer to the monitor. The faces were small.

"Can you do something fancy and tighten up on these two faces for me? Not for your master tape, just for my benefit. I want a closer look at those faces."

I pointed out the ones I had in mind.

Vince used the mouse on his computer to mark a rectangular portion of the stilled image and blow it up for me. It lost some definition in the blow-up, but the larger size confirmed their identities for me.

"How's that?" Vince asked.

"Perfect," I said.

Dr. Willem Kirst was there in the audience, looking red in the face and absolutely livid as he watched Karel and Jared making out. Sitting right next to him was Juliet Logan, looking every bit as angry and upset as Kirst.

"That's what I was looking for," I said. "Can I ask you guys to do me a favor and make a copy of that whole segment, unedited, with Karel and Jared kissing? Along with a blow-up of that image from the audience? I know it's a lot of trouble, but I want to show it to the police. It could be important."

"If you say so," Vince said. "It shouldn't take us too long to put that together. You want it on regular VHS, don't you?"

"Yeah."

"What's so important about it?"

I told him I wasn't sure.

Once I had my VHS tape in hand, I had a strong urge to go. But I couldn't be sure there wasn't something else important on *The Betsy Morgan Show*, so I stuck around to watch them do the rest.

Betsy had gone to a commercial break after Karel and Jared got out of hand. When she returned, she turned to Jared:

"Jared, I understand you've always been drawn to horror movies, gothic music, and anything and everything to do with vampires. Do you have any idea where this impulse come from?"

"I used to think it was just a natural part of me," Jared said, shrugging. "You know, something bred in the bone. I had my friend Lucrezia over there hypnotize me. She was going to take me back to my past lives to see if there was some clue to who I might have been in some other age. But first, she took me back to my childhood, and we learned something more important."

"What was that?" Betsy Morgan asked.

"My father sexually abused me from when I was six years old

until about the age of twelve. He would come down into my bedroom late at night and rape me. My own father. I think that's where my sense of alienation comes from. Those memories were repressed in my mind until Lucrezia brought them out. I never really felt a part of my own family. I always felt like some alien who'd fallen out of the sky, like David Bowie in *The Man Who Fell to Earth*. I mean, when your own dad thinks so little of you that he takes that innocence away, what do you think's going to be left? Nothing, really. That's what I feel inside, a big nothing. I keep getting deeper and deeper into the goth scene because I'm looking for ways to fill up that void my father left inside me. Dad, if you're watching, I hate you."

Jared flipped his middle finger at the camera, at his dad.

"We'll have to cut that," Curt said.

"Or maybe just digitize it," Vince said.

"The viewers will still know what it is. I'm not sure we ought to obscure it. Just cut it. He already said he hated his dad. What more do we need?"

"You're right," Vince said. "We'll cut away to Betsy."

"Maybe I should have you back on one of my other shows," Betsy Morgan said. "Jared, that's just tragic, and happens all too often, I'm afraid. I feel for you, I really do."

"Yeah, sure," Jared said. "My dad felt for me, too. All too often. I don't want to come back on some other show. I've got it off my chest, and now I feel better. Thanks, Lu."

Jared looked over at Lucrezia, whose powdered face was dripping with black mascara tears. Vince cut to her face.

From there, Jared went on to say that since his memories of abuse had returned, he had begun sleepwalking on occasion at three or four in the morning—the same time of night that his father used to sneak into his bedroom. He talked about learning hypnosis techniques from Lucrezia. He spoke of how he tried hypnotizing people he met in the clubs, trying to impose his will on theirs and get them to take him back to their apartments for sex. He said he liked to be in control of others, and the thing he liked least in life was to lose control of himself.

Betsy Morgan had had enough of Jared, so after the next commercial break, she turned to Lucrezia:

"You're what they call a psychic vampire, is that correct?"

"You can call it that, Betsy, if it makes you feel any better," Lucrezia said. "I feed off other people's lifeforce."

"What do you mean, exactly?"

Lucrezia sighed and tried to explain it all in terms Betsy's spiritually bound mind could comprehend, all the while staring Betsy down as if she were draining the lifeforce from her. The audience tittered every now and then, amused by the seriousness with which Lucrezia talked about her psychic abilities and the sixth sense. Lucrezia gave them all broad, powerful glares.

"So you're not the kind of vampire who sucks other people's blood," Betsy Morgan concluded.

"Duh," Lucrezia said.

"Unlike our next guest, who calls himself Theophrastus. I have to say, sir, I love your name."

"Thank you, Betsy," he said. "And thanks for the 'sir.'"

Betsy referred to her four-by-six cards. "Theophrastus is the owner of a popular goth club called The Loft—"

"The Lot," he corrected.

"Oh, The Lot, I'm sorry. Theophrastus says he enjoys drinking blood, but he generally restricts himself to the blood of virgins. Boys and girls?"

"Just girls." Theophrastus was terse.

"And those two along with you are Darcy and Marianna?" Betsy Morgan said, smiling at the girls. "Which one's which?"

They got this sorted out.

"And how old are you?"

They both claimed to be sixteen.

"And you go to Theophrastus's club? Aren't you too young to be doing that?"

"We don't drink," Darcy said. "What's wrong with that?"

"And you let Theophrastus drink your blood?"

"Why not?" Marianna said.

"What does this do for you, Theophrastus? Why virgins?"

"Virgins don't have AIDS," he said. "And I like drinking blood. It tastes good. It makes me feel stronger, more virile."

"I know in Asian countries, older men like to hire underage prostitutes," Betsy Morgan went on, "some as young as twelve, for the same reasons you describe. They want to avoid sexually transmitted diseases, but they also believe that by taking the girl's yin, they're feeding their yang. Or is it the other way around? I forget. Well, anyway, you're saying you get some kind of erotic satisfaction out of it?"

"You got it, Betsy," Theophrastus said.

"What do you do, bite them on the neck?"

"She seems inordinately interested in this," Vince put in.

"No, I just make a little incision on their wrists. Don't let Karel fool you. He doesn't bite people, either."

"I never said I did," Karel said.

"And his butt buddy over there—" Theophrastus said.

"Are we leaving in butt buddy?" Curt asked, stopping tape.

"Leave it for now. We'll run it for Betsy later and see."

Curt backed it up slightly and let it run.

"And his butt buddy over there, Jared—we'll have him sucking blood before you know it. Of all the kids I've met on the scene, he's the one I'd vote Most Likely to Suck. He's gone from one thing to the next, and now he's into psychic vampirism. The next thing you know it, he'll be drinking blood every night and sleeping in a coffin."

"Jared, is that true, what Theophrastus just said?"

"I don't have any interest in sucking blood," Jared said.

"Oh, come on!" Theophrastus said. "Get down off your high horse! I bet you've done it already."

"I've tasted it," Jared admitted. He had the air of someone erecting a deliberate front. I could see why Kirst thought he'd be suited for the dramatic arts. Every actor I'd ever met had erected a kind of wall around themselves, which they only took down while they were on stage. I was always uncomfortable around actors. They were always performing. They never let you get close. I got the impression that everything about Jared was an act. He liked being in costume. He liked playing a role. He liked the attention. He didn't want the curtain to come down.

"Once you've tasted it, you'll never go back," Theophrastus said. "It's like nectar. All you out in the audience, you'd better watch out for Jared the next time you're walking the streets of New York at night. He'll stalk you to your lair, get you to invite him in, cast a spell over you, and suck you dry."

"I will not," Jared said, laughing amusedly.

"Leave him alone, Theophrastus," Lucrezia said.

"You don't know what you've wrought, Lucrezia," he retorted. "You tapped into something in Jared that's yet to see its full expression. All of us here are just goths, but I'd like to predict right here on your show that Jared will be a vampire."

"Well, if so," Betsy said, not taking any of this very seriously, "we should inform our next guest. We're going to take a break, but when we come back, I'll introduce you to Professor Harold Jurgen, a self-described vampire hunter who claims to have located and destroyed—yes, destroyed—six actual vampires. When we return."

Harold Jurgen was brought out, taking a seat at the foot of

the audience, across from the row of his sworn enemies. He was a mousy-looking man in a bow tie and thick-lensed spectacles, with a comb-over haircut sweeping from one ear to the other.

"Professor Jurgen," Betsy Morgan said. "Is there really such thing as vampires?"

"Oh, absolutely!" Jurgen said.

"And you claim to have destroyed what, six vampires?"

"Yes, I have."

"How, with a stake through the heart?"

"Oh, no," Jurgen said earnestly. "It takes much more than that. The stake through the heart is only the first step—once you've found the vampire's lair and opened the lid of the coffin, of course. After the stake, you have to cut off the vampire's head, stuff garlic into the mouth, turn the head upside down, and exorcise the evil spirits that have taken over the poor soul, so that the soul can be freed to ascend up to heaven."

"I see," Betsy Morgan said.

"Is that guy your Downtown Vampire?" Vince asked me.

"No," I said. "This guy's a joke. He's crazier than the rest of them."

"Professor Jurgen, take a look at my guests, if you will. Do you think that any of them are real, actual vampires?"

"Only that one," Jurgen said, pointing to Jared.

"Oh, please," Jared said, rolling his eyes.

"That one has the vampire's curse," Jurgen said.

"Yeah," Jared said. "My father gave it to me."

After a final commercial break, Betsy Morgan came back to wrap up the show with her comment of the day:

"What have we learned from this? I guess, if anything, we've seen that there can be such thing as taking a lifestyle choice too far. For some, being a goth means wearing funky clothes and staying up till all hours at the clubs. For others, well, as you've seen, they seem to have shed their very humanity in favor of some other existence—a way of life that, at least as far as I'm concerned, is not worth living. Are there vampires among us? Obviously, there are. It could be your next-door neighbor. It could even be your own son or daughter. So take my advice. Listen to your children. Hear their cries of pain. Don't let them go down the dark paths of life. And from all of us here at *The Betsy Morgan Show*, have a safe Halloween."

"Oh, brother," Curt said.

Vince leaned back in his chair and stretched. His arms came close to touching me. He swiveled around and said, "Satisfied?"

"Yes," I said. "Thanks for all your help."

Vince stuck out his hand, looked me in the eye, and said: "Pleasure meeting you, Greg. Here, let me give you my card."

"Pleasure was all mine, Vince," I said, shaking his hand again. His grip was firm and warm, and he held on for too long.

Curt swiveled back to face the monitors, whistling softly.

I broke the handshake hastily, pocketed Vince's card, and handed him one of mine. I didn't have time to keep flirting.

"Give me a call if you need anything more," Vince said.

Like a shoulder to cry on, I thought. I told him I would.

THIRTY-FOUR

I PARKED THE 'CUDA a block from my office and kept looking over my shoulder as I walked down Eighth Avenue. A cute, muscular guy walking his pug thought I was trying to catch his eye. I was only looking out for Gloria or Theophrastus or Kirst or Orjuedos or anyone else who might currently have something against me.

My office was still locked up tight, with no signs on the door that anyone might have attempted entry. Still, I opened the door with caution, Glock in hand. There were no dark shapes within to take a potshot at me. No one was hiding under the waiting room chairs or behind the coat rack or under my desk. The windows were locked up tight. The air was stale, as usual. The gray chinchilla hairs Gloria had left behind yesterday were still clinging to the cold steel chair. Nothing was disturbed.

Nothing except maybe me—paranoically so. I had these delusions that every gay hunk I met wanted my body and that every slimy character I crossed wanted my corpse, sooner or later.

But they weren't delusions. I had proof. I had marks all over my body to prove malice towards me on the part of Gloria and Theophrastus. Moreover, I had phone numbers in my wallet for Nick at Café Giotto and Vince at Hell's Kitchen Studios; they wanted to see me again—and not to talk about the weather.

I sat at my desk, laying my Glock on my blotter before me. I played back the messages on my answering machine:

Beep. "Mr. Quaintance, this is Gustav Grosse. Evelyn and I are checked in at the Howard Johnson's on Lexington Avenue. It is now twelve-twenty, and we are about to go meet with Detective Orjuedos. He is taking us over to identify Karel. Evelyn and I would like very much to speak further with you regarding Jared. Please leave us a message. We are staying in room 407."

Beep. "Greg? This is Sebastian de Leon. Something's come up. I'm not sure how private your machine is, so I'd rather not get into details. Give me a call back—or better yet, come on over and have a look for yourself. I'm at Anastasia's apartment, helping her cleaning up the place. Hope to see you later. Bye."

Beep. "Greg, Tavo. I spoke to you harshly last night. I'm not going to apologize, but I want you to know I've softened up a bit. I'm not happy about what you did, but I might be willing to forgive you if you'll come in today and make a complete statement regarding your actions last night. I think we can get the D.A. to overlook your illegal entry into Karel's apartment on account of the fact that you were hired to find Jared Foster and you were concerned about his safety. But I need you to describe what took place in the apartment so we can sort out the evidence. We got a lot of good evidence off the bed. I believe a lot of the blood evidence we found on the floor and in the bathroom sink is from you. I appreciate all the good cooperation you've given us so far, and I want you to keep it coming. I hope you're all right, by the way. I saw a lot of blood on the floor. If you're still in a cooperative mood, come on in, and let's talk. Okay, buddy?"

I liked the buddy part. It kind of made my day.

I drove over to Avenue D, parking the 'Cuda in front of the Chinese restaurant. It was already reopened for business, with a fresh crew of indentured workers that included a man, a woman, and a fourteen-year-old girl. Chinese gangsters had an endless supply of people literally at their disposal. No one was ever going to remember the two brothers I'd met. I'd probably forget them myself before long.

I pressed Anastasia's buzzer. Sebastian talked to me and buzzed me in. I bounded up the stairs with my hand in my jacket, on my Glock. I knocked on 4B.

Sebastian undid the locks and opened the door, tossing his blond hair back off his face and looking at me in amazement:

"Jesus, Greg, what happened to you? Somebody beat you up?"

"You don't mind if I take a quick look around?" I said, withdrawing my Glock and pointing it up, alongside my ear.

"Go ahead, but it's safe. I'm the only one here."

"Where's Anastasia?" I said, checking the kitchen.

Sebastian followed along behind me. "At her day job."

"And she's got you doing this shitwork for her?" I asked, crossing the living room, through which Sebastian had cleared a broad path through the broken glass and debris. I peeked into Jared's cleaned-out bedroom, then his closet, and found nobody.

"I'm going to move in here," Sebastian said. "Anastasia's giving me a break on my first month's rent if I help her clean."

"Isn't that a little premature?" I asked, going across the hall to check the bathroom. Sebastian had cleaned most of it up. "It's still possible Jared might be coming back to stay."

"I hope so. If he does, I'll sleep in the living room."

"What about all your stuff?" I asked, checking Anastasia's bedroom. It looked exactly the same as the other night, the stained mattress lying untouched. I looked again in her closet, piled with the clothing Juliet Logan had torn from the hangers.

"We'll sort it out," Sebastian said.

"I guess you were right," I said, replacing my gun. "No one here but us chickens."

"What, don't you trust me?" He acted hurt.

"I don't trust anybody, Sebastian," I said. "No offense, but for all I know, someone could have wanted me up here for a reason. I got kicked around a little last night, and I don't want to go through it again. I'm only being careful."

"I understand," Sebastian said. "You look terrible."

"Thanks. What did you want to see me about?"

"Come back out to the living room, and I'll show you."

Sebastian led me back out along the cleared path, reached across to the computer desk, and picked up a large picture frame.

"Is this the one you said was missing?" He handed it to me.

I held it between the palms of my hands, at the corners. It was Sebastian's photograph of Jared in vampire makeup and Byronic shirt, lying in the coffin with his arms folded across his chest and blood on his lips. The glass and the frame were intact. I held it up to the light and noticed several latent fingerprints.

"Are you trying to say it was here all along and that I overlooked it?" This seemed to me a distinct possibility.

"No," Sebastian said. "Theophrastus brought it over a few hours ago. He said he knew it belonged to Anastasia, and he wanted to return it to her. He said for me not to ask him any questions about how it came into his possession. I said okay, and he handed it over. I called you just after he left."

"Why not the police?" I asked, still studying the picture.

"You know why," he said, shifting his weight nervously.

"You're still afraid of Theophrastus? Well, don't be."

"Why not?"

"Theophrastus didn't kill Karel Janáček or Henry Foster or anybody. He certainly didn't steal this. Not from Anastasia, anyway. He stole it from the person who stole it from her."

"I thought you said that was Henry Foster," Sebastian said.

"Theophrastus could have been the one who interrupted him and Juliet Logan after they cleaned out the place. Couldn't he?"

"Could have been, but wasn't," I said. "I'd better put this down. You've touched this with your fingers, haven't you?"

"Whoops," Sebastian said. "Sorry."

"What about Theophrastus?" I took the picture into the kitchen and laid it on the table. "Was he wearing gloves?"

"As a matter of fact, he was."

"He's no fool," I said. "This might still have the killer's prints on it. As long as no one else accidentally smeared them."

"I said I was sorry." Sebastian was penitent.

"I didn't necessarily mean you," I said. "Could be one of Theophrastus's biker-burglar pals mishandled it this morning. I'm going to take this to the police, if you don't mind."

"Go ahead," Sebastian said. "If it'll lead you to Jared."

"It will," I said. "Trust me."

THIRTY-FIVE

I WENT INTO the Sixth Precinct carrying a black canvas book bag, which I set atop the formica counter for an overweight uniformed officer with a bristly mustache to search. He was unimpressed by the framed photo in the Ziploc freezer bag and the unmarked VHS videotape. He advised me that Orjuedos was in, but he was busy talking with some folks from California. I said Orjuedos would want to see me. The officer told me to wait behind the counter.

I stood there for a while, watching deskbound cops taking reports of damaged property and stolen bicycles over the phones. One was a young, good-looking black man with his arm in a cast—temporary shit duty because of disability. The rest were healthy enough but older and fatter, put behind desks because they were near retirement anyway and not much use on the streets anymore.

Orjuedos appeared from down the hall and lifted the hinged countertop for me. "You look like shit, Greg," he said.

"Relax, Tavo," I said. "I'll tell you all about it."

"Come on back, and I'll introduce you to the Grosses. We just came back from the M.E.'s. They were just about to leave."

I followed Orjuedos back to his desk, in front of which were seated a middle-aged man and woman, holding hands and whispering to each other and looking indescribably sad.

"Ah, Mr. Quaintance." Gustav Grosse dropped his wife's hand and stood up to shake mine. He was a foot taller than I and a hundred pounds heavier, and his big hairy hand crushed mine the way it might a head of garlic. His cheeks and nose were ruddy from burst capillaries, framed by a disheveled head of gray hair and bushy white mutton chops. He wore a cheap, thin-gauge brown leather coat and gray polyester slacks over black cowboy boots. Evelyn Grosse remained seated in a black dress, nude hose, and black pumps, with a black handbag across her lap. A simple gold crucifix hung on a thin chain at her neck. Her face had a sagging softness around the jowls, offset by a terse mouth and a hard pair of eyes. A lot of doors had closed in her life. With the deaths of Karel and her ex-husband, she'd just witnessed a few more. From the grim look on her face, I'd say she was expecting another. Gustav sat back down and held her small hand.

"You still haven't found my son, have you?" Evelyn asked.

"I'm getting closer," I said. "I'll find him yet."

"I don't want any false promises." She was solemn. "All I want is Jared back, safe."

"We all do," I said.

"Detective Orjuedos here wants to put him in jail," Evelyn said, darting an accusatory glance across the desk at Orjuedos.

"No one else could have committed these murders," Orjuedos said confidently, leaning back in his squeaky chair. "And Jared seems to fit the psychological profile we've developed."

"Nonsense!" Gustav said, slamming his fist on Orjuedos's

desk. Loose paper clips jumped up in fright. "If Evelyn says Jared is no murderer, then you had better fucking believe it!"

Evelyn must have given Gustav a talking to on the plane over. He'd seemed ready enough to believe it before.

"Jared hasn't killed anyone," I said. "I'm sure of it."

All three of them looked at me expectantly.

"Mr. and Mrs. Grosse," I said, "I'm sorry, but I'm going to have to go over these matters with Detective Orjuedos in private. You're staying overnight at the Howard Johnson's, right?"

"We are staying until Jared is found," Gustav proclaimed.

"Then I hope to be in touch with you later this evening."

They took this, appropriately enough, as their cue.

Orjuedos shook their hands and thanked them for their cooperation. I gave them my condolences over Karel Janáček.

After they were gone, I took the seat closest to Orjuedos, rubbed my hands up my face and back down, and said, "Shit, Tavo."

"Time for you to explain yourself," Orjuedos said mildly.

"Yeah, thanks for the phone message, by the way. That was real generous of you."

"I didn't want you running scared from me. Of course, if I think you're obstructing my investigation, I'm still going to bust your ass."

"You won't have to do that," I said. "I'm going to tell you everything I know, starting with a guy named Willem Kirst."

"Willem Kirst?" Orjuedos said. "Never heard of him."

"He's your man," I said. "I'm sure of it."

"How sure are you?"

I shrugged, then hedged: "Maybe sixty percent."

"What about the other forty?"

"That I'm reserving for someone else."

"Jared Foster?"

"No," I said. "A giant chinchilla."

Orjuedos scowled. His goatee morphed into something ugly.

"I'll explain," I said, "if you want to get cozy with me and a stenographer in an interview room for the next couple hours."

"I've got just the guy," Orjuedos said, picking up his phone, running down a list of support personnel, and calling a four-digit extension. "Bernard? Tavo. Get in here. I need you." He slammed the phone back in its cradle and smiled.

"Good steno?" I asked, raising an eyebrow.

"You'll like Bernard, Greg. He's fast, and he's cute."

THIRTY-SIX

I LET THE 'CUDA rumble into a parking space on East Sixteenth Street, killed the engine, and doused the headlights. The sky was black, but the streetlamps gave off enough light to see by. Construction, or destruction, of the townhouse next to Willem Kirst's was at a standstill. No more junk had been piled upon the dusty heap in the giant garbage receptacle. The scaffolding was still up and awaiting the sandblasting crew. The plastic drapes breathed in and out with the shifting breeze.

Kirst's townhouse was as quiet as the dead one next door, with only one window illuminated, on the second story. I kept watch through binoculars while smoking a chain of Luckies.

After half an hour, a black Jaguar sedan double-parked in the middle of the street, ahead of the garbage receptacle. The horn was tapped a few times. No one got out. I spied a black male driver wearing a cap and a man in the back seat with male pattern baldness. The license plate was personalized: SRPRTNR.

The second-story light went out. A faint light came on, barely making it through the first-floor curtains but shining brightly in the angled panes over the entrance. The stoop light came on. The front door opened, and Willem Kirst emerged in a gray suit, black tie, and open overcoat with swinging belt, turning to lock the door behind him. He went briskly down the steps and into the back seat of the waiting car, where the balding man reached over to slap him on the back. The brake lights came on as the driver slipped into gear. The Jaguar zipped up the street, turning south onto Irving Place.

My watch said 7:50. The schedule was being followed roughly to the minute. After I divulged all the known facts to Orjuedos, he agreed that Kirst should be questioned. If indeed Kirst had been burglarized, he had not made a report of it to the police. It was the most telling fact of all, as far as Orjuedos was concerned. The photo of Jared and my tracing of its possession was condemnatory; unfortunately, the picture, being illegally obtained, was insufficient evidence for obtaining a search warrant. The most Orjuedos could do now was question Kirst. He got Kirst on the phone (while I listened over the speaker) and asked him if he would agree to come to the station to answer some questions related to the disappearance of Jared Foster. Kirst blithely agreed, claiming it would be no problem and he was happy to be of assistance. He agreed to meet Orjuedos at eight o'clock at the Sixth Precinct house. He added parenthetically that he would be accompanied by his attorney, some kind of senior partner with Morris, McNulty & Jahns. Looking across at me, Orjuedos told Kirst that would be fine, and they hung up. Orjuedos didn't like the idea of the lawyer; the Constitution gave him no choice.

I rolled up my window and put the binoculars back in their case. I grabbed my black gloves from the glove compartment and slipped them on. I took out my large flashlight and tucked it in a deep inner pocket of my jacket. I got out, locked up the 'Cuda, and approached Kirst's house, watching for witnesses.

I couldn't be involved in the official questioning of Kirst. My presence in the precinct house would tip him off that the police knew more than they pretended. It was a happy thing for me that Orjuedos was getting Kirst out of his house. Orjuedos asked me what I was going to do; I told him it would be better for him if he didn't know. He nodded and told me to be careful.

I went up the steps casually, as if I had routine business with Kirst, in case any neighbors were peeping. In addition to the stoop light, the light within the foyer was on. I could make out the security alarm box on the wall just past the second set of doors. I recognized the unit as one manufactured by Vetrex Controls. I'd installed a few of their systems myself before getting my private detective's license. I didn't have the technology to beat Kirst's system, but that hardly mattered in this instance. I could tell by the steady green LED on the Vetrex box that Kirst hadn't turned the unit on.

I doubted it was an oversight; people with high-end security systems were in the habit of using them. Kirst had left it shut off deliberately. If the alarm were to go off while he was at the police station, his security firm would be on the scene before him. If he was hiding something in his house that he didn't want anyone to know about, security was the last thing he wanted. They would come over and search for whatever had tripped the alarm and find something they oughtn't. I also had to consider the possibility that Kirst had left someone behind in his house as a guardian.

It was a chance I had to take.

My lock-picking tools would be of no use. Kirst had a high-security Medeco lock on his doors, unpickable except by a real pro. It would not be difficult to break the glass, reach in, and undo the locks, but the street was too well lighted and too well populated; the noise itself would draw attention to me.

I went back down the steps and stood before the house. I had no way of knowing how long Kirst would be at the Sixth Precinct. Now was my only chance to get in and have a look.

The plastic tarpaulins rustled dully on the house next door. I took a quick look around; for the moment at least, no one was coming along the sidewalk. Washington Irving High School across the street was dark. I hopped the low fence into the garden of the gutted house and ducked under the shadow of the scaffolding.

I climbed up the crossbars to the first level of planking and pulled myself over. I was protected from view by the opaque plastic sheeting. It was like a giant jungle gym, and fairly easy to climb. I grabbed the thick horizontal overhead bars and inched my way up the crossbars to the next level, and the next, and on up, until the scaffolding ran out, about ten feet from the elaborate cornice at the roofline. I lay flat on the upper planks, trying to figure out how to scale the rest and get on the roof. The brick face gave insufficient fingerholds, and I saw no protrusions I could reach and hang onto. I'd fallen short.

Up here, though, I was high above the streetlamps. I was dressed all in black and was not likely to be seen by anyone. There were three windows along the level. The first one I tried seemed to be locked, but when I tried forcing it, it came unstuck from the crumbling paint that had been sealing it. I thrust it halfway up. I covered the lens of my flashlight with my fingers and shone the subdued light inside. The floorboards had been taken up, leaving the exposed floor beams spaced a foot apart, ready to be lined with insulation. If I'd simply vaulted over, I would have fallen through to the next floor, if not farther. I stepped over the sill with care, planting one foot and then the other squarely across the narrow beams.

I shut the window and played the light around the space. The walls had been stripped of plaster, cross-slats, and wiring and were down to two-by-four skeleton frames and open doorways. I could see the entire length of the floor, to the back. The staircase ended at the far right. A brick chimney ran up along the left wall, over a sealed fireplace.

I walked carefully along the creaky roof beams, keeping one hand against the wall, until I found the hatch in the ceiling that was the roof access. A short iron ladder was bolted to the wall just beneath it, and I had to stand on my toes to reach the bottom rung. I pulled myself up, hoping the bolts would hold, and went hand-over-hand to the top rung, hooking one arm around so I could undo the latch with my other hand. I threw back two lengthy deadbolts and pushed the hatch open, onto the roof.

A blast of cool air blew in my face. I pulled myself up and looked out across the rooftops. I saw no sign that anyone was watching from anywhere. I came out onto the roof and shut the hatch, hoping I wouldn't need to return this way—I would have to be careful climbing back down that ladder and letting go.

I walked across the tarred roof and stepped easily over a low row of bricks, onto the roof of Kirst's townhouse. His roof hatch poked a few inches out of the tar but was held firmly shut. I stepped over to a domed skylight of clear plexiglass and shone my flashlight in, finding iron bars fixed beneath. I wouldn't be able to gain entry without a power drill and a hacksaw.

I walked down the slope, to the back, and looked down. Most of these townhouses had a deck, and Kirst's was no exception. It lay below me two stories down—all of redwood, with a covered jacuzzi, wrought-iron furniture, and a barbecue—built over the lower floors of the house, which extended deeper into the garden.

I wished I'd had the foresight to bring some rope. A two-story drop was more than I was willing to risk, even if I could manage to land on the jacuzzi cover. There was a rain gutter along the roof, and a drainpipe extending down from it, but I took one look at it and shook my head no. It looked unstable.

I kept standing there, though, unable to do anything else. If I didn't risk going down by drainpipe, I'd have no other choice but to give up. I'd have to go home and stick my head under my pillow and not answer any phone calls. I might never know what became of Jared Foster. No matter what I did, I was a fool. Better to take my chances with the drainpipe.

I got down onto my belly, grabbed onto the edge of the roof, and slowly lowered one leg and then the rest of my body over the side. I hung there for a moment, then transferred one hand around the drainpipe. I pulled at it, and it came away from the wall a bit—too flimsy to support my weight. My only chance was to try to slide down it like a firepole. I looked below me to make sure I had an unbroken trajectory. I planted my toes on either side of the pipe, then let go, grasping lightly onto the pipe with both gloved hands, and slid all the way down.

I bent my knees to break the impact but landed on the deck with a thud, falling against an iron chair and knocking it over.

A dog barked in response to the clatter, in someone else's garden. I crawled across the deck and looked out onto the lighted yard a few houses down, where a yellow lab was straining against his chain and barking deeply in my general direction, his tail sticking straight up, a ridge of fur raised along his back. A door opened, and a gray-haired man in reading glasses stepped out, saying, "Baxter, hush!" Baxter kept barking, but the man didn't bother to look up at what at. Instead, he unfastened the chain and escorted Baxter inside. The yard light went off. I heard one last muffled bark from Baxter, then silence.

When I stood up, my left shin gave me a sharper pain than it had last night. It was bleeding through my Band-Aid, staining my jeans. I could barely put my weight on it. I wondered if the knife thrust had nicked my bone. I limped over to the sliding glass patio door and had a look at the lock.

Kirst had not bothered with a sophisticated Medeco lock back here, though I would have advised him to if I were consulting on his security. I also would have advised him to block the track of the sliding door with a cross post, but my visual inspection showed he had none. I got out my tools and picked the lock with no more difficulty than I'd managed Karel's. I slid the door open and stepped through the drapes onto a yielding carpet.

I closed the door behind me. I took out my flashlight and shone it around with my left. It felt clumsy, but I needed my right hand free. I pulled out my Glock and held it at the ready.

I was in a long den or party space with a bar and barstools, leather couches and chairs, and an empty walnut entertainment center that would have once held assorted stereo components, a couple of VCRs, a laserdisc player, and a giant-screen TV. I guessed at the laserdisc player because a few shiny twelve-inch discs were lying on the carpet out of their sleeves: *The Greatest Show on Earth, The Great Waldo Pepper, The Great McGinty, Great Expectations, The Great Escape,* and *Grease.* The last one had a long crack and bore the imprint of a boot sole. Theophrastus and his boys must have cleaned out Kirst's entire library; these six had fallen out (in alphabetical order) and no one had bothered to go back for them. There were no other laserdiscs in the room, or anything else of value. The bar was cleaned out of its liquor. Any beer was gone from the refrigerator. Hooks and dark markings on the walls indicated where several framed prints had once hung.

I went up the stairs, intending to start at the top floor and work my way down. I searched each room thoroughly—guest bedrooms, a home gym, a library, a darkroom, bathrooms, closets —everything was in disarray, with items strewn on the floors and certain things obviously missing. The darkroom had no enlarger.

The home gym had an outmoded, elaborate, pulley-driven weight machine in the center, but the dumbbells were missing from their rack. In every room, pictures had been removed from the walls. Knickknacks and vases lay broken on the wood floors.

Nothing was any help to me until I found what had to be Kirst's bedroom, taking up the front half of the second floor, with all three windows facing the street. It was a masculine room, with dressers, bed, night tables, and an old wardrobe all of dark mahogany. The bed was a queen-sized four-poster that stood high off the floor and was made up with a black leather cover neatly tucked around the pillows and draped over all four corners. At the foot of the bed was a trunk whose lock had been busted open. I lifted the lid and found it practically empty. The canvas-padded interior smelled strongly of leather. In the nearest corner, one thing had been left behind—a chromium ring two inches in diameter: a cock ring. The trunk would likely have held other sex toys, at least until Theophrastus stumbled onto them. I figured one of the items had been a black leather full-head hood with rawhide lacings crossing up the back like a shoe, the kind someone had been wearing the night of October Fifth.

I hesitated a moment before opening the wardrobe. The doors were taller than I was, starting three inches off the ground. Just about anything could be inside. The doors opened to reveal a lot of empty hangers from which Kirst's suits had been taken.

I opened the walk-in closet and tossed my light around, with similar results. Kirst's clothes looked as if they'd been picked through, leaving only the most boring and least valuable ones behind. A few worn-out shoes littered a three-tiered shoe shelf that had probably held about thirty pairs before last night.

I went through his dresser drawers, but they were all half-empty as well. If he'd kept anything of Jared's, like wallet and identification, they had probably gone with Theophrastus.

I was about to leave Kirst's bedroom, when the light of my flash fell onto the glossy wood floor to the right of the bed and showed up pale scratch marks—shallow cuts freshly dug into the wood, swinging out in a slight arc. The largest arc was toward the foot of the bed, with a smaller one at the head. Both arcs ended abruptly in sharp diagonal lines that cut downward and appeared to be of identical length. They were the markings of a long, heavy box that had been dragged out from under the bed, moved across the floor a few inches, then picked up at both ends.

I got down on my knees and shone the light under the bed. There was nothing there now. It may have been another trunk, and perhaps Theophrastus had taken it away. But if it was kept under the bed and occasionally dragged out, there would be other markings on the floor. The fact that there was only the one set made me wonder. . . . No one liked to step off their bed onto a cold floor. Kirst probably kept rugs on each side, or else a large rug under the entire bed. Theophrastus would have taken up any rugs that were worth anything. Either he had taken the other trunk, or Kirst had moved it himself after his rugs were gone.

Trunks were seldom longer than four feet, though. These scratches were a little over six, made by an oblong box.

I picked up the black phone on one of Kirst's night tables. I dug out the business card Xerxes had given me and called the number of The Lot. A sexless voice answered.

"I'd like to speak with Theophrastus," I said softly.

"Who is this?"

"Tell him it's Greg Quaintance from last night."

"I'll see if he's busy. Hold on."

I stood with my back to the wall. I set the flashlight atop one of the pillows, pointed at the door of Kirst's bedroom, while I held the phone slightly away from my ear, trying to stay tuned in to any sounds that might arise in Kirst's house. I kept my Glock in my right, aimed at the darkened doorway.

"You've got a lot of nerve, you fucker," came Theophrastus's voice over the line. "I catch up with you, you're dead meat."

"You'll have to order the hit from Riker's Island," I said.

"Don't think I won't."

"Don't count on being successful. Look, Theophrastus, you know and I know your days are numbered. The narcotics squad is onto you, and we all know about the burglary you pulled."

"What burglary?"

"Willem Kirst. The guy I got you onto. He told me all about it. Anyway, you were heading over here last night, and he was burglarized. If not you, who?"

"I told that fuck if he told the police I'd blow his fucking brains out. If you see him, you tell him he's dead, got that?"

"He didn't tell the police," I said. "But he did tell me. I'm calling you because I need a few more pieces of information out of you."

"Fuck you."

"If you cooperate, maybe I'll appear for the defense as a character witness at your drug kingpin trial."

"Why would you want to do that?"

"I don't know. You knew that photo belonged to Anastasia, and you returned it to her. That shows you've got character."

"Fuck that, too. I'm still pissed at you, Quaintance. Jared Foster wasn't over there at Kirst's. I was ready to come back to my place, stick that pin in your dick, and slice your fucking balls off. I'd still like to. You sleep on that."

"You don't need my balls. You got some consolation prizes. That loot you stole from Kirst probably more than covered what Jared owed you. I'm not holding a grudge against you."

"Then you're an idiot."

"Why don't you wipe the slate clean and let Jared ride?"

"Jared wasn't square with me," Theophrastus said. "That shit still owes me bigtime. Got nothing to do with Kirst. And you got two strikes against you, Quaintance. First you take Lorelei Matheson from my brothers, then you go and corrupt my Darcy and Marianna and wriggle out of my basement."

"You would have done the same, if someone was going to come back and slice your balls off."

"I guess so," he said. "But you spoiled all my fun."

"Truce," I said.

"No truce. You just watch your back."

"If that's how you want it."

"I won't be happy till I've got Jared's money."

"I'm still looking for Jared," I said. Then I went on and lied: "Maybe I can recover your money."

"I'm not hiring you, if that's why you're calling."

"No, all I want is some more information. Can you tell me where in Kirst's house you found that picture of Jared?"

"Ted found it in Kirst's bedroom, on the dresser."

"There was also a trunk in Kirst's bedroom. It's still here. The inside smells like leather. Probably contained S and M sex toys, but it's empty now. You know anything about it?"

"Ted took them. I've got the stuff over here in a sack."

"I want to know if there was a leather hood—full-head thing, laces up the back. You've probably seen them before."

"I know the kind you're talking about," Theophrastus said. "But there was nothing like that in the trunk. Wrist and ankle restraints, some rope, some cock and ball toys, tit clamps. No hood, though. Nothing much else."

"Okay," I said. "One more thing. Did you or Ted or one of your boys remove a large box from under Kirst's bed?"

"You're not talking about the trunk?"

"No, something more like a coffin."

"I didn't see nothing like that."

"Maybe Ted didn't bother to look under Kirst's bed?"

"All I know is, we didn't remove anything that big."

"That's all I wanted to know," I said.

"You say you're over there now? At Kirst's house?"

"I never said that."

"You didn't have to. I've got caller I.D. I'm sending someone over to get you. Maybe myself. We're not far away. You've got maybe two minutes' headstart, if you want to run."

"I'm not afraid of you," I said, fingering my Glock.

But Theophrastus had already hung up.

I set down the receiver and listened to the house.

THIRTY-SEVEN

BUT THERE WERE no sounds. I was all alone with my ghostly marks, the only evidence I had of Jared's presence. He had been kept here under the bed until at least this morning. The burglary spooked Kirst, and he'd decided to move Jared to a better hiding place. Barring secret chambers or walled-up rooms, I was sure I would find it. Given enough time. I'd been here more than half an hour, and there was no telling when Kirst would return.

I searched the rest of the bedroom floor but found no other scratches, nor did I detect any loose floorboards. The walk-in closet and the master bath had dull-thudding walls of solid plaster, with no detectable secret panels. The box had to have been carried out of the bedroom altogether, by two persons— unless it had been stood on a dolly and wheeled out upright.

I quit the bedroom and quickened the pace of my search, rapping on floors and walls, opening every door, trying to spot anything that looked like it might be out of the ordinary. The rest of the second floor was made up of Kirst's home office, a walk-in linen closet, another bathroom, and a small bright empty room that looked as if it was already empty when Theophrastus struck. It might have made a nice nursery or hobby room for anyone with a child or a hobby.

I went down the wider stairs to the main floor, touching the polished mahogany post at the base of the balustrade. The light over the stairs was the only one Kirst had left on. While I was down here, I double-checked the alarm box to make sure it really was off. It was. I made a quick circuit of the front room where I'd interviewed Kirst. Persian rugs, liquor, prints, and *objets d'art* were gone, and I found nothing to help me.

I opened up the coat closet just off the foyer and drew my Glock on the gray chinchilla coat I found hanging inside. It was Gloria's, all right, but for once she wasn't in it. She wasn't hiding behind the other coats, either. I couldn't see her leaving without her coat. She had to be around somewhere, in one form or another. I searched her coat but found no wallet or anything else helpful—only a pocket pack of Kleenex.

I closed the door and saw gray hairs clinging to my hands.

I went back and made a glance of the sparkling stainless steel kitchen that took up the entire back half of the first floor. It had a back door to the garden and another door on the far left wall, probably to a pantry. The kitchen was an unlikely spot for hiding anything of size, unless it was cut up into bite-sized pieces and put in the refrigerator.

I skirted the kitchen for now and opened the door under the stairs, to a more likely spot—the basement.

The stairs gave under my boots and creaked woefully, but they seemed sturdy enough. I kept my flashlight in my left, my Glock in my right, like a two-gun cowboy, and made my descent. The cobwebbed ceiling sloped low and steep above me, forcing me to cock my head down to one side. A cool, moldy dampness wafted up around me. My wide beam caught a scarab-sized black beetle scuttling home across the gray concrete floor.

The stairs ended in an open area of the basement Kirst was using for storage. Cardboard boxes were stacked all around, along with old junk like upright vacuum cleaners, electric fans, and an assortment of ceramic pots. I poked my way around the stacks of boxes. None were longer than two feet. They were stacked in rows for easy access and were not hiding anything. I opened up a couple of boxes and found old books, Christmas ornaments, decades-old issues of the major medical journals.

Along the far wall were a Maytag washer and dryer. A load of white garments still sat damp in the washer, smelling strongly of bleach. I picked out some items—briefs, socks, undershirts—but saw no bloodstains or anything else of interest. I put them back and checked the dryer, which was empty.

The concrete floor was solid throughout, stained with the use of many years, with no evidence of recent repair. If there had ever been an old well, it had long since been covered up.

There was one last door down here. I opened it and found the boiler room, filled with a large upright tank with multiple pipes protruding and warm, steamy air surrounding me. I scanned the dark corners with my flashlight and saw some old tools lying around, but otherwise nothing but solid stone walls. There were no more doors, no breaks in the floor, nowhere to hide a man.

I went back up the stairs. When I closed the basement door behind me, I heard a car door slam outside and footsteps tripping up the front steps. A shadowed figure stood at the door, digging out a key. I could be seen with a mere glance through the glass.

I dashed around the corner, into the kitchen, and headed for the back door. It would be easy to go out, into the garden, and scale the fence into someone else's backyard. But I stopped as I was undoing the chain lock and deadbolt.

The door to my left had a similar set of locks, not the kind one would put on a pantry door. It was a newer door, not of wood but of white, wood-grained aluminum. The frame around the doorway was of pale, unfinished wood. It even smelled new.

As I thought about it, I realized there should be no door here at all. It was the farthest wall of the house and ought to be right up against the house next door. It was a door that ought to lead nowhere.

The front door squeaked open and slammed shut. The locks were put in place. The inner door was being unlocked.

I undid the chain and deadbolt on the left-hand door and opened it to find another door, like a communicating door in a hotel room. There was less than a foot of space in between. I tried the handle of the communicating door, but it was locked. It was a simple lock, one I could pick and open, provided there were no more deadbolts on the other side.

Someone came in the inner foyer door, whistling. I heard the rustle of an overcoat being shed. I was sure it was Kirst. His lawyer must have cut short the questioning. I would have.

I closed myself in the space between the doors, pressing my face flat against the second one. I dug out my tools, slipped the long, skinny tongue along the bottom of the keyhole, and poked the crooked tool along the upper ridge. My first try didn't work. The lock held firm.

A light came on at my feet. Kirst was whistling in the kitchen, opening the door of the refrigerator.

I tried again, hastily. It took another minute, but when I tried the knob, it turned, and the door gave. I lifted the door slightly to keep its weight off the hinges. It opened quietly.

I stepped inside the gutted house next door, landing on a slab of plywood that had been thrown across the exposed beams.

I closed the door behind me. It had no deadbolts on it, or I would have thrown them to try to keep Kirst out. He was going to discover soon enough that the chain lock was dangling loose on his new door, the one that led into his unfinished property.

My flashlight showed me long pieces of plywood thrown about the floor, making navigable paths. One path led from the front door to the stairs. Another led from where I stood to intersect with a cross-path. From the cross-path was a fork that went to the basement stairs. I went out to the cross-path and scanned my light around but found nothing.

My instincts next door had been correct: what I wanted was probably in the basement — only I'd had the wrong basement.

The plywood rocked noisily as I went toward the stairs. I peered around the lip of the hole, shone my light down into it, and had the barest glimpse of the corner of a coffin.

THIRTY-EIGHT

Two IRON BRACES were padlocked together, holding the coffin shut. I set down my Glock and hammered at them with the butt of my flashlight until they broke from the wood, falling onto the floor with the lock still attached.

I raised the lid of the coffin and shone my light inside.

An emaciated young man lay within, his naked figure embraced by red satin. His wrists and ankles were bound to the sides of the coffin by leather restraints and padlocks. His eyes stared up at me wide and frightened, pleading for help. The rest of his head was fully encased in a black leather hood, with reinforced eyelets at the nostrils. A thin plastic tube hung out of the left nostril, with a yellow plastic connecter at the free end. It looked to me like some kind of feeding tube, in which case the other end went down the young man's throat, to his stomach. The inside of the tube showed spotty red bloodstains. Another, smaller-bore tube—a surgical catheter—was poking out of his urethra and snaking through a hole in the side of the coffin to empty into a rusty metal pail on the floor.

It was Jared Foster, dragon tattoo slithering up his right side, shrunken head etched on his left pectoral, hawthorn branches creeping up his arms. His stomach was sunken, his pale skin stretched taut around ribs and pelvis.

"Jared, I'm getting you to a hospital," I said.

He nodded, straining against his gag to say something.

I set down the flashlight and unfastened the gag. The flashlight rolled away from me in an arc. I assumed Jared's first words would be something like, "Help me."

But his raspy voice whispered, *"Watch out!"*

I glanced up in time to hear the shot and see the lick of flame shoot from the end of a gun across the room.

A slug burst through my leather jacket, searing my shoulder. I felt the slicing burn of a graze wound.

I winced, grabbed up my Glock, and dove onto my stomach.

Another shot was fired, whizzing over my head and ricocheting off the stone wall behind me.

I fired in the direction of the gun flash.

A woman screamed out, and a gun clattered onto the floor.

I found my flashlight with my left and aimed it toward the corner where the woman was moaning and whimpering. The light picked up a mangy blonde with leathery skin in white jeans and a gaudy Versace blouse. Her right shoulder was thoroughly ripped open and bleeding profusely where my hollow-point round had impacted. The bones would be shattered into small fragments, the deltoid pulverized, arteries and veins severed and useless.

Gloria sat shell-shocked against the dank stone wall, her right arm lying limp at her side. She didn't move.

Her gun, a semi-automatic, lay two feet out of reach.

I went over, picked it up, and put it in my pocket.

I reached down toward Gloria, and she shrunk away like I

was going to strike her. I only patted her down for more weapons, careful not to jar her wound, which would be painful but not life-threatening if I could get her prompt treatment.

"He—he gave me no choice," Gloria said pathetically.

"Shh!" I said, hearing a noise and looking up.

Plywood boards clattered overhead. Someone was running toward the basement stairs. Gloria followed my gaze and drew a sharp breath. The he she was talking about had heard our shots.

I doused my flashlight and stood to the side of the stairs, my Glock aimed up at the opening, where the dark outline of a man stood holding the silhouette of a gun. I heard him breathing.

"You're caught, Kirst," I said. "Throw down your gun."

"Who's that?" came Willem Kirst's voice. "Quaintance?"

"It's me. Throw down your gun, or I'll shoot."

The figure stood motionless, deciding.

"I've got a bead on your chest, Kirst. I'm not aiming for your kneecaps. And don't count on Gloria to help you. I've already taken away her gun. Now you give me yours. I said *now*."

Without a word, Kirst swiped his gun arm down in the direction of my voice. He didn't want to give up.

I fell to one knee and fired simultaneous with him.

Another bullet whizzed over my head.

Mine hit Kirst in the upper chest, making him arch his back and go weak in the knees, arms flying into the air, body falling forward onto the stairs in a belly flop. He bumped and rolled halfway down before tumbling over the side, onto the floor at my feet, and emitting a dull groan.

I stomped on Kirst's wrist and made him give up his gun with open fingers. I kept my boot on him, reached down, picked up his semi-automatic, and found another pocket to put it in. I was developing a nice gun collection.

Kirst was still breathing, but he had a glazed look in his eyes, and he was bleeding from a hole that I'd pierced through his suit coat and Oxford shirt, in his left lung, fairly close to his heart. He might hang on long enough to reach the operating room. Or he might not. Depended on how soon I called for help.

"Don't believe . . . everything Jared says," Kirst said. His breathing was shallow. His eyes fluttered up into his head. He was still with me, but barely. "He wanted to drink their blood. Don't think . . . don't think it was all me. . . . Jared . . . he went along . . . I wasn't forcing him."

"That's not true!" Gloria shouted from her corner. "He's keeping Jared prisoner! He wants him for his own sick purpose!"

"How did you get Gloria to guard Jared for you?"

Kirst laughed, but it came out a wretched gurgle. Blood bubbled out of nostrils and lips and oozed down his cheek.

"You've got the tape of her and Karel, don't you?" I asked.

Kirst tried to speak but coughed instead.

"How can you know about the tape?" Gloria demanded.

"Shut up," I told her, then turned to Kirst: "Where is it?"

Kirst laughed and said, "Stolen. . . . Theophrastus."

"He was going to send copies to my country club, to everyone in Hartford!" Gloria screamed. "How can it be stolen?"

I turned and shushed her. When I turned back to Kirst, he was no longer breathing. I felt for a pulse but found none.

I went back over to the coffin and shone the flashlight on my face so Jared could see me. He didn't know who I was.

"I'm a private detective. Your father sent me after you."

"He's dead," Jared said. "Kirst made me drink his blood."

"Kirst's dead too, now."

"Get me out of this box."

"Can you hang on a few more minutes?"

Jared nodded. "He's kept me in here for the last week. A few more minutes won't kill me. Just promise you'll let me out."

"I promise," I said. "You can trust me. I'm going to go upstairs and call ambulances for you and your wicked stepmother. Gloria, don't you dare move till I get back, you hear me?"

"I can't," Gloria said. "You killed my arm, you bastard."

I went back upstairs, across the plywood, and through the open door to Kirst's kitchen. A white phone hung at the wall by the door. I went to it, picked it up, and dialed 911.

"What's your location?" asked the female 911 dispatcher.

"Put the phone down," said a gruff voice behind me, and I heard the hammer of a revolver click into cocked position.

"Hello?" asked the dispatcher.

"I said put the phone down." It was Theophrastus.

"Shit," I said and hung up the phone.

It rang again: the dispatcher calling back.

"Don't answer it," Theophrastus said. "Put your gun down, arms away from your sides. Don't turn around."

I did everything he asked, dropping my Glock on the counter next to Kirst's stainless steel Kitchen Aid mixer. Theophrastus stood behind me in the kitchen doorway. I could see a weirdly distorted reflection of him in the Kitchen Aid, but nothing else. If he pulled the trigger on me now, I'd never see anything more.

"How'd you get in?" I asked.

"I took Kirst's duplicate keys. What's it to you?"

I felt cold air swirling in around my feet, coming from down the hall. Theophrastus had left the front doors open.

The phone kept ringing: 911 was persistent.

"You don't want to kill me," I said.

"I don't, huh? Why not?"

I heard footsteps on the front stoop, already coming through the doors before Theophrastus could react. Then he turned the gun away from my head and pointed it back down the hall.

"Police! Drop your weapon!" came a familiar voice.

I turned my head and saw Theophrastus hesitating, his pistol aimed at Orjuedos, who stood in a firm stance down the hall with his shiny .38 Special pointed at Theophrastus. It was a draw.

"Drop it!" Orjuedos repeated, baring his fine teeth.

I snatched up my Glock and pressed its nose deep into the jungle of black hair at the base of Theophrastus's head.

"I've got him covered, Tavo," I said.

Theophrastus's hand opened up. His revolver fell on the floor and fired a slug into the wall.

The phone was still ringing.

Orjuedos came around and slapped cuffs on Theophrastus.

"Thanks, Greg," Orjuedos said. "What's going on here? I was following Kirst back to his house and got gridlocked. What's this clown doing here? Where is Kirst, anyway?"

I picked up the ringing phone.

"Did you call 911?" the dispatcher asked.

I gave her the address and ordered two ambulances to go.

After turning over custody of Theophrastus to some backup units, Orjuedos rode in the back of the ambulance with Jared on the way to St. Vincent's. I rode in the back of the other ambulance with Gloria. An EMT stabilized her bleeding, gave her an IV, and injected her with painkillers. The EMT allowed me to talk to Gloria while he attended to my grazed shoulder and bleeding shin.

"Kirst was the one who wanted you to pay me off, wasn't he?"

Gloria nodded her head and said, "Willem called me Sunday afternoon at the Plaza. I was already talking with those cops you sicced on me. After they left, I went to see Willem."

"And he showed you the videotape," I said.

"I still don't know how you know about the tape."

"Never mind how. I also know what's on it."

Gloria closed her eyes in shame. "He blackmailed me into helping him. He gave me no choice. He told me he'd killed Karel and Henry. He claimed his tape was a copy. He sent me over to Karel's apartment to look for the original. I didn't find it. I heard you picking the lock. I hid under the bed, and you came in. I couldn't let you find me, so I stabbed you. I'm sorry."

"That's okay. You made up for it just now by shooting me."

"I had nothing to do with the murders." Gloria's eyelids fluttered. Her head lolled. She was drifting away with the painkillers. "The only thing I ever killed was that damn dog."

"Pardner," I said.

She didn't hear me.

THIRTY-NINE

ELEVEN DAYS LATER, Orjuedos was sitting across from me at a narrow table in a small Chelsea restaurant crowded with hunky men in fresh haircuts and tight designer shirts. Tacky orange-and-black decorations were still up, though Halloween was over two days ago. The waiters had been hired for how they looked in snug blue jeans and T-shirts rather than for their serving ability, if any. They were slow but friendly enough, and cute. They were all in the habit of making strong, direct eye contact, in the hopes that you might turn out to be a Hollywood agent slumming.

My eyes usually spent a lot of time roving, but not tonight: I had the hottest guy in the place. Orjuedos had spent some time putting himself together for me. He was svelte in a black Donna Karan shirt. His hair, goatee, and nails were immaculate. He wore a heavy silver identity bracelet and a Tag Heuer wristwatch. The bags under his eyes were gone, miraculously—but then his case had reached its end, and he hadn't yet gotten involved in anything else nearly as hairy. Tonight he was off. So was I.

It was Friday, ten o'clock already, and the noise level in the restaurant was high, but somehow Orjuedos and I were able to hear each other, and no one else was paying the slightest attention to what we were saying.

"Someone told me this was All Soul's Day," I said, drowning the taste of grilled red snapper with a hefty gulp of beer.

"Of course it is," Orjuedos said, chewing on a chunk of rare steak. "A.K.A. the Day of the Dead. You're not Catholic?"

"I'm nothing, if you must know. I'm not good at religion."

"That's okay. I'm not the best Catholic in the world."

"The Day of the Dead," I said. "In Mexico, don't people go around dressed as skeletons?"

"Some do. It was always my favorite day of the year as a child, even though I'm second generation and grew up in Passaic."

"I caught *The Betsy Morgan Show* on Halloween."

"Oh, yeah?"

"They didn't run the one with Jared and Karel."

"Of course they didn't. They've got a court order not to."

"Funny," I said. "Betsy Morgan came on first to describe the show she'd been planning to run, and how it was tied in to the recent events in the news. She claimed they weren't going to show it, out of respect for the murdered Karel."

"What a load of bull. Judge issued a temporary restraining order. It won't last forever. They'll show it. Wait and see."

"They reran a show about women who'd caught their husbands cheating on them with the family pet, but still stood by them."

"Great," Orjuedos said, rolling his eyes.

"How are you guys doing?" asked our waiter, smiling in a pose suitable for a glossy head shot. "Get you another beer?"

I said I was fine. Orjuedos asked for more water. The waiter left us in the hands of a short Mexican busboy who poured with a flourish, like he was also waiting to be discovered.

"We charged Gloria Glendenning-Foster with unlawful imprisonment for helping Kirst with Jared," Orjuedos said. "We also charged her with assault for stabbing you in the leg."

"Good," I said. "How did she get in Karel's apartment?"

"She says she'd been there before and knew he kept an extra key in his mailbox. The mailbox could be jimmied open with just about anything. She used her nail file. Kirst put the idea in her head to go over there, supposedly to look for the original of the videotape. He wanted her fingerprints all over everything. He was setting her up. He had the original anyway, at least until early Monday, when it was stolen by Theophrastus. It ended up with all the rest of the stolen loot in the storage room of The Lot. We recovered all of Kirst's property, by the way, and also found Theophrastus's drug stash. Narcotics arrested Ted and all the other members of his gang. They shut down the club."

"I don't care about that. What about Gloria?"

"Kirst never told her the tape was stolen. Without it, he had no power over her. He had her come over to help him after the burglary, early Monday morning. He was worried that his neighbors might have witnessed it and called police. He was also beginning to worry that he might be hit with a search warrant. He couldn't keep Jared in the house. He got Gloria to come over. He wanted her to help him move Jared and make sure nobody discovered him until he could come up with a more permanent hiding place. He owned the house next door and was renovating it, intending to expand—"

"More megalomania," I said. "Who needs all that space?"

"He called off the construction crew for that day. He and Gloria moved Jared down to the other basement, and he planted her there as an armed guard. He had classes to teach. Had to keep up appearances. In her own mind, Gloria doesn't see herself as an accomplice to anything. My guess is, Kirst was only going to use her for a day. He was hoping to frame her for the killings. That, or he was going to kill her and feed her to Jared."

"Ugh," I said. "How is Jared doing?"

"St. Vincent's released him today," Orjuedos said. "He's flying back with the Grosses tomorrow, going to recuperate with them out there. Physically, he's okay. Mentally, I don't know."

"D.A.'s office isn't charging him with accessory, I hope."

"No, your arguments won out. Jared says he had nothing to do with Kirst's crimes, even if he did drink the victims' blood."

"It was forced down him," I said, as I'd been saying over and over to the relevant authorities. "Otherwise, Kirst wouldn't have resorted to the coffin, the restraints, and the feeding tube. Jared was his victim as much as the others were."

"I told you they agreed with you. What more do you want?"

"You don't agree. You're still suspicious of Jared."

"I don't know." Orjuedos exhaled sharply through his nose. "Jared got mixed up with Kirst willingly enough, seems to me."

"He was desperate for cash," I said. "He didn't know what he was getting into. He was only worried about what would happen to him if he didn't pay off Theophrastus. With reason, Tavo."

"I guess so, after what you told me." Orjuedos squirmed in his seat. "But Kirst had *raped* him—supposedly—at the sleep clinic. That's the part that just doesn't gel. No one would want to have anything to do with anyone who'd raped them."

"Jared didn't know anyone else with any money. Gloria had failed him, and his father had cut him off, and Evelyn Grosse didn't have that much, and none of his friends had any. He didn't like the idea of going to Kirst, but he had no choice."

"He gave in easily enough," Orjuedos said.

"That's just it," I said. "Jared wasn't the type to give in to anybody. His friends said he was an aggressive, independent guy who liked to control others. Anastasia told me Jared wasn't her type, that she liked her men passive and effeminate. I can't see Jared simply giving in to a guy who was old enough to be his father—especially Kirst, who'd betrayed his trust. Kirst held the money out for him like a carrot on a stick. It was a trap."

"You may be right, Greg."

"I think I am. Kirst was obsessed with Jared. He had been for months. He'd been spinning these dark fantasies in his head— something to do with making Jared his very own somnambulistic sex slave in a box, like Dr. Caligari's kept boy."

"I've seen that movie, Greg, and I didn't ever notice that the sleepwalker was Caligari's sex slave." Orjuedos's voice dripped with sarcasm, like molasses. "Much less a kept boy."

"Well, that's how Kirst saw it," I said. "While Jared was still a student, he told Kirst everything that was going on in his life. Kirst followed Jared's descent into gothdom, and it fascinated him. Kirst got a kick out of it. He befriended Juliet Logan to learn more about Jared. Then came the incident at the sleep disorders clinic, and Jared's complaint against him. His professional career was collapsing around him. His license was threatened. He could have lost his practice and his teaching position. So when Jared came to him begging for money, it played right into his hands. He could kill two birds with one stone: keep Jared's complaint from being properly followed up, while keeping Jared for himself, literally. Forever, I guess."

"He was just plain nuts," Orjuedos said. "I still don't get what the blood had to do with anything—or the murders, for that matter. Kirst had Jared already. Why bother?"

"It was about power and control. Kirst killed people who were close to Jared in some way, and he made sure Jared knew whose blood it was. He wanted to bend Jared's will to his own. He encouraged Jared's fantasies of being a vampire. He hoped to

wipe out Jared's identity and turn him into a slave. Call it
brainwashing, mind control, whatever. Kirst was a neurologist.
He knew a thing or two. Given enough time, he might have
succeeded. Unlike Jeffrey Dahmer, who gave his victims home
lobotomies with a power drill, hoping to turn them into zombies.
They both had delusions of grandeur. Two classic psychos."

"Jared said in his statement that it started as a kind of sex
game," Orjuedos said. "Bondage and discipline, giving in to
Kirst's demands. Jared was over at Kirst's house for three weeks
before he was ever put in the coffin. Kirst kept him on a chain in
that empty upstairs room. He could have opened the window and
called for help. How do you explain that?"

"Jared didn't want any help. He didn't want to go out and be
seen. He was too afraid of what Theophrastus would do to him.
But Kirst never came through with the money—only with the rent
money for Anastasia. He put on the leather hood and
accompanied Jared, bought him some food at the Chinese
restaurant, and took him upstairs to deliver the cash. Jared could
have run, but he thought he had nothing to fear. It was all still a
kind of game to him, and he still hoped he'd be able to pay off
Theophrastus."

"He was having fun," Orjuedos said. "He liked it."

"Up until Karel was killed, maybe. But Jared says he loved
Karel. All his friends say he did. He didn't have any reason to
want him dead. Kirst did, though. Karel was a threat to his
supremacy over Jared. For that matter, so was Henry Foster."

"You're saying Kirst killed off his main rivals for Jared's
affection?"

"I think so, yes. And it was when he was ready to kill Karel
that he locked Jared in the coffin. Jared might have died if I hadn't
found him. All Kirst had given him to eat for a week were those
sixteen pints of blood from Karel and Foster. Kirst didn't trust

Jared enough to keep him chained upstairs anymore."

"Oh, well. Whatever happened, we don't have enough evidence to charge Jared as an accessory. No jury would ever convict him. Kirst's dead, and we'll never know the whole truth."

"You'd believe Kirst's word over Jared's?"

"No," Orjuedos said. "But it might be helpful to hear his side of the story. No chance of that now, thanks to you."

"It was either him or me."

"I'm not blaming you, Greg. I'm glad he didn't kill you."

"Thanks, Tavo."

"Finished?" asked our waiter. He removed our plates and asked if we wanted dessert and coffee.

I asked for the dessert menu.

"Sure," he said, and went to get them.

"Maybe just coffee," Orjuedos said.

"That's what I was thinking," I said. "But I've had their coffee. It's nothing special. I've got better at my place."

"Coffee at your place, Greg? I thought you'd never ask."

When the waiter returned, I refused the menus and asked for the check. The waiter said sure and went away again.

I reached across the table and held Orjuedos's hand.

"Tavo," I said, "what comes after the Day of the Dead?"

Orjuedos smiled, narrowed his eyes sexily, and said:

"How the hell should I know?"

We paid our check and got out of there fast.

THE END

ABOUT THE AUTHOR

JOHN PEYTON COOKE was born in Amarillo, Texas, in 1967, and grew up in Laramie, Wyoming. His other novels include STINK LAKE, OUT FOR BLOOD, TORSOS, THE CHIMNEY SWEE-PER, HAVEN, and THE RAPE OF GANYMEDE. His short fiction has been published in several magazines and anthologies, including *Christopher Street, The Magazine of Fantasy & Science Fiction,* and *Best American Mystery Stories 2003.* John currently lives in Toronto with his husband and their dog Ricky, a toy poodle and petty thief.

If you enjoyed *THE FALL OF LUCIFER*, check out the first
Greg Quaintance novel, *THE RAPE OF GANYMEDE* ...

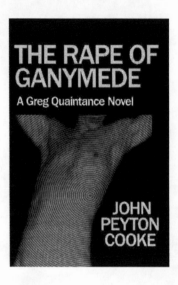

$18.00

Published by
Éditions Cuir Noir

cuirnoir.com

ISBN
978-0981004716

Available at
Amazon.com

From the author of THE CHIMNEY SWEEPER and TORSOS
comes a novel of a gay private eye working the mean streets of
New York City's Chelsea circa 1998....

Greg Quaintance sports a Desert Storm tattoo, packs a Glock, and
drives a Plymouth Barracuda, but only those who know him best
see the wounds etched in his heart. As a P.I. in Manhattan's
Chelsea neighbor-hood, he is hired to thwart an extortion attempt
aimed at Jimmy Gilbert, a billion-dollar man-child musical
superstar accused of having sexual relations with a teenage boy.
But when Gilbert's accuser turns up dead and the boy goes on the
run, the bodies of the rich and not-so-famous start piling up. From
the canyons of Manhattan to the halls of presidential power,
Quaintance must now penetrate a minefield fused with greed,
depravity, and violence.

2047677

Made in the USA